THE FIRE LORD TRILOGY

The Last Voyage of the Betty-Lou

Dr. Benjamin Stewart Johnson

Dr. Benjamin Stewart Johnson

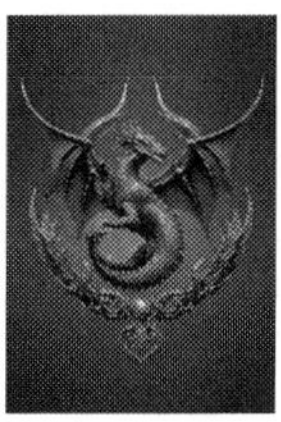

ISBN-13: 9798562859167

Cover design by: Melanie D. Johnson
Library of Congress Control Number: 2024900588
Printed in the United States of America

CONTENTS

INTRODUCTION

I am sure that you will enjoy the Fire Lord series because I enjoyed writing it. As with all authors, I write about what I have observed and experienced, what I have imagined and what I have dreamed. This series is no different. I write about how evil persists like a stubborn stain and how heroic people struggle to eradicate it. The battle between good and evil is really only about one thing: Freedom. Living in these times, maintaining our Freedom has never been more critical to survival. This trilogy parallels our current situation and aside from being an engaging adventure, has another message that is best explained by Gideon Livingston, the Fire Lord, himself:

We must fan the flames of freedom so
that they burn brightly in the hearts and minds
of all sentient beings through all of Portus!
We must continually shine that
brilliant light of freedom in every dark corner
so that tyranny has no place to hide.
With the light of freedom, we must
expose those despotic men and women who
tread on others for personal gain.Finally,
we must fuel the light of liberty in the
hearts of our children, their children and
their children's children so that never again
will evil despots darken our free lands!

How to Read this Book

I have written this book as a fictional history similar to Don Quijote. The individual stories are put together by scholars on Portus who depended on records, journals, memoirs and legends to recreate the historical experiences. In most books where there is a note introducing the chapter, reading this note is optional. In this trilogy, it is required because each chapter is written from a unique perspective and you must read the chapter note in order to know from whose perspective you are experiencing the action.

Another thing about this trilogy that sets it apart from other young adult science fiction and fantasy is that this book is safe to read for all ages. It is a wholesome rip-roaring adventure. I drew inspiration from authors I admire; Ender's Game by David Eddings, FableHaven by Brandon Mull, Martian Chronicles by Ray Bradbury, The Count of Monte Cristo by Alexander Dumas and even the Westerns of Louis L'Amour. All of these authors wrote about heroes, male and female, and their writing was more about the story or the adventure and any political or social message was secondary. The Fire Lord Trilogy is a rip-roaring adventure and just like in Louis L'Amour westerns, the good guy wins, and though he may fall off his dragon, his hat stays on.

So find a comfortable recliner, sofa, or bean bag and get ready to read this family and brain friendly series, because once you start, you will not want to put these books down.

Dive into the world of Portus, a planet with new and familiar creatures, unique technologies and powerful forces. Become part of the desperate struggle for freedom. Join the rebellion and follow the Fire Lord in overthrowing the rule of despots..

The Fire Lord Series
Volume I: The Last Voyage of the Betty-Lou
Volume II: The Dragon and the Maelstrom
Volume III: The Battle for Portus

To keep up-to-date with the other books as I prepare them for publishing, see https://wordpress.com/page/ benjohnsonedd.wordpress.com/182

Enjoy!
Dr. Benjamin Johnson, Ed.D

GEOGRAPHY OF PORTUS

Eight Continents of Portus

- Scryberg
- Southern Marches
- Fernland
- Fenfold
- Foldfen
- Gladewater
- Asombre
- Montara

18 Civilized Kingdoms of Portus and Major Cities

1. Bergland
    - Sky Forest
    - Miller's Pond
2. Scryberg
    - Twin Stones
    - Noonday
    - Gran Saline
3. Starfold
    - Tempston
    - Portsmouth
4. Turrin
    - Shrebrite
    - Foldfen

5. Cutterston
    - Hapsfel
    - Bridgeland
6. Thirrston
    - Dayhill
7. Stonehold
    - Fernland
8. Idylwild
    - Bluerock
    - Fenfold
    - Zurrin
9. Meridian
    - Meridian
10. Granberry
    - Grandberry
11. Gladewater
    - Gladewater
12. Sparfeld
    - Sparfeld
13. Marshton
    - Marshton
14. Ironfeld
    - Ironfeld
15. Asombre
    - Sulmana
    - Lejanosa
    - Ladoso
    - Polgro
16. Montara
17. Kingdom of the Scrybeasts
    - Scryland
18. The Kingdom of the Guardians of the Sky

Notes about the Kingdoms

Ironfeld-was later recognized as the 14th kingdom- It was

an independent kingdom and was never conquered by the overlord. After the Battle of Gran Saline, the Fire Lord, Gideon Livingston sent his grandfather, After ratification by the council, Ariel Livingston and the Goodwill Ambassador ship Horacio with Captain Petro Fitzgerald made the formal invitation, which King Tilmut Houndrock III eventually accepted.

Little was known about the Western Continent of Asombre which was also never conquered by the Overlord, being esteemed of little value and not worth the effort. Only due to the efforts of the Goodwill Ambassadors and Gideon Livingston, the Fire Lord II, the Kingdom of Asombre was added as the 15th kingdom. Montora was added as the 16th kingdom.

The Kingdom of the Scrybeasts was accepted into the republic after the fall of the Bridgers and became the 17th kingdom. Scryland is an island off the coast of Ladosa where the main population of Scrybeasts resides.

The Kingdom of the Guardians of the Sky (formally known as Sky Devils because of their vicious appearance) were accepted into the republic after the fall of the Bridgers and became the 18th Kingdom.

Shanti- Remains a secret place. At some future time they will reveal themselves. Perhaps then they will be accepted into the Republic as the 19th Kingdom.

The Shoals- The only place in Portus where it is safe to swim due to the shallow water and coral formations that protect the inland shores from the large predator creatures of the open ocean and has become a popular vacation spot.

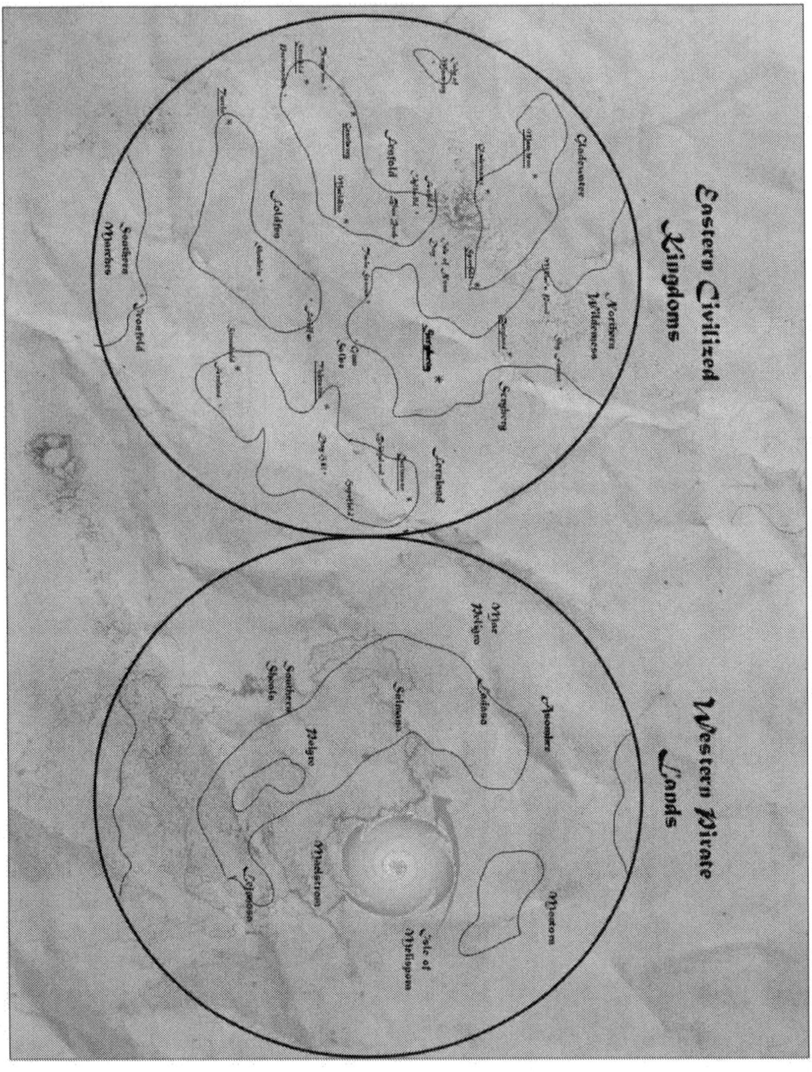
Eastern Civilized Kingdoms
Western Pirate Lands

ACKNOWLEDGEMENTS

Presented to Your Honor, President Jasper Ariel Livingston in the rotation 2230 *al*:

Volume I of III

Through many cycles of research and the dedication of many historians who sifted through leagues of parchment and tapestries we are proud to finally present to your Honor the complete history of the Fire Lord. We are most appreciative of your beneficent support and patience in this important project and fully appreciate your keen interest, as the great, great Grandson of the Lord Gideon Livingston, the Dragon. Since the Landing, we have not known such enthusiasm and excitement about any project.

We acknowledge also the cooperation and technical assistance provided by the Royal Universities Meridian and Scryberg. Were it not for their timely advice and extensive libraries, these manuscripts would not have come to light. Also, great accolades should be given to the Regents of the following locations for their cooperation in allowing access to their historical documents and communications: Isle of Noonday, Miller's Pond, Melispora, and Asombre. Most assuredly, thanks are due the Livingston Family Association, the Descendants of Bragg Incorporated, and the Estate of Sir Percivel Kendrick the Third.

Finally, we owe much gratitude to the family of Portenza Grizbol of Sulmana who graciously donated to the

National Museum of Asombre documents and the original logs written by the Fire Lord himself which contain the only account of his early adventures and his early life. Truly this has been a multi-national endeavor and because of these many happy circumstances, this history is now in your hands and ready for distribution at the 200th anniversary of the establishment of the Portus Republic.

Most Humbly submitted,

Dr. Torrance Cloudjumper
Chief Historian of the Executive Council, PR

CHAPTER 1 RESCUE MISSION

(Taken from the Memoirs of Captain Ariel Livingston)

"Captain Livingston:

I know you are retired but we desperately need your services here at Noonday. The Adjudicator McFarland and his Boar Riders raided one of our safe houses and confiscated our coded ledger. Though he cannot read it, he is threatening to break the code or destroy it if he can't. Either would damage the resistance tremendously.

The morale of our troops is plummeting. The Adjudicator is bearing down in the most vicious manner on anyone suspected of being loyal to the rebellion, or anyone aiding suspected rebels. He has destroyed their businesses, burned their homes, confiscated their land and has stolen their property. Anyone who complains about the Overlord or the Adjudicator taxes is suspect. The Boar Riders kill any who resist; men, women or even children. His jail cells are filled with townsfolk suspected of being rebels and because of this ultimate injustice, they have now joined other rebels who have also had their fill of the Adjudicator's atrocities. What is most egregious is that every few rotations, McFarland has held public executions to keep the townsfolk in fear. So many have died already, hanged, or beheaded, we cannot endure it any longer. Please help us!

We have a plan to free these people, but we need you and the Betty-Lou to lend your aid. Loyal people are in place at the jails and in McFarland's residence, but we need you to get into McFarland's home. Everyone who had knowledge of the secret entrances is either dead or in prison. We need you and the Betty-Lou to help cause a distraction and retrieve the ledger while we free the captives. Upon your arrival, all attention will be for you and the Betty-Lou. But most importantly, we need you and the Betty-Lou to give hope to the resistance at Noonday and in the surrounding areas. Come with all haste. Do not risk replying to this message as all message birds are shot and the messages confiscated.

If you cannot come, our only hope is that the prophecy be fulfilled and the Fire Lord Returns.

Sincerely,
Sir Percivel Kendrick."

"Curse Julius McFarland! I should a never let'm live!" I shouted as I slammed the coded message on the table, making the whey hens squawk in fright and fly to other roosts.

"Would that I'd burned me own house ta the ground, with him in it, instead of selling it to that blaigeard! T'would'a been a fittin' recompense," I growled and then sat in the worn piglin-fur chair in the whey-hen enclosure on the roof of the house.

"I'm too old fer this! We need some young blood to take over," I muttered to myself as I glanced down at the road.

"There, walking with his friends, be Gideon, ma grandson. Tall, strong and handsome he's come out ta be. That's the kind'o rebels we be needin'!" I reflected.

<What say ye, Betty-Lou? Ye think I should recruit me own grandson?> I pondered as I watched him holdin' his own with the two boys that were attackin' 'im.

<Ye canna keep this from 'im. He'll find out sooner or later. He's got too much 'o his father in 'im,> she answered.

<He's a fine lad. Too young fer war. Should we not let'm live his life carefree?> I asked to myself.

<With the Adjudicators, Boar Riders, 'n the Overlord there'll be no carefree livin'! We need 'im. If we don't stop the

powers that be, there will be no carefree life for none'o us!> Betty-Lou interjected. <Aye, he be young, but he's got skill!>

<Ye be right', 'o course. I weren't no older than Gideon when I went off ta find m'fortune,> I responded mentally.

<Now tis Gideon's turn,> Betty-Lou commented.

<D'ya think he be ready?> I asked Betty-Lou.

<Do ye not see 'im teachin' those other boys a lesson? He can takes his lumps, but he can also give 'em. He be ready,> she countered.

<His mother will object mightily. She raised him proper 'n he e'n speaks proper, as if he were born in a palace. She'd keep 'im from the rebellion if she could," I said.

<Sadie-Belle knows. She sees what good 'n bad be in 'im just as you do. Bein' able ta speak like a gentleman be a grand attribute but he canna stay here 'n be happy 'n there be no better cause than freedom.>

<Aye, there be no other way. When can ye be here?> I asked her.

<By tomorrow.>

<It be decided then. Tis a good thing I been storin' supplies for a long while now. I will ready m'self and convince Gideon ta come along.>

CHAPTER 2 HONOR

(Extracted Directly from the Personal Log book of Gideon Livingston, the Fire Lord)

Oslo, a chubby scoundrel from school and Keppler, his skinny side-kick, followed me as I casually walked toward my house after a morning nine-ball practice.

"Hey, Gideon. There be yer Grandfather, ole' 'Loony' on the roof o' yer house. He be waitin' fer the Betty-Lou? Ha ha ha." Kepler joked and pointed with his thumb. "How do'ye deal with that doaty old man?"

"If he misses that ship so much, then he shouldn't have let 'er go." Oslo laughed.

"A fortune he threw away, 'n fer what? Jest ta keep it from ye!" Kepler jabbed.

"What an old dobber! How could he be believin' that the Betty-Lou were alive?" Oslo howled, holding his sides as he chortled.

"What were worse be that Gideon believes 'im 'n is more a fool than he be!" Kepler guffawed and pointed at Gideon.

That was going too far. I responded to the typical derision of my grandfather with anger, "Shut your traps! Do you really want to do this? You don't remember the last time you decided to run your mouth about my grandfather… how you ended up begging me to quit beating on you? Apologize!" I growled.

I grew up with these kids and adults jeering at me and making fun of me and my grandfather. The kids at school called him "Loony Livingston" just because he claimed that his airship, named the Betty-Lou, was alive. I used to get beat up, a lot, defending his honor, and mine, but then I grew up and got strong…very strong. I have worked very hard to control my temper. Ma said it would be the death of me, not being able to ignore insults and taunts. She'd tell me as she cleaned up my cuts and bruises from the frequent fights, "Ye should just ignore'em. They want ta see ye get angry 'cause they know that ye will be the one in trouble."

"I was pretty successful at following my mother's advice… until today," I reflected.

Oslo responded, "That was five cycles ago when we were kids. We're bigger now an we know yer nothing but a frightened squabbler. What'cha goin' ta do about it if we dunna want to apologize?" He sneered as he cracked his knuckles and Kepler picked up a metal bar and smacked it in his palm.

I clenched my fists and without thinking, and like a moth drawn to flame, I walked over to the two boys, "I've had enough of you and your stupid harassment," I growled. "My grandfather was the world's greatest sky merchant and adventurer. He's seen and done more amazing things on Portus than any since the Fire Lord. And as far as the Betty-Lou goes, if he says that she is alive, then she is alive. You've no right to question what you don't know!"

"So, Gideon…how does it make ye feel that Looney Livingston did'na want ta leave ye the most famous airship in Portus. He jest let it drift away 'cause he thought ye could'na handle it?" Oslo taunted, as he motioned with his pudgy fingers as if they were drifting.

"Maybe it be 'cause 'o Gideon pretend'n ta be all noble with his formal speak'n," Keppler added for good measure. They never did like that my mother had insisted that I speak formally and not "gutter language" and this also set me up for persecution.

I gritted my teeth as their jibes hit sensitive nerves. It did hurt that Grandfather just let her go. My thoughts involuntarily went back to when Grandfather set the Betty-

Lou free, ten cycles ago. Instantly I felt the memory of that fateful day.

It was a calm spring day. I was only eight cycles old, but just like everyone else, I thought Grandfather was making a big mistake letting the Betty-Lou go. The townspeople gathered just to see if he would really do it. Julias McFarland had even sent a troop of Boar Riders, dressed in their red and black military uniforms with the scrybeast emblem blazened on their chests.

Grandfather walked up to the Betty-Lou and placed a gentle hand on her green hull. The Betty-Lou was unique among airships. She was ornately designed in the form of a dragon, complete with the long neck and the graceful head of a magnificent beast at the prow. All the wood was stained dragon green, and to top it off she had billowing sails that took the form of dragon's wings as she flew.

Then Grandfather turned to the townsfolk assembled around him. "Thanks ta all 'o ye fer comin' ta the final voyage 'o Betty-Lou. I know y'all think I am crazy ta do this, but I'm doin' it ta save my family 'n yer families. As long as the Betty-Lou be here, ye be not safe."

"Give'r ta me! I'll take good care 'o 'er, I will!" someone shouted.

"Somebody stop 'im!" another shouted and there was a rush towards the landing platform.

Grandfather then looked at the Betty-Lou and said tenderly, "As a last gesture of good will, I set you..."

Grandfather moved to cut the mooring line but a Boar Rider guard grabbed Grandfather's arm and loudly proclaimed, "In the name of Adjudicator, Julias McFarland, we confiscate this ship and all its contents."

"No! You canna do that! You dunna have the right!" Grandfather shouted and struggled to get free.

"We have every right!" The Boar Rider growled as he struck him with a club. Grandfather fell to his knees. "Make the ship fast and prepare to board!" He commanded the dozen other Boar Riders standing nearby.

Just then the Betty-Lou gave a great heave and the mooring lines snapped with a loud crack. As if alive, the thick rope whipped the Boar Rider in the left side of his face and then the right side, knocking the guard to his knees in pain. Then the rope slipped through the retaining ring and the Betty-Lou drifted off, carried by a light breeze.

The crowd laughed at the Boar Rider who had been whipped by the mooring line. Some ran to try to catch the Betty-Lou.

"free to roam the skies of Portus forever." Grandfather Livingston moaned just before he passed out.

My mother, Sadie-Belle, ran to the platform to tend to my Grandfather. As she held his bleeding head in her lap she snarled to the Boar Riders as they ran after the Betty-Lou, "Better free than in the hands of the likes of you or the Adjudicator!"

My thoughts returned to the question Oslo had asked and I turned and faced them, "It was his ship and he could do with it as he pleased," I said and started to walk away, but then like a piglin-head I couldn't leave it alone and said, "But If I had the Betty-Lou, I wouldn't hang around with losers like you two, who want nothing more than to be the adjudicator's puppets and be 'gantin' on the back of those bristle-backed pigs he calls the Boar Riders!"

"That's better than being one o' them rock scrapers. Serves ye right since ye want to be a jewel-smithin' spend yer time handlin' other men's jewels?" Oslo sneered.

"Oh that's funny. Did you think of that one all by yourself, Olso?" I countered and could feel my anger rising and I consciously took deep breaths to calm myself. "If I had the Betty-Lou, I wouldn't need to study how to cut gems and match stones. But I don't have her…do I? That's why I enrolled in the Jewelstone Academy in Meridian, to get away from this stinking place and squash-brains like you. You can stay here and play with your hogs. I can see why you are attracted to them. There's quite a resemblance." I turned and walked away, pleased with my self-control and that I had not been drawn into a fight.

"Ye'll pay fer that Gideon! Yer just runnin' away from

duty, ye spineless coward!" Oslo clamored back and chucked a hand-sized stone which hit me hard in the back.

Oslo's grandad was Julius McFarland, the town Adjudicator of Noonday, and Kepler's father was the adjudicator of Miller's Pond. which was why they felt that they could get away with "pokin' the fire lizard", my nickname from all the fights I'd had.

In a flash of anger, I turned and threw a fist at Oslo. He was expecting this and dodged while Kepler connected with his pipe on my side and retreated out of striking range. Oslo had picked up another stone and both were then facing me.

More wary this time, I feinted a lunge at Kepler, who swung and missed and I tackled Oslo, knocking the rock out of his hand.

"Now you listen to me!" I said, and open-handed slapped Oslo in the face. "That was for insulting my grandfather." Then I backhanded him on the other cheek, "And that is for insulting me!"

Taking advantage of the situation, Kepler swung his pipe at my back, knocking me off of Oslo, and taking away my breath. I lay on my side in pain, trying to breath and Olso scrambled to his feet and grabbed a large river stone in each hand.

Kepler and Oslo laughed, "Not so tough now! But the fun be just beginnin," he said and prepared to hit me again with the pipe.

I rolled towards Oslo and grabbed his legs, knocking him off balance. He fell hard and dropped the stones. Anger did not fully describe what I was feeling as I jumped up to face Kepler.

Kepler swung the bar viciously at my head, which I ducked and before he could swing it back, I grabbed the bar with my right hand and held it firmly. In vain he tried to twist and yank the bar, but I continued to glare at him as he struggled to get the pipe free. I could feel vast amounts of fury boiling inside of me as I held onto the pipe. I exulted in the feeling that the years of frustration, hatred and anger were going to be released. This torrent of retribution flowed through my arm and onto the pipe. I was preparing to yank the pipe from his hands and let him feel a double portion of the pain he had inflicted on me.

But my revenge was halted when Kepler yowled in pain and let go of the pipe, shaking his hands as if they were on fire. He scowled in fear at me as he tried unsuccessfully to help Oslo off the ground using the backside of his hands.

Still not understanding what happened, I looked closely at his hands and they were covered with blisters as if he had been badly burned.

"A, ah! That be it! You bloody assaulted us! I'll have m'grandpa put yer ass in the pen fer bein' a rebel 'n conspirin' ta revolt!" Oslo shouted with a look of triumph as he finally got off the ground.

"He's been trying to do that to us for many solar cycles now. Just because his porky grandson and his rock weasel of a friend go home crying to papa, do you think that will make a difference?" I lunged toward them as I said this, and they both scampered backwards. I turned and walked inside.

"There'll be no good comin' from this! Why can't ye just leave 'em be? My mother, scolded through the galley window. "Though they be deservin' this fer some time, fer sure ye'll 'ave hell ta pay fer doin' this! Ken ye imagine them as Boar Riders with that crooked adjudicator? Fire Lord protect us!"

"You know what I really wanted to do?" I said. "I wanted to unleash my full anger on them. You know, let them have it all."

"No one would'a blamed ye. But ye need ta be as smart as ye be strong. Tis a combination that be hard ta be contrarywise" my mother laughed. "Have some red bean tea ta calm yerself while I look at yer wounds."

I gave my mother an awkward hug due to the tender ribs and back and accepted the tea from her. As I sipped the hot spicy liquid, I thought about how Grandfather Livingston was not just a merchant airman. He was an adventurer. He boasted all the time about how he and the Betty-Lou fought pirates, and avoided the Overlord's flying tax collectors, the armada. I was always proud of Grandfather Livingston and I had no regrets about defending his honor, especially against stone brains like them.

CHAPTER 3 THE CHOICE

(Compiled from the memoirs of Sadie-Belle Livingston, Ariel Livingston and the personal journal of Gideon Livingston, the Fire Lord)

"I just got word from the Jewelstone Academy," I shared with Mother as she prepared my favorite meal of squash root and moor beast stew. "I've been accepted. I start in the fall after harvest."

"Congratulations, ma dear! I knew they had'ta let ye in. Ye be the best student in the whole school, and right handsome ta boot! Besides, I hope it'll keep ye from the constant fightin'!"

I stood half an arm-span taller than her so she gave me a hug and then pulled my head down so she could stand on her toes and kiss my cheeks.

When I first spoke to my mother Sadie-Belle, three cycles ago about attending Jewelstone Academy and avoiding the draft, she was pleased, "Jewel-smithin' be better than losin' yer life ta the skies as a merchant 'n ye dunna want ta be one 'o those idiot pig riders. I'm glad ye finally came ta yer senses. Flyin' as a sky merchant like yer father'll bring nothin' but heart ache 'n sorrow. At least now, we've nothin ta argue 'bout!"

Ever since my father died, she would not let anyone talk of sailing, airships, or even traveling. The mere mention of the Betty-Lou prompted tears and the reproach, "Why do ye speak of her in this house?"

I went upstairs to see if Grandfather Livingston was still

above. He was sitting in his study filled with charts, wind gear, and mementos of his cycles as an air merchant. He was reading a whey hen message.

"Good morning, Grandfather."

"Hello, my fine young lad." He set the message down and continued. "Just the person I be needin' ta talk to. Do ya have a moment ta chat?"

"Of course, Grandfather." I responded and took a seat on a nearby stool made of swamp lizard skin, with three spines from a small fin fish as legs.

"I've been watchin' ye and see that ye have turned into a right fine young man. Tall, handsome, built sturdy with broad shoulders and healthy smile. Ye have an easy manner 'bout ye and get along well with all sorts of folks. Ye be smart as a cloud fox 'n strong as a rock serpent. Yer not 'fraid of hard work and when ye see injustice, ye strive to right the wrongs. When I see that red hair 'o yers with those bright green eyes, I think 'o your grandmother. Ye look much like 'er. I think ye be ready." Grandfather finished praising me with a gleam in his eye.

"I know what you are doing, but it won't work." I responded with a stern grimace.

After the fight with Oslo and Kepler, I was in no mood to be patient. I continued with more anger than I intended, "You want me to take those cheap piglin furs that you bought and try to sell them for more at the market! Nobody's fool enough to buy them. I don't know why you bought them in the first place!"

Grandfather looked surprised. "I did it ta help a friend. But no, that not be it, jest let me explain…"

My emotion was rising and I growled, "Oh then you want me to go and purchase that prize delivery hog that you've been eyeing over at the mercantile." I followed up with even more force, "Our hog is good enough for what we need and we don't need an expensive, spoiled hog to take care of, especially if I'd be the one caring for it!"

"Now calm yeself a moment. I dunna want no hog!"

Grandfather responded in frustration and continued in a calm voice, "I truly think the world 'o ye and those comments be sincere. I just wanted ta ask ye a simple question."

Grandfather held out his hands, then asked, "Will ye accompany me on one last journey?"

My ire at being manipulated vanished. I was shocked by his question. I had always dreamt of going with him on one of his excursions, but when he let the Betty-Lou go, I thought that I would never have the chance.

"You're planning to book passage on an airship?" I stammered. "To what destination? You know we don't have a lot of money and..."

Grandfather interrupted my questions with firm words, "Ye be mistaken. We need no passage," he paused and smiled, "we be takin' the Betty-Lou! She be here right now!" and then he gave a captain's order, "Get above to the landing pad on the roof of the house and welcome 'er."

"What? Really? Uh...alright." I stammered, taken aback by the firm tone of his voice.

I went above and as I opened the hatch to the landing pad on the roof of our home, I nearly fell down. To my amazement, I could see that the Betty-Lou was approaching the house. I had to look twice because I just couldn't believe it.

I called down to Grandfather, "She's here, Grandfather!"

I watched as she glided not 20 lengths away. As I viewed her magnificent emerald keel with the fierce dragon head with its long, curved horns, and the large pointed teeth in her gaping jaws leading the way, I could not help but wonder what it would be like to fly in such a ship. Compared to this, jewel-smithing seemed mundane and boring. Then remembering that I was supposed to greet the Betty-Lou, my mind raced, *What do you say to a living airship? Have you had a nice trip? How was the weather? I hope you are in good health.*

"Don't be a moron!" I chided myself, "Those all sound stupid!"

I left the hatch and stood on the mooring platform. On

instinct, I took off my hat and luckily as I did so, words came unbidden into my mouth, "Hello Betty-Lou! I'm Gideon... Bert's boy... Captain Livingston's grandson. Welcome home."

As she turned around for another pass, I saw her in her full majesty. Her green-wood hull and stained-glass windows gleamed emerald in the afternoon light. The wooden dragon's head at the prow seemed to smile, while the sails and banners waved as if in joyous greetings. She was a long and wide merchant vessel, unique among all others because her buoyancy tanks, full of xeoxyn gas, were hidden within her structure instead of being above the ship like a large puff gourd like most other ships.

"She be feeling gentle-like today," Grandfather said. "When she comes 'round again, grab hold of the mooring line 'n make it fast."

I jumped a bit at the sound of Grandfather's voice. I had not realized he was behind me.

I was still in shock and all I could say was, "The Betty-Lou is back!"

As the Betty-Lou approached on the second pass, I jumped to reach the mooring line and tied it off on the mooring post that extended above the landing pad. I extended the pneumatic stabilizing supports and grappling hooks.

"Well, what think ye lad?" Grandfather asked with the same gleam in his eye that I only saw when he spoke of the Betty-Lou.

"Well, sir, she is even more beautiful than I remember as a boy," I responded and reminisced, "You know, when I was a boy, I dreamt of traveling with you on the Betty-Lou to see the tropical Isle of Manning to the West, the icy shores of the southern marches, or verdant forests of Fernland to the East. I even dreamt of visiting the desolate lands of Asombre and finding firestone along the beaches. But that all changed when you let the Betty-Lou go. I had to come up with other dreams. My plan is to be a jewel-smith, not an air merchant."

"Dreams be a fleeting thing, m'lad, always changin',"

Grandfather quipped.

"Aren't you too old to take a voyage on the Betty-Lou?" I questioned. "Wait a moments, are you thinking this will be your final voyage, like a journey to the afterlife?"

"Aye lad, I be old but this be no mystical last voyage ta the afterlife. Tis a rescue mission in more ways than one. I'll be needin' yer strong arms and courage ta bring aide to some needy folk. Besides, this be a good reason for ye ta see the world a bit. There be many things ye need ta learn, and the best way to learn 'em be on Betty-Lou. Far too long has the truth been kept from ye. But now that ye are of age, tis a problem I will rectify on this journey.

"So what be yer decision, will ye come with me?"

"How long of a trip will it be?" I asked.

"Tis hard to say, but, for certain twill be more 'n three lunar cycles."

"Three lunar cycles! That means I'll have to give up my spot at Jewelstone Academy!" I groaned. "Jewelstone Academy is my future. Once I graduate, my plan is to earn lots of money making jewelry, designing farsight scopes, or creating decorative frames for light stones.

"Ye gotta be kiddin' me! I canna imagine ye stuck in a cramped room, workin' all day with tiny things, 'n makin'trinkets. Tis not in yer nature. This be yer opportunity ta see fer yerself. Then ye can make the decision."

"But, I can't leave mother alone. Who will take care of her?"

Grandfather shook his head and replied, "She be fully capable ta care fer herself fer such a short bit."

"She won't agree to it," I parried.

"Tis not her choice, tis yours."

"I can't. I've got too many plans to take off on three-cycle journey. I've got to practice for the nine-ball tournament, I've got to hunt for scholarships, I've got to get the books and supplies for the Jewelstone Academy and besides, I've studied to be a jewel-smith, and don't know the first thing about flying the skies!" I stammered.

"That be yer mother talkin'. All those things can wait. What say you? Will ye take a chance on a grand adventure... seein' all manner of strange places and visit'n all them places ye dreamt about?" Grandfather encouraged.

The more he talked, the more I wanted to go, but my plans felt like a stone anchor holding me back. "I just can't." I groaned.

"The lad I've seen growin' up would've liked nothin' better than ta see the world and fly the skies. Seems ta me that he's been associatin' with other fellows what be spineless and a bit 'o that has rubbed off on 'im" Grandfather chided. "Yer not made ta be a jewel-smith. Adventure 'n excitement be in yer blood, boy!"

"Spineless?" I challenged, now angry once again, "Who was it that had to remove the rock wasp nest from the eaves of our house? Who had to fight off rock weasels when they entered our piglin pens? Who was it that had to untangle you from the stinging tentacles of a wind floater? Who was it that has been defending you at school and everywhere since I was a toe dodger? I did all those things. I am not spineless!"

"So, ye will be comin' along, then? Grandfather watched me closely as I worked things out in my mind.

I responded, "Hang on a moments. It's not that easy. I can't turn my back on everything I've worked for without thinking it through."

Grandfather grinned and slapped me on the back with the vigor of a much younger man and said, "That be another thing I be likin' about ye lad. Ye have ta think it out fer yerself. But remember, ye will'na be losin' anything if ye take this trip with me. Ye'll be just postponin' it a bit. Ye can pick up where ye left off when ye get back."

I began working through the decision by thinking out loud like I used to do with grandfather when I was younger.

"On the one hand, I could finally ride the Betty-Lou and help Grandfather rescue whoever he needs to help, on the other hand I'd have to wait to attend the Jewelstone Academy the next semester or the next cycle. I held my hands out, palm up one by one as Grandfather trained me to do in order to logically talk through a problem.

"On the one hand again, I'd be able to aide in Grandfather's rescue mission and help him fly the Betty-Lou. On the other hand, I'd be leaving mother alone and she would feel abandoned..."

"On the one hand again, mother would want me to be my own man and see the world, but on the other hand she hates the Betty-Lou and sailing the skies and would beg me to not go.

"On the one hand again, I could learn how the Betty-Lou works and grandfather could teach me about sailing the winds and I could decide if I like it or not. On the other hand, I could stay home and play nine ball, while trying to not beat Oslo and Kepler into squash root.

"On the one hand again, I'd be able to see places and peoples I can only imagine now. On the other hand, I'd be stuck in Miller's Pond biding my time until I go to the Jewelstone Academy.

"On the one hand again, I'd be happy and enjoying the journey, and on the other hand, at home, I'd be bored as a predator wasp in front of an empty rock wasp nest."

"Well, lad, seems ta me that ye've arrived at a decision. Ye best go below and discuss it with yer mother."

"You're right. If I don't go, I'd hate it here and I would never forgive myself."

I went below to find my mother. She was still in the galley, making final preparations for lunch.

"Ahem... Mother, can I have a moment of your time?" I asked.

Without turning, she responded, "I'll be done in a jiffy, I've just got'a finish gettin' these smash roots inta the pot a'fore we can talk."

"Let me help you and we can talk while I peel," I offered

and grabbed a root and the peeler.

"That'd be grand," she smiled.

"So, you know that I've been accepted to the Jewelstone Academy for next session."

"Yes, and so happy that has made me feel. Me boy is becomin' a man!"

"I'm excited about it too. But...Well, I'd like to postpone that till the next cycle."

The clay pitcher she had been holding fell to the stone paved floor and shattered. We both bent to pick up the pieces and I went to fetch the broom and dust pan.

"Why would ye be doin' that may I ask?" Mother asked with her hands on her hips.

"I'd like to take a trip with Grandfather."

"What kind of trip and how will ye be travelin'?"

"To be truthful, he said it was a rescue mission. Apparently, some friends of his have gotten themselves in a bit of a jam and they could use the help," I guessed on the last part. I supposed they were his friends. Grandfather did not mention what kind of trouble.

"What be the mode of transportation?" Mother asked now with a raise eyebrow.

I braced myself for the response from Mother as I replied, "We'll be flying in the Betty-Lou."

Tears ran down her cheeks as she glared at me with fists clenched. "Impossible, that ship be long gone or destroyed these past ten cycles and if not, ye've no business boardin' her cursed decks. I thought I'd taught ye with enough sense. Flyin' the skies be a fool's errand 'n will cause the death of ye, just as the skies took yer father from us. I'll not lose another to the wind. Ye canna go. I forbid it!"

"It's a short trip and I'll be back before you know it. Besides, I'll be careful. It's not like I am changing careers to become a sky merchant. I just want to go see a bit more of the world than what Miller's Pond can show me."

"The skies are bewitchin' and beguilin'. Best not tempt

fate, stay on the ground fer pity sakes. What about Jewelstone Academy?" Mother begged.

"I will let them know I'll be postponing my entrance. It's only a short trip. Not long enough to be beguiled by anything."

"I did'na raise ye ta talk like common-folk, nor ta act like 'em. I taught ye ta have some sense 'n now yer goin' ta throw it all away?"

"Just think of it as a vacation, I'll be back soon. I've made up my mind and I'm going. I'll be staying in touch by whey hen. I just wanted to let you know and say my goodbyes. Love ya mom. You know that right?"

"Yes. I do lad and that be why ye must not go. I canna handle the loss 'o ye both. I did'na raise ye as best as I could, teachin'ye ta speak 'n act proper so's ye could throw yer life away in the skies."

"Mama!" I raised my voice, trying not to shout in anger, "You must understand! I am 18 and I will never have the opportunity to travel and see Portus if I do not take it now. Later, I will be busy with school and then when I graduate, I will need to find a job, save money for my own shop, and who knows, have a family," I reasoned, "Besides, you can't stop me anyway. I've made up my mind. I'm going.!"

Mother wrapped her arms around me and broke down crying. "Ye canna, canna canna!" she sobbed.

"Ma, I'm coming back!" I explained softly in her ear, "It's not like I'm being conscripted into the land or air forces and you won't see me for many rotations. It'll be just a few cycles," I consoled her as best I could, patting her back and squeezing her.

Then mother stopped crying and stood apart from me. She wiped her eyes and fiercely looked me in the eyes, "Seems pig-headedness runs in the family. Yer father was the same, once he had his mind set, there was no movin' im. I tried my best ta convince ye otherwise. Be it on yer own head!"

This time I gave her a hug, and she cried, and I cried. Then I went back to peeling and tried to talk about other things, but the conversation always came back to me leaving her alone and mother giving me a reproachful look.

When we gathered for dinner, Grandfather had more skill at keeping the conversation light and hopeful. As we ate, he spoke about the journey and how soon we'd be back and that I would continue at Jewelstone Academy. Overall, we had a good lunch. Then grandfather announced, "It be time."

That news sent mother crying to her room, refusing to come out.

"Leave 'er her be lad. She'll be alright. Go above and let's get the Betty-Lou loaded."

Grandfather and I went above and took in the sight of the Betty-Lou.

"Go on, do what ye've been achin' ta do since ye could barely walk. Board the Betty-Lou!" Grandfather encouraged.

I mounted the gang plank and walked towards the Betty-Lou. When I grabbed the rail and put my foot on the deck, I was not prepared for the sensation that ran through my body. It felt like I had a shock fish wrapped around my leg and arm. I could not move because of the agony as the fire coursed through my body. Then I collapsed on the deck when the sensation left me.

Grandfather rushed to my side and picked me up. "Be ye alright?"

"I'll be fine. Just give me a moment to catch my breath. Is that normal to get shocked when boarding the Betty-Lou?"

"Tis a grand thing ye be about ta do. Perhaps a we-bit overwhelmin'."

"No, that's not it. I literally felt fire surge up my leg and through my arm. It came from the Betty-Lou when I touched her for the first time."

"Is that what ye feel now?" Grandfather asked with concern.

"No, it stopped and I'm fine now. It was probably some residual cloud static that she picked up."

"Well, in all my cycles flyin' the skies, I've ne're heard

of anyone what got shocked from cloud static. It be mighty strange."

"I can't explain it either, but I definitely felt it though there's not a mark on me and I did not get burned."

"Alrighty lad. We need ta get the Betty-Lou loaded right quick...Er...when ye be ready, that is, we'll be needin...." and Grandfather began listing all of the things that he would be needing on the journey. When I'd recovered enough, I busied myself following his orders retrieving foods and sundries from the pantry and his hidden stashes of supplies. It would have been loaded quicker if my ribs and back were not still sore from the beating received from Kepler's pipe. Collecting medicines, plants, whey hens, fishing tools, clothing and much more.

"I'm surprised that we had everything you listed. Mama kept telling us that we had to watch our money. Where did all this come from?" I asked Grandfather.

"Ta tell ye the truth, I've been preparin' for this journey several rotations now," Grandfather replied.

In less than a watch bell, everything was loaded and stowed. Grandfather did the final inspection below deck. When he came above, he commented, "I think we be ready." He gave the signal to cast off, a chopping motion with his hand.

CHAPTER 4 THE INHERITANCE

(Extracted Directly from the Personal Log book of Gideon Livingston, the Fire Lord)

As we climbed, we entered what I could only describe as a ceiling of clouds. Since I had never flown among the clouds, I was unprepared for the experience. The sun disappeared and everything turned somber and gray. I was shocked with the realization that clouds are wet, not dry and fluffy like piglin fur. Swirling white and grey, the moisture in the clouds made our faces wet as we traveled up and up. Then we broke through the layer of clouds to brilliant sunshine and we sailed on the blindingly white clouds as if they were storm tossed seas.

I watched as Grandfather spoke to the Betty-Lou as if she were a person, a lifelong friend, a lover. I was awed that the Betty-Lou spoke back to him in her own way; in the dulcet tones of the swaying of the sails and rudder. But there was more than that.

In response to a subtle question from Betty-Lou, Grandfather said, "Yes Betty, this is my last voyage. We've enough air below us now, take us where we need to go."

Her response was immediate. With a sudden surge of speed, I was thrown against the forecastle.

He really can talk to her... and she answers! I thought.

As we zoomed through the skies with all the sails extended to the sides of the ship like great spikey dragon wings, Grandfather turned to me and said, “It’s time we had a chat.”

We entered the captain's cabin which was elegantly decorated with paintings on the walls, ornate wooden carvings of dragons and vegetation on the crown moldings and corners. A bronze-cornered navigator's desk made of green ebony and large conference table of inlaid wooden patterns surrounding a carving of a dragon in battle. All of it was stained dragon green.

I was drawn to the observation windows at the stern complete with green cushioned window seats. I was mesmerized by the view as the orb of the sun reflected on the expanse of white clouds that surged behind us in swirling eddies caused by Betty-Lou's incredible speed.

Grandfather motioned for me to join him at the large captain's table. I sat down next to him and he began telling me things I have never forgotten.

"Gideon. I invited yeh on this journey for a multitude of reasons. First of all, ye be my grandson and I have tried to raise ye as me own son, but I could'na because of my respect and love for yer mother. Ye know how she be feeling about sailors and especially the Betty-Lou. I would'a loved to have brought ye on many a journey but she would'na allow it. But finally, ye be here beside me, even when I am old, but better late than never, I say. Another reason be that airmen be in our family a far-ways back. Tis in yer blood lad and I could'na deny ye that. I believe ye will take to the wind and sails as a natural. I've been watching ye and I know that yer caliber be grand. I expect great things o' ye lad, and it all starts with this journey. Another reason fer invitin' ye lad is that I have some final business to transact and a canna do it by me lonesome. Aside from yer much-welcomed help, I would love to have yer favorable association and company so as to discuss the ways of the world, the rotations ahead, and the rotations past. I expect to teach ye what I know about sailing and living, and share enough wisdom ta help ye make yer own choices. Gideon, this here, in truth, be my last journey and I fully expect ta not return from it. I wish ye to know Betty-Lou like I know her.

Afore it be all over, and listen careful now," he paused then continued, "I want ye to be the rightful captain of the Betty-Lou."

"Me? Captain? But everything I have learned was to help me be a jewel-smith or a stone-wright. I can't captain a ship! I don't know the first thing about navigation, wind, or sailing the skies." I moaned, though inside I was excited because this is what I always wanted, but the glaring truth was that I was not prepared. How could I be? I spent my entire life off of airships.

"O'course ye be not able to captain a ship right now," Grandfather agreed. "Tis why I brought ye along; so's ye ken learn 'n see what I been tellin' ye. Ye were made ta fly the skies! As far as the other crafts, truth be told, ye never had it in ye. Since ye were a knee-higher, ye be climbing trees and explorin' whilst the other lads stayed indoors. Cloud jumping be in yer blood, lad!" explained Grandfather with a large smile.

"How can I be a captain without a crew?" I complained.

Grandfather just shook his head and said, "Ye've got much ta learn, or ta un-learn 'bout Betty-Lou."

The anger welled up inside of me as I thought of the only question that I needed to have answered. I felt the unjustness of it all burn in my throat. "Why did you release the Betty-Lou if you meant to give her to me?" I demanded.

"Ye be wise beyond yer cycles. Twas a hard thing ta do, fer certain, but givin' the circumstances, twas necessary. Ye were but a toe dodger at the time, 'n I felt yer mother needed help with ye. So I gave up bein' a sky merchant so as ta provide a stable place fer ye 'n yer mother. I could'na help her if I were travelin' the skies. If I'd kept the Betty-Lou idle so I could be with yeh all, knowin' the adjudicator, he would'a found a way ta take her from me by force. The best thing ta do, then, were to let her go free. I knew she could take care 'o herself 'n had no worries she could come back at any time I needed her. Well, ye witnessed what resulted the day she was set free. Besides all 'o that, I could feel the tiredness in ma bones and needed a rest. But now... I feel energized and ready fer an adventure."

Grandfather explained with a grin.

I asked Grandfather to tell me more of what he meant but he simply responded, "All in good time lad, All in good time. While there's light, let me show ye the Betty-Lou."

I followed grandfather around the deck like a tamed water pup. He showed me mechanisms that opened and closed the side sails that catch the wind for added speed. Grandfather demonstrated the use of the guide ropes, safety ropes and forward sails lines. He instructed me on how the helm's wheel worked and let me steer the Betty-Lou for a bit. He showed me everything from the graceful dragon head at the bow to the officer's quarters in the stern. We mounted the forecastle in bow, and the quarter deck in the aft. He showed me how to use the capstan for the anchor and the windlasses for loading the ship with heavy cargo. I listened carefully as he demonstrated how to load the harpoons, razor disks and shafts for puncturing buoyancy tanks.

"Most ships dangle from their buoyancy tanks by ropes and chains. That makes them an easy target. The Betty-Lou's tanks be part 'o the ship between the bulkheads 'n that provides tremendous speed, stability 'n strength." Grandfather explained. "It be hard ta sink the Betty-Lou."

We went below and Grandfather showed me the empty crew's quarters with swinging beds stacked three high- ten rows of 24 bunks, enough for 240 crew members, the sulfur cannon enclosures, the large cargo storage holds, and how to open the secret compartments. I already knew where the pantry, the water tanks, and the whey hen and animal enclosures were because I had helped fill them. As we passed hidden buoyancy tanks, Grandfather pointed them out. He showed me the access passageways for ship repairs and where spare masts, timbers and other repair materials were kept. At the bottom of the ship, next to the keel he showed me the ten iron cages that composed the brig and beyond that, the well-stocked armory which contained enough swords, spears, darts, lances, and fire shields for 200 crew members, as well as an assortment of explosive stones, blinders, shards, arrows, bows and crossbows. Finally, Grandfather showed me how the waste plumbing and the bilge operated.

After the tour, we sat and chatted. He told me about fighting off pirates, braving terrible storms, and nearly getting captured by the western savages. After a while Grandfather began to doze as he sat in the captain's chair and so I let him peacefully nap, with a blissful smile on his lips.

CHAPTER 5 THE STORY OF THE BETTY-LOU

(Extracted Directly from the Personal Log book of Gideon Livingston, the Fire Lord and the memoirs of Ariel Livingston)

The journey continued through the afternoon into the evening. I marveled that the Betty-Lou was navigating and flying by herself without any assistance. I had been taught about the discovery of the xeoxyn gas that filled her internal ballasts and that provided the tremendous lift allowing her to travel through the skies, but of the specific workings of how the Betty-Lou operated as if she were alive, I was just beginning to see.

I left the cabin and looked over the side of the ship. For the first time, I saw vast expanses of dark blue sea. I had heard the tales of the leviathan and the sea monsters that dwelt there, but discounted them as exaggerations.

"Tis a beautiful sight, is it not?" Grandfather said as he joined me and slapped me on the back.

"Did you have a good nap?" I asked.

"Aye, lad." He chuckled and continued, "Naps be the friend 'o the old and decrepit."

"Not so decrepit to me!" I rubbed my shoulder where he had slapped my back. "Grandfather, what do you know about the seas below us?" I asked.

"Not too much m'lad, but enough to know there be

terrible dangers lurking in those waters." Grandfather warned and continued, "E'en the bravest souls dare not venture upon the waters. What's more lad, those that have, were ne're seen again."

"What have you seen in those waters?" I pressed.

Grandfather looked at me squarely and replied, "Understand me lad, tis not worth yer life to go explorin' the seas when we can explore the skies, which be dangerous enough, mind you. What dwells in the depths be of no concern, except for those unfortunate enough to fall into them. I remember as if it were yesterday. Twas a beautiful clear day, much like today. We were locked in a terrible battle with pirates. Our ship returned fire and breeched their airship's buoyancy tanks with a razor disk. We were over open waters as we be now. I watched the pirate ship descend until it splashed upon the waters. While I watch with mixed feelings of vindication and pity for those poor sailors scurrying about on the wrecked ship, beneath the ship a dark shadow circled. The pirates could'na see the danger, but from our vantage point above them it was plainly visible. In the water, this sea creature appeared to be at least thrice the size o' the ship, but when it rose, I saw it to be much larger 'n that. I'll never forget when I saw the huge gaping maw o' the beast, rising from the depths to swallow the ship and its crew whole. I remember the fish's eye as it turned to go back to the depths. It looked straight at us as if ta say, 'I see you and I'll be waitin'.' That leviathan be the reason no man has sailed upon the waters."

I searched the water below and thought I saw a huge dark form undulating under the shimmering waves and dark swirling shadows.

I shivered at the awful sight and said, "I'd always wondered why we travel the skies and not the sea. Now it makes perfect sense."

"Aye lad, the seas be too awful dangerous." Grandfather responded and slapped me on the back so forcefully that it took my breath away.

As the sun disappeared at the end of its rotation, Grandfather adjusted the glow stones set in a framework on the wall of his cabin. The two stones glowed with more light as Grandfather twisted the lever to bring them closer to each other. To pass the time, Grandfather and I played games of castles and stones on the playing surface inlayed onto the wooden table in the captain's cabin that also served as the captain's cartographer desk and navigation table.

"I'm getting a bit tired." I told Grandfather as I stretched my arms after losing another game. "Where do I *bunk*?" I felt I needed to emphasize using the word "bunk" instead of "sleep" to show my impressive nautical vocabulary.

"Tired of losin' eh? Canna take the heat, eh lad? Well, you will be *sleepin'* in the first mate's cabin below, first door on the right." Grandfather emphasized the word "sleeping" as he gave me those directions just to show me that I had no understanding.

"Good night Grandfather," I stated as I directed my truly sleepy feet to the ornate cabin door.

"Night, Gideon. Be your sleep peaceful and restful. I'll be seein' ya bright 'n early in the mornin'." Grandfather responded kindly.

I entered the room and saw that it was small, with two stained-glass portals on the left. The furniture left little room to walk in the center of the room. On one side under the portals stood a small table and an ornately carved old-fashioned sailor's chest. On the other side rested a single bed with railings carved to look like horned adders. The bed's four corner posts looked like small trees with roots as the feet of the bed and branches supporting the thick green curtains surrounding the bed. The curtains were tied back with a golden tassel. The bedspread depicted a flying creature that I had never before beheld. It appeared to be reptilian, but it had the beak of a marsh hawk and the flat tail of a swamp lizard. Its scaled wings were spread wide and its long red talons extended, as it appeared to be attacking a bearded man armed only with a sword. The striking features of the man were his green eyes and bright flaming red hair.

"That's strange! He and I both have red hair and green eyes. I wonder if he is an ancestor of mine...mmm." I commented out loud, but had I not been so tired I would have studied it more. Instead, I pulled back the covers, took off my boots and changed into my night clothing it seemed in one swift motion. I jumped, or better stated, fell into the inviting covers and slumber came swiftly.

The bright light of morning hammered its way into the room via the portals. At least that is how it felt with the blinding light and warmth shining directly on my face. As I awoke, I noticed that I had neglected to close the bed curtains and made a mental note to not forget this in the future. I quickly readied myself to see Grandfather.

I found him on the emerald deck above. He was seated and enjoying a steaming cup of red bean tea in the fresh morning air. He was seated at a curiously designed octagonal table of the same color as the deck.

"Morning to you Grandfather." I greeted him warmly.

"Likewise my good lad. Have a seat." He said as he motioned to the table.

He chuckled at my confusion because I could see no seats to be had. The only seat visible was the one he sat upon. What I saw was an eight-sided box with intricately carved wooden lattices for sides. "Push the button on the side." Grandfather motioned with his chin.

I located the circular button with the shape of a dragon on one side of the octagon. The pewter dragon was coiled in a spiral, jaws gaping wide, ready to jump up or out of the button. When I pushed it, the section of the table slid out revealing a seat of the same shape as the segment of the table. "How ingenious! Eight seats concealed in a table with such artisanship. The builders of the Betty-Lou were masters."

I exclaimed in admiration and surprise. I thought I knew everything about the Betty-Lou.

I sat in the chair, which to my amazement, though connected to the table, swiveled for easy access and egress. "So, Grandfather, where are we going?" I asked hopefully.

"We be headed to the Isle of Noonday, and as of this moment, yer training tis about ta begin." He winked at me and continued sipping his red bean tea.

"What direction would that be?" I pressed.

"We are heading due southeast, following the transcontinental current." He took another sip from the straw that extended into the steaming liquid around the beans in his cup.

"How can you tell?" I queried, "All the clouds look the same."

"That is where ye be wrong lad." He pointed ahead and to the right to a dark cloud-mass billowing up like the thousands of flower buds of the white caul plant. "That be a static rumbler cloud. At this time of year this only occurs in the south. Look at those clouds over there." He pointed behind us. "See how they follow us? The only current big enough for all of those to be following us is the transcontinental." Again, he winked. "Besides, I looked at the guide stone when I woke up." He pointed to the pedestal with a round top covered in a bubble of clear crystal.

I walked over to the pedestal and saw a map of both hemispheres of Portus with an oblong stone the color of a sunrise marking our location and direction. The stone was slowly moving down toward the center of the Eastern hemisphere. I clearly saw that we were headed from Miller's Pond, far to the northeast on the continent of Bergland, to the Isle of Noonday West of Bergland. Below that, I saw the twin continents of Foldfen and Fenfold and to the East, the continent of Fernland. Then I looked at the Western hemisphere. Though continents and a few cities were visible, it was much less detailed than the Eastern hemisphere. In the center of the western hemisphere was a spiral as large as a continent labeled "Maelstrom". The continent of Asombre seemed to form a barrier like a nine-ball glove to hold the Maelstrom from coming further West.

"So this is how you steer the ship!" I exclaimed.

"Naye lad. Ye've got it all wrong. The steerin' happens at the helm, with the rudder wheel. The guide stones just help the navigator 'n the capt'n to set the direction, among the other signs such as the wind, the clouds and the stars. Matter 'o fact, ye dunna need the guide stone if ye know how ta read the other signs. If ye read the signs wrong, however, even by just a wee bit, could set ye off course by leagues and bring ye disasters untold. More 'n a few ships end up runnin' out 'o supplies afore they can get back on course. Some end up in places they should'na be, surrounded by pirates and worse." Grandfather explained.

"Speaking of pirates, have you been to the Western lands Grandfather?" I asked him while I studied the maps.

Grandfather peered at me from behind the mist of his red bean tea and replied cautiously, "Aye lad, I've had to travel there on several occasions."

"Do not many people live there? Where are all the cities? Why is the Western map so empty?" I continued my train of thought.

"Well, lad, that be for many reasons, the largest bein', they do not want us knowin'. There be a large population in the Western provinces. Ye know of the pirates and outlaws that dwell in those lands, and they be unwilling to divulge their numbers or their dwellings. Government surveyors and map makers rarely return from expeditions to map the western regions. What little we know be from those lucky few what have returned, myself bein' one 'o those few," Grandfather shared.

"So what is the maelstrom?" I asked referring to what I had seen on the map.

"That be a perpetual tempest the likes of which ye've

ne're seen. Devours anything what comes near it. That be another reason fer not knowin' much 'bout the Western lands," Grandfather Livingston responded sadly as he took another sip of his tea. "Too many a soul've tried to navigate in those skies and have ne're been heard of again."

I pondered on the terrible maelstrom for a moment longer. Then my eyes were drawn to the outside of the pedestal. I noticed that the external lip of the circular top was marked with directional symbols and that the whole device swiveled to be able to take a bearing based on the direction of the point of the guide stone. "So that is how navigation is done," I said to myself.

I returned to my seat and asked the questions that I had asked hundreds of times before but had only gotten, "You will learn when ye be ready" as an answer. "Grandfather, how did the Betty-Lou come to be? Why is she called the Betty-Lou and not the Adventure, the Lightning Bolt, or the Cloud Jumper, like all of the other ships. Why does she look like a dragon instead of a regular air-ship?"

"Hold on there, lad. One question at a time. I do believe that you be finally ready to hear and understand the answers. But before I get my story-tellin' machinery in motion, I be needin' some nourishment. How about we fix a bite of breakfast for us first?"

I realized that I was hungry too, so I gladly went below with Grandfather to make a tasty breakfast of some piglin sausage, springlot cheese, squabbler eggs, and tubers, that Grandfather showed me how to cook over the heat stones in the galley. These consisted of two dark red stones set in an iron framework. The frame of each stone was attached with a lever that allowed the cook to slide the stones so they nearly touched each other. When the stones were slid close to each other, they began glowing red hot. The closer they got, the brighter they glowed and the more heat they produced. Notches on the framework indicated the temperatures for each setting. I set the stones to medium-high and placed cooking pans on the framework.

"More than one ship has burnt to the keel 'cause of a careless cook or boatswain," Cautioned Grandfather as we added the ingredients to the sizzling pans.

After breakfast, Grandfather and I cleared the galley table, scoured the dishes with cleaning sand, and then we returned to the octagonal table above, but it was not there.

Grandfather smirked at my confusion and simply pulled a lever next to the entrance. To the noise of clanking, the octagonal table arose from the center of the deck; all the chairs tucked neatly into its eight sides.

"How ingenious!" I remarked once again. "This air-ship is certainly full of surprises."

The Betty-Lou gave a sudden lurch, and Grandfather sternly said, "This ship has a name and it be Betty-Lou. Be ye well advised to show respect and stay on her good side."

"Grandfather, you talk about the Betty-Lou as if she were alive. How can this be?" I asked as I pushed a button to release my chair.

As we sat around the table again Grandfather looked at me intensely. "Yeh really want to know the answers to those questions now, do ya lad? Tis fer this reason ye be on this here voyage. There be much ye need ta learn a'fore takin' over as captain."

"I'm still getting used to the idea of me being the captain. But go on. I'm all ears."

"I must impress upon ye the serious nature of what I'm 'bout ta tell ye. Tis worth more 'n me life ta reveal these secrets 'n only one other person knows what I am about to tell ye and that be my son, Bert, yer pappy. Should anyone else find out this information, our lives and that of the Betty-Lou would be in mighty peril," Grandfather said these words as he leaned forward and added, "Yeh must promise me lad, ta never tell no-one 'bout this, not e'en yer own mother. Agreed?" He extended his weathered hand.

"Agreed," I responded as I shook his hand and by the

force of his grip I was once again reminded that Grandfather was still a strong man.

"It all began when I were a young sailor aboard the air-ship Westover. We ran into a mighty terrible storm that blew us about for two full turns. By the time it was spent, we might've been hundreds of leagues from our original course. What were worse, our guide stone had stopped working. It lay at the bottom of the map, immobile and useless. We had no idea where we were at. The captain determined to descend from the stratosphere above the clouds to get a visual landmark bearing. Down we went. But as we descended through the clouds, it were darker and darker, and the misty clouds, they never lifted. It was so nearly dark as ta seem night.

"Is that unusual, to be surrounded in a cloud?" I interrupted.

"No, tis not out of the ordinary... mists and fog abound in many parts of the globe. But remember lad, we had no means to know in which part of the globe we were, seein' how our guide stones were inoperable and we could'na see the stars."

"So, to continue, lad; finally, from fear of grounding, after what seemed an eternity, the captain called for a sounding. To our amazement, it was called out as only 100 ship-lengths. The captain called for a full stop. Since it could be the peak of a tall mountain, or we could be on the lip of a bottomless pit it were not safe to land our craft. The captain ordered the light stone be brought on the deck. The light stone was installed in a tube with refracting lenses to shine concentrated beams of light. He unshuttered the tube and a brilliant beam of light shot from the end and extended into the misty darkness. As the airman moved the light beam, it illuminated something. Another air-ship floating just beneath us. It appeared to be abandoned. "I need a boarding party," the captain announced. When I volunteered to go aboard the other air-ship, little did I know how that would change my life."

"How did it change your life Grandfather?" I

interrupted again in my excitement.

"Hang on lad, there be more ta tell yet!" Grandfather Livingston grumbled as he was in full storytelling mode and disliked to be interrupted.

"So we boarded the air-ship and with our stone lanterns we looked around a bit. It was an old air-ship, maybe 200 cycles or so. Everything seemed functional, and even more strange, it did not appear to be in disrepair. We figured that it must have had a crew recently. We did not find any clues or anything useful for that matter. The captain went to grab the logbook and the rest of us, we returned to the Westover. That is when things began to happen. That old ship, she came alive just as Captain Sorenson was going to step on to the ladder to return to our ship. The old ship sank just enough so he could not reach the ladder. He called up to us,'Lower the ladder more.' And we did... and the ship sank more each time. We tried to hoist the captain aboard with ropes. The ol' ship's masts moved to knock them away from his reach. We tried to keep the ship from dodgin' and sinkin' by fixin' grapplin' hooks and mooring ropes to her. But she did'na want that and glided beyond our reach each time we cast the ropes."

Grandfather took a sip of tea and continued, "When it was done playing with us, as if it grew tired of a child's plaything, it simply flew off with our captain. We tried to follow, but in the deep mist it was impossible. We used the light stone all the rest of that day and into the night till we were exhausted and gave up the search."

"On the second bell, the night watch woke up the first mate. By that time, all of us were awake given the racket he had made. We rushed to the deck and witnessed, as the light stone spun around us, that our ship was surrounded by at least 20 old ships of all shapes, sizes, colors, and styles. All of them appeared to be in the same pristine condition as the first. Right in the middle was that old ship that had taken the captain, and there he were, standing on the deck. He came aboard the Westover as a man on a mission. Changed he were. Gone were the customary scowl, the furrowed brow, and the angry stare. Only one word could describe his visage, that were 'peaceful'. He spoke to us, 'Ye all know me to be a serious man, not given to believe the yarns and tales that abound in taverns and drink halls. Yet one tale I have come to believe now. Tis the tale of the ghost ships. Ye all know of it, and here they be before ye.' He gestured around to the vacant ships surrounding the Westover. 'They be alive.'"

"'All of ye be my crew; ye work for me. I work for Sir Mayfair, the owner of the Westover. What do we get for it? We work far away from family, friends. We brave the elements, e'en riskin' our very lives. For what, I ask you?... a few silver ingots, or if we be in luck, a gold stone? Which one of us is satisfied with our pitiful lot? The only one getting wealthy be Sir Mayfair, the owner.'"

"A few of the sailors raised their fist and grunted and cheered in agreement. Captain Sorensen fixed each one of us in turn with his passionate gaze a'fore he continued, 'This be a gran opportunity gentlemen, the likes of which will never occur again in our lives. All of these ships be lost to history, no owner, no captains, yet each one has been searchin' for someone. I read this here logbook,' Captain Sorenson had a wild look in his eyes as he held aloft the old leather bound logbook. '...and ye know what I found? I found that this here ship has a soul, that each one of these vessels has a soul, and can fly without a captain, but what they want more than anything else be the companionship that only an airman can give.'"

"'What say ye then? Will ye take yer destinies into yer own hands get yer own ship, or do ye want to stay workin' for wages on the Westover?'"

"There was a lot of murmuring amongst the crew members sayin' things like: 'He's gone mad he has.' 'How can a ship have a soul?' 'But there they are, surroundin' us. How do ye explain that?'"

"'Who will it be amongst ye that has the nerve to take

what they're offerin' ye?' Captain Sorenson called again."

"No one moved. At the time I was just barely conscripted and held the rank of yeoman. It would be cycles before I could even think of raising that rank and more cycles after that to make it to captain. I spoke up seeing as I had nothing to lose, 'You mean to say that these here ships want us be their owners, to man them and pilot them?'"

"'Blessed be. I always knew you were a bright boy. But ya got it all wrong lad. These ships cannot be 'owned' by anyone. They be looking for a companion, a partner, a friend. It's all right here in this journal. The last captain of this airship wrote it all down.'"

"Embolden by his words, I spoke again, 'So all I have ta do is choose an airship and then board her and that be it?'"

"Not quite lad. The ship will be picking ye if ye be willing and it be a life-long commitment. So, be ye ready?' Captain Sorenson smiled when I stepped forward."

"I be willin' and ready.' I said as he motioned for me to step to the edge of the Westover."

"They be waitin' to meet ye.' The captain smiled and gestured to the waiting ships."

"The airman manning the light stone widened the aperture of the light and we could see that one by one the ships were approaching me and then departing. This took a few moments until one ship did not depart after approaching. It was the oddest-looking ship I had ever seen. I wondered that it had no visible buoyancy tank but what struck me most was its elegance and grace. 'Hello', I said to her, 'My name be Ariel Livingston. May I come aboard?' She obliged by turning port and extending her walk way. I boarded her and never regretted it. I dunna know if I were the only one, besides the captain that boarded a ship that mornin', but I heard the First Mate shout, 'The fun and games be over. Now get below deck, we have a long day tomorrow and you are goin' ta need yer rest.'"

"That is amazing Grandfather. So you were chosen by the Betty-Lou! What do you suppose became of the captain and the other ghost ships?" I wondered.

"We stayed among the other ghost ships that day and night, and I bid farewell to Captain Sorenson the next morning. That is the last I saw of him or the other ships. Be it my understanding that we had found one of the uncharted floating islands," Grandfather grew quiet and his eyes gazed off in the distance as he remembered that event from long ago.

I interrupted his silent reverie, "Next question Grandfather. You didn't tell me why she is called the Betty-Lou."

As if awoken, Grandfather blinked and looked around, then recalling the question grinned and gave me a wink as he answered, "Why it was the name she chose for herself. I thought it were a good idea to allow the ship to get to know me a bit. I chattered like a school-girl telling her about me life, me ambitions, and me family. I could tell she were listenin' 'cause she were swayin' an creekin' in rhythm ta me words. She seemed to chuckle at the funny parts by flappin' her sails or clappin' the portal covers. Soon enough, I realized that if we were ta be conversin' that I needed a name by which to address her, as a sentient being, in some fashion other than 'ye ship'. Since she could'na talk as we do, I attempted to discover a name for her by reciting a few names to see how she responded."

"'Be ye liking Lightin' Stalker?' She shuddered, 'Fair Cloud?" Another shudder, "Drifting Mist?" A jerk and a shudder as a hound would make when shakin' off the water."

"I tried several more names that she did not like, given the shudders, jolts and shakes I suffered. It came to me that someone did know her name, and it had to be the former captain. I went to the captain's cabin to see what he called her. I found the captain's journal located in a crystal enclosed bookcase. I opened the logbook of Captain Clarence Elder and flipped to the end and there it be, she was called 'Betty-Lou'. I asked her, 'How do you like the name 'Betty-Lou'?' I should have hung on to something because Betty-Lou started bucking and spinning like a lassoed meercat. From then on, I addressed her as Betty-Lou. As far as her origin, that is a story for another day. Betty-Lou is as unique as her name. In all my travels, I've never seen the like of her."

CHAPTER 6 THE DRAGON

(Extracted Directly from the Personal Log book of Gideon Livingston, the Fire Lord and the memoirs of Captain Ariel Livingston)

That morning Grandfather and I sat and chatted about his tales of sailing as a merchant in the southern drifts, how he acquired a crew, and his first encounters with pirates and scoundrels. I could have listened to him all day. In fact, that is what I intended to do. We had lunch and I was anxious for him to continue. He had just begun a story about his visit to the frosty Southern Marches when he announced, "We've arrived."

When he saw the mountain peak above the clouds, Grandfather stopped talking and his eyes misted over. In silence he used his sleeve to wipe tears that threatened to fall.

"What's wrong Grandfather?" I asked.

"Tis nothing. Tis just that this place holds many a fond memory and many a sad one," he continued softly, "When I were a young sailor on this very ship, we came to port here and this be where I first met yer grandmother, bless her soul. I did'na know it at the time, but I was to return here often, drawn by the beautiful brown eyes and flowing auburn hair of Milly McBride. She had a smile that could warm even the coldest sailor, but what I liked most be that Betty-Lou were mighty fond of her too."

"So you lived here?" I asked.

"Yes, m'lad. Betty-Lou has brought us to the Isle of

Noonday, economic center of trade and commerce for the twelve kingdoms, and largest city in the Eastern Hemisphere."

"Yer grandmother and I were married here and we lived here a good long while. Yer dad met his darlin' here too," and then Grandfather got serious, "and here is where he was taken from us."

"Grandfather, I was always told that he died in a terrible storm just as he arrived here. Struck by lightning because he did not wear his grounder," I said, but I sensed there was another reason for my father's death.

"Aye lad, tis a sad tale, and it breaks my heart to recount it to yeh, but now ye must know the truth. Your father was a brave man, contrary to what ye have been told, and that bilge of a story about him having an accident was not my idea, t'was your mother's; crafted to persuade ye to not consider the skies as a profession. Ye know she despised the life of airmen 'n she could'na bear for ye to be one either. She preferred a man with his feet firmly planted on the ground. Yet she loved your father like no other and he loved her. She was willing to wait to see him every time he came to port because her love was so strong. Yet as time went on and ye came along, her patience waned and she longed to have yer father at home fer good. While ye were yet an infant, one day yer father announced, "I have one more voyage to take that will provide for us in a way that I will never have to leave your side," she was overjoyed.

He was gone for six lunar cycles and when he returned, tragedy struck. A storm arose like none I had ever seen before or since. Suddenly, the full fury of lightning struck the helm near where your father manned the till. But that is not what did him in. T'was mutiny. He had a traitor in the crew that wanted to steal the hard-earned rewards your father had acquired. It was his own first mate, Josiah Jorgenson. The scoundrel took advantage of the distraction of the lightning and threw your dad in the brig, and turned the Windlass into a pirate ship," as Grandfather pronounced these words, the Betty-Lou shuddered.

"But how do you know this if he was taken before he came to port?" I pointed out.

"I knew ye were bright. There be logic in yer thinkin'. The ship's navigator, Kendrick, escaped overboard before the mutineers gathered all of Bert's supporters and locked em in the brig. He lowered hisself down a rope as far as it would take 'im and had ta jump the rest of the way. Injured his legs in the process but he made it to us, riskin' his life so as we could mount a rescue. Apparently when they saw that he were missing, they turned tail and flew to escape. Of course, we tried to find them, and kept looking for many turns and for a full cycle, all to no avail."

"The Windlass wasn't seen or heard of again for ten cycles. When word came back to me t'was found as a wreck on the air shoals south of the Ilse of Manning . There were no sign of yer father either. During that time yer mother wasted away 'cause she couldn'na stand not knowing. Your mother could never forgive me for encouraging my son to be an airman and hated Betty-Lou for being an airship like the one that stole her love. She refused to come aboard or to ever see it again. So the last voyage of your father was never mentioned again and no one knows the full story, but Betty-Lou knows and I believe that she wants to show you."

The Betty-Lou descended into the clouds slowly and soon enough we reached the municipal docks of the Ilse of Noonday.

"Here ye be lad," and Grandfather gave me a small dagger and a curved sword. "We canna be too careful. Always watch yer surroundings and stay close."

We disembarked and Grandfather immediately began the grand tour, showing me the town of Noonday. "Here is the chapel where we were wed. Over across the way is the school yard your father attended."

We wandered seemingly without purpose and Grandfather Livingston told me the history of every building, statue, and fountain. Then we stopped. Grandfather had brought us to his old house. “This be where ye were born,” he stated.

We were looking at a three-story wooden home, white washed from top to bottom. A balcony opened up on the second floor supported by thick spiral carved columns. The third-floor roof did not come to a point as other houses, but was flat to accommodate a landing pad and the tall mooring post. Flowers were planted in the window boxes and white lace curtains hung on all of the windows. The white picket fence surrounding the manicured yard extended all the way around the property. It was obvious that the house was inhabited and well cared for. A large white signpost announced, “Office of the Adjudicator, the Honorable Julius McFarland, Audiences by Appointment Only.”

Grandfather’s jaw tightened as he saw the sign and said, “I built that house and it were ma pride and joy. It broke ma heart ta sell it. But fer the health of yer mother, we would still be there. She could’na handle the bad memories. That be why we relocated far north to Miller’s Pond. Besides, it were just three of us and we had no need of such a large habitation.”

“Thanks for bringing me here. I have been wanting to know about our family history for a long while. Mama would not talk of her life here, and so I know little of what happened. How did grandmother really pass?”

“I suppose ye were told that she died of consumption. That be true, but that were not the whole story. She died from complications giving birth to yer father. We never wanted Bert to feel that he had caused her death. Twas her idea and last request to protect her son.”

“Is there more that I should know about my family?” I asked.

“Well, there be a wee bit more, that be why we be here. Let’s go have dinner at the Keel where we can talk more,” Grandfather offered.

We walked down the cobble stone streets back to the town square. As we walked, I noticed a shop with a sign that showed a green dragon that seemed very familiar. I couldn't place it but I knew I had seen that symbol before. We arrived at another building that looked like a ship upside down with a sign labeled with the words, "The Captain's Keel" in white letters. No sooner had we entered the door than we were embraced savagely by a stocky woman with her hair in a bun and bright red cheeks. "Yeh must be Gideon. I have'na seen yeh since yeh were pint sized. Yeh have much of your father in yeh," she said as she looked me up and down. "Give me a squeeze!" A rock serpent could not have squeezed tighter.

"Bless my soul. I'm so glad to see yeh Captain. What brings yeh to Noonday? I thought ye'd be forever rid of this place that caused so much grief for yeh."

"Penny Stonewright, tis a pleasure to see ye. Ye have'na changed a bit. There be some things that I need ta take care of 'n I brought my grandson Gideon ta help. How be Cappy?" Grandfather inquired.

Penny's face darkened a bit. "He passed away a few cycles back. Nothing unnatural, just that his old injuries caught up with'm. He died peaceful like. He spoke of yeh on his death bed. Wished yeh'd been there."

"Sorry ta hear that, Penny. Looks like ye took over right well."

"The Keel be all we had. I felt duty bound to keep it a go'in," Penny changed the subject, "So how can I help you two fine gentlemen?"

"We'd like some dinner, whatever the special is, and a quiet place to chat," Grandfather answered with a knowing smile.

"Right as rain. I'll have my daughter Miel take you to your table and I'll fetch yeh somethin' ta eat," she said as she motioned to a girl that seemed her twin. "Miel, I'd like yeh ta meet the finest captain that ever sailed the skies and his grandson. Captain Livingston 'n Gideon. Please make 'em feel comfortable and take 'em ta booth one," with a wink she was off.

"Pleased to make yer acquaintance," she said in a velvet voice that was completely opposite of her mother's husky voice. "Follow me this way."

She led us to a booth in the back of the dining floor on the side of the large brick fireplace protected from view by a heavy wooden trellis. "Can I get yeh both somethin' ta drink while yer dinner is being prepared?" she asked sweetly as we sat down.

"The usual," Grandfather said and then caught himself, "ah, no, I better have just your famous dragon fruit punch, and one fer ma grandson too."

"Very well," she smiled and bustled off in an instant.

I admired the dark wood table and the ornate benches surrounding the booth where we sat. On the wall above us was a beautiful painting of none other than the Betty-Lou braving a terrible storm.

Carved on the top of the table was the same dragon symbol from the shop on the road to town. "What is the significance of this symbol?" I asked Grandfather as I ran my fingers across the dragon's neck.

Grandfather chuckled, "Tis the symbol of assurance, strength, and honor. This dragon crest has been used for ages and I am ignorant of its origins. During the first revolution, it came ta mean somethin' else."

"I saw it on a shop's door on the way here."

"Did'ja now? Well, that be interesting. We will have to visit that shop after dinner."

Just then Miel came back with the drinks and table settings. "Will there be anythin' else?" she asked.

We both shook our heads and she departed. My eyes followed her through the carved trellis that separated our booth from the dining hall. She greeted three scruffy men dressed in black leather jerkins and knee-high sailor's boots. She was not smiling as she did so.

"Careful boy, lower your gaze a bit. I know their kind; always lookin' for trouble," Grandfather warned. "There be no use in causing a stir. I'd like my presence here ta not be known at present." Luckily she led them to the other side of the dining room and they paid no attention to us seeing as we were mostly hidden.

Lunch was delicious. The tender moor beast was the best I had ever tasted and the roasted bashroot was so tasty, I had several servings. We did not chat much as we ate, which really was an indication of the quality of the fare. I took a last swig from the mug of dragon fruit juice and sat back with a sigh. Grandfather began simply, "I had many enemies in this town, mostly due ta jealousy, but some men, and even some women be pure evil, driven by greed and envy ta do horrible things in the dark, behind the backs 'o decent folk and under the very noses of the law. That be the cause of the trouble with my Bert. He being much like me in character, but bolder and less cautious."

Now this is what my ears had been aching to hear and this was the perfect place. "Tell me more about my father. Mama would not speak of him for her grief."

"She forbid me to speak of it to you lad. But here is the tale that even your mother does not know and surely if she did, t'would'a added ta her grief a tremendous load," he said as he shook his head.

"My intention were always ta pass the Betty-Lou on ta ma son Bert. She and he being fast friends due to the many voyages we had taken with Bert as cabin boy. Yet Bert was a stubborn lad and got the notion that he wanted ta be his own captain and not live in my shadow. When he came of age, he conscripted with a fellow with the name of Shultz as an airman. When he came back from his first voyage, he was already a shipmate first class. Aye, he had some ambition in him."

He took a drink of dragon juice and continued, "Bert had some friends from his school rotations on that boat who conscripted, just as he did. I suppose that when he were advanced and they were not, the seeds of envy were planted, never to be rooted out. One in particular was Granger Rockland who was the closest thing Bert had to a brother. They could always be found together and spent many bells right here at this table talking of their future plans. It was here, in The Captain's Keel, that Bert met Sadie-Belle as a waitress. That were the final straw for Granger for he too had become enamored of Sadie and when she chose Bert over him, he vowed revenge on Bert and became his most bitter enemy," Grandfather paused a moment to glance around the dining hall. His eyes lingered on the three unsavory characters chattering loudly punctuated by loud guffaws and back slapping.

"Good. They be self-absorbed and have'na noticed us yet," he continued. "Well, Bert moved up the ranks eventually ta first mate on the Windlass, a fine ship. Granger had left the Windlass for another ship called the Wrath of Kendor. He too had moved up ranks and was the navigator. On their next voyage, the captain of the Windlass fell ill and died, leaving my son ta captain the ship back to port. In the end he was commissioned as the captain of the Windlass. This did not sit well with his former friends, seeing as their advancement progress had not been near as rapid. Secret plans were made ta cause my son misery and grief and strip him of what he had earned. I tried to warn him of the rumors I had heard but he was more stubborn even than I. He would'na take the necessary precautions. After all, they be his friends, and he blindly refused to believe that Granger were really his enemy."

Grandfather looked at me sternly and said, "When it comes to money 'n women, remember lad, ye have no friends. I know this from sad experience and my son experienced this to his doom. Were it not for Betty-Lou I would have suffered a similar fate many times over. Now that you know the history, you will understand that it were Granger what paid the Windlass' first mate, Josiah, who also was a former school mate, to suborn the crew and throw those loyal to Bert in the brig with him. His fortune was stolen and he was taken away, never to be seen again," Grandfather had not taken his eyes off of the three men. "Tis time to go Gideon. Gather yer belongings now."

I turned to see what he was looking at and saw that one of the men was pointing in our direction and laughing. "Push the button," Grandfather said pointing to the side of the table where I sat.

I looked and beheld the same dragon symbol that I had seen on the Betty-Lou. I pushed the button and the bench tipped silently forward and Grandfather and I slid down an opening under the table. We landed on a soft cushion and Grandfather put his finger to his lips, "Shhh" and he pointed upward.

We could hear shouts of angry men. "Where'd they go? I did'na see them leave! Lord McFarland told us they was in here."

"This way," Grandfather motioned and I followed. Once again, I was reminded that Grandfather did not seem that old as I tried to keep up with him through the dim passages that wound among barrels and crates of who knows what.

We came to a small grated hatch about knee high, that led downward. At the end of the small tunnel the exit was filled with moonlight. Grandfather got on his knees and found the dragon symbol and pushed the button, releasing the latch of the grate. On all fours we crawled through the grate. We barely fit single file in the rough-hewn tunnel and more than once a jagged edge of rock caused my knees considerable pain. We stealthily went down what I realized was a ship-length long drainage culvert that led to the creek. We wriggled out of the exit with wet and bruised knees, glad to be able to stand again.

We secluded ourselves under some overhanging bushes and Grandfather turned to me, "Remember that name, Julius McFarland. He were the most powerful man in this town, and he be mine enemy. I believe that he were also involved in the mutiny aboard the Windlass. Tis he who lives now in my house."

Without another word, Grandfather left the protection of the tree and began following the uphill course of the creek.

"Don't we want to go down to the Betty-Lou?" I asked perplexed and pointing the other direction.

"Betty-Lou can take care of herself. They know better than to try and board her or capture her, and if they try, I pity the poor fools. No, she be fine. We have to check out the dragon symbol you saw in the street."

Once again, I did not quite understand. "What was so important about the dragon symbol. It looked like any simple decoration, and it wasn't even very detailed, "I thought to myself, but I followed my Grandfather up the creek to a path hidden by a tall, large-leafed hemphoria tree. This once well-worn, but now deteriorating path led us up to an alleyway behind the main road. Grandfather quickly turned up the alley and then onto the street. "Where be the shop that had the dragon symbol?" he motioned with his hand. "We must hurry."

"Well this is it, but the symbol is not there anymore," I stated, as I pointed to a bluish shop with an over-hanging porch. Now I was even more perplexed than before.

"Come on! We have no time to waste," Grandfather grabbed my over-cloak and pulled me to the shop entrance. He knocked in a peculiar pattern and the door opened. Grandfather pushed me in as he watched the street outside. Then he entered and barred the door with the heavy wooden beam that stood in the corner.

Grandfather took off his hat and slapped it against his thigh, "Curse me for a fool. Why did I not see that symbol on the door? I would not have stayed so long at the Keel!"

"Not a fool Ariel. Only old," cackled a hoarse feminine voice from the darkness of the room.

CHAPTER 7 THE FIRE LORD REBORN

(Extracted Directly from the Personal Log book of Gideon Livingston, the Fire Lord, the memoirs of Lady Mercedes Stewart and the memoirs of Captain Ariel Livingston)

"Quickly! We must get below. Here, follow me," the hoarse voice whispered. I heard a door creak open and I followed my Grandfather down a short wooden staircase that ended on a platform. The door silently closed above us, leaving us in complete darkness. I heard a click and grabbed the railing to keep my balance as the platform began descending slowly. For a few moments the only sound we heard was that of well-oiled pulleys as we went lower and lower. When we arrived at the bottom, our host struck a spark stick on the wall and lit a well-used lantern attached to a post on the platform.

We had arrived at the bottom of a long natural cavern perhaps two ship's lengths below the shack above. The cave extended for as far as the limited light could reach. Our host grabbed the lantern and led us back to an iron grate set in the wall of the narrow cave. This chamber opened up into a large and spacious cavern with multiple side rooms that appeared to have been carved out of solid rock. Above the door grate was a large, metal depiction of the same circular dragon symbol that was on the banner; a green dragon making a spiral and looking up with its gaping jaws wide. As I walked, I looked around and I was astounded to see that inside this cave were the complete furnishings of a garrison, mess tables--able to seat fifty, and at least that many bunks, stacked two-high, lined the walls. By the look of it, many people had left in a hurry. The tables had cups and the dishes sported half eaten dinners. On the left was a full galley, and in the back were racks and racks of swords, axes, spears, stout battle shields, curved overshields, and multiple varieties of throwing darts.

"How be ye Mercedes?" my Grandfather addressed our host, "I am glad ye be still watchin' over me. Ye warned me ta be careful by putin' the symbol on the door and I was too stupid and arrogant ta notice it. Thank ye. I should'a been on my guard at all times. Tis not a mistake I'll be makin' again. Thank goodness my grandson saw it. Oh, by the way, this be Gideon. Gideon this be yer great aunt Mercedes Stewart, me elder sister and a dear friend."

Grandfather motioned for our guide to come forward. An old lady with silver white knee-length hair stepped out of the darkness into the light of the lantern that she had hung on a bar set in the wall for that purpose. She wore an old shopkeeper's leather apron over a tattered skirt and well-worn blouse. Her face was deeply wrinkled, but her bright blue eyes smiled as if she was much younger. She had the same strikingly blue eyes as Grandfather.

"So, this be my grand-nephew! I remember ye Gideon when ye were no more 'n a toe dodger not even a knee higher. My you've grown. If I were 50 cycles younger, I would'a loved ta spent some time with a tall, handsome red-head such as ye. Come 'ere and give me a hug."

She only came up to my shoulders but she grabbed me with surprising enthusiasm. For the second time that day I had the sensation of being squeezed by a rock serpent. "Being old hasn't reduced your strength one-bit Auntie Mercedes," I said when Mercedes released her hold on me. "I take it you've lived here a while."

"Aye, lad. I've lived here since the first opposition," she took a knowing glance at Grandfather Livingston who nodded at her. "That be when we were obligated ta go underground durin' the Overlord's occupation," she motioned around her as proof.

"Underground? You mean you were rebels? You fought in the rebellion?" I could hardly believe it. I was amazed that I never had a clue. The rebels of the war were still being hunted and each rebel they found or each poor soul who they thought was a rebel was executed on the spot. *That could have been us!* I thought.

"I wanted ta tell yeh, lad, but I had ta protect ye and yer mother, Sadie-Belle. Ye could'na known and lived normal, and with spies and tattler's everywhere, twas too dangerous. I could'na trust anyone. But now yeh know where I'd been goin' all those cycles on Betty-Lou," Grandfather explained.

"Ariel! Ye brought him here without tellin' him what this was all about?" Mercedes questioned, alarmed, "Ye canna tell him more without assurances. We already be mightily expose if he were caught 'n tortured."

"I thought I might'a had more time. But the symbol changed that. He's got ta make his decision now," Grandfather responded to Aunt Mercedes with equal intensity.

Then he turned to me and stated firmly, "Gideon lad, I'm sorry to put ye in this situation. Ye've already seen more than ye should'a. But here be the rub, lad. There be no goin' back from this point. Now that ye be of age I am givin' ye a choice. Join us and be the rightful captain of Betty-Lou on the one hand..." He held out his empty hand and continued, "...or on the other hand ye can live a life of blissful ignorance as a jewel-smith and we help you forget you ever knew us or Betty-Lou," he held out the other hand that had a small bottle of greenish liquid, "What will it be lad?"

My mind was reeling. Now things were making sense. The ruffians in the Captain's Keel were not merely looking to cause trouble. They were hunting rebels; they were hunting us. This information, together with my grandfather's deep-seated animosity of Julius McFarland all came to focus, I blurted out, "Julius as the Adjudicator in this town is not just an annoying rival. He is the enemy of the rebellion! Your blood must boil to know that the murderer of thousands, lives in the house you built and that he has yet to be punished for his part in the disappearance of my father."

Grandfather nodded and smiled, knowing that I now understood.

I continued angrily, "I've seen plenty of injustice imposed by adjudicators who were supposed to be the town protectors. Each time I tried to go to the aid of my friends, or even strangers, both my mother and you, Grandfather convinced me to stay out of it. You said, 'What good would it do? They would just throw you in irons just like your friends. Then what could ye do to help them from the same jail cell?' After each event I still felt cowardly and weak regardless. If you were a rebel, why did you not invite me then?"

"I canna say I did'na think of it often. Then me better judgement told me ta keep ye safe until ye were of age. We've no underage rebels 'ceptin' those what have the permission 'o there parents, 'o their parents be rebels too. Since I had no authority, only yer mother Sadie-Belle could'a decided 'n she never would'a consented, I could'na invited ye if I wanted to. 'Sides, yer mother would'a had me head on a platter had I done it," Grandfather explained.

Grandfather waited for me to say something, or to respond, but I was thinking. I remembered all the times that I had dreamt of being a rebel fighting against the Overlord.

"Ahem," Grandfather grunted intruding my thoughts.

In a furious tone, I blurted out what I had been thinking, "So, I've been a rebel all my life and did not know it. All my family is part of the rebellion, except for me and my mother!"

"Aye lad, ye have the rub of it," Grandfather agreed.

"You said that we were going to rescue some friends of yours. These friends are rebels, am I right?" I challenged.

"Along with innocent town's folk," Grandfather added.

"I wish you had told me the whole story before we left!" I growled.

"Would ye have come if I had?"

"Most likely, no. I would have stayed."

"But ye did come, and now ye be here, makin' a gran decision."

"Yes, the decision," I sighed and stuck out both of my hands. "Either I turn my back on my career as a jewel-smith and become a rebel and risk my life to fight the Overlord," I held out one hand, "or forget about you, Aunt Mercedes and the Betty-Lou and live in blissful ignorance as a jewel-smith until I have to deal with the thieving Boar Riders and the greedy Adjudicators, then I'll probably end up fighting them and risking my life anyway." I said as I held out the other.

Grandfather and Aunt Mercedes waited patiently.

"Whenever I heard tales of the rebellion and their daring acts of bravery, I dreamt of being like them," I held out my left hand, "but now, when the real opportunity presents itself, my childhood dreams seem like fairytales!" I groaned and held out the other hand, "I wish I had more time to decide."

I balled my fists, knowing my future was being made right there at that instant.

"Actually, it sounds like ye have already made yer decision," Aunt Mercedes spoke up. "Which would ye rather do, fight the Overlord and his Adjudicators as part of a rebellion, or fight 'em as a solitary citizen? Choose ye careful laddy."

"She's got a point there, m'lad." Grandfather chimed in.

"You are right, except for one thing. I have no choice. I end up fighting the Overlord either way!" I pointed out.

I was having trouble controlling my emotions at being kept from the truth, but then finding out that the truth was so unbelievable. Other pieces of the puzzle began to fall into place as I my emotions churned. I asked point-blank the question that arose from my thoughts, "But tell me this, Grandfather, the story of my father's death you recounted to me just morning...there is more to it, isn't there? He was a dragon rebel also, am I not correct? He was given the same choice that you are giving me, at this time, tonight. Am I right?"

"It seems only yesterday that he were standing in this very spot, choosing which way ta go," Aunt Mercedes reminisced.

"You see, Mercedes, this boy has his father's intellect. We need him among us if we are to succeed. You and I, we are the old guard. We need ta train a new crew for Betty-Lou," he spoke to Mercedes and then turned to me, "Yes yer father were a valuable leader in the rebellion and his death were not just one of jealousy, though that played its part, but he were captured so the Boar Riders could locate the rebel leaders and murder us publicly, once and for all. He did'na give them anythin' or we'da been exterminated."

An anger towards the Adjudicators, the Boar Riders, and the Overlord, washed over me. I was also angry that I had never known the truth about my father and my family. I was angrier than I was when Kesler hit me with that bar. I had never felt this angry before. I was so mad that my blood seemed to boil up within me and that hot anger centered in my chest and felt as if it would burst. I looked fiercely into my Grandfather's eyes and growled with clenched teeth and balled fists, "I will join the dragon rebels, and I will find and punish those responsible for my father's death!"

Rather than being pleased, my Grandfather and Mercedes gasped and looked shocked and apprehensive. I maintained my anger and growled, "Isn't this what you wanted? A new recruit? Why do you not welcome me?"

"Why yes lad, we be right pleased, but beggin' yer pardon, there be grander things to consider at the moment," Grandfather simply pointed to the cave wall behind me. I turned to look and saw that the dragon symbol I had noticed before was outlined in glowing green flames.

"Mercedes, what does it mean?" Grandfather questioned my aunt.

Mercedes grabbed Grandfather by the cloak lapels, "Ariel, why did yeh not tell me? The legend...he be the one!"

"Me own grandson? I did'na know. I had no idea this was to happen. But yet, I see it and hardly believe it!" Grandfather replied, a shocked look on his face.

Still full of rage that was turning to confusion, I responded, "What legend? What am I supposed to be?"

"We have ta test 'im. You know the rules!" Mercedes insisted.

Grandfather could tell I was becoming frustrated and held up his hands to calm me, but to no avail. I was still furious at the Overlord and his cruel government, and I was becoming even more angry at being kept in the dark. I balled my fists again in impatience.

"Gideon, lad," Grandfather said slowly as he approached me, "Now, this be a new situation I had'na foreseen," my Grandfather carefully said, "There be an old legend about a man who bears the dragon seal and canna be hurt by fire. He is said ta command supernatural forces that will change the course of the war. We must see, Gideon, if ye be the one. Please take off yer shirt."

I did not need to take off my shirt to know something was different. I felt the strange sensation in my chest building. I un-balled my fists and I took off my over cloak and vest. I unfastened the first few togs of my shirt and I heard the gasps. In the center of my chest, the same green flames burned around an incomplete version of the symbol on the wall. I watched with keen interest as the green flames slowly completed the circle and began to outline the full dragon on my chest. I felt no pain but the blackened and scorched skin was obvious to see and smell.

Grandfather lit a torch from a sconce on the wall and said, "Hold out yer arm."

"Now wait a moments," I said nervously as I backed up. "I'm just as flammable as the next guy."

"What about that on your chest? Does it hurt you?" Grandfather asked and point at my chest.

As I glanced at my chest, he grabbed my right hand and

put the burning torch under my elbow before I could react to stop him. "Then this shouldn't hurt either," he said.

I watched in wonder as he held the burning torch beneath my elbow and I did not feel it. Just then I did feel something but it was not in my elbow. I felt molten lava flow up from the ground beneath my feet and go up my legs all the way to my chest. At the same time, I felt a surge of cold crackling power like a lightning bolt run down my head and in from my arms. The two agonies met in my chest. I screamed out in pain.

"It hurts!" I roared. Grandfather quickly removed the torch.

"Not that, this!" I pointed to the dragon on my chest.

Grandfather shook his head and smiled as he let go of my arm.

"Ye be the one! Yer Majesty!" Mercedes cried and fell to her knees.

I fell to my knees too, but for different reasons. I was in pain. My chest ached liked I'd been kicked by a 20 hand tall delivery hog.

When I caught my breath and the pain diminished I spoke, "Ok, I need you to explain what this is all about. What just happened?"

"Tis simple Gideon, ye be the Fire Lord, reborn. Ye will bring a time of peace and prosperity to Portus, the likes of which we've ne're seen since the landing," Grandfather explained, "Yer strong emotions must'a brought the change upon yeh."

"The Fire Lord? I thought he was an old legend. I never thought he actually controlled fire. You say I am him reincarnated?"

"Nay, yer Majesty, ye be his descendent."

"Does it still pain ye?" Grandfather asked.

I explained the different types of pain I had just felt. Before I finished, though, Aunt Mercedes jumped up, grabbed the torch from Grandfather and went into another room, leaving us in the green glow of the dragon symbol on the wall. She came back a moment later with a stack of what looked like old carpets.

She said, "Right here it explains the legend in old speech. See the symbol," she pointed to circular symbol on the bundle. It was the same dragon symbol on my chest, on the wall, on the buttons on the Betty-Lou and the Captains Keel. It was embroidered on the front cover of the rugs.

"How old are those carpets?" I asked as she quickly flipped through several rugs.

"They be hundreds o' cycles old, Gideon, and they be called tapestries," she continued explaining, "Now look at this," I saw a picture of a man with the green symbol of the dragon on his chest. The tall muscular man had fiery red hair, a full beard and was holding a flaming green sword. He was facing a creature that I had only seen once before. It was the same creature woven into my bed cover on the Betty-Lou. The orange winged beast had the curved beak of a marsh hawk and a reptilian tail. Fire jetted toward the man as the creature beat its taloned wings, positioning itself to strike the man with its spiked tail.

"What is that creature?" I asked, "My bedcovers have the same picture on them, well, everything but the flaming green sword."

"Tis a symbolic creature called a scrybeast. The symbol, it be used by the Boar Riders on all of their uniforms. Twas a symbol of nobility, loyalty and honor until now," Grandfather said bitterly and continued, "The Grand Overlord has ne're a drop of loyal blood in'm. Brutal conquest makes no man noble. Now, behold that man, Gideon? That be you."

"What? You mean to say this tapestry shows the future, not the past?" I blurted out not believing what I had just heard.

"Tis so, my Lord. The ancients used what be called the scrystones what can show the past 'n the future. They recorded what they saw in tapestries to keep fer future generations. That symbol on yer chest confirms it. Ye be destined to lead the fight against the Overlord and his corrupt government," Grandfather explained, pointing to the burned emblem on my chest that still throbbed with pain.

"So what happens in the battle with the scrybeast?" I eagerly asked, pointing to the next woven tapestry.

Mercedes gingerly flipped the cloth over amidst clouds of dust. Coughing, she smoothed out the tapestry and pointed. The picture was faded and part of the cloth was damaged. What was visible was that the beast was lying down, mortally wounded and also plainly visible was the lower half of a serrated sword dripped with blood. The sword was emerald green.

"It dies, the good guys win! Yeah!" I shouted exultantly, raising my fist. I received a shock when I looked up at my hand, "Yow! My hand is on fire!" I shook it and tried to pat it out with my other hand but it did not go out. When I realized that it did not hurt, I just looked at it, mesmerized, by the green flames that covered it.

"Do ye believe me now?" Grandfather Livingston asked, laughing.

Aunt Mercedes stared with her hand over her open mouth. "Oh my blessed soul!" she exclaimed.

"Now, control yer flame Gideon. Ye could seriously damage things," Grandfather said between chuckles.

Once again, I tried to snuff out the flame. I put my hand in my pocket but it did not go out. I even found a bucket of water and the flame kept burning with my hand immersed.

"Concentrate, Sire!" Mercedes commanded. "Use yer will ta shut it off. That be no ordinary flame."

I concentrated and nothing happened. Then I imagined my hand back to normal, with no fire. No sooner had this thought entered my mind than the flames disappeared.

"Ok, back to the records. Tis not as easy as simply killing the beast. Look closer at the tapestry," Mercedes instructed as she pointed out the many dead and dying people around the scrybeast. "Ye be now the central figure in a centuries-old struggle. You be now a marked man. Ye've joined the rebellion 'gainst the most powerful army that Portus has e'er known. Anyone seeing that symbol on yer chest will know. What happens next will depend on how ye choose to act and...", she looked at me and scowled at the green flames now engulfing both hands, "and fer pity sakes pay attention and snuff out the flame in yer hands!"

"Oh sorry. You were saying..." I un-balled my fists, took a deep breath, and shook them till the flame died.

"I was saying ye will need ta learn how to be a leader and use yer powers for more than lighting yer hands as torches."

"Of course, I agree," I responded. "Though hands that burn green are awesome, how is a blazing symbol and resistance to fire going to help the rebellion?" I questioned. "You do realize that I am only 18? I might be big for my age but I do not have leadership or any fighting skills. I was the captain of the nine-ball team and once in a while, things would get rough but that is not life and death."

"Bein' modest...another gran quality. Yes, tis a rough game, but that night against the Rupert Royals, what did ye do? Remember I was there!" Grandfather pointed at me.

"I stopped it," I simply said.

Nine-ball was a game of strategy in which two teams struggle to gain control of all of the balls. The balls have to be kept in the air and cannot be held for more than the time it takes to throw a ball to a team mate. Each team tried to intercept the tosses of the other team.

"My gracious lad, ye did more than stop it. The opposing team had supposed that the rough play would be too much fer yer team. They were vicious beyond measure and intercepted tosses by tacklin' yer team mates and the game judge did'na call one penalty for foul-play. Then they started a brawlin' because ye and yer teammates were not intimidated and refused to hit back. But when one o the Rupert Royals began beating on yer forward player, that was when ye went into action. Ye were a whirlwind, tripping, punching, ducking, and flipping...all to protect yer teammates. In less than one moments the nine members of the opposing team, and their alternates were on the ground, or bent over in pain and yer team had all nine balls," Grandfather grinned and continued, "I remember the stupefied look of the coach of the other team and that of that ill begotten game judge. The fans cheered and shouted and you got carried out on your teammates' shoulders. Dunna doubt me, Mercedes. This boy can fight."

"But, Ariel, he is right. He needs training so he dunna kill himself nor others. This here be no game," Mercedes countered.

"We've not the time, Mercedes. They know we be here. Betty-Lou is at the dock. We canna stay," Grandfather argued.

Mercedes had stopped listening because she diverted her attention to the pile of tapestries that she had in front of her. She carefully lifted one tapestry then another until about halfway through the pile she shouted, "Tis here! I've got it!"

"Tell me you found a way to wake me up from this dream!" I said half-jokingly and half-seriously. There was no way that I was the superhero savior of the rebellion.

Ignoring my comment Mercedes showed my Grandfather the tapestry and they both began the Kelta dance, hopping and skipping around the room.

Frustrated at being kept in the dark, I went over to the tapestry. I saw a picture of a white room with a man in the middle that wielded a green sword. A single ray of light was bouncing off the sword he used to defend himself. "What is this place?" I demanded.

"Tis a training room...right here in this very hall!" They both replied with glee.

Mercedes grabbed my elbow and we danced around the hall. It was either hop and skip to the ancient Kelta rhythm, or be trampled. So, I danced along as best I could.

"I thought you decided that we did not have time to train me. Why do I need a training room?" I asked between stomps and skips.

Grandfather and Mercedes stopped dancing which meant I could stop dancing. Grandfather bent over and grabbed his knees and between huffs and puffs he answered my question, "Tis not so much that ye need training. What ye really need right now be confidence. Confidence in yerself. Confidence in yer abilities. Confidence ta command. Confidence ta finish what ye start. This here room will show ye what ye've got."

Then Mercedes led me and Grandfather to the back of the hall. She selected a curved sword from the rack, and with a little effort, located a dragon button on the wall of the cave. When she pushed the button, a door appeared where I had thought there was just solid rock. We pushed the stone door open and entered a completely round room carved from the rock itself. When I entered the room, a ghostly green light began to glow from the dragon symbol on the opposite wall. As it got brighter, I immediately recognized that it was the same room as depicted in the tapestry. Mercedes tossed me the sword and she and Grandfather quickly ran to a recessed protective cage near the door.

I looked at the blade in my hand and swung it around a bit. It was heavy and I was obviously not used to swinging a blade. "Am I supposed to do something?" I shouted but I did not have to wait long before I was forced to do something.

I felt a searing pain in my left leg. Reflexively, I swung the sword and a white light bounced off the wall while the pain subsided. White rays of light began striking all around me, emanating from the large spinning jewel in the ceiling. I limped as fast as I could to the center of the room, dodging the white beams of light. I felt a beam strike me on the shoulder and jumped away to only be struck by another beam on my left thigh. I dove and I reached the dark circle at the center of the room, directly beneath the spinning ball. Both legs were stinging with pain and my left shoulder was sore as if scorched by heat stones. Despair started to bubble up as I saw the white shards of light striking all around me. "I can't do this...it's too much!" I shouted.

I looked over at Mercedes in the cage and saw the worried and anxious look on her face, almost pity. Then I winced in pain as I got struck once more and stole a glance at Grandfather. His face told another story. A frown and a furrowed brow told me that he was unimpressed with my performance so far.

"Stop that!" I shouted when I got struck by another beam of painful light from the white ball.

The despair evaporated and was replaced with anger. I angrily batted the next beam of light away from me with the blade. Again, and again I swung the sword to deflect the rays headed directly for me. As I did so, I notice the blade, my hand, and my entire body was engulfed in green flames.

As if on cue, the white lights came faster and more directed. Without any mental thought I went into action. I spun, jumped, twirled, and swatted away the lights with the sword. My movements came faster than I believed I could move. I instinctively protected myself from the myriad of shafts of burning white light, flicking them with the sword as if it were a part of me. The shafts began raining down on me in torrents and my arm moved so fast that I wove an impenetrable barrier of green flame with the sword. And then it stopped. I sank to my knees, once again, totally shocked, exhausted, and in pain from the initial jabs of light.

"Yeh see, I told you he was natural born to it. Dunn'a worry your mind," Grandfather told Mercedes confidently as they exited the cage.

"He be truly amazing. Ta think that I have lived to see the Fire Lord reborn, and from me own family no less!" Mercedes exclaimed, giddy with excitement.

"Yeh did great lad. Now be the time to rest and plan," Grandfather went to the center of the training room where I had collapsed. I had not the strength to even lift my hand. After a few moments lying there, they both helped me stand and then led me back to another room right off the dining hall. He pointed expectantly to a large ornately wrought iron chandelier full of candles hanging from the ceiling.

"Yes, it is a pretty chandelier, and what about it...?" I responded still recovering from my ordeal.

"It be a large and loathsome task to light each one of those candles individually..." he paused for effect.

It took me a moment to comprehend exactly what he was saying to me. "Oh..." I nodded slowly. Then I concentrated on my right hand till it turned green with flame. I tossed the ball of flame in the air and caught it again to be sure I could do it. Then I underhanded the flame toward the chandelier.

A ball of green flame made a lazy arc from my hand and then I willed it to enlarge itself to envelope the iron chandelier. Fifty candles burst into flame, filling the room with light.

"Thank yeh lad. I be much obliged," Grandfather slapped my back and Mercedes joined us. "Ye see lad, while some thin's I kept from ye, I did reveal the whole truth as to why we came upon this voyage. Tis a rescue mission, an we needed ye ta help us free the prisoners in the adjudicator's jails. As it turns out, with yer powers, our prospects of bein' successful have much improved. As soon as we free 'em 'n leave this place, ye can begin learnin' how ta use yer powers."

Aunt Mercedes was watching from the door and commented, "I found this ring amongst the papers. What would happen if ye would try ta light it with fire?"

I put it on and it fit perfectly. I concentrated, and nothing happened.

"Mayhaps ye should not think of fire, but light from fire," she proffered.

I tried again to concentrate, but this time thought about putting light into the ring's jewel. Slowly, the jewel began to glow green. "Of course! I was expecting white or yellow light, but the fire I produce is green, so the light would be green!"

"My Lord, ye should probably practice some more with that ring. It could come in handy in dark places," Auntie Mercedes suggested.

Under the glowing candelabra and the glow of my green jeweled ring, we sat down to plan the details of the rescue and our escape from the Ilse of Noonday.

CHAPTER 8 THE DARING RESCUE

(Extracted Directly from the Personal Log book of Gideon Livingston, the Fire Lord, the journal of Camphoria Livingston, and the memoirs of Ariel Livingston)

I concentrated like I had practiced at the garrison when Aunt Mercedes gave it to me,
and green fire lit the clear stone mounted in the ring on my left hand. We walked along in silence. Grandfather Livingston walked quickly and I struggled to keep up. He kept his gray hair neatly trimmed under his captain's cap, though it ended in a small pony tail at the nape of his neck that bobbed up and down as he walked ahead of me. Though he was as tall as I, at 12 hands, the stoop in his gate spoke volumes of the hard life he had lived. I noticed that his shoulders that were once broad, now were more rounded. He had the boney look of an aged man, nevertheless, as old as he was, he had not lost much of his energy but seemed to have gained even more this past week. The bags we carried clanked with each step. The glow stick Grandfather carried lit the narrow tunnel in which we walked and cast grotesque shadows on the wall. We hurried because we had little time to accomplish our task. Soon the 8th morning bell would sound and we would set our part in motion just at the turn of the watch.

Gratefully we arrived at the ladder at the end of the tunnel. Grandfather ascended first and I followed, careful to not bang the bag on my shoulder against the wall.

No use in alerting them of our presence earlier than necessary, I thought. Then Grandfather Livingston rapped a peculiar rhythm on the trap door...it opened with a creak.

As I came up the ladder through the trap door in the floor strong hands helped me enter the basement of the home. In the flickering light of the glow stick, I saw that those hands belonged to a young lady with hair red enough to match my own. Her eyes sparkled in the glow stone's light as she smiled and introduced herself.

"Hello, I am Camphoria. I work in the Adjudicator's mansion but I have pledged myself to the resistance."

"I..."

Grandfather interrupted me as I was about to respond, "Formal introductions can wait. We must hurry."

He stepped between us and continued to the stairs at the far end of the room. I lowered the trap door and I was amazed that it completely blended with the tiles on the floor, making it impossible to discover if you did not know it was there. I made a mental note of its location then silently followed Camphoria up the stairs.

"Be careful your Lordship and good luck be with ye. Dunna think bad of me for what is to happen next," Camphoria whispered. She deposited a piece of parchment in my hand and walked ahead of me. I stood there for a moment not comprehending her words. It was so dark, I couldn't have read anything even if I had time to spare, so reflexively I put the parchment in my vest pocket and followed.

Grandfather and Camphoria went left to the kitchens and I went to the right to access the second-floor stairs. I set my bag down with as little sound as I could and took out the two round clay pots. I struck a spark stick and ignited the wicks extending from the side of each pot. Grandfather had told me exactly where to put the smudge pots for greatest effect: right under the stairwell in the center of the house. The chemicals in the pot would produce volumes of smoke and stinging fumes that would force anyone out of the building.

I quickly scooted the lit pots to their hiding places and withdrew the wet translucent cloth from the pouch on my hip. I placed the cloth over my head. It was cool on my face and smelled of the chemicals that counteracted the effects of the smudge pot which would allow me to see and breathe without difficulty for a short time.

I saw that Grandfather Livingston had donned his wet cloth also and had grabbed a pot and a metal spoon for both of us. As the smoke filled the hallway near the stairs, the 8th watch bell rang in the distance. We walked by the servant's quarters on the first floor and it dawned on me that Camphoria was not with us.

"Where's Camphoria? Isn't she coming with us?" I asked.

"She'll be along in a bit. She's goin' ta wake the other servants when we sound the alarm."

Our mission was to draw all the Boar Riders to the house to put out the fire. While the Adjudicator McFarland was busy saving his house, we would board the Betty-Lou and quietly slip away. We stopped on either side of the door to the room where the guards slept. It was helpful that Grandfather knew the house so well because black smoke already filled the hallway. At a signal from Grandfather, we banged as loud and as fast as we could on the pots while we shouted, "Fire! Fire!" Simultaneously we heard a woman's voice shouting the same thing from the servant's rooms. We dropped the pots and headed for the basement. Soon, we heard above us other's joining the shouting of, "Fire!" and we heard feet pounding as they rushed to exit the building.

After the sounds died down, Grandfather Livingston said in a casual tone, "I've a small matter to attend to. I'll be but a moment. When we knock thrice, let us down," he bounded up the stairs, "Keep a weather eye for trouble, would ya now?" He called down not waiting for a reply.

I didn't have to wait even a second. "Wait, I'm coming with you!" I called up, but Grandfather had gone.

Besides not being able to see clearly under the wet rag, the smoke that still billowed from the smudge pots made visibility almost impossible. I concentrated a bit more and the stone in my ring glowed brighter, lighting no more than a barrel length in front of me. I could hear some noise on the second floor and headed up the stairs. I had no expectation of finding anyone else still in the building so I was completely surprised when I was struck a vicious blow from behind. Lucky for me my concentration was broken and the light in my ring went out. I fell to the floor and instinctively rolled to the left because of cycles of nine-ball training to avoid being trampled. This saved my life as I heard the whoosh and crunch of an axe biting into the floor where I had fallen. Instead of rolling further away, reflexively, I rolled back towards the axe, knowing that my assailant was trying to remove it from the floor. I grabbed the axe handle and aimed a swift kick at where I thought his head would be. I was rewarded with a sharp crack as my hobnailed boot connected with his skull. That was not a nine-ball technique.

I relit my ring and saw my attacker unconscious on the floor. He also wore a protective cloth on his head. From this I surmised that the adjudicator knew we were there and that we had been expected. I rushed to the next room where I saw my Grandfather struggling with two burly men, also wearing wet cloths. The scene was eerily lit by Grandfather's glow stick on the floor. One attempted to stab my Grandfather from behind with a sword and the other menaced him with a spear in front. I shouted, "Behind you!"

As if in slow motion I saw my Grandfather step aside as both men attacked simultaneously. Grandfather drew his sword and diverted the spear just as it thrust towards him. A gasp of surprise escaped the man behind Grandfather as the spear entered his chest. The attacker in front of Grandfather faired equally as poorly with Grandfather's sword in his heart. It was over in a blink of an eye.

Grandfather then rushed to what was obviously the

adjudicator's office. He pulled a black cylinder from his backpack and in large black letters wrote, "The dragon has returned!" directly over the smirking face of the adjudicator's self-portrait. Grandfather then grabbed the large book that lay on the adjudicator's desk and stuffed it into his bag. As if noticing my presence for the first time, Grandfather whispered, "Quickly, we must hurry. The building is surrounded."

"And Camphoria? She's coming with us right?" I asked him.

"I think not me lad. We'll chat later. Now, run!" Grandfather growled.

I refused to move. "We can't leave her!!!" I shouted angrily.

"Shhhh. We dunna have time ta talk about this. We must go! She'll not be comin'! Do ye hear me?" Grandfather whispered ferociously.

I burst into green flames as my anger took over. "She has to come with us!" I demanded.

Grandfather was as angry now as I was. "Quit bein' a petulant child 'n understand what I tell ye. She betrayed us 'n will'na be comin'! Now douse yer flames 'n let's go!"

It was too late to douse the flames because the floor and wall had caught on fire. I was confused and could not believe that we had been betrayed, but my own eyes had seen the men with the wet cloths, waiting for us. I numbly followed Grandfather and concentrated on turning off the green flames.

We hurried down the stairs and to the basement just as we heard running feet and shouting overhead. "They have to be in here! Find them! Fire! Bring water!"

I headed towards the location of the tile that was the trap door, but Grandfather grabbed my arm. "We cann'a be goin' back that away lad. If Camphoria has sold us out and that path be compromised. Follow me."

He went to the opposite wall and twisted one of many hooks on the wall. The floor tile on which he stood folded beneath him and he disappeared into the depths. I followed by twisting the same hook and found myself sliding down a chute as I had at the Captains Keel. I landed painfully on something hard and by the loud grunt realized that it was Grandfather.

"Yeh could'a waited for me to get out 'o the way, lad. Ye be a might heavier than ye appear," he said as he took off the wet cloth and rubbed his back where I had landed on him.

"Sorry Grandfather, are you ok?", I asked as I removed my wet cloth and returned it to the pouch at my waist.

"I'll be fine in a jiffy. We dunna have time to waste. Hurry lad. Time be on our side now, whilst the adjudicator and his soldier be tryin' to trap us in his home," Grandfather turned and then said, "Er...be a good lad and shine yer light a bit brighter please. I lost me glow stick in the struggle above."

I obliged by concentrating and making my ring glow bright as a green spark rocket and we headed down a tunnel at a quick trot. Though I had only just met her, I could hardly believe that Camphoria had betrayed us. I still felt it was wrong to leave her at the mercy of the adjudicator.

I was not surprised that Grandfather had installed two escape routes in his home. Without this kind of preparation, the resistance would have been discovered and destroyed long ago. We came to the end of the tunnel and ascended wooden stairs leading up to the right. At the top of the stairs Grandfather unnecessarily turned and put his finger to his lips, "Shhhh," he motioned for me to extinguish my ring.

Quietly he opened the thick ironwood door and we stepped out into the ravine in the moonlit early morning. I realized immediately that this was the same ravine that we had traversed while escaping the Captain's Keel. The shaded path lay before us, hidden from view by a thick wall of woody grass that extended far above our heads. We hurried down this path escaping the growing noises coming from the adjudicator's mansion. "Fire! Bring buckets of water! Put it out!" men and women screamed.

We had traveled about 300 paces when I clearly heard

a click of metal on stone. We both froze in the gloom of the path. Grandfather withdrew his sword and I mine. He struck the stone of the pathway twice with his sword. As soon as he had done this, two men disconnected themselves from the darkness and greeted Grandfather with hugs and backslaps.

"I be Jasper Bragg, and he be Sir Percival Kendrick your excellency."

The largest of the men pointed to his companion. They both swept their broad brimmed hats off their heads and performed a deep bow. Jasper Bragg was more than a hand taller than the Percival and was built like boar wrestler, with massive hands and broad shoulders. Percival Kendrick, was a more average size, but was obviously athletic and in good shape. Both sported beards. In the dark I could tell that Brag's was scraggy, while Kendrick's was pointed and well groomed.

Addressing Grandfather, he continued, "The adjudicator's men've surrounded the Betty-Lou all day, waitin' for us to make a move. Yer plan worked perfectly and the main force were drawn to the mansion when the 8th bell rang. We had no problem overcomin' the few men that remained guardin' the jails."

"We still expect to find that other ensnarements have been laid, but so far we have been able to discover them before any one has been injured," the older man named Kendrick shared.

On closer examination, both men wore the outer cloak of noblemen yet their demeanor was not that of effete nobility, but rather the hard-bitten determination of seasoned soldiers.

"This way yer majesty," Bragg motioned for us to follow.

"They've tried ta capture and even destroy the Betty-Lou but as ye would know, they've so far been unsuccessful," Bragg explained as he led the way. "Ha...when some Boar Riders tried to get aboard the Betty-Lou, she threw'em overboard right away. Another poor soul she shot out through the bilge tank. She had a right good time of it. She tied others with ropes, or snapped'em with the ends till they screamed in pain and jumped off. Then from a distance, they tried to burn her with flaming arrows. She dodged most of'em, and she put the ones that landed out with a simple flip of her sails. They even tried the flame thrower but the ship flapped her side wings like a nectar bird and returned the flame in the same direction, setting several Boar Riders ablaze."

Kendrick added, "Sire, our men warned us that troops are ensconced in other boats, and the dockworkers actually are soldiers in disguise. They will attempt to eliminate us before we embark on the Betty-Lou, but we have already laden all the accoutrements and only awaited your highness, you, and Camphoria."

"Camphoria betrayed us. They were waitin' for us inside. We left without her," Grandfather shared.

"Na, that canna be true!" Bragg choked. "Nay Captain, ye were not betrayed by my own daughter?"

"I couldn'a believe it myself," Grandfather replied and put his arm on Bragg's shoulder consolingly. "We must hurry a'fore they realize that we are not in the mansion," Grandfather headed down the path after them.

"I'm goin' back ta fetch me daughter!" Bragg announced.

"Ye canna. She be discovered 'n captured already. Ye'd just get captured yeself. We'll rescue her when we've made it aboard the Betty-Lou," Grandfather stated firmly. "How many new recruits did ye rescue from the jails?" he asked Bragg, who appeared to be some sort of commander.

"Only 47 have been gathered aboard the Betty-Lou. Many of the original resistance be too old or infirm. Even still, we have far too few able-bodied men. Most of the men we freed from the jail be terrible afraid o' what the Boar Riders will do ta their families and though they promised ta keep the fight goin' here, they ran ta protect their families.

"Also, with all the preparations, we had little time to recruit from neighboring lands," Sir Kendrick reported dejectedly. "We did convince 16 men from Sparfold, and six from Blue Rock to join us as soon as they could settle their affairs.

Both Bragg and Kendrick walked ahead and I and Grandfather followed.

"Grandfather, I have been wondering, why do they address you as if you were nobility?" I whispered.

He chuckled a bit, "Tis not I they be addressing as a king but ye."

"What? Why would they do that? I'm not royalty!" I objected.

"Did ya' forget the legend so quickly now? We've been waitin' fer a new king fer many centuries, and then ye shows up. Ye canna blame Captain Bragg nor Sir Kendrick for being excited about the prospects," Grandfather kindly explained and slapped me on the back, "You'll make a fine king, when the time comes."

Full realization of my role in the resistance came to me with a shock. Not only was I going to topple the current monarch, but I was to take his place as supreme ruler. How I was supposed to do this, I didn't have a clue. What I did know was that I knew nothing about ruling a kingdom.

I suppose that Grandfather could tell I was overwhelmed with the idea of being the king. "Dunna worry about this now. Ye will have plenty of time to prepare. Just focus on what be ahead of ye...one step at a time," he said encouragingly, "Trust yer instincts lad. Leadin' be in yer blood."

We arrived at a gap in the side of the hill where there was a narrow door hidden by trees and bushes. Grandfather knocked his peculiar rhythm and the door opened.

"Come in quickly now, the adjudicator has troops scouring this hill looking for all ye," a voice whispered from the darkness.

One by one we entered through the narrow door; purposefully narrow so that only one person at a time could enter and making it easily defended. There were at least 20 people in the narrow passageway. I lit my ring and there were gasps of surprise and murmurs of, "It be true then!" We followed in single file up the winding stairs until we arrived at the small room at the top of the stairs.

"On the other side of this door, rests the Betty-Lou, not 20 feet above us. Upon a signal from Captain Livingston, she will drop rope ladders and we must swiftly climb. Once aboard we will set sail at yer discretion yer majesty," Captain Bragg explained.

One by one we exited the hidden door and made our way directly beneath the Betty-Lou. Without warning, five rope ladders slithered down to us. I was surprised that I did not hear any signal from Grandfather for Betty-Lou to do that.

Before any of us could ascend the ladders we heard a man's muffled oath and a girl's voice, "Run it's a trap!" and then a man's voice, "Catch her! She must not escape!"
Then a beam of light shot from the opposite side of the ravine fully exposing me to fire.

"That's Camphoria!" I said ignoring the light, "We must save her," I pointed to the direction of Camphoria's voice.

I was tackled by Captain Bragg just as several arrows and stone projectiles hit the lighted area where I had just been. Strong hands quickly dragged me back into the hidden entrance, that was not so hidden anymore as arrow shafts and projectiles hammered the door.

"Let me go! We cannot leave her!" I growled as I struggled to get free.

"Dunna be a fool, lad. She sold us out and this be just another ruse for us to follow. Why do ye think that they brought her?" Grandfather scolded angrily.

Captain Bragg spoke solemnly, "Though, my Camphoria would never betray us, I agree with Captain Livingston. That be not the way to save her."

Only when I stopped struggling did I notice that several of our company had been wounded, including Captain Bragg, who had received a shaft in his arm. "Thank you for risking your life and saving mine Captain Bragg," I said breathlessly, to which he simply nodded acknowledgement.

Then a thought struck me and I voiced it, "Captain Livingston, Camphoria had said something to me as we entered the house. 'Dunna think bad of me.' Why had she said that? There was something else...she gave me something. I remembered her strong hand in mine... a parchment. It was dark, so I decided to read it later. I put it... where? Aha!" I shouted pulling the parchment from my vest pocket.

Every eye was now upon me as I read the parchment aloud:

Most honorable Lord Gideon:

They know you are here. Do not go upstairs. Men are waiting for you. Find another way out. I will escape and wait at the right spot.

Camphoria

"You see! My Camphoria tried to warn ye but ye were too dense to understand! She be not a traitor!" Bragg pointed out enthusiastically.

"Watch yer tone when speaking about His majesty!" Sir Kendrick growled menacingly with his hand on his sword.

Bragg blanched when he realized what he had said. "A thousand pardons yer Excellency. I meant no disrespect," Bragg bowed low and did not rise.

Knowing that I had to say something, I walked over to Captain Bragg, frantically thinking, *What would a king say?... Look, he is shaking in fear. Oh no! He is thinking he might be killed.*

"Rise Captain Bragg. Your insult is forgiven. I know you were concerned about your daughter Camphoria. The task at hand is discovering how we will board the Betty-Lou and then devise a plan to retrieve your daughter. I cannot afford to waste good men like you over unintentional slights."

Captain Bragg stood up shakily, much relieved.

Grandfather spoke, "They will be surrounding this location in a moment. We can stay here and fight our way onto Betty-Lou, or we can seek another avenue to board her. What say ye m'Lord?"

This was the first time that Grandfather had addressed me in this fashion. I was so shocked that even he regarded me as something more than a lad, it took me a second to reply.

"We cannot stay here. We cannot fight because they have the high ground and we cannot see how many there are. Lead us to your second escape route," I pronounced. It was a total shot in the dark that sounded kingly. I clung to the hope that since there were two escape hatches in the mansion, there would be two here also.

"Right away m'Liege. This way."

He rushed down the stairs, and all of us followed suit. He stopped abruptly at a door that I failed to notice on the way in. He pried it open and entered. We followed him up the steep stairs. Arriving at the top, Grandfather motioned for us to be silent, remain still, and extinguish our lights as we stood in the small room. He then opened a door and exited silently. We could feel the cool morning air rush into our cramped space.

A moment later he returned and whispered, "Nice call about the second escape route. Betty-Lou will be here shortly. We must be prepared to board her. Follow me."

We heard a commotion of angry shouts from below followed by the concussion of explosive fire shafts and high velocity shrapnel weapons designed to cripple airships. Based on the amount of cursing we heard, the Betty-Lou easily avoided the threats.

Not daring to illuminate ourselves, we had to trust that the Betty-Lou knew where we were. After a few anxious moments, Grandfather whispered, "She is here. Grab the ladders."

I was the last to make my way up the ladder and heard the shafts and stones zoom past me. I swung my foot over the side of the ship and as soon as my foot touched the deck, I felt the same powerful surge of energy I had felt the first time I set foot on the Betty-Lou, but this time it was 1000 times stronger.

Everyone gasped loudly. Not only was I enveloped in green flames, but so was the Betty-Lou! That was not all, however. We heard a loud grinding noise and fell to our knees because deck of the Betty-Lou trembled and shook as from a land quake. The Betty-Lou had transformed from a wide and elegant merchant vessel into a sleek and ferocious looking fighting ship. Two different sides of the same dragon!

I stood up and I came to my senses. "No!" I shouted. "We cannot be seen!" I concentrated furiously to douse the flames, but it was too late.

Though it was only a second or two, it seemed like an eternity—enough for the troops of the Adjudicator to fire their weapons at us. There was no time to relay orders to the helmsman. We had to move out of the firing range now!

How the Betty-Lou responded to Grandfather's requests without words, I did not know, but I guessed that the Betty-Lou and Grandfather had a special mental connection. Perhaps he knew her thoughts and she his. I didn't have time to make a request to Grandfather for him to make the command--we had to move immediately. So for the first time I attempted to communicate in my mind to the Betty-Lou the urgency of moving away from the spot we now occupied.

"Betty-Lou, I need you to move out of danger immediately or we will all die," I thought forcefully.

The response was instantaneous. The Betty-Lou shot forward so quickly that everyone was knocked down to the deck once again. The scatter shots and the deck slicers missed the Betty-Lou by less than the breadth of a hand span.

"Thanks, Betty-Lou! We are not out of trouble yet, keep moving about, and keep out of range," I thought.

I could not be sure but it seemed I heard her reply, "You are welcome."

Grandfather stood by my side and whispered, "If ye need my help 'n dunna know what ta do, just ask, I'll be right here. Ye be in command now!"

"I'll do my best. Thanks!" I replied and then I called to the helmsman, "Do you know the 'Right Spot'?"

"Pardon m'Lord, but we canna go there right now. We

were betrayed and it be just another trap," Grandfather advised in a whisper.

I blazed green in anger, this time only me, and shouted, "Am I not in command?"

As soon as I said those words in that way to Grandfather, I knew that it was wrong. I was starting off my command poorly.

"Of course yer excellency. Helmsman take us to the right spot." He relayed the command.

The helmsan looked at me quizzically and then Grandfather Livingston stepped to his side and explained to him the location. "Yes, your Excellency. I can take us there, but we'll be vulnerable ta be attacked if we moor there. It be on a hill where all would be able to see us in the moonlight."

"Leave that to me. For now, take us out of range of those weapons!" I said grimly. I had an idea. It occurred to me that where there was fire, there was smoke. As sure as I could use my power to create green fire, I believed that I could create a smoke screen as well. I pulled out my sword and instead of thinking about covering it with bright green flames, I concentrated on smoke instead. Sure enough, my sword began exuding copious amounts of green smoke.

"Wow!" I said as I swung it through the air leaving ribbons of smoke, "This could be useful in battle."

Though I had never been in a battle, I envisioned what it might be like. The closest thing to a battlefield in which I had much experience was the nine-ball pitch. Still swinging the smoking sword, I wrote my initials in the air "GL"

As I watched my initials dissipate in the air, I spoke what I was thinking, "Green smoke won't do. We will still be seen. There has to be something else."

Since I was the Fire Lord, I thought the answer might be once again found in fire itself. Then I started thinking more about the anatomy of a fire. I lit a spark stick and a flame erupted from its end. I brought it to my eyes to observe it in detail. "Closest to the wood burning the fire it is completely transparent, then blue, then yellow, then the smoke," I muttered, "I wonder...?"

I pulled out my sword and focused my thoughts on the transparency below the flame. The sword became as transparent as a stinging cloud floater.

"Ah ha!" I exclaimed.

Once again, I became aware that all eyes were upon me, awaiting instructions and mesmerized by what I had just done. "Er hum...It is set, then. We will have to fly by sight only," I told the helmsman. I didn't know if that was possible, but I figured that if we were transparent it would be impossible to see our instruments.

"Yes m'Lord, so it shall be done," the helmsman responded nervously. I saw that Grandfather Livingston was trying to calm him down.

"Captain Bragg, assure that everyone has a station and that everyone on deck is fitted with a safety line. We are going to rescue Camphoria. We may have to move quickly and cannot afford to lose men overboard," I instructed, "Let me know when you are ready."

My thinking was that Captain Bragg would know where everyone was supposed to be. I also guessed that there were safety lines that could be attached to the crew above deck.

"It will be done, my Liege," Captain Bragg bowed and then turned to begin giving orders to the multitude of people on deck.

Apparently, I had said the right things because everyone now moved with purpose and their attention was elsewhere besides being fixed on me. I approached Kendrick and asked, "I would like to stand in the forecastle for best visibility, what safety lines can be attached to me?"

"If you will allow me Sire, I will show you," Sir Kendrick said with a bow and indicated the way to the forecastle.

Soon I was stationed at the light stone controls and was connected with a harness that would allow me to be remain standing on the deck regardless of what kind of flying the

Betty-Lou was doing.

"Kendrick, let everyone know that it is going to be difficult to see on board the ship in a few moments. Tell them to have their weapons and tools at easy reach," I requested.

Kendrick returned and said, "M'Lord, all the crew be prepared."

"Thank you and get to your own post. Ok, Here we go!" I responded.

I concentrated on making the whole ship just like the invisible part of the flame. The ship began fading until all of its timbers, sails, and weapons became transparent and the sleek form of the Betty-Lou became hazy and was soon lost to view completely. I could feel the energy draining from my body and wondered how long I could maintain invisibility.

I called out to the helmsman, "Fly us straight and true to the right spot."

"Aye, aye yer Majesty!" he replied.

The Betty-Lou descended from the clouds, completely invisible. She picked up speed and the only thing visible was that she left a cumulus trail in her wake.

I had no idea where the "right spot" was, but I trusted my Grandfather and the helmsman knew.

Just then, the helmsmen nervously shouted in my direction, "Sire, we be above the location, what be yer orders?"

"Hold your position for now...uff," I responded, now struggling to focus on maintaining invisibility. The effort was taking all my attention and my strength.

Though we could still see the hazy outlines of the ship, we could see right through it to the ground below. It was also an eerie feeling—not being able to see oneself. But there was one person we could see in the moonlight. She was running full speed to the top of the hill where the rocks formed a small landing pad and a tall tree served as a mooring pole. She was being pursued by several of the Adjudicator's troops.

"Helmsman. Get us closer," I ordered and furiously tried to think how to get her aboard. I knew I could shoot flames at the pursuing men and roast them alive, but I also knew that they were just following orders. "What do we have to help her?"

As all the ideas seemed to be coming today, it started with a simple thought. Ships have nets to catch food like sky crawlers and jelly pods. "Ah, ha! We can lower the nets and catch ourselves some troops," Then I thought, "What do we want the troops for? Let's catch Camphoria!"

I spoke quickly to the Helmsman, "Move us right above Camphoria."

"As you wish Sire."

"Kendrick, prepare to lower the nets over Camphoria," I said as we approached unseen, not ten body lengths above her.

"Right away m'Lord," he responded and issued his own commands to the crew.

"Ye know where the nets be, e'en though ye canna see em. Reach out 'n touch'em... Move them into place now. Well, done lads."

The troops were gaining on Camphoria, I had to slow them down. I pointed my sword and shot a bolt of green fire in front of the charging men. They jumped back in alarm as green flames erupted in front of them. The discharge of energy left me panting for breath and my knees began shaking from the strain of holding the ship invisible. I could see the ship becoming visible again. I refocused all my attention on becoming invisible, but to no avail...I could not do it. I was too weak. Then I felt a surge of energy rise from my feet and instantly the ship was invisible again.

As I looked at the men dousing the flames that had gotten on their clothing, I wondered how I had fired the flames right through the hull of the Betty-Lou. I prayed that I had not done her any damage.

"Lower the nets now!" I shouted.

Translucent nets were lowered onto Camphoria and she screamed in shock and fear. Violently she struggled to be free of her invisible bonds. "Grab a hold of them and we will pull you aboard!" I shouted to her.

Her struggling stopped and she questioned in disbelief, "Lord Gideon? Be that you?"

"Yes, this is Gideon and the Betty-Lou. There's no time to explain. Grab ahold tight," I shouted down.

"Sir Kendrick, reel her in!" I ordered, wondering if those were the right terms.

Camphoria squealed a bit when her feet left the ground. The pursuing troops were even more shocked for when they saw her floating in the air they turned around and ran.

"Bring her aboard carefully, Sir Kendrick," I knew I didn't have to say that as soon as the word left my mouth, but I felt that is what a captain would say.

"Helmsman, we have to raise the Betty-Lou up to the clouds. Call Captain Bragg to the deck," I knew I did not need to give those orders either. Even though he was below, Captain Bragg could well see his daughter floating beneath the ship as the nets were drawn in.

Camphoria was shivering with fright as invisible hands brought her aboard an invisible ship. "What magic hath wrought this? I can feel ye and hear ye but I canna see ye," she looked around wide-eyed, "Be I aboard the Betty-Lou?"

I responded, "Yes Camphoria, you are aboard the Betty-Lou."

"My Lord! Help me. I be bound with invisible cords and held fast with invisible hands." She pleaded in the direction of my voice.

"Be patient Camphoria. We had to use the nets to retrieve you, but the men are having trouble untangling you because they cannot see anything either," I explained.

As we gained altitude, I stopped the invisibility so the men could safely handle the netting and the winches. I was becoming accustomed to hear the audible gasp from the crew as the ship became solid again. I was amazed that I could hold the invisibility. Before the infusion of power from the deck, I had exhausted all of my strength and could barely stand. I could feel the energy coming up from the ship, fortifying me and replacing the energy that I had expended. "I will have to investigate where this energy came from later," I thought.

I disconnected my safety harness and left the forecastle to help with bringing Camphoria aboard. The winches were just being drawn into the deck of the ship with Camphoria securely within the nets. Captain Bragg stood by, anxiously awaiting his daughter's release from the nets. Sir Kendrick and his team efficiently lowered the nets to the deck and successfully disentangled Camphoria.

As soon as she was free a shout of triumph rang from all on deck. Captain Bragg loudest of all, held his arms wide open to hug his daughter as she ran towards him. Camphoria ran past her father and to my surprise gave me a hug that once again reminded me of the constrictive strength of rock serpents.

"I knew you would come for me Lord Gideon!" she said as she took my face in her hands and she kissed me full on the lips.

After the surprise of it, I cannot say I did not enjoy it, but I barely knew her. Luckily her father came to my rescue when he saw my confusion and said, "Camphoria, dear. Mind your place. You be huggin' and kissin' His Worshipfulness. Tis not befittin' yer station."

She right away disengaged and a red flush filled her face. "Please pardon my affrontery m'Lord!" She bowed low, with her arms out to her side.

"Rise Camphoria. There is nothing to pardon," I grinned, "I am just as glad to have you back again... doubly so," I casually touched my lips, "Here is the man you should be hugging and kissing whose bravery and loyalty only match your own," I pointed to her father.

"Thank ye my Lord," she said as she stood and then rushed over to give her father a big hug.

CHAPTER 9 A FIERY ESCAPE

(As recorded by eye witnesses in The Fire Lord Reborn by Eliud Mejilla, the personal journal of Gideon Livingston, the Fire Lord.)

"Navigator. Take us to the nearest port at top speed!" I commanded. I had no idea which one that might be, but I had faith that he did.

"Aye, aye Sire," the navigator responded. The ship started but then halted abruptly. "Look Sire!" He shouted.

It was too late, a whole flotilla of ships surrounded us above and beneath. They must have been anticipating an escape attempt.

I wracked my brains thinking, "What do I do now? Even if we were invisible we could not have safely passed through the ships. There were too many of them.

"Captain Livingston," I called. I felt uncomfortable calling him Grandfather with my new station.

"Yes, your Majesty," Grandfather said with a cold bow.

"I apologize for my angry outburst," I whispered. "I need your help. What do I do?"

"Apology accepted. You must fight. It be the only way."

"What weapons and protection does Betty-Lou possess?" I asked him. "This is a warship, correct?"

"Aye, m'Lord, a mighty one at that. Though I've ne'r seen Betty-Lou in this form, it won't be hard ta find the war machinery," Grandfather replied.

"We have cannons, correct? What other things might a

warship have?" I probed. I had no clue other than what was fired at us just a few moments before.

"A well-prepared war vessel would have a ballast blower, mast cleavers, razor disks, lightning spikes, and sulfur cannons," Grandfather listed on his fingers.

"Ok, I need you to find those things on the Betty-Lou. I need a hole blown through that blockade in the direction we were heading before they can tighten the circle and blow us all to bits."

The armada continued closing in uniformly in all directions. They would be in firing range in one or two moments. I had to act fast and I knew exactly what to do. I pulled out my sword and lit it in green flames. I pointed to the deck and the whole ship was covered in green flames. Not expecting this, the crew gasped audibly once again. Though they had seen this once before, it was still quite unnerving to be standing on a burning ship and not be consumed. While it made us more visible to attack, I was hoping that it would also make us more intimidating, giving us a few moments longer while the armada weighed its chances against us.

It appeared to work but for a different reason than I had imagined. Cheers of victory could be heard from the many ships that surrounded us. Some even began turning around to depart. Then the reason dawned upon me. "What would I think if I saw a wooden ship burst into flames, albeit green ones?" I answered my own question, "The armada's ships paused most likely thinking that their work was done. They think that the Betty-Lou was destroyed and will be consumed by flames."

"Well, it's best to let them think they have won for now," I said to the crew on deck who I just realized had been listening intently to the conversation I had with myself.

I felt a need to encourage them as if they were my nine-ball team facing an unbeaten rival. I shouted to reach as many ears as possible, "We are facing the entire might of the Overlord's armada. For some of us this is our first battle. I know you feel fear. Courage is not the lack of fear, it is the domination of it. The will to keep struggling and fighting when facing a terrible foe is the essence of bravery. We have something they do not. Our cause is right. We fight for our freedom, for our families and our children. And that my dear comrades, makes all the difference, for the God of truth and right will help us and send his angels to watch over us. Do not falter! Do not hesitate in performing your duties. I promise you as Fire Lord, I will fight to protect each and every one of you with my last breath. What say ye? Will ye fight beside me?" As I asked this last question, I raised my sword into the air and as if on cue, was covered in green flames.

Everyone on deck raised their swords and shouted in chorus, "We will fight!" As they did so, to their amazement, they too were enveloped in green flame, which only made them shout the louder.

"Captain Livingston. Are the weapons ready?" I shouted out.

"Aye, they be ready, m'Lord!" Was his enthusiastic response.

Then I walked to the light stone and opened the shutter to form as wide a beam as possible. I willed flame through it and aimed the beam at the ship closing in right in front of us. I had no wish to kill all the crew, just to disable the ship so it could not block us or harm us. I aimed at the ballast tank and as soon as the green beam touched it, it burst into flames and the ship slowly headed towards the ground.

I heard a cheer from behind me and realized once again, I was the center of attention.

The armada ships in front of us scattered while they assessed what just happened. The other ships, as soon as they realized that the green flames were not consuming us, they once again began tightening their circle. I doused the green flames mentally and the Betty-Lou returned to her normal dragon green color.

"Now would be a good time to unleash the weapons,

Grandfather," I said as I aimed at the next ship to our port. Green flames ignited the ballast tank and another ship sank in flames. The crew began following my example with the light stone. The Sulphur cannons began igniting ballast tanks of ships on the starboard and port sides.

Due to my inexperience, I was so concerned with the ships in front of us, I neglected to keep an eye on the ones above us. Two large ships had begun their descent and were preparing to drop avalanches of explosive stones upon us.

Suddenly a loud clicking noise came from a pair of dark brass columns that I assumed were decorations. I turned to see that a crewman was madly trying to crank them into position. They swiveled upward and then with a woosh, two shiny disks zoomed straight at the ships above us, narrowly missing our own sails and hitting each of the enemy ships squarely in the keel. A loud cracking noise filled the air followed by loud shouts of dismay from the enemy ships. The razor disks had disabled the ships but in doing so caused them to descend more rapidly towards us, threatening to collide with the Betty-Lou.

"Navigator," I shouted. "Full speed ahead!"

In response, the navigator shot us forward almost as fast as when I had asked the Betty-Lou to save us. The sinking ships barely missed us as they fell.

Since I had not noticed the ships above us, I had the sneaking suspicion that ships might be preparing to fire on us from below. I thought of the invisible part of a flame again and willed that only the part of the ship through which I was looking become transparent. This revealed two ships pointing their razor disk throwers up at us.

Without thinking, I threw two flaming balls of fire at them. The balls passed through our ship and landed on their decks, causing immediate panic. But even with this, one of their determined crewmen fired the razor disks at us anyway.

I could clearly see as if in slow motion the two razor discs leaving their fusile, hungry teeth ready to bite into the

Betty-Lou. Once again there was not time to relay a message to the navigator. <Move or we all die!> I shouted mentally. The vision of a flame flickering and jumping came to mind.

What happened next has no rational explanation. One moment we were about to be struck by two razor blades, and the next moment we were out of harm's way and the ship above us was struck by the razor blades meant for us. We felt no movement, but in a blink of an eye we had jumped a ship length.

Once again, I heard the familiar gasp of the crew at the sudden shift.

Grandfather and his crew were furiously firing the four sulfur cannons from both sides of the ship to keep the ships out of range, but their field of fire was too limited and there were too many armada ships approaching at angles they could not reach. We were outnumbered a hundred to one. In a few heartbeats they would all be able to fire upon us and there would be nothing we could do. The light stone I was wielding was only one weapon and as soon as I dispatched one ship, another took its place. My fireballs were a hand-to-hand weapon and a hundred ships close enough for fireballs would already be firing on us. There had to be something else.

The reality of the situation descended upon me as the heavy blankets of dismay and despair threatened to overcome me. I had faced unbeatable odds before as a nine-ball captain, but the outcome of losing was never utter destruction and death. "I'm no leader! Who am I fooling? I don't know what to do or what to say to save these valiant men and women!" I groaned inwardly. "In the end, it won't matter. We'll all be killed." I said out loud, fortunately, no one heard because of the noise of sulfur cannons, ballast blowers and razor discs all going off. "No, don't be an idiot!" I shouted at myself. "Keep fighting until there is no more fight left in you!"

I fired the green light at ship after ship and then they were in range and began firing back at us. A cannon ball whizzed by my head. "Evasive maneuvers!" I shouted, but did not need to. Sir Kendrick had masterfully moved the Betty-Lou and avoided the first volley of sulfur cannons from the enemy ships.

Unexpectedly, I felt rather than heard the word <Firestorm> and my attention was forcefully drawn, as if by a powerful attraction stone, towards another device I presumed to be decoration. It appeared to be a convenient parasol providing shade for lounging on the deck but given our present circumstance, that thought seemed to me to be out of character with a war ship. A metal pole supported the half dome made of sheets of thin brass connected to the curved rigid framework. I had no idea how this device functioned but I noticed decorative spikes protruding outward along the ridges of each triangular section of the dome and the memory of my first test with the light beams in the caverns jumped into my mind.

I called mentally to Betty-Lou, "Lower the sails and stow the wings before they are destroyed."

The sails began sliding down the masts and the side wings began folding themselves along the sides of the ship neatly into their protective housings. I unstrapped myself and ran to the pole. I took three steps and was struck by shrapnel from an explosive stone that had burst in the air above the Betty-Lou. My right thigh was impaled by a splintered rock. I knew enough to not pull it out right then. I stood and fought through the pain to hop to the parasol. I grabbed the pole of the domed device to steady myself and then ignoring my pain, I willed green flame into it and out of it. Just as the spinning jewel in the cavern had shot beams of light in all directions, I willed this device to do the same. Beams of green fire shot from the spikes in the dome above us and also unexpectedly from below us as hundreds of similar decorative spikes spaced about the entire ship's hull began blasting away with green beams of fire.

Shouts of amazement came from the crew as they witnessed the sky fill with shards of green flame as if the Betty-

Lou were the center of an exploding color rocket showering green sparks in a wide circle. No less surprised were the crews of the armada who instead of closing in for an easy kill, now piloted their airships into a whirling mass of green death.

The closest ships burst into flames as the green flames strafed them. As fast as they could reverse directions, the armada ships that remained, turned and departed at their highest speeds. Even still, the green flames caught fleeing ships as they retreated, causing one after another to fall smoking and burning to the ground.

When all the ships had either been destroyed or had fled, I let go of the pole and fell to my side completely exhausted. It appeared that I had exhausted whatever extra source of power that was helping me as well as my own. I hoarsely commanded, "Navigator, take us from here."

I felt strong hands lift me up onto their shoulders and then I heard the cheering and shouts for joy. "Long live the Fire Lord! Long live the king!"

"Let him be! Are ye daft?" Grandfather shouted above the clamor. "He be injured 'n all but dead!"

"I am fine. Let them celebrate and I will regain my strength shortly," I responded as they paraded me around the deck shouting and singing and I faded from consciousness.

CHAPTER 10 WISE COUNSEL

(Extracted directly from the Personal Log book of Gideon Livingston, the Fire Lord)

I awoke in my Grandfather's quarters. My Grandfather sat at my side, much relieved that I had regained consciousness.

"Be ye well laddy?" He asked.

"I feel a bit tired and my leg hurts, but I am fine," I responded.

I tried to sit up and was forcefully reminded that I been injured by the sharp pain that greeted me as I swung my legs to the side of the bed.

"Why am I in your quarters?"

He said, "Ye be the leader with the most authority now. Even Betty-Lou listens ta yeh."

I looked around at the captain's large stateroom, the quarters that Grandfather used to claim as his own. "This is mine?" I wondered aloud.

I felt excited and exhilarated that the escape had worked, but I also felt uneasy about how it was done.

I turned to my Grandfather for advice, "Grandfather, most of that escape had to do with blind luck and not skill. I did not know how to control my new powers and I definitely did not have the strength to maintain them for long. The crew trusted me and expected so much out of me. Up to now, I had been able to amaze them with my powers and bluff them into thinking I knew what I was doing. What do I do now?"

He calmly replied, "Sooner or later, ye will have ta take the real mantel of kingship and lead them."

"But I know nothing of being a politician and statesman. How could I? those are things they simply do not teach you in the school-house," I complained.

"You'll be needin' help, 'n lots of it," he agreed.

I worriedly hobbled accross the cabin floor. "I just don't know enough," I groaned. "How can I lead these people without knowing what to do?" I sat down on the bed and put my head between my hands to concentrate.

<When ye be lacking wisdom, what can ye do?> asked a beautifully melodious woman's voice.

I jumped off the bed and tried to find the source of the voice. "Who said that?" I demanded. "Did you hear it Grandfather?"

"I did'na hear a thing," he smirked as he said this. "I'll be takin' my leave to attend ta the crew. Ye'll figure somethin' out. Just put yer brain to it 'n ye'll see it through. I'm here ta help, but it be upon yer shoulders now."

He bowed and left the cabin.

<Calm yeself, laddy. Twas I, Betty-Lou.> The words came unbidden into my mind. <Now be answerin' me question. What be your next step if ye dunna know fer sure what ta do?>

"Er...Um...I suppose I need to ask someone who does know, and he just walked out saying that I had to figure it out," I said as I spun around, not knowing where to look as I addressed the Betty-Lou.

<Be still, Gideon. It dunna matter where ye look. Be ye within or without, I be always here.>

I felt something touch my head. I turned and saw it was a cord from the bed curtains.

<You are in my head?> I did not bother to say the words out loud this time.

<Ariel always believe ye to be a bright lad. Now who

should ya be askin' fer assistance?> Betty-Lou responded in my brain.

<I suppose my Grandfather and the leaders of the crew? > I responded in thought.

<Right ye be. Dunna forget that yer not in this alone. There be many people who can help ye. Quit yer fussin', and begin actin' like the king yer pretendin' ta be. What'er ye waitin' for? Summon yer war council 'n get on with it!> Betty-Lou demanded.

I headed towards the door and was stopped mid-stride by a gentle but firm bed curtain cord around my waist.

<Do ye not know anythin'? Ye've not but to pull the cord and yer first mate be runnin' ta answer ye,> Betty-Lou explained and released the bed cord around my waist as I turned and saw the gold cord hanging by the captain's table.

I pulled the cord and a deep gong was heard below. In a few moments, I heard firm rapping on the door.

"Enter!" I commanded.

"Captain Bragg at your service, M'Lord," Captain Bragg bowed deeply and remained so until I motioned for him to rise.

"I wish to convene a war council. Please summon all the leaders of the resistance that are aboard and have them here before the next bell strikes," I said in my most authoritative voice.

"As ye wish Sire," Captain Bragg said as he bowed again and backed out of the room.

<How did I do?> I queried Betty-Lou.

<Tis obvious ye be born to it. Leadership becomes ye,> Betty-Lou replied in a voice tinged with sarcasm.

<I have so many questions. Who are you and how did you become a ship? How can I communicate with you?> I asked mentally in rapid fire.

<I would gladly answer all of yer inquiries, but then ye would'na be ready for the war council, would ye? What kind of leader would ye be then?"> Betty-Lou chided.

<By the blue skies of Meridian! They expect me to have

a plan!> I cursed myself inwardly. <Why'd you tell me to have a war council then if you knew I was not ready?>

<Goodness sakes Gideon. Ye be misinterpretin' me words. Bein' a leader dunna mean ye've all the answers. The answers be comin' from the council—from all yer leaders what know their business, ye dunna have ta worry 'bout that. When I said bein' ready fer the meetin', I were thinkin' more practical-like. Do ye think to have the meetin' in yer night clothes, on your bed?> Betty-Lou clarified with a chuckle.

Now I was really confused. The only furniture in the room was the captain's desk on the port side with built-in cabinets, a large bed in the center of the room, a wardrobe on the lee side, and a reading chair with an attached side table nearby. The stern of the room was composed of a built-in divan under the observation windows.

"When Grandfather and I were in this room playing castles and stones... there had been a large table with chairs. Where had they gone?" I asked myself.

I looked around the room and found no clues. I sat at the captain's desk and tried to think. Then it came to me. When Grandfather and I had been playing stones, there was no bed. <So, from where did this bed come?> I wondered.

I walked over to the bed again and sure enough, I saw the same dragon symbol button that Grandfather showed me on the deck table. I pushed the button and the bed began receding into the floor. As the bed lowered to eye height, I understood what happened. The bed was the table.

My question "Where were the chairs?" was answered as the bed disappeared into the floor and the ceiling to which the bed curtains were connected became the new floor under the table. The large table was supported by legs that were in reality, a continuation of the four bedposts. The wooden folding chairs were stacked neatly underneath the table in several piles.

<We are going to need a writing board or map table to make significant plans,> I mentally queried Betty-Lou.

<Right ye are. There be a large paintin' on the wall by the captain's desk. Pull it over by the table,> Betty-Lou instructed.

I hadn't paid much attention to it before, but the painting was at least as long two arm spans and a bit more than one arm span tall. It depicted an airship that resembled the Betty-Lou but different, more sleek and fearsome, firing all sulfur cannons at several attacking ships of the traditional style, all flying the Boar Rider's banner. <That must be what ye look like now> I thought.

<Right ye be,> Betty-Lou answered.

When I grabbed the side of the painting's frame it gave a creak but did not budge. I looked around the frame for a release latch and finally found it at the bottom of the frame... another dragon symbol.

I pushed the button and the frame pulled away from the wall easily. It was mounted on extendible wooden lattice that scissored out to permit the frame to be moved away from the wall, left or right.

"This is well and good, Betty-Lou, but it is still a picture of an old airship in a forgotten battle," I remarked trying to be funny. "I still need a writing board."

<Tis not forgotten ta me. That were Battle of Mile-High and that were me as the flagship 'o the fleet. Many a good men died that day,> Betty-Lou gruffly responded.

<Forgive me Betty-Lou. I should not have made light of a terrible incident. You can tell me about the story of the picture another time.>

<To change the picture, just tap the glass twice on the upper left corner with the black end of that stick on the side 'o the frame. To leave your mark on the surface, use the white end of the pointing stick. To erase all marks, run the black end of the stick from one edge of the frame to the other,> Betty-Lou replied with a definite chill to her voice.

<Thank you. I've much to learn especially about treating lightly things of great significance. I plead for your

patience with me and I apologize again. I feel more ready for the war council. I am much obliged to you for your help!> I responded as sincerely as I could think.

I found the pointing stick and noticed that the black end of the stick contained an attraction stone covered in short fur to not damage the glass on the picture. The white pointing end of the stick ended in a flexible resin covering a repulsion stone. I used the stick and tapped twice on the glass. I heard a rustling noise and the painting was replaced with a uniform light grey. I flipped the stick over and signed my initials, leaving the GL in black. I ran the fur across the glass and the picture was gone.

<Ye plan ta impress the council in yer new fashion of night clothes, do ye?> She chuckled. I could feel her displeasure eased entirely.

<Oh my, I'd better get dressed! Close your eyes Betty-Lou!
>

<I canna. Ye best get used ta it.>

I finished putting on my boots as I grunted with pain, just as I heard a timid knock on the door.

"Enter!" I bellowed with all the authority I could muster.

In walked the beautiful Camphoria, her father, Captain Bragg, Sir Kendrick, Mercedes, my Grandfather, and five other men I did not know.

"Please retrieve a chair and let's begin," I said as I motioned to the chairs under the table.

CHAPTER 11 THE OVERLORD

(Composed from the private writings of Octavius Rumford, III, great grandson of the Grand Overlord, Octavius Rumford)

"What do you mean one ship defeated an entire armada? That is not possible!", raged the Overlord as he slammed the whey hen message on the ornate table. "Such things have not been seen since the Fire Lord himself set up the Overlords to rule Portus!"

The Deputy Minister, Forldon McWhorter, winced as he stood before the supreme ruler of the twelve kingdoms. "Yes, it is incredible. The trap was perfectly laid and the rebellion would have been crushed forever. But not even your royal prognosticators could have anticipated the weapons that the rebellion used to escape."

"Why didn't you know? You have been following that ridiculous-looking dragon-ship for an entire year. You know everything about it, but when you finally have it cornered you discover it has weapons you never knew about?" A scowl formed on the Overlord's face. "How could that be? Maybe I need a new Deputy Minister, Forldon... one that can actually do his job!"

"My most humble apologies, your majesty. I must explain... You see...The ship burst into green flames, yet was not consumed. What ship can do that? It destroyed three of our best ships with gouts of green fire. It moved faster than any ship could move. Deadly shards of green light decimated our armada in a matter of heartbeats. No ship possesses any weapons like these m'Lord," the Deputy Minister stammered.

"Well one does! Where is that infernal ship now?" The Overlord demanded.

"It is in route to Meridian, your Majesty, where we have a full battalion of ships waiting," the Deputy Minister said with a smug smile.

"So they can get destroyed too? You idiot! Get them out of there!"

Shocked out of his gloating, Forldon replied, "Yes, right away sire."

CHAPTER 12 THE COUNCIL OF WAR

(Compiled from notes taken by Lady Mercedes Stewart, and the personal journal of Gideon Livingston, the Fire Lord.)

Everyone presented themselves to me one by one with a bow or curtsy. I knew Captain William Jasper Bragg, Sir Percivel Kendrick, Champhoria Bragg, and my aunt, Mercedes Stewart. I did not know Colonel Hars Cloudjumper who proudly introduced himself as the weapons master, Lieutenant Sperry Shipwright who stated he was the communications master, nor Munford Devlin who introduced himself as the master cloudsman. I had no idea what a cloudsman does but I was determined I was not going to reveal my ignorance at this meeting. The sergeant at arms, and the quartermaster introduced themselves also. I sat down which served as the signal for everyone else to sit down around the table. They all looked expectantly in my direction.

I squirmed uncomfortably under their gazes. I needed more information and I knew that these people would be able to provide it, so I plunged ahead, "Captain Livingston, uh...,please report our current status," I was hoping that he would set the tone for a positive and productive meeting.

"Yes, your Majesty," he pronounced as he stood and walked over to the drawing board picture frame. With expert ease he tapped it and it replicated a map of Portus on the gray surface and with the pointer, he indicated where we were headed.

"We have a company of 67 persons, 47 of whom be

new recruits. Aboard Betty-Lou there be some of the most experienced members of the rebellion. We be well provisioned with supplies, but because of your victorious battle with the armada we be needin' munitions for our arms. Minor repairs to Betty-Lou be proceeding on schedule. The Betty-Lou can carry over 200 passengers and crew 'n much more if double bunked. To be fully manned, we should acquire more airmen in Meridian. We've resistance fighters ready to mobilize in each of the other eleven kingdoms and our numbers be growin' daily. The news that the Fire Lord has returned will certainly swell our ranks as well. We be nearly prepared to put in motion our plan to topple the Overlord," Grandfather explained with the confidence and ease of much practice.

He continued after a pause, "As yer Excellency be aware, we'll be arriving at Meridian in approximately two bells. Meridian has always been a stronghold for the rebellion and till this current time, has been considered by the Overlord as a faithful and compliant province of the kingdom of Fenfold. Our arrival there will undoubtedly make Meridian a target. Our original plan involved undermining the populace support of the Overlord and his tyrannical government by usin' our network of lithographers to publish the atrocities, cruelty and injustice of the Boar Riders and the adjudicators. At the same time, we'll continue to lead attacks on the storehouses and munitions depots to break their supply chains. Of course, we will also continue recruiting rebels in every province and kingdom. The transformation of Betty-Lou, as well as the humiliatin' defeat of the armada at the Isle of Noonday will've already been reported to the Overlord and he will double his efforts to destroy Betty-Lou and yerself m'Lord. We know that we'll be needin' ta make adjustments to our original plan, but that be where we are at present."

"Thank you Gra...., I mean Captain Livingston. Now Captain Bragg, please provide your security report."

"Thank you, Sire. We've already done the impossible, but the enmity of the Overlord knows no bounds. His retribution will be swift. My sources have informed me that the Overlord has doubled the naval forces not only at Meridian, but also at Grandberry and Portmouth, the two cities that be closest. Somehow the Overlord has foreknowledge of where we will be goin'. It worries me that either we might have a spy in our forces, or we be watched from afar."

"Captain Bragg, what are your plans to discover the answer to your two questions?"

"Well stated, your majesty," he smiled. "Me thinks that we be observed from afar by a ship in our tailwind. They be awful careful ta not be seen. Regardless, I will set watches with far stones to scan the skies for ships and maintain a tally of all the whey hens. So far none are missing. I have also tallied the sky stones where by a floating message may be left for a following airship. All are accounted for."

"Thank you, Captain Bragg. Sir Kendrick, before you give your report, are you related to the Kendrick that served with my father?" I asked the question that I had wanted to ask ever since I met Sir Kendrick.

"The very same m'Lord," he responded with a bow.

"Then I owe you a great debt of gratitude for your service to my father. A truer friend he never had. Thank you," I stated and I awkwardly stood and bowed to him, though it hurt to do it.

"M'Lord, please rise. You need not honor me so. Your thanks are abundantly welcomed but not in the least necessary. Robert Livingston was a great man and I would have given my life for him," he responded, blushing and flustered.

I stood upright again with a gasp of pain and gingerly took my seat. "So, to continue, what are your plans to evade these airships that are pursuing us at a distance?"

"That will be a hard thing to do, your majesty, in our present state. I believe that it would be wise however, if it please your majesty, to use your amazing capacity to conceal the ship strait away and plot a course that would bring us to Meridian by a lesser used route. Undoubtedly our position and course have already been observed and reported. But we cannot stay in Meridian unless we wish to be surrounded like we were at Noonday!"

"Thank you, Sir Kendrick. Let me know when you are ready and I will conceal the ship. If we do not stay at Meridian, where else should we go?"

"I propose that we set a course straight for the rebellion headquarters," Sir Kendrick responded to gasps of amazement.

"We canna go there! We'd be leadin' 'em right to it," said Colonel Cloudjumper, as he stood and forcefully pointed.

"I misspoke," Sir Kendrick interjected, "Following an obtuse route, we should eventually arrive at the headquarters. We have not been there for some time and we must use the talk stones there to contact the other bases and inform them of what has transpired. We have to regroup and prepare ourselves. Once we are there, we will find sanctuary and respite, of which we are in dire need in order to gather our forces and prepare for the inevitable conflict."

"Any other opinions from the council?"

Lieutenant Shipwright stood and said respectfully, "Yer Majesty, I believe that Colonel Cloudjumper speaks wisdom. We dunna dare reveal our base. Tis too dangerous. Too many lives hang in the balance and we have already lost some of the best blood to keep it secret. I do have a proposal if ye may hear it m'Lord."

I nodded and he continued, "I propose that we return secretly to Noonday. We've a full garrison there, well stocked with provisions and weapons. They'll not be expectin' us to do this, to be sure. We would be safe and protected. What think ye, m' Lord?"

<A ship be not built for the harbor,> Betty-Lou interjected in my thoughts.

"We're not talking about ships and harbors!" I said out loud, to which the group responded with politely curious looks.

<Ye need ta mind to whom ye be speakin',> Betty-Lou responded with a chuckle, <It could get mighty confusin'>

"You don't..." I started to reply to her, but then I caught myself and continued my statement to Lieutenant Shipright.

"I mean, thank you, Lieutenant. Yes, they would never expect us to do that, though I cannot see any advantage to be gained by the rebels by hiding under their very noses. I believe we would have to spend more energy being hidden than actually helping the campaign," I replied.

He bowed as he sat down.

"Captain Livingston. What is your opinion?" I queried.

Grandfather stood up, bowed, and then he began speaking, "These be dangerous times for sure, 'n precautions must be taken. However, the more we flit about avoidin' the Overlord's ships and spies, the more time be lost to prepare ourselves. Tis a risk we must take. We should set course for the fortress. Nowhere be safe now, not even at the headquarters, but Sir Kendrick speaks wisely, we must communicate with the other rebel outposts."

"Thank you for expressing your concerns Mr. Cloudjumper and Mr. Shipwright. I agree that extreme care must be taken. We will stop at Meridian only long enough to get supplies and pick up more volunteers, then we will go to the headquarters," I tried to be diplomatic but I knew the decision was up to me anyway.

Rather than belabor the point, I changed the topic, "Lady Stewart, as historian, what else do we need to know?"

"You honor me M'Lord," Mercedes curtsied. "I, your most humble servant, have been reviewin' the ancient records we discovered recently at Noonday. As ye be aware, the tapestries left by the ancient scrystone masters be incomplete. The records howbeit, contain invaluable information that'll help us to decipher the messages left by the ancients. So far, tis all we know."

With a sudden inspiration I asked pointedly, "What do your scrystones tell you?"

Everyone gasped and looked expectantly at the Lady Mercedes.

"Tis obvious that the wisdom of your Lordship knows no bounds." Mercedes bowed deeply as if accustomed to courtly manners, in contrast to her shopkeeper's leather frock and worn clothes. "I did'na want to reveal my skills just yet, but seeing as nothing can be hid from your Majesty, I will share what I know. There be dark forces we know not of gathering in the West. The danger threatens the whole world of Portus. The threat is as much to the Overlord as well as to the rebellion."

"What details can you provide that will guide our decisions at the present?" I inquired, now very concerned. It was bad enough that I was a central figure in the rebellion against the Overlord, but now I was being threatened by an unknown force and tasked with saving the entire world of Portus. "How could I, untrained and inexperienced, be able to survive?" I thought.

<Don't be daft lad! Did ye not listen ta me. Ye be not alone. We all be there ta help ye!>

"I know that, but I ...," I said, but then switched to thinking instead <It is easy to forget. I feel overwhelmed, and as you stated, the only way I might make it, is by leaning heavily on you and these people.>

<Yes, it be a large burden, but give yerself some credit also. Ye've got skills 'n talents ye dunna know. Twas ye that saved me, 'n I be mighty grateful.>

I was brought back to the meeting when Mumford Devlin stood up with a scowl on his face and waiving his arm with a dismissive gesture. "Ya canna believe this half-crazed lunatic yer majesty. Tis obvious that tryin to use the scrystones has addled her brain. No one has successfully accessed their power for ages, M'Lord!"

I was angered by the outburst and though I barely knew Mercedes, I knew that Grandfather Livingston knew her and trusted her. I could not allow Master Devlin to malign or challenge her, but at the same time I could not alienate one of my key leaders. I mentally reached out to Betty-Lou for support.

<Temper fury with gratitude> she responded.

I slammed my fist on the table and the table instantly burst into green flames. Once again, I heard the now familiar audible gasp from the group as they quickly removed themselves from the glowing surface. "That's enough!" I shouted and continued in a calm and controlled voice, "The rebellion is thankful and well aware of your zeal, Master Devlin, but I cannot condone such effrontery towards one of the rebellion's most trusted and faithful leaders. You will apologize and state your concerns in a more respectful manner."

Master Devlin quickly bowed low and awaited my command to rise. I let him squirm a moment. "Arise," I succinctly stated.

"Forty thousand apologies yer Majesty. My passion for the rebellion got the best of me," he turned towards Mercedes whose face was a stone. "I chose m'words poorly. I know yer heart be right and I had no cause to belittle ye. Please accept m'humble apologies," he bowed in respect to Mercedes who nodded coldly in return.

I did not release the green flames until the apology was complete.

He now turned to me and spoke more cautiously, "M'Lord. I have heard of the scrystones and the dangers that abound ta'those that use 'em. Many a well-intentioned folk have lost their very sensibility due to tryin' to speak to the powers that be in those cursed rocks. Aye, and e'en some have pretended at gettin' answers and have led believin' soldiers ta their dooms. Sire, I am only sharing what every soul aboard this vessel knows. I beg ye to listen. I would'na trust what she be sayin'."

"Thank you, Master Devlin. Your warnings are appreciated and noted. Lady Stewart. Please share with the council the precautions you have taken to protect yourself and the rebellion from the dangerous powers of the scrystones," I motioned in Mercedes direction hoping that I was not wrong.

"Thank ye Sire. Master Devlin speaks the truth. But here be where we part ways. My story follows a different path. I found the scrystones with the tapestries in the chambers below on Noonday. I knew what they be and I knew the tales of their terrible power. I would'na touch 'em, ne'er use the scrystones. I kept searchin' in the records ta see how to stay clear o' their playin' with reality. I came across a script so old it near crumbled to breathe upon and I used webjuice to firm the pages so as to read them. I found in them the proper use of scrystones. Here be the rub. One stone be for the past, the other for the future, but most importantly, one stone and the scryer both must be grounded in the present. One stone in water, one in fire, and the grounding stone in earth. The stone in the earth protects the scryer from losing her way back to the present. Tis but once I have done this and followin' this pattern, I have suffered no ill effects. I ne'er would attempt this by m'self and made sure to have someone standin' by to break the connection should it go awry."

"If what you say is truth, what is this danger you discovered and how must we prepare for it?" I pushed.

"The scrystones are not an exact science, and I am the first to attempt it successfully in many hundreds of cycles. I have no more than I told ye, Sire," Mercedes said apologetically.

"Then we must move forward with what we know and can control... and keep a weather eye on the West," I affirmed with a nod at Mercedes.

<What is the direction of the headquarters?> I asked Betty-Lou to not show my lack of knowledge about where the base was.

<West laddy,> she replied and I felt like she curtsied as she did so.

I thought to myself, <How am I not surprised? It figures we would be going straight from the frying stone to rock fire.>

<Well, you bein' the Fire Lord…should'na be a problem. Be I mistaken?> She quipped.

<Hmmmph> I grunted.

"What is the voice of the council. Shall our destination be the headquarters?" I queried the group.

"Aye" responded the group in unison.

"Camphoria, in the service of the Noonday Adjudicator, what did you learn? Please give us your report," I asked.

"As ye wish your highness," she said with a small curtsy as she stood. When Camphoria spoke, my heart skipped a beat as I heard her soft melodious voice, "I have'na had an opportunity ta beg forgiveness of yer Highness for nearly killing ye and yer Grandfather. I had hoped that yer Worshipfulness would read the note and take precautions. As it turned out, my feeble attempts to protect yer majesty were unnecessary," her face blushed red as she stated this.

I gulped and tugged at my collar that had all of the sudden become uncomfortable. "Ah, er… Apology accepted," I stammered and wiped my forehead with a pocket cloth.

Camphoria continued, "As ye know, I were a servant in the house of Julius the Adjudicator. When the Adjudicator began askin' fer me in particular, showin' me special favors, and lettin' me see documents that servants should'na see, I suspected that the adjudicator had knowledge that I be a spy from the resistance and only waited 'til a plan had been formed to take action against me.

"I were not privy to direct information bein' only a servant, but I did see strange fellows comin' and goin' at all times. I did'na recognize their dress and took them to be foreigners. There be one man that came much: tall, built very strong, short black hair, long pointed beard that he were always playin' with, shifty eyes, and always dressed in black robes. They referred ta him as the 'Deputy'. As far as spies, there be many, 'n all the servants be mighty afraid to speak their minds to anyone.

"It be three rotations past when the Adjudicator Julius

McFarland, asked me if something might happen at his mansion. To make 'em think that I be on their side, I let slip that the dirty rotten rebels might be preparin' something. I had to give 'em something or my life were forfeit. I also knew that ye would read the note and know what to do."

"He did'na read the note till we arrived at Betty-Lou," Grandfather said with a smirk, "But we managed without it."

"I'm so glad to see that ye be both well and things worked out. Adjudicator McFarland laid plans to capture ye, Captain Livingston, and he mightily wanted the Betty-Lou. He knew that ye would be there from a whey hen message to Captain Livingston which he had intercepted and he informed the Overlord of such. As ye saw, the Overlord had an entire armada waiting. Fortunately, he is only now becoming aware of the abilities of our king... and our determination," Camphoria managed to say with beauty and grim determination.

<No need ta be blushin', laddy, though she be a bell at that,> Betty-Lou chuckled in my head.

"I'm not blushing," I growled in response, then realized that all had heard it and collectively were holding their breaths...all eyes on me.

I took a breath and followed up with a correction, "What I mean, to say, is that I am blushing from your high praise and confidence, Camphoria. The Overlord has much to learn yet about our abilities and our determination," I responded and continued, "I...ah...personally thank you for risking your life at the Adjudicator's mansion and for your great service and loyalty to the rebellion."

At that, I stood, careful of my leg, and bowed to her while the whole company did the same.

Now it was Camphoria's turn to blush, "Just do'in my duty, m'Lord." she curtsied and quickly sat down. She could not hide her beautiful smile as she looked at me with a bit more than appreciation.

CHAPTER 13 THE DEPUTY MINISTER

(Compiled from the eye-witness account in journal of Serephina Joyston, linen servant in the Overlord's palace)

"But your Majesty, the rebel ship just disappeared. One moment the sky gazers beheld the ship and in the blink of an eye it was gone," whimpered the Deputy Minister. He trembled from head to toe as he wrung his hat in his shaking hands.

"Where did it go? No ship can disappear! Do you think I am an imbecile? You're simply trying to cover for your spy's incompetence. Are you so simple to think that I would believe such an idiotic story?" The Grand Overlord shook his fist as he shouted at the cowering Deputy Minister.

"Yes... er... I mean no, your Majesty," the Deputy Minister seemed to wilt. "We searched everywhere. It is not in the sky, my Lord."

"Well then, if it is not in the sky, search the town of Meridian. Find it or you will find yourself without a head!" Bellowed the Overlord as he pointed to the door.

The quivering Deputy Minister backed out of the room bowing profusely. As soon as he passed the guards at the door, however, he transformed from the cowering government lackey, to a towering and imposing personage in black flowing robes. He stamped purposefully towards his office as he fumed. He balled his fists in fury, "Get out of my way imbecile!" he roared and raised his hand to slap the unfortunate linen maid who happened to be in the hallway delivering sheets. Instead his foot swept out and toppled the linen cart out of his path. "Pick those up and be quick about it!" he fumed as he stormed past.

"Imbecile! Yes! That describes the Overlord. Ha! I should help the rebels get rid of him! The only reason I don't is that the Overlord is sitting on my throne and I have worked too hard to get it. Blaming it on the rebels though...hmmm," he stroked his black pointed beard as he entered his luxurious office.

The Deputy Minister sat behind his ornately carved wooden desk and tapped on the largest talk stone nestled in a crystal case with 20 or so other talk stones. After a few moments the egg–sized green stone began to vibrate. The Deputy Minister placed the stone in a shiny circular foil dish suspended in an ornate wooden frame. The vibrations from the stone were amplified by the foil dish and the words, "What be yer bidding m'Lord?" rattled in a metallic cadence.

"Tell me what you have learned about the rebel ship, the Betty-Lou," the Deputy Minister demanded.

"Reports indicate that it made port in Meridian but be already departed to destinations unknown," the tinny voice replied.

"We must find that ship!" the Deputy Minister growled. "Use every ship at your disposal. Contact every informant from here to the South Marches. Do not fail me!"

"Certainly, yer Lordship."

The Deputy Minister removed the stone from the dish and tapped a peculiar rhythm on a small jade colored stone and placed it in the dish. After a moment, the stone vibrated its answer, "I be in position m'Lord Deputy Minister."

"Good. Are you prepared to execute the plan?" the Deputy Minister queried.

"Yes, my Lord. All be in readiness. She only awaits yer command," the distant voice responded.

"Let it begin, then. Report back on the 8th afternoon bell," the Deputy Minister picked up the jade stone with grim satisfaction and placed it back in the crystal case.

"We'll see who the imbecile is now!" The Deputy Minister purred as he stroked his pointed beard.

CHAPTER 14
CAMPHORIA

Dearest Mother,

It has already been a score of rotations and I feel like I need to write and tell...

"No. That's not right. Sounds like I am forcing myself to write," I scowled and crumpled the parchment. I placed it in the metal bowl and sent a green spark from my finger to ignite it. I pulled out another small parchment from the desk drawer and began again.

Mother Dearest,

It has only been a score of rotations and I miss you. I am enjoying the journey with Grandfather. We have seen many things and I have learned so much. I and Grandfather are in fine health and good spirits. I do not know how much longer the journey will take but I can't wait to tell you about our journey in person.

With love,
Your son Gideon

"Yes. That will do," I said as I sprinkled writing powder on the parchment.

<Tis a bad idea writin' home! Dunna do it!> Betty-Lou intruded in my thoughts.

<I know I have to be careful to not reveal any indication of our location,> I mentally retorted.

<Ya. That be just one of the problems...>Betty-Lou fired back.

<What other problems might there be?> I asked.

<What about them followin' the return whey hen right back to us?> Betty-Lou responded triumphantly.

<Who's going to follow a whey hen from a mother to a son?> I asked now getting frustrated.

<Ye be forgetin' that ye be no ordinary son and that makes yer mama a fine target,> Betty-Lou made her point.

<All right, you win,> I thought. Then I pulled out the parchment again. "Hmmm..."

> *P.S. Don't send this or any other whey hen back. The distance is too great. I will communicate when I get closer.*

<Does that satisfy you?> I mentally asked Betty-Lou.

<Ye still be courtin' troubles,> Betty-Lou warned.

Of course, I did not want to worry my mother and secondly, I had no intention to jeopardize our situation should the message be intercepted by our enemies. I rolled up the parchment and placed it in a small leather cylinder. This I tucked in my vest pocket as I grabbed my jacket and left my quarters.

"Good mornin' yer Majesty," Captain Bragg said with a smile.

"Good morning to you, Captain Bragg!" I returned his salute as we passed.

I went down the stairs below and on the way to the whey hen enclosure, I encountered Camphoria taking care of the other animals. She was dressed in a work dress of blue canvas with a long-sleeved blouse covered by a light piglin leather vest.

This day is just getting better and better! I thought.

"Good to see you...ah...hard at work," I stammered cursing myself.

<Just say what be in your heart,> Betty-Lou interjected.

"Now is not the time!" I responded out loud.

"A thousand pardons m'Lord. Time for what yer Majesty?" Camphoria said with a look of confusion.

"Ah, well, ah, I mean that you need not do extra chores that others can do. Your skills are needed elsewhere," I looked in her large green eyes and saw the reflection of what I felt.

Camphoria smiled, "I be at yer service m'Lord. How may I help ye?" She bowed as she said this, but she never lost eye-contact.

I thought, <She wants to help me! What do I need?>

<Ye need time to be with her,> Betty-Lou interjected.

"What? Yes I do," I muttered out loud.

"Pardon Sire. How may I assist ye?" Camphoria patiently waited, still bowing and looking at me.

"Oh, I was saying that yes, I do need your help. I am preparing to send a message to my mother. Will you accompany me to the whey hen enclosure?" I reached out my hand to her chin and gently raised her to a standing position.

"With gladness m'Lord," Camphoria blushed yet her eyes never left my own.

"Lead the way," I motioned for her to walk in front of me. I could not help but notice the sway of her dress that could not hide her lithe figure as she walked ahead of me.

We walked to the stern of the ship where the whey hens could have open access to the skies through small portals.

"Here we be yer Majesty. What be yer wish?" Camphoria's voice was as sweet as the nectar from a citrix flower. Her beautiful smile was also reflected in the twinkle in her eyes.

"Er,...I wish to send a message to Miller's Pond, to my mother's home. Please choose for me the correct whey hen," I requested, though I could have done it myself. The whey hens are birds of habit and always roost in the same spot. Though they appear to be slow and incapable of flight because of their size, the whey hens are some of the swiftest fliers, and their sense of direction is without equal in the animal kingdom. The whey hen will return to its birth place without fail, but those born on an airship will somehow find the ship wherever it may be. On board a ship, their eggs are a delicacy.

I admired Camphoria's beauty as she gracefully reached out for the whey hen in the roost labeled Miller's Pond. Not only was there great beauty in her well-proportioned frame, but I knew there was strength there too. Camphoria turned and caught me gazing at her and blushed again, but I could not remove my eyes from hers.

<Quit yer admirin' and start yer talkin'!> Betty-Lou interrupted my thoughts.

"Quit telling me what to do!" I said to Betty-Lou out loud.

"Yes M'Lord. As ye wish," Camphoria said confused as she turned to face me with the whey hen in hand.

"I, ah, meant to say…", I cleared my throat, "Camphoria, please tell me about yourself. We have not really had time to be properly introduced to each other."

Relieved, Camphoria pointed to the large whey hen in her hand and asked with a glint of a smile, "The message, yer Majesty."

"Oh,… here it is," I handed her the container from my vest pocket and for a brief moment our hands touched and lingered.

As she deftly tied the small cylinder to the whey hen's leg and opened the hatch she said, "I be the only daughter of Jasper Bragg. We've a small farm in Bergland not far from Miller's Pond. My three older brothers have served the rebellion since they were mid-conscription age. Yet my father would'na allow me ta help and bade me stay home ta care for our farm and beasts. We've got the finest piglin wool in all the twelve kingdoms. Twas not till I became of conscriptin' age that I were able to convince him that I could be of help in the rebellion. My first assignment was ta serve in the adjudicator's mansion on Noonday. I had only been there ten rotations till ye and yer Grandfather arrived," she then flung the whey hen out of the portal which took to flight with a flurry of wings.

For a moment we both watched as the whey hen disappeared from view. "You are brave to be involved with the rebellion when you could be safe at home," I told Camphoria and I lightly placed my hand on her shoulder.

She brushed my hand off her shoulder as she abruptly turned to face me sternly.

"NO WHERE be safe while the Overlord lives!" Camphoria responded with a ferocity that matched her fiery red hair. "I be only doing what needs to be done. Being a woman, ye think that I be fit only for stayin' at home, cowering?"

"No, that's not what I meant, I just thought you needed to be protected."

"So, I am a weak and dainty girl that needs protectin', now?" Camphoria was angry now, hands on her hips, waiting my answer.

<What do I do now, Betty-Lou?> I called out mentally.

<Ye stepped right into it lad. Ye be on yer own,> she chuckled in my head.

"No, it's just that you shouldn't think that you have to fight if there are men to protect you," I said in my feeble attempt to be gallant.

"I be needin' no protectin' from men, m'Lord. I ran the farm, cut the piglin wool, planted crops and cared for the bills, all while pappy 'n my brothers played soldier, in the rebellion. No Sire, women be stronger than ye think! When the need arises, females show courage in equal quantities as the men, e'en more so."

Defeated, knowing it was a lost cause, I continued, "I still feel it was very brave of you to join the rebellion."

"Thank ye kindly, m'Lord for the praise and the illuminatin' conversation," she said coldly and with a curtsey, "If ye will not be needin' me for anything else, m'Lord, I will take my leave to finish the chores that other less qualified folk should be doin'," she turned and left in a flurry of skirts and straw dust.

<How poorly did I do, Betty-Lou?> I asked sheepishly as I stood in the whey hen enclosure.

<As well as a moth flying around the flame perhaps. Not so close as to singe yer wings, but close enough ta provide illumination,> Betty-Lou replied.

<That bad?> I asked.

<Ye've much to learn 'bout women-folk,> Betty-Lou counseled.

CHAPTER 15
THE WEST

(Extracted directly from the Personal Log book of Gideon Livingston, the Fire Lord)

All the troubles, worries, and pressures of leadership only added to the dark angry feelings that I had after meeting with Camphoria. I headed up the stairs to talk to the navigator about our position.

"Good morning Mr. Pulsey. What news do you have sir?" I pretended to cheerfully ask.

"Mornin', yer Majesty. We be on course and makin' good time," Granite Pulsey responded.

"Sir Kendrick is not here?" I asked a little irritated.

"He be below takin' a well-deserved rest. May I be of some assistance, m'Lord?" Mr. Pulsey offered.

"Thank you. Let him rest. Would you be able to tell me our current location, Mr. Pulsey?"

"Part o' the way between Meridian of Granberry and Tempston in the Kingdom of Fenfold, Sire."

"Very good. When will we arrive at Tempston, Mr. Pulsey?"

"Eh, my Lord? Tis not our destination. Do ye recall? Tis ye'self what gave the order to go to the safety of the rebellion headquarters?"

"Right you are. How long will it take to get to '*you know where*'?" I asked, not wishing to reveal my ignorance of not knowing where the rebellion headquarters resides.

"We should be to the place that '*we cannot*

mention' (wink, wink) by the 4th afternoon bell, eight rotations from now," Mr. Pulsey replied with a smile.

I mentally congratulated myself because that left me plenty of time to try to get to know all of the guests and crew on board. Eventually, I would need to actually find out where the headquarters was from my Grandfather, but first, I needed to fix the mess I made with Camphoria.

<Mayhaps, an indirect approach be better at this time,> Betty-Lou suggested.

<Good idea!> I responded, not being in the mood to confront an angry Camphoria and not trusting myself to not get angry with her in return.

I went down to Mr. Bragg's post by the mid-ship armory and found him sitting at a small octagonal table that probably served as something else if the need arose and the right button was pushed.

I opened a conversation. "Good morning to you, Captain Bragg. Do you have a moment to chat?"

"Of course yer Lordship."

"Wonderful. Thank you for saving my life. How is the wound healing?

"It be mending just fine, m'Lord. Thank ye fer askin'," he responded genially.

"I just chatted with Camphoria. My she has some fire in her!" I commented. Based on the recent conversation with her, I knew that to be an understatement.

"Aye she gets that from her mother," he chuckled.

"Say, I'm trying to get to know everyone better, would you mind telling me a bit about yourself then?" I asked.

"Not at all yer Majesty. There's but little to tell. I was a merchant captain n' sailed nearly the world over. I'd seen the good and the bad. But mostly had a good go of things. Then one day, the Overlord's ships detained me and my crew for supposedly aiding the rebellion. They confiscated my ship with all its contents. I were not part of the rebellion then, but that be what turned me to it." He paused as he unclenched his fists and did his best to keep his emotions under control. "Twas just after that, my wife left us, leavin' me, my daughter, who was a baby at the time, and twin boys of four cycles. I ne'er laid eyes on her since that ill-begotten time."

"I am sorry for your loss. That had to be hard on all of you. Thank you for sharing with me your story."

He was right. Though his tale was sad, it was short...too short. Was there something that he was not telling me? I probed for more information, "Camphoria, she is 18 right, so that would make it roughly 17 cycles ago that you joined the rebellion. Am I right?"

"Right ye be."

On a hunch, I asked, "What kinds of things were you carrying the day that your ship was confiscated?"

"Er, it...well...it was mainly rock rum, m'Lord," Captain Bragg looked a bit fearful as he revealed this.

Rock rum was hard to come by and the Overlord placed severe penalties on those who tried to get around the tariffs and taxes.

"Black market rock rum?" I pushed more.

"Aye m'Lord. Tis obvious secrets cannot be withheld from ye," he looked around to check that we were alone and lowered his voice to a whisper, "Ye see m'Lord, I was a pirate, or if ye prefer, a more civilized term, a privateer and we had just acquired a shipload of rum and were headed to the southern shoals to trade it in for supplies and arms."

I tried not to look shocked. This revelation was much more than I had thought he was hiding. "A pirate? I cannot imagine you as a ruthless and bloodthirsty pirate!" I whispered back.

"If ye'll pardon me m'Lord, the term of 'pirate' be much maligned in my book. Daring we were, but we were not for killin' nor did we lack for mercy on our victims. Aye we did plunder, but we never took it all and we only harmed those what did not see reason. Among ourselves, that be another matter. Only the strongest pirates could lead the others and that required ye ta be vigilant and wary at all times."

On another hunch that Captain Bragg was being more humble than necessary, I pushed, "You were their leader and you defected? That must have caused a bit of confusion!"

"Once again, m'Lord you astound me with yer insightful nature. Please to come into me office where we can talk private-like," he stood and led me to the door to the armory, which he unlocked with a key. Inside there was no table or chairs, but Captain Bragg sat on a barrel of explosive sand and motioned for me to sit on another.

When we were both settled, he continued, "Now here we can speak a bit more freely. Aye, I was their king and my wife their queen. And none of them took my decision to leave well, least of all my wife. I made my escape and I have kept a weather eye out for trouble from them ever since."

"It is hard to believe that you joined the rebellion because of one lost load of rock rum. There had to be something else," I prodded.

With a chagrined look on his face he responded, "Thrice now, m'Lord, you have me at an intellectual disadvantage. I beg yer mercy and forgiveness in not providin' all the details."

"Why did you take sides? The Armada certainly has taken ships from you before?", I asked.

"Aye, the Armada and those cursed Boar Riders, that be a ruthless and bloodthirsty lot. In the name of the grand Overlord, they kill and maim without remorse. According to their rule of law, they destroy with vicious hunger, everything they touch. I had reached my fill of their butchery and determined to rid the world of them. But one night, when I laid before my darlin' queen a plan to make it happen, she objected."

"Says she, 'Why do ye think to risk life and limb to help a people that shun and fear us and would'na lift a finger to help us?'"

"I replies, 'The Boar Riders 'n the Armada be given our lot a bad reputation. All the killin', burnin', and viciousness they be blamin' on us, when it be they that done it! Just fer pirate's sakes we'd be doing the world a favor by riddin' it of these beasts.'"

"She responds, 'Nay, I will not let ye risk yerself! Let em kill each other and when they be all dead, we will be ready to take over. Best tell no one 'bout your fool hardy plan, neither. They be much less patient than I.'"

"I says, 'I see yer point. It still bothers me fierce to have the good name of pirate maligned.' I thought that we was in accord and the conversation be over."

"Later I got word that my dearest wife had planned a mutiny on account of my crazy idea. I grabbed my two sons and Camphoria and we barely escaped with just what we had on. Twas your father what found us and took care of us till we could get settled in Bergland."

"That is quite a tale. How many pirates would you say there are and where are they located?"

"There be a good number, nigh unto ten thousand. Most of the pirates take berth on Islands and shores in the west, the unexplored territory...where we be heading at the present moment."

"Since we are headed in that direction, what do pirates think of the resistance, especially given your departure from their ranks?"

"Pirates be a non-political folk. They try to keep a neutral stance seein' as their clients may come from varying political persuasions. Tis bad for business ta take sides."

"Neutral to all but the highest bidder. Interesting. Last question Captain Bragg. Who knows what you have told me?

"None but yerself and the pirates that be alive. Not even my boys nor Camphoria know the truth."

"Your secret is safe with me, Captain Bragg. You have been of immeasurable help these last few rotations. It is good to know that I can count on your support and trust," I shook his hand and stood to leave. On a whim, I thought I should talk with Captain Bragg about Camphoria. Maybe he could help me smooth things over. "One more thing Captain Bragg."

"Yes, m'Lord?"

"I had a conversation with Camphoria this morning and it did not go well. She took offence to somethings that I unwittingly said to her. Please let her know that I am sorry. As a token, please give her this ring," I pulled off the ring that Auntie Mercedes had given me.

"Yer Majesty, I will be talking ta her 'bout her behavior to yer Lordship. There be no need ta be givin' her a gift." Captain Bragg said and grimaced, holding up both palms.

"No. Please. You don't understand. I was at fault and I want her to have this with my apology," I requested and tried to put the ring in his hand. He would not accept it.

"Beggin' yer pardon Lord, but ye have nothing ta apologize for. Whatever it be, it be the fault 'o Camphoria," Captain Bragg bowed and would not look at me.

<Betty-Lou, can you help me? I'm drowning here!> I mentally pleaded.

<He thinks ye be angry with Camphoria. Most nobles would be. He knows not yer real intent, so tell him,> Betty-Lou chuckled.

<It's not funny>

<Aye lad, it is. Good luck to ye!>

I grabbed Captain Bragg's shoulders and he flinched a bit as I did so. "Please look at me."

He complied with a look of dread.

"Camphoria is not in trouble and neither are you. I want you to give her this ring and tell her that I am sorry for my insensitive remarks. I want you to do this because... well, because I am attracted to her and I do not wish for any bad feelings between us. I know this is unusual for nobles to do, but I feel that I must ask your assistance in this matter. Will you help me?"

Relief was evident on his face. As I finished, his frown was replaced with a wide grin. "M'Lord, I understand yer intentions and will help ye. Beggin' yer pardon Sire, knowin' me own daughter, I've had me own whiskers singed a few times. If that little conversation did'na turn ye away, be ye warned, there be more where that came from," Captain Bragg said as he accepted the ring. "If I know 'er, 'n I do, she be cussin' herself fer her temper right this moment. But know this. There ne'er existed a more kindly lass, nor one more fiercely protective 'o family. She be worth the effort ta get ta know 'er."

He gave me a wink and put the ring in his vest pocket.

With a sigh of relief, I turned to go see Grandfather...we had much to discuss.

CHAPTER 16
MAELSTROM

(Extracted directly from the Personal Log book of Gideon Livingston, the Fire Lord)

"Grandfather. I just talked to Mr. Pulsey, the pilot, who says that we are headed into the pirate lands of the West. Is that true?"

"Aye, that be our destination," Grandfather confirmed with a nod.

"So the main base of the resistance to the Overlord is in pirate territory?" I confronted my Grandfather.

"Ye be correct once again. Where else do you think t'would be safe to come and go at will? We could'na had it in Noonday... well ye saw fer y'self that it be too heavily guarded," Grandfather Livingston responded.

"Pirates are safe? What about all of those stories you told me about blood-thirsty buccaneers and all those times that you barely escaped from them with your life?"

"Those stories be true, every one of 'em. Pirates be much like spider wasps. They dunna bother ye, unless ye be botherin' them, or be it that ye possess items that they be partial to. Besides, we bought the headquarters at more than a fair price and we've helped them out of a few tight spots."

"The resistance bought a pirate fortress?

"Aye, we did and there we will be safe from the Overlord and the Boar Riders for a bit."

"But we're headed for uncharted lands, full of pirates. What's safe about that? Is there anything else I should know

Grandfather?"

"Well, there be the northerly gales, the shoals on the North East, and the maelstrom in the very center of it all. Na, that be all," Grandfather shrugged his shoulders and then looked me in the eyes. "Best remember lad, ships be built for the open skies, not for the safety of port. Safe and secure be the Overlord's way, but in return ye lose yer freedom and be the worse off for yer safety."

His words struck a chord that reverberated in my head. "Now I get it. I always wondered why smart, hardworking folk would put up with the Overlord. They mistake peace and happiness as results of safety and security, when in fact the opposite is true. Peace and happiness come from taking risks and enjoying the results of freedom, the good and the bad," I mused. "Ok, that also explains why the western skies are uncharted. Timid souls will not knowingly place themselves in danger. No one in their right mind wants to end up a shipwreck on the shoals or be torn to pieces by the maelstrom or the gales."

"Aye lad, those be mighty dangerous skies to be sure, and there be no safe passage from the East, due to the gales and the dastardly shoals where be blown many a foolhardy ship to their doom. It be not much better from the West for the Maelstrom, what be a perpetual cyclone the size of a continent, deadly to all and it be unnavigable by even the most experienced pilot unless ye know the secret way. Aye, the resistance fortress be well protected."

"I'm supposing you know the 'secret way'. Am I right Grandfather?" I confirmed to which Grandfather nodded.

I took a sip of steaming bean tea and sat back in my chair to think. Now things were making sense. In the West the pirates were free to live untouched by the reach of the Overlord. We knew their secrets and that gave us an advantage. The feelings of vulnerability and insecurity were being replaced by a growing sense of confidence. I mused out loud, "You know, we might just have a chance to make this work."

Grandfather nodded in agreement with a wide grin on his face.

Pleasant rotations past as we journeyed West. I was able to practice more with my powers by increasing my ability to concentrate on what I wanted to do with fire. Because I hadn't seen her, I made a point to talk to Camphoria on the morning of the third rotation since we left Meridian.

"You've been hiding from me." I chided when I found her working oddly enough, in the same place she had been working the last I saw her; feeding the animals on board.

She stopped what she was doing and bowed as she said, "What be yer pleasure, m' Lord?"

"Please rise," I did not touch her chin as before.

She stood and faced me with a timid, serious look.

I figured I should not hunt for wind wisps but instead, I should get right to the words I had rehearsed a hundred times. "Ms. Bragg, I come before you to apologize for my insensitive behavior the other rotation. I know your courage and your sacrifices for your family and your country. I had no cause to belittle them in any way. Please forgive my thoughtless remarks and know that I meant no disrespect or harm. I am deeply sorrowful and would like to make amends in any way possible to perhaps be considered a friend."

I knelt down on one knee and lowered my head. Then I saw what I had placed my knee upon: a pile of animal excrement that Camphoria had been scooping up just before I arrived.

I heard a gasp, then, "Please, my Lord, stand up."

"I will not stand until you have forgiven my insult," I responded, holding in my laughter.

"I forgive ye, though there be no need. Twas I the one at fault, my Lord, 'n it should be me kneeling in piglin poop asking for yer forgiveness."

At that, I stood and said, "Thank you Ms. Bragg!"

I began laughing and then Camphoria laughed with me until tears came to our eyes. She found a rag and we cleaned my left knee as well as we could.

We sat on bales of dried grass and I asked her, "Your father gave you the ring, I suppose?"

"Aye, my Lord 'n I keep it safe. Ye did'na have'ta do that m' Lord. Right after I exploded at ye, I did the same ta m'self fer actin' like an angry squabbler. I thought ta never see ye again. When my da gave me yer ring, 'n explained what ye'd said, I could'na believe it. The next few rotations, I stayed clear o' ye so as ta not provoke ye. I should'a known I could'na hide from ye m' Lord."

"Well we both felt miserable for a few rotations. Let's promise to not do this again."

"Agreed, m'Lord."

We sat on the bale chatting about her life and my life and what we both wanted to do eventually. I felt comfortable talking with her and hoped that something more would develop as we spent time together.

For the next few rotations, Camphoria and I found time to meet and took walks on the deck and watched the waves beneath us as we listened to the rhythmic flapping and clapping of the propulsion sails as they opened to let air through on the forward stroke and closed on the back stroke, or often we simply sat on that same bale of grass and just talked. On the eighth rotation since leaving Meridian we were sitting on that bale and I was explaining to her about my original thoughts to be a jewel-smith, which she found incredible.

"I canna imagine yer Lordship as a jewel-smith, trapped indoors, looking through enlargement stones all the time!" she shared.

"Frankly, I was glad to have an excuse to not do that. Though a profitable and well-respected profession, I don't know if I could actually do it. Of course, I had no idea of my heritage, nor the resistance. I only wanted to be free of Miller's

Pond and thought that being a jewel-smith…"

A loud clang interrupted my sentence.

"That be the warning bell. Ye need to get topside to your station," Camphoria urged.

I bade Camphoria farewell and hurried up the main stairs.

"Problems?" I called out to Grandfather.

"Nay m'Lord, it be the borders of the maelstrom and all hands be needed at their assigned stations. Standard procedure, as a precaution only. Mr. Pulsey be well acquainted with the route. There should be no problems."

"Ah humm... Where is my station?" I blushed as I did not know.

"The captain of the ship takes the wheel during times of crisis. That be yer station."

"I well, uh,...., I've never piloted a ship before," I stammered.

"Betty-Lou will help ye. Trust yerself," Grandfather said encouragingly.

Mr. Pulsey was there and he saluted and motioned for me to take hold of the large wheel with spindles all around it. Then he strapped me in place.

It felt good to have the steering spindles in my hands. It was a moment that I had always dreamed of. I had always imagined myself at the helm, free to go where I wanted, the wind blowing in my face, the clouds racing by....

My daydreaming was interrupted by an insistent, "Yer Majesty!"

I looked up and saw the most horrific thing in my life, the Maelstrom. It was a massive wall of seething charcoal gray straight ahead of us. I froze. How do you escape such a monster? As we approached the fury of the winds increased and so did my terror.

"Your Majesty! You must guide us through!" Mr. Pulsey shouted.

I glanced at Mr. Pulsey. He motioned with his hand as if

he was going to chop the deadly swirling winds in half. “You want me to go straight into it?” I repeated the sign back to him and he nodded his head and pointed directly at the center of the Maelstrom.

Then I remembered Betty-Lou. <You’ve been here before. So, I go straight into the Maelstrom?> I thought as loud as I could to cover the noise of the wind in my ears.

<Ya dunna need ta shout, there be no wind in your head. Aye Laddy, the path lies directly through the Maelstrom. But do not falter or change course no matter what ye see or feel. Tis more than wind and rain ye be battling.>

<Huh? How could it be more than wind and rain?> I countered.

<Portus be an angry world and the maelstrom be the evidence of that wrath. If ye try to ride the maelstrom, we will be torn apart and devoured like the pods of ripe kettle peas when the hordes of rock jumpers fill the skies with their devouring mouths. But the screams of the dammed and the nightmare visions be worse by far than any physical suffering, though there be much o’ that also.>

<What will I see?> I asked.

<I canna say. Tis different for each person. What do ye fear most in all the world? Times that by ten and that be what your eyes and ears will behold,> Betty-Lou tried and failed to sound cheerful and optimistic.

<Do I steer toward the exact center of the maelstrom?> I asked.

<That be the target, but do not waiver. Ye must be steady and firm. Trust not your ears nor your eyes. They can deceive ye,> Betty-Lou warned.

I spread my feet, squared my shoulders, checked my deck harness for the hundredth time. I grabbed the spindles of the wheel firmly and steeled my nerves. With a grimace of determination, I pointed the prow of the Betty-Lou directly into the center of the darkest fury of the maelstrom. The powerful rear fins of the Betty-Lou pushed us in.

The wind whipped at my jacket and stung my face with its ferocity. I could feel how it clawed at me as if it were a huge animal and were it not for my safety harness already straining to keep me on deck, it would have played with me as a meercat plays with a tiny bilge mouse it intends to eat. Anything not tied down would have been quickly lost in the torment, but the crew was prepared. The sails had been retracted to their protective housings and all essential loose equipment had been stowed below deck. Only myself, and the helmsman, Mr. Pulsey remained above deck. Mr. Pulsey wore a harness like myself.

The darkness began to envelope us as we flew straight into the heart of the wild beast. The Maelstrom roared and howled, the noise was deafening, and I had to squint my eyes to protect them from the onslaught of the wind. My instinct was to turn the ship into the wind in order to stay on course, but I held back. I could feel the ship being tossed and blown as if it were a puff gourd floating on the breeze. <How can I keep it on course? The Maelstrom is too powerful!> Bettty-Lou did not reply, I was on my own.

She said to not trust my senses. <Am I being deceived now?> I closed my eyes and thought about wind and fire. <Wind only makes a fire stronger and larger.> I concentrated and for a moment, a wall of flame appeared before me, lighting everything with a green glow. In my mind's eye, between the whipped clouds and mists, I could see we were traveling straight ahead as glimpses of mountains, valleys and rivers flew by us. The vision began to flicker and felt myself getting weaker and weaker. I had to hold the steering spindles tight to keep my knees from giving way. It was as if the Maelstrom was drawing away my power to stop me from using it.

I let go of the vision and opened my eyes to the chaos. I was able to stand straight as my strength quickly returned. Even though I knew I was being deceived it took all of my will to not correct the Betty-Lou's course. I fixed my gaze on the devouring blackness ahead and held the steering spindles unmovable.

Then I began to hear the screams of agony, the pleas for help, and the wretched moans of anguish from the port side of Betty- Lou. Almost by reflex, I began to steer towards them but then I remembered Betty-Lou's warning. I told myself with gritted teeth, <Hold true. If there are souls to be saved, I cannot save them without endangering the ship and all my crew.>

Without warning, I heard a woman's voice rise above the tumult. "Gideon! Where are you? I need you!" It was my mother, Sadie-Belle.

I was about to turn the ship and find the source of the voice, then Betty-Lou spoke to me. <Do not heed it!> I heard in my mind. <Tis but illusion to snare the feebleminded.>

With bleary eyes I squinted and I saw a face rise up through the near total blackness. It had a look of terror and a scream frozen on the mouth, the bright red hair matted and limp, and the green eyes... "Camphoria!" I shouted and with one hand reached out to her. I turned the wheel in her direction.

"Hold tight Camphoria! I'm coming!" I shouted.

No sooner had I turned the wheel than the ship began to buckle and jump in response to the wind. Up to now it was just the wind that tried to destroy us, but now, the Betty-Lou twisted, jolted and bucked like a lassoed meercat.

Though I had turned the Betty-Lou in the direction of Camphoria, we were no closer.

<Get back on course! Think lad! Where be she now?> Betty-Lou nudged in my mind.

<She is safe below,> I answered and the dagger of fear that I felt in my heart slowly disappeared, only to be replaced by a new terror. <I've doomed the ship and the crew!> at these words I froze and could not move.

<Gideon! Control yerself!> the Betty-Lou shouted in my brain. This was the first time she had used my given name and it shocked me out of my paralysis. Drawing on the power I had left, I pushed the flames ahead of the ship and in the green haze

pushing away the Maestrom's illusions, I saw that I needed to turn starboard or be smashed by an oncoming peak. I yanked the wheel to the right, and then a bit to the left to get back on course. I let the fire subside as my knees trembled from the effort.

For the duration of a bell's watch, I held my arms solidly on the steering spindles of the Betty-Lou -- rigidly maintaining a straight course while the wind battered myself, Mr. Pulsey, and Betty-Lou. Even more exhausting than the physical strain from fighting the wind was the mental and emotional battle. I saw terrifying visions of on-rushing jagged mountain tops and had to resist the urge to avoid them. I heard sobbing pleas for help from mothers, friends and added tears of anguish to my already watery eyes. I endured threats of the overlord's warships firing their weapons and nearing to board us. Just as in all the other visions of the Maelstrom, at the moment I felt that we were doomed to be destroyed by the volley of explosive stones, it faded and was replaced by a new terror. I glanced back and saw that though Mr. Pulsey said nothing, the grim look on his face showed he was also being taxed to his mental and physical limits.

After what seemed to be an eternity of agony and wind, the darkness lifted suddenly as if the cover of a light stone had been removed. The wind was now a gentle breeze, though at the stern, just a few ship-lengths behind us, it continued boiling with fury.

I called out, "Your status Mr. Pulsey?"

To which he replied, "Here My Lord, I be of sound body and mind, though much shaken and distraught in both. And your Lordship?"

"Likewise. Are we on course?"

"Aye, your Lordship. By my reckoning, the...," he paused as he took another bearing, "the base be dead ahead Sire. Shortly it will be within a stone's gaze."

"Make the call to come topside and prepare to dock."

The deck of the Betty-Lou became a hive of activity as

men and women bustled about preparing the equipment and gear for the headquarters.

Soon I saw, rising out of the mist, the jagged spike of the Mount of Sorrows, or so Mr. Pulsey told me was its name. It appeared as a pointed hat with a thin brim of land surrounding it, slightly tipped to one side as if blown by the wind.

Mr. Pulsey guided me, "Yer Majesty. Steer Betty-Lou to the larboard side of the mountain to the secret entrance."

I turned the spindles left and on the starboard side the ship approached the mountain. The mountain was a black barren rock with scraggy bushes and a few trees clinging to the stone for survival. The Mount of Sorrows formed the edge of a small island called Melispora, which appeared to be thrust up from the bottom of the sea, as a jagged black splinter. A few leagues of forested scrub and grass extended from the base of the Mount of Sorrows to the ocean on the opposite side. The rocky volcanic soil barely supported the stunted trees and bushes on the plains, but the lush tropical growth flourished along the several streamlets radiating out to the sea. Other than the hidden headquarters as a base, the island was uninhabited. From the side-view, the blackened tip of the mountain extended out at an angle over the rough sea called Mar de Peligro, or Ocean of Danger, and pointed East, directly into the perpetual Maelstrom. From the tip of the Mount of Sorrows to the icy water was at least 100 ship lengths.

I unstrapped the frame containing far-stones from the side of the steering column and brought them to my eyes. I gazed through the far stones and found nothing that looked like an entrance, " Mr. Pulsey. It is a barren rock! I see no entrance."

"Aye, yer Majesty. Tis difficult to find, which has certain advantages."

Finally, Betty-Lou approached a fairly level outcropping of bare black rock that was located midway up the mountain on the south. With the far stones I saw that this had served as a landing platform with large metal hoops affixed to the side of the mountain which could serve as mooring anchors. On closer inspection, I located other similar hoops at intervals along the rock platform that could be used to secure airships. I nodded in approval: the mooring platform was purposefully small for defensive purposes.

"Engage the descent pumps!" Mr. Pulsey commanded in order for xeoxyn gas to be pumped from the main ballasts to compressed tanks where their lifting power is reduced. "Full stop!" to reverse the vanes in the propulsion wings so that they could push air forward instead of behind.

The Betty-Lou lowered in altitude and slowed to hold position over mooring area. The gang planks were lowered and the crew began to disembark. The small platform was soon full of the resistance crew and crew of the Betty-Lou. Captain Bragg headed directly towards a jagged spire leaning against the mountain at an angle. Beneath the shadow of the rock was a narrow gash that stretched at least a ship's length up the side of the mountain. This was the opening that led into the rocky lair. The small entrance had been carved out of the volcanic stone and was secured by a sturdy iron and wooden door. The inconspicuous entrance opened to a large reception room at least three ship's lengths deep and at least one length high. The room would be nearly completely dark were it not lit by glow stones in sconces on the wall and an ingenious series of light tubes that gathered the light outside of the fortress and funneled it using tubes, reflector stones and concentrating stones so that every corner of the room was well lit. On the East wall, round observation portals the size of flat-bread pies, mounted with clear crystal, gave view to the ocean toward the Maelstrom and the mooring platform. A chandelier hung from the center of the ceiling and provided perpetual light from its hundreds of glow stones mounted in a silver and crystal framework that resembled the swirling maelstrom. The rough black walls extended upward to a point, continuing the natural cavern formation. Several passages, some natural, some carved interrupted the west wall. The floor of the reception hall was bare stone polished black with the soles of thousands of boots over the millennia.

As he pointed to the passage ways Mr. Pulsey shared, "This stronghold hides a honey comb of rooms, dwellings, and meeting halls above and below this chamber."

"Is this the only entrance?" I asked.

"Tis the main entrance. There be others, less used and less convenient."

"Where is everyone? Is this base not manned?" I asked the question everyone was thinking.

We should have been aware that something was amiss when there was no greeting party, but we blindly blundered into the open headquarters (and that was the other detail that should have raised the warning signs-Why was it open?).

No sooner had the words left my mouth than we were surrounded by heavily armed pirates that funneled out of the many passageways.

"Surrender sus armas and you weel be not harm-ed," the pirate captain shouted with a thick accent I'd never heard before.

We had few weapons because we assumed it was our own base, nigh impregnable. We were at their mercy.

CHAPTER 17 ESCAPE FROM THE BRIG

(Compiled from the personal Journal of Gideon Livingston, the Fire Lord and personal documents of Capitan Mejilla, donated by Portenza Grizbol of Sulmana)

The pirates made a terrible racket as they played Stones on the lone table. The point of the game was to end up with all of the stones being played. To gain stones the pirate had to correctly predict which stones his stone would touch. They made wagers on whether the claim would be accomplished or not. Each stone that was touched and correctly predicted became the property of the thrower. While each stone that was tossed that either was not touching the predicted stone, or touching one that was not predicted was set in the stone pot. The winner of the game won all of those stones too. Some of the stones were very valuable. They could be gems, or richly decorated with yellow ochre or rose metal, or have some special quality. These were poor pirates as demonstrated by the simple tumble stones they used which were easily found in any wind-swept mountain cleft. There was certain skill in throwing the stones, to be sure, but the real skill in winning at stones was to see who could cheat the most and not get caught.

Some stones vibrated when rubbed and others spun on their axis. Others attracted or repelled stones. Some stones were extremely light and almost floated when thrown, while others were incredibly dense and refused to bounce or slide. Inserting a "power stone", as they called it, into the game of stones gave the thrower significant advantages. Inserting a fake power stone in the game was equally advantageous. The game was all about deception; making a show of tossing a stone in order to not reveal, or pretend to reveal the stone's unique quality.

I watched, intrigued, as the pirates, some were clumsy while others greatly skilled, feinted, hid, and dissimulated to gain advantage in the game.

I and a few crewmates had all been placed in a dank cell carved out of the mountain. A sliver of a window ran up the side of the wall behind us. The floor and walls were of rough granite, with seams of black basalt crisscrossing the surfaces. The rest of the crew of the Betty-Lou was deposited in the 20 or so smaller adjoining cells that lined the basement of the headquarters. So far, I saw no signs of the pirate leadership. I had assumed that they would be down to gloat over their easy victory. As far as I knew, the headquarters had been taken without a fight. The pirates undoubtedly knew a secret way in to the base so as to catch the base personnel by surprise. I realized that we had walked into a well-planned trap when I noticed that the occupants of the headquarters were already situated in cells when we were brought down. Thankfully, none appeared to be injured.

"I demand to speak to your leader!" I shouted to the pirates, engaged in their game.

"Shut yer trap. Ye be in no position to demand. Our captain will be speakin' to ya soon enough," the largest and ugliest pirate retorted, not taking his eyes from the game.

We were all chained to the walls by manacles on our wrists through which a thick iron chain was strung above our heads through iron hoops fixed to the wall. I spoke to Mr. Pulsey, who was on my right side and asked him to pass a question down the line to discover where my Grandfather, Captain Bragg, and Camphoria might be. He leaned his head to Mr. Cloudjumper who immediately leaned his head and whispered the query, and so on until I could not see who was responding. After a few moments, I saw Mr. Pulsey lean his head closer to Mr. Cloudjumper, and receive the answers.

Mr. Pulsey leaned his head to mine and whispered. "M'Lord, Captain Livingston, and Camphoria be five cells down. Naught is known of the whereabouts of Captain Bragg."

I worried that the pirates had found Captain Bragg, their former leader, and were planning on taking their revenge for his defection.

I reached inside my mind to seek the Betty-Lou. <How are you?> I asked.

< Fit as a fiddle, with ne're a care. The pirates be seeking me, but they be easy to avoid. What be yer status?> She queried.

<We are chained to the walls in the brig of the headquarters. Captain Bragg is somewhere else in the base. We have to do something before they kill him,> I answered.

<M' Lord Gideon, I dunna think they know who ye be, otherwise ye would be in the same danger as Captain Bragg,> Betty-Lou pointed out. <Bein' unawares, mayhaps it be time to reveal yerself to 'em, seeing as pirates be a superstitious folk and easily swayed.>

<That gives me some ideas. Thanks Betty-Lou,>I responded.

<Don't mention it. I'll just keep playin' tag with these here pirates while ye make yer plans,>replied Betty-Lou matter-of-factly.

I began to think of different options out of this predicament. I could make myself invisible, but I would still be chained to the wall. I could do the same for everyone, but it would not change our situation, to be sure, it would frighten our guards, but put ourselves at risk of being stabbed by a pirate's saber. I could use brute force. I could fill the room with smoke, kill all of our guards with blasts of fire, and then melt the bars of our cell, but I had no idea where Captain Bragg was... and the pirates would be expecting attempts to break out.

I determined that I had to do first things first, I needed to find where Captain Bragg was being held. Betty-Lou had pointed to the best solution; superstition. Armed with this thought, I created a plan that would get us free, free Captain Bragg, and gain the cooperation of the pirates.

I informed Betty-Lou and then waited for the right time.

Just after the 7th bell, I began my plan.

"There she be!" Shouted the pirate from the look-out dangling from the bottom of the ship. This was the best position because the egg-shaped buoyancy tanks from which the ship was suspended obstructed the view below. The disadvantage was that the view above was obstructed.

Betty-Lou was stationary, as if asleep, drifting with the clouds upon which she rode.

"We've gotcha now! Prepare the razor discs. We'll bring 'er down good and proper," the pirate wrung his hands in anticipation.

"Belay that order!", the pirate captain bellowed. "Our orders be not destroying this barco, only to be taking command of her."

The Betty-Lou had not moved and appeared unconcerned about the close proximity of the pirate ship.

"For certain, they be aware of our presence. Why do they not responding?" The captain pondered aloud. He was a tall but swarthy man, Sulmanian by birth, which explained his dark complexion, "Board her and be taking possession. If any resist, kill them," he shouted to his men as he pointed his scimitar at the Betty-Lou.

Betty-Lou allowed the pirate ship to come alongside her and then the men rushed aboard her.

They spread out on the top deck, part went to the forecastle doors and the rest headed down the main hatch. Betty-Lou had a few surprises for them. The first pirate rushed down the stairs, shouting and waving his shooter and cutlass in the air. Betty-Lou snapped him in the rear with a tie-down. He jerked around to accuse the pirates that followed and was nearly impaled by a rushing crewmate. "Whoa there! Why'd you whack me on me backside?" He accused threateningly as he nimbly dodged the cutlass that would have run him through.

"What you talkin' 'bout? We ain't touched you!" they replied.

"It were someone, 'n I've got the welt ta prove it," the first pirate stated and rubbed his backside.

More carefully, the pirates searched the first level below deck. Odd things kept on happening to them. One pirate took a wicked fall over a bottle that just happened to move right when he took a step. Another pirate broke his nose when he ran right into a door that suddenly opened in front of him. Several pirates found it hard to stand when a full keg of water broke loose and rolled over them. A pirate smashed his toes when he walked behind the wheel of a cannon just as it rolled back on its track. One pirate got tangled up in a sleeping hammock and could not get out.

Guide ropes and tie-down whipped around like snakes, snapping, snagging, and snaring the pirates every time they turned away. Amidst the shouting and cursing of these apparent accidents, three pirates disappeared through a sudden hole in the floor, accompanied by a flushing sound. A full side of smoked moor beast swung loose from the rafters and slammed into a poor pirate, sending him flying head-over-heals into the galley wall. A pirate ran for his life as a large and vicious looking meat hook nearly impaled him as it swung free from its place on the wall.

After being beaten, whipped, tripped, paddled, slammed, and skewered, the pirates huddled in a circle to protect themselves as they cautiously moved around the barrels, boxes and equipment lashed to the deck. A gust of wind blew out all the lanterns the pirates carried and at the loud bang caused by all the doors slamming at once, the pirates ran for the stairs, causing more damage to each other as they tripped each other and fought to get out.

"Tis haunted by evil spirits down there! We barely escaped with our lives!" One pirate shouted to Capitan Mejilla.

Captain Mejilla scowled and drew his sword. With measured words he commanded, "Ye ne're will escape with your lives if ye are not bringing back the hombres of this ship in irons. Be ye more fearful of fantasmas than me?"

Captain Mejilla was interrupted in his reproach of the crew when, just then, three bedraggled pirates shot out of a vent hole, landing at Captain Mejilla's feet.

"Arhgg! What is it that is smelling so horrible?" Captain Mejilla pulled out a handkerchief and covered his nose. "Where is it that you have you been?"

The three untangled themselves and began praying and giving thanks. One pirate said, "Capitan, do not make us go into that foul ship again. It ate us and we spent time in the dark belly of the beast before it coughed us up."

"Spending too much long in the bilge, more like," Captain Mejilla said with a disgusting look. "You three, must be cleaning yourselves immediately. Be gone."

"We searched the ship from top to bottom, no one is aboard Captain Mejilla!" the first pirate reported as he quavered uncontrollably. All of the others who were physically able to moves, also vigorously shook their heads in agreement.

Captain Mejilla noticed for the first time the miserable state of these pirates: bloody noses, limping, mangled fingers, swollen faces, and some of them were completely unconscious.

"I am not comprehending this. What has being done to yous?" Captain Mejilla asked, thoroughly confused.

"Set upon by a terrible force we were," the spokesman explained. "We were attacked from all sides at once. We fought like lions but t'were no use. We saw the beast eat those three and before the beast could devour us, we escaped."

"Ye are being fools and frightened niños," the captain furiously shouted. "If there be no one aboard, who attack'ed you? How did the crew be escaping? I saw no escape launches. They must to being on the ship somewheres. I, yours Capitan, will search it and find them myself. First-mate, you is going first," Captain Mejilla growled and signaled for the first-mate to enter the ship.

"Wait! First, I be talking to them," Captain Mejilla, being a careful man, decided to see if he could draw out the crew of the Betty-Lou.

"Valiente crew of this ship. I am Capitan Mejilla. I know that you is here!" He shouted as he paced the Betty-Lou. "I need to speech with your Capitan," as he shouted these words, he wandered the deck while his first-mate took a protected position facing the stairs to the main hatch in order to shoot anyone exiting from below deck.

"Come arriba now for I to be merciful. You are surrounded and there is nowheres for you to be escaping," Captain Mejilla lied. "Spare your crew by surrendering unto me."

There was no response. The captain and his first-mate waited a few moments and then the captain signaled to his first-mate to follow him with weapons drawn as he began the descent into the Betty-Lou.

When the first-mate and Captain Mejilla were both on the stairs, the Betty-Lou twisted the stair steps so they formed a flat slide, sending the two pirates hurtling and screaming on their backsides into the galley wall.

The pirate crew on seeing their captain and first-mate disappear screaming into the maw, turned tail and boarded their own ship as fast as they could, helping the lame and unconscious as they went.

The captain and his first-mate untangled themselves and looked at the stairs, which were back in their normal positions. They heard a noise below and cautiously, the two men crept around to the entrance of the second set of stairs. The captain shoved the first-mate so he would go first in the dim light. Nothing happened as they descended and headed towards the animal stables and the whey hen enclosures. A loud thump made them stop. At this point, the floor dropped out from beneath them and they plummeted directly into the brig, landing heavily on top of each other.

I concentrated and sent a tendril of green smoke along the ceiling of my cell. It flowed like an upside-down river of water over the bars and into the corridor. The pirates at the table were still playing stones boisterously and didn't notice the green ribbon of smoke over their heads silently making its way down the hall and into each cell and room. I could only make out a fuzzy image in my mind of where the smoke was going due to the poor lighting from torches mounted in the wall. I guided the smoke to check the contents of each room. Once certain that Captain Brag was not at this level, I directed the tendril of smoke up the stair entrance-way along the ceiling.

I methodically checked all the rooms on this level and discovered that Captain Bragg had to be on the ground floor. The smoke tendril quickly obeyed my will and I was pleased to find that my mental vision became clearer due to the increased light. As quickly as I could, I searched the rooms until I encountered Captain Bragg seated on a chair, bound and gagged. He was badly beaten and sported a black eye, swollen cheek, and caked blood under his nose. Though obviously in distress, the set of his jaw told me that he was unbroken.

"Are you alright?" I whispered.

Startled at the voice, he opened his eyes and looked for the source of the sound. His eyes widened even further when he saw the outline of my body in green smoke.

"Whmmffwa haffafawun!!" He groaned.

Which I took to mean, "What the blazes, I be

hallucinatin'!!"

I thought of a surgeon's scalpel made of flame and carefully sliced through the knot at the back of his head, holding the gag in his mouth.

"Wait, it's me. Gideon. I'll explain later. Are you able to travel?" I whispered.

"Aye m'Lord. But I be bound good and tight," Captain Bragg croaked.

"I'll have you free in a moment," I said and then directed the smoke to the leather bands holding his arms behind the chair. I concentrated to create a flaming knife that my apparition used to cut the bonds as if they were made of paper.

"Let's go!" my apparition said as it motioned for him to follow.

I checked outside by sticking my apparition's head through the door and seeing the corridor clear, I melted the lock with a burst of flames from a smoky finger.

"Go directly to the mooring rock and wait for the Betty-Lou. She will pick you up. Stay aboard the Betty-Lou. I will cause a distraction so you can leave unnoticed," my ghostly apparition explained.

I went ahead of Captain Bragg, motioning him to wait as I returned to my ribbon of smoke on the ceiling. Captain Bragg gaped incredulously at what he was seeing, but he obeyed.

Ahead, I knew there were guards at the door to the mooring rock. I had to get beyond them and then cause a disturbance. As the smoke stream I guided turned the corner, I saw the two guards rigidly on either side of the door.

Good, they will be alert and will be easy to distract, I thought.

I saw that they had lit the torches in the sconces in the darkening evening and knew that I had found my distraction. I directed the tip of the green smoke to the flickering torch and gave it a burst of flame, at which it exploded and caused a large noise and clattering as it fell to the stone floor. To my disappointment, only one guard came running. I had to do something else.

As the lone guard saw the sputtering torch on the floor and bent to pick it up, I scorched the other torch with a blast of flame and it shot out of its sconce and landed on the pirate's behind. He let out a cry of surprise, "Fire!" He shouted, which immediately brought the other guard to the smoke-filled hallway.

As my smoke tendrils returned down the ceiling of the hallway, I noticed that Captain Bragg had been attentive and had made it safely out to the mooring rock, which afforded a hiding place until the Betty-Lou arrived.

I released the smoke and allowed it to dissipate in front of the two mystified guards and then in my cell opened my eyes to once again get my bearings of where I really was. Now for part two.

I waited for it to become dark outside as indicated by the slits in the wall that served for fresh air and light. Then I closed my eyes again and mentally I travelled to the Betty-Lou. I imagined the form of the red-haired man with the serrated sword that I had seen in the tapestries. I made the green form of the Fire Lord emerge from the wall of the Betty-Lou and walk, sword in hand, directly in front of the brig.

I pointed the flaming sword at the two quavering pirates and bellowed in my deepest voice, "I am he who is your doom. I am the destroyer of board and ballast. I am the savage flame. I am the smoldering spirit of this island born of the deep belching fire. Who dares to enter my realm? Who be the captain of this miscreant crew?"

The two men were so terrified that without hesitation the first-mate pushed his captain forward.

"What be your name?" I continued fiercely.

"I am being Capitan Mejilla," he responded, shakily removing his hat and bowing his head.

"Who commands ye?" I demanded.

"My comandante is being the Pirate Queen, Cirulea," Capitan Mejilla's voice trembled as he gave this information.

"And what be her bidding? Speak truth or face my wrath!" I roared.

Capitan Mejilla blanched and responded with quaking knees, "My tasks were the capturing and the holding of the forces of the rebellion and be capturing this barco for small time when my Queen could come and take them."

"WHY!" I shouted and swung my flaming sword in the air above my head.

"Ay! We are being humble mercinarios, your majesty. Whoever is paying the most, that is who we be following orders. I do not know who is being our master now," Capitan Mejilla responded in terror.

I glared at him but softened my voice a bit. "Here be your new task. Swear fealty to me and you will be richly rewarded, fail me and your life ends in flame and torment. Release the prisoners in your dungeon. Protect and care for them as if they were your own. I will await the arrival of your queen. Dare to leave this sacred place against my will and you will perish in flames. Do not send any message to your queen. Gather your soldiers in the great hall that I may visit them. Go now!"

I waved my hand at the cell door and Betty-Lou did me the favor of opening it.

The two pirates fell to their knees and bowed deeply, then as one ran up the stairs to their ship.

CHAPTER 18 PIRATE CONVERSION

(Reconstructed from eye-witness testimonies and the records of Capitan Mejilla and Gideon Livingston, the Fire Lord.)

The pirates were as good as their word. Capitan Mejilla returned to the island and immediately released the prisoners, fed them and provided for all of their needs. They were astonished at how Captain Bragg had gotten loose and were sure that the Fire Lord had released him when they saw the melted lock and burned leather straps.

Once all of Capitan Mejilla's pirates and our crews were assembled in the great hall, I found a quiet place where I would be able to concentrate and brought the Fire Lord apparition out to them again.

I thought it best to keep it a secret that I was the Fire Lord at the present time, especially since according to Captain Livingston, they did not recognize him and thought that he was the captain of the Betty-Lou. He of course did not reveal anything different to them and they looked to him as the captain.

The hall consisted of wooden tables and chairs sufficient for hundreds of troops arranged in a semicircle facing a raised circular platform. For dramatic effect, I sent my Fire Lord apparition rising up from the center of this circle.

All the chatter stopped as eyes riveted upon the flaming green apparition. I did not conjure a sword for the apparition to hold, but instead I imagined that it stood with empty hands outstretched to the sky.

"Hear me and tremble. Behold me and quake," I once again used my deepest voice for effect, "For I am the bringer of doom to unrighteous enemies and usurpers. Fear my wrath and beware my anger. I am the Fire Lord, born of molten rock and flame. Merciful to those that serve me and kind to those that protect the weak and forlorn. Men and women of many nations heed my words. Those who have cast you out and scorned you do not deserve your service, even for a price. Uphold your honor, stay true to your loyalty to me, and you will see the day when you will travel freely in the skies and walk tall in the cities of your enemies. This day is the day of your redemption," I expected first fear, and anxious looks and then relief in the faces of the pirates, but all I saw were looks of curiosity and confusion.

<These be pirate folk; most cannot read and are uneducated. Best be usin' simpler vocabulary,> Betty-Lou communicated.

I regrouped my thoughts and tried again, making two flaming swords appear as I growled and pointed at the pirates, "Ye will all die for attacking my ship." Now I heard the groans and anguish and continued, "But I am merciful. Join my crew and you may be saved. Be false with me and face my anger!" I finished by shooting green flames from both the swords into the stone dais.

At those words, all the pirates, including Captain Mejilla, knelt down and offered their swords to me, as the apparition. Captain Livingston went with a parchment and pen and wrote the names of all the pirate crew members and had them make their mark on the paper.

CHAPTER 19 THE DRAGON TREASURE

(Compiled from the records of the Fire Lord, Gideon Livingston, King of Portus, Protector of the 18 realms. The headquarters is now a museum in honor of both of the Fire Lords. The treasure is no longer there and has been spent, lost or moved to parts unknown.)

Back aboard the Betty-Lou, I sat down alone with Captain Bragg as he recovered in his quarters.

"How are you faring?" I asked him. Camphoria had cleaned him up and placed poultices of herbs on his swollen face. She also bandaged his bruised ribs. He looked much better than when I rescued him.

"Fair to middlin'," he replied with a smile, which disappeared as soon as he felt the pain in his face.

"Though I would prefer not to bother you as you need your rest, I must prepare for the arrival of the Pirate Queen, your former wife. I promise to not be long, and if it hurts, please tell me," I said trying to show my concern and kindness.

"Sire, it does hurt, but not for the reasons that ye be thinkin'. I never stopped loving her and my heart aches every day for her," Captain Bragg said with red rimmed eyes. He continued. "Sire, if I may be so bold, ye be makin' a large miscalculation if ye think ye can negotiate with Cirulea. She be the most vicious and cunning pirate of them all. I could not pretend to match wits with her. You say the pirate crew now belongs to the Fire Lord. I say all will change once Cirulea arrives. Dunna trust them nor her. She has plans within plans and ye cannot win at this stage," Captain Bragg nearly pleaded. Though his face was bandaged, I could see the concern in his eyes.

"If I cannot negotiate with her, what course of action do I take?" I asked.

"Pirates only understand two things: power and money. Someone with power and money has bought and paid for her service and commands her loyalty. To negotiate you must have more of both. She will come with many ships full of pirates loyal to her. We have only one of her ships that may be loyal to us. Though, with your strength, we may win a battle with them, they are prepared, unlike the Overlord's armada at Noonday. She can be a tenacious enemy and a fearsome friend."

"I get the point. I am asking for your advice...options," I interrupted.

"Yes, Sire. Though I am loath to tell ye this, knowin' of yer Majesty's valor, I believe that the best we can hope for now is to escape so we can find out who it is that has bought the Pirate Queen's services."

"Then we give up the base; we cannot return here with Cirulea as an enemy. The rebellion needs allies, and if what you say is true, she would be a fearsome one. Power and money you say...Hmm," my last words trailed off in a mutter.

"M'Lord, do not underestimate her cunning," Captain Bragg pleaded, guessing at what my course of action would be.

"Thank you for your advice Captain Bragg. Is there anything else I need to know?" I asked as I stood up to leave.

"Just one thing, yer Excellency, I wish to thank you for saving me and keepin' me apart from all this. If Cirulea were to know that I were involved, things would get more complicated indeed," Captain Bragg said sincerely, shaking his head at the thought of his wife's fury.

"I was glad to do it and will be glad to do it anytime and anywhere. Take care and get well my friend," I said and retired from the quarters.

<Any advice Betty-Lou?> I thought.

<Listen careful to Captain Bragg's counsel, but follow yer heart,> Betty-Lou replied.

<Cryptic as usual. Thanks,>I thought sourly but grinned inside. Betty-Lou was getting to know me for sure.

<Just curious, do you know where I can get a hold of a lot of money, fast?> I asked.

<There be things that I know that the oldest pirates dunna know. For sure I know where there be loads of treasure, but none of it close nor easily retrieved, 'ceptin' perhaps one place,> Betty-Lou responded tentatively.

<I'm listening. Tell me more,> I pushed.

<Tis close, but well hidden. Not one of my captains has ever simply asked me for money, and had they, I would'na told 'em nothing. But ye be different. I see in yer heart that ye would'na use it fer personal gain, so I'm gonna tell ye where ye can find it.> Betty-Lou said with conviction…and love.

Overwhelmed by what I felt from Betty-Lou, it took me a moment to respond. <Ah…Your trust in me, an unexperienced novice, is astounding and much appreciated. What I feel from you, though, I have only felt once before, and I will carry it in a place of honor in my heart. Thank you. I hope you feel the love I have for you also,> I responded solemnly.

<Aye, laddy, I do> Betty-Lou answered and quick as lightning changed pace. <Time's a wastin'! This is how ye can do it.>

Betty-Lou explained where the treasure was and how to get to it and I listened carefully, memorizing all the mental maps she drew for me. I called a council of war by ringing the bell in my cabin and laid out the plan to all the leaders. Always keeping in mind Captain Bragg's words, I prepared several possible options for interacting with the Pirate Queen and several possible alternative means of escape. I told no one about the treasure or that part of the plan; that was something I had to do myself. To keep up the ruse and hide my identity, I had my Grandfather meet with the pirate crew to find out what needed to be done to prepare for the arrival of the Pirate Queen, to belay their fears about us, and to pump them for any information that might give us the upper hand.

Everyone, both pirate and rebel, were given assignments and they went about completing them with enthusiasm. The headquarters was buzzing with activity. Decorations had to be found and then hung, food prepared, and accommodations cleaned and readied (pirates are not known for being tidy). We were going to have a feast the likes of which the headquarters had never seen. While everyone was thus busy, I undertook my task to find the treasure.

The base was located within the bowels of the Mount of Sorrows on the island of Melispora. Who knows who carved out the myriad of tunnels and rooms because the knowledge of the labyrinth creator has been lost to time. As everything in Portus, history is shrouded by eons and what was fact, oft turns to legend, then turned to myth. The dragon's treasure is the greatest myth that everyone knows about and no one has found. That is what Betty-Lou has sent me to find. According to her, it is located right here on the few hundred leagues of Melispora. It is understandable that no one has found it, seeing as this island is the hardest to find and only the mythical floating island is more elusive. With Betty-Lou's mental map in my head, all I had to do was to sneak out, without anyone seeing, and follow it to the treasure. I told my Grandfather that I would be very busy the rest of the evening and that I should not be interrupted for any reason.

My quarters in the secret base located in the mountain, happened to be on the second level. I concentrated on the part of flame that is invisible and I disappeared from view. I quickly walked up the stairs into the third, fourth and fifth levels.

The fifth level of the base was uninhabited and dusty from lack of use. The characteristic rounded ceilings of the passages and rooms indicated that the same builders had carved this level out of the mountain as the rest of the levels in the base. At one time it may have been a sumptuous dwelling, but the furniture was all broken, gnawed, and falling apart. Wall coverings were ragged and torn, and so old that a good wind would blow them to dust, while litter and rat droppings could be seen everywhere.

I grabbed two seat cushions that nearly disintegrated at my touch and I whacked them together to emit clouds of dust to cover my tracks. Though I was invisible, I still left footprints. The stench made by the rats was unbearable. I shivered as I heard the scattering of rats feet and I continued following my mental map holding a face cloth to my mouth, wishing that I still had the cool refreshing smudge pot cloth to put over my head to filter out the smell.

"No wonder why no one came up here," I complained to myself.

As I entered more of the interior of the level, I made to light my ring to provide more visibility, but then, I remembered I had given it to Camphoria. I lit my finger instead. Following the map in my head, and periodically dusting the floor with the pillows, I turned into a narrow corridor, then turned right. I faced an elegant and unusually sturdy door that opened into a large alcove covered in a mural. I saw disintegrating benches and what looked to be the remains of a podium.

"This may have been a place of worship, perhaps a theater," I thought.

I stepped up to the raised platform and walked right up to the far wall. At the end of the alcove I turned right. Just as the map in my head had indicated, behind a wall that was painted to match the surrounding mural so that someone could stand there undetected, there was a door of a castle painted on the wall in fading paint. The rest of the painting depicted a pastoral scene with trees, flowers and grazing piglins. I reached out to the door and found the handle, though painted in the form of a dragon, it turned out to be an ingenious latch.

Following the instructions that Betty-Lou had given me,

I opened it, or attempted to. After ages, or who knew how many cycles of unuse, the door, not of wood but solid stone, mightily resisted my efforts to move it. Inch by inch I managed to swing it out. I extended my flaming finger into the darkness and I saw the steps leading downward. Cautiously, I stepped into the winding stone staircase leading down only one flight of steps. I found myself in a study complete with desk, leather bound books, and moth-eaten seats; perhaps the room for a clergy to prepare the sermon for the day.

I thought, "What an inconspicuous place to hide a fabulous treasure!"

Then I wondered if the former occupants even knew it was there.

I stopped ruminating about the history of the place and came back to myself and my purpose. I turned to my left and viewed a spectacular reflecting stone. It was 14 hands tall, framed by two, long and sinuous golden dragons, one on each side with their heads meeting in the middle. In the reflection of the reflecting stone I was startled to see a candle-less floating, green flame. Then I realized that I was still invisible, I released the concentration and became visible once more. I approached the reflecting stone and knew that I had arrived at the destination. I searched with my fingers around the edges of the reflecting stone for the secret latch that would swing the reflecting stone open. I had to increase the light shining from my finger to get a better look but found no obvious latches or buttons. Everything appeared to be solid. The dragon's themselves affixed the reflecting stone to the wall with their claws, refusing to relinquish their hold.

I recalled what Betty-Lou had said about this part of the treasure hunt, <The reflecting stone opens to whom the secret is revealed.>

"This is the dragon treasure. Betty-Lou knows about it because she was part of its discovery and safe-keeping. Dragon symbols are all over the Betty-Lou and open and close multiple things, both mundane, like chairs and beds, but also secret, like weapons or escapes," I thought, knowing Betty-Lou could not help me.

I saw two dragons on the reflecting stone, looking out. "In order to see what is revealed you need eyes," I thought.

With excitement I reached up and pushed a dragon eyeball. Nothing happened.

I knew it was too good to be true. It could not be that easy to have stayed hidden all these cycles, right under the very noses of the people who would have plundered it. Another thought occurred to me.

"To see well, you need two eyes," I thought, feeling a little giddy about finding the clue so easily.

I reached my hand up and pushed the eyes of one of the dragons simultaneously with two fingers. Nothing happened.

"There are two dragons, each with two eyes," I conjectured, now grasping for answers. "Maybe I have to push four eyes simultaneously."

I reached up with both hands and pushed the four eyeballs together. Nothing happened.

"What is needed to reveal? Truth? Knowledge? What truth or knowledge had I been given?" I frantically thought.

I knew I was running out of time. I still had to transport the treasure to its final resting place tonight in order for my plan to work. The Pirate Queen could arrive at any moment. I had to be ready. I began to feel panic that I might not answer the clue.

"Who am I fooling? The smartest minds on Portus had probably wrestled with this same clue and they could not figure it out. Why do I think that I can figure it out?" I asked myself.

"This would be a perfect time for Betty-Lou to chime in," I thought, "but she warned me that I had to figure it out on my own, without her help."

I sat on the desk chair in frustration. I heard a crack and then chair disintegrated in a cloud of dust, dumping me on the floor unceremoniously. I stayed there for a moments with my eyes closed frantically trying to find the answer. I opened my eyes to discover I was in complete and utter darkness. I had let the concentration on my finger lapse and it had stopped burning. Then the answer hit me.

"In order to reveal something, you need light," I murmured.

I concentrated on my finger to burn bright again, but then I realized that I had tried that and the light had not revealed anything.

"I need another kind of light," I told myself. "A dragon light!"

I unbuttoned my shirt and concentrated on the symbol burned into my chest. It had originally glowed with green fire the first day I got it. I had to make it do it again. I imagined that only the symbol on my chest was glowing in green fire. I looked in the reflecting stone to see the results of my efforts. I saw a dim circle in green begin to appear and it glowed brighter and brighter. I willed every ounce of energy I had into that dragon symbol and suddenly I felt a surge of power outside of myself assist me. The reflecting stone reflected the light as it grew until the whole room was lit in a bright green glow. The brightness of the symbol on my chest became so intense that I could not look at it, and then it happened. The eyes of the dragons on the reflecting stone began to glow green and I saw all their claws that dug into the wall to hold the reflecting stone in place retracting with a grinding noise. The Dragon Reflecting stone swung open of its own accord.

A soft <I knew you could do it.> echoed in my mind from Betty-Lou.

The symbol on my chest was still brightly glowing I saw into the cavern that lay beyond, mountains of gold bars, gold coins, gems, and golden goblets and rings. My attention was drawn to a woman's golden crown, made from a single dragon that formed the circle of the crown. I was delicately embellished with red rubies as eyes and crowned with a large diamond in the center held up by dragon claws. A curtain of diamonds dangled from the entire edge on golden chains.

"There is no way that I need all of this gold. How do I move enough for what I need tonight? Gold is extremely heavy," I wondered.

Then I began to think on how I discovered my other abilities with fire and how my reserves of strength had increased by that practice. I thought about what fire does and is, "I had never heard of fire lifting heavy objects though. Fire could melt the gold, but having a golden river running down the corridor would draw attention. Fire vaporizes water, and I had practice controlling smoke. Maybe I could vaporize gold and control where it goes, without having to lift it."

"Let's practice with a coin," I said as I found a golden coin on the floor.

I pointed my finger at the coin and a gout of flame erupted, instantly melting the coin, then vaporizing it into a golden mist. I concentrated on moving the superheated mist to another location and willed it to congeal into the coin again. First a round puddle appeared a few yards away, then the outline of a coin. I went over to look at the coin and realized it was round, but it was featureless. Smooth and round. I came to understand that this was going to take a lot more practice. More practice than I had time for.

"I'll stick with the bars of gold," I determined.

I practiced on one of the bars of gold and found that I could move it and reconstitute it into its basic shape fairly easily. I separated a suitable pile of gold bars that would have been worth a fortune and began the work that would take me most of the night. I vaporized and reconstituted in the Pirate Queen's guest chamber, one bar after another until the entire pile was gone. Exhausted, I collapsed on the dusty carpet to catch my breath. I picked up the golden crown and exited the treasure room. Now in the study, I concentrated on the dragon symbol again and the eyes glowed green while the dragon claws firmly grasped the reflecting stone frame. I used the diamond on the crown to shine with green flame, so I could see in the darkness.

After closing the reflecting stone door and the door to the secret study and all the while covering my footsteps by banging two extremely dusty pillows together, I quietly retraced my route. Unseen by the guards and the staff, I stumbled back to my quarters a few bells before dawn and immediately fell asleep on the bed only to be awoken what seemed a few moments later by a frantic knocking on my door.

"Sire, she be arrived!" Mr. Pulsey announced.

"Huh, what, who?

"The Pirate Queen, M'Lord. Ah... I have the clothes you requested m'Lord."

"Hmm...Thank you. I will be right down," I called through the door.

I tried to shrug off the grogginess of sleep and quickly dressed in brown furry breeches made from giant marmot fur, a white shirt with a brown piglin vest, hobnail boots and a yeoman's white cap; sailor clothes that Mr. Pulsey had brought. I called through the door to the guards, "I'm leaving in a moment. Report to Mr. Pulsey in the main hall."

When they had left, I quickly left the room. I ducked my head and my used the floppy brim of my hat to cover my face when I passed anyone.

I stopped by the suite of rooms that the queen would take that evening and placed the golden crown in an ornate box that I had found earlier and placed it on the chest. I checked the chest at the foot of the bed and wiped off a bit of gold dust on the lip. I placed the embossed message scroll that I had written next to the box on the chest. I hurried down the stairs to the look-out stations in the main entrance way. I saw through the portals that there were hundreds of ships surrounding the base and fortunately, the Betty-Lou was nowhere to be seen.

CHAPTER 20
SECRET PLANS

(Reconstructed from the memoirs of Deputy Minister Forldon McWhorter and the unpublished manuscript, "My Life as a Pirate Spy" by Pockmore Piddleton.)

The tinny voice from the stone rasped, "They have been captured as you anticipated and everything is working as planned, your Honor."

"Good. Now see that the queen fulfills her part of the agreement," the Deputy Minister chuckled.

"This was just too easy," the Deputy Minister said to himself as he twisted his black goatee. "These rebels have no idea of who they are dealing with and they are following my plan to the letter. They will weaken the Overlord's forces to such an extent that they will be decimated. In doing this, they will expend every ounce of strength and resources they possess and will be too weak to defend themselves. Just when they think they have finally toppled the Overlord, I will snatch their victory from their uncomprehending hands and throw them in prison for their part in the coupe. I will be called a hero and there will be no one who knows the wiser. I have a plan to take care of these pirate loose ends too," he chuckled.

"The only thing that has worried me is that ship, that infernal ship that almost ruined all of my plans by making the Overlord too cautious. But now, that is taken care of and I can concentrate on weightier matters. Like, what am I going to wear at the coronation! Ha ha!" the Deputy Minister cheerfully said as he put away the small green talk-stone and placed the larger talk stone in the foil dish. He tapped it and it rattled obediently.

"Yes, your Honor," a voice replied.

"What news about the rebels is there?" The Deputy Minister asked.

"Nothing new, your Honor, just that word of the rebel victory over the armada has spread. Oh, there has been talk of the resurrected Fire Lord of legend, sir. They say it was him that won the battle," the tinny voice explained.

"That is wonder… I mean, I wonder what that means?" The Deputy Minister caught himself. "Keep me posted if anything new arises in Meridian."

"Yes sir."

"This gets better and better! The legend of the Fire Lord will keep the populace looking in the wrong place. They won't even notice when I have moved in with my secret forces. But not yet. I must be patient," the Deputy Minister gleefully intoned.

CHAPTER 21 BATTLE OF WORDS

(Compiled from eye-witness accounts collected by ancestors of Portenza Grisbol of Sulmana, the journals of Ariel Livingston, Cirulea Bragg, and Gideon Livingston the Fire Lord.)

"They appeared just moments ago," Mr. Pulsey stammered nervously.

"All is prepared. Have courage!" I told him while I patted him on the back. "Please direct me to where I might find Captain Livingston."

Following his instructions, I found my Grandfather barking orders on the first level.

"Good morning Captain Livingston!" I greeted enthusiastically.

"Good mornin' ye'self. Quit yer lollygaggin' and get busy. We've..." Grandfather stopped in mid-sentence when he realized who I was.

"Oh, tis you. My apologies, m'Lord," Grandfather said as he was about to bow.

"No, no, no. You cannot do that," I put my hands up to stop him. I stood and saluted him, "What be yer pleasure sir?"

Grandfather winked and said, "Grab that mop o'er there and get busy swabbing the decks by the portals, 'n be quick about it!"

"Right away sir," I said with another crisp salute.

I hurried to grab the mop by the window, as this was the plan so I could see what was going on and assist without being suspect. I began mopping the floor, all the while keeping an eye on the ships that were visible through the round window openings.

The pirates and rebels had done a marvelous transformation of the base. Bright colored ribbons and bows hung from entrances and window ways. The floor was polished to a shine, and many cycles of grime had been removed to show that at one time, this place had been quite respectable, perhaps even palatial given what I had seen on the fifth floor. There must have been a storeroom full of items for banquets and celebrations, though I couldn't imagine pirates or rebels taking much interest in that. I glanced into the grand hall and was amazed to see that the individual tables surrounding the dais had been arranged into a series of ten long tables, covered with fine linen and decorated with ribbons. Someone had gone to the tropical streams and they had gotten a hold of hundreds of bouquets of bright, beautiful flowers to place in the vases on the tables. Pirates and rebels stood in attention on either side of the entrance to the grand hall.

Captain Mejilla, returned to the base on his scout ship, looking confused and frustrated. He rubbed his cheek where the red imprint of a woman's hand could be clearly seen. "The Queen is arriving here in a momento," he glumly shared with Captain Livingston.

"Are you alright Captain Mejilla?" Captain Livingston asked.

"Be ye ware is all I can be telling you," Captain Mejilla mumble.

"Much obliged," Captain Livingston responded and nodded amiably.

The Pirate Queen's ship approached the landing pad and once it had moored, hundreds of pirates, armed to the teeth, spilled from its interior. Though pirates wore no uniforms, they appeared to have similar tastes when it came to dress: loose fitting long-sleeved shirts or bare chest, leather jerkins, tight fitting pantaloons with lots of buttons down the legs, and sturdy boots or clogs. The only measure of rank it appeared was the quality of the head gear they wore. The pirates barking the orders seemed to have the best hats. They formed a fast-moving wedge of pirates with their projectile weapons aimed directly at us. When they reached the purposefully small entrance to the base, they flowed inside two abreast until most of them had entered. The last to enter was the Pirate Queen, followed by her rearguard of twenty pirates. These pirates wore wide brimmed, red hats with a long white dow-feather streaming behind, red leather jerkins, and black boots with their blue pantaloons tucked inside.

The Pirate Queen looked every bit the part. She wore a velvet black gown that revealed her lithe figure. The split at the sides of the dress that went up to her knees did not hide her black knee-high boots. At her waist she wore a golden chain from which her ornate jewel laden cutlass hung. Slung over her back she carried a portable razor disk launcher. Her scarlet hair was crowned by a red hat with a white feather, just like the ones her guard wore. Her bare arms were decorated with tattoos and silver and gold bands encrusted with glowing jewels, red being the predominant color.

As the Pirate Queen and her entourage made their way to the center of the great hall, all of Captain Mejilla's pirates bowed low as she passed them. The rebels stood stoically upright, withstanding the withering looks projected at them by the passing pirates. When the queen's troops had all entered the great hall, a throne was procured from a secret location and placed on the circular dais. The Pirate Queen gracefully sat down and slowly looked around the room.

Captain Livingston took several firm steps toward the pirate queen and without hesitation, swept his hat off and bowed to her. "It be our grand honor to welcome ye to our humble abode."

The queen looked amused at the change of events. She had laid a trap and expected that when she arrived, she would take possession of both her husband and the Fire Lord, but nevertheless, now she did not show her displeasure but instead, appeared amused. The tone of her voice and her demeanor oozed charm and confidence as she spoke.

"Tis much appreciated, though quite unanticipated. Ah, Captain Livingston, I heard that ye be retired. I be much surprised ta be seein' ye so far away from yer comfortable home," she crooned in a teasing manner as she absent-mindedly twirled a lock of red hair in her fingers.

"Yer highness, twern't long ago that I realized that retirement was not fer the likes of me. Ye can understand that the open skies be my home," Grandfather replied with a smile. "In like manner, yer majesty, I be much surprised ta behold yer beautifulness in these parts m'self."

As I watched them both, it occurred to me that a battle was about to begin, though no physical weapons were being brought to bear. This was going to be a battle of words and wit. By the looks of anticipation in both Grandfather and the Queen this was a battle that they relished.

"I feel just as ye Captain Livingston, long confinement to a single place, regardless of the comfort afforded, chafes me as sure as shackles and prison bars," she fired the first volley, referring to her expecting them to be in the dungeons below.

Grandfather appeared calm and confident as he replied, "Aye, no such prisons be made yet that can confine our fiery spirits, even if that prison be made by friends."

The queen was unshaken by the jab at her treachery and the trap that was foiled by the Fire Lord. "Tis a strange coincidence that our simple pleasure trips bring us to the exact same location in the empire, at such a judicious time of year. (Translation: I know that the Overlord and the adjudicators are looking for you.)

Grandfather skillfully replied, "This be my thinking altogether, and it were in our best interest to hasten to a place of peace and tranquility and leave behind the concerns of bitter encounters."
(Translation: We have escaped their grasp and yours.)

The queen's smile flickered, but she countered effortlessly. "The winds bring fleeting tales of such fire and indignation that one can hardly believe them. (Translation: I heard about the destruction of the fleet by the Fire Lord.) Such were me understandin' till we chanced upon yerselves and desired to bid ye greetings. (Translation: I was surprised to see you free when I arrived.) Beguiled I was, till this chance to flame our past friendship were renewed. (Translation: The Fire Lord is a worthy foe whom I would like to meet.)"

Not breaking a sweat in this battle of words, Captain Livingston kept the queen off balance tempting her with information then providing her nothing. "Yer Majesty knows 'bout the winds that swirl and amplify things beyond recognition. We highly esteem yer friendship and shall pass yer warm regards to all the crew and passengers till the flame of friendship be ignited once again (Translation: Do not believe everything you hear. The Fire Lord knows you are here). We be but travelers prepared for a long journey, full of happiness and confidence that ne're a worry could invade our peace. (Translation: We are not afraid of the Overlord nor you.) The fire of hope for a glorious journey burns bright within us and we will'na put it aside." (Translation: We trust the power of the Fire Lord and will not allow you to harm him.)

With a hint of steel, and less of a smile than a grimace, the queen countered, "Tis so delightful and enlightening ta be chattin' with ye all peaceful-like when the winds of fate be howling about us like ravening scrybeasts and their offspring." (Translation: The Overlord and the Deputy Minister will find you and your hope is unfounded. You will be captured.)

As ready as a cloud jumper for a storm, Captain Livingston saw the opening and took it with these words. "The wind in such turmoil picks up all manner of filth, I should not be surprised to see yer sails stained by the tempest and a grand sum it would cost to have them cleaned." (Translation: I understand that you are in league with them and offer to pay ye more than the Overlord or Deputy Minister have paid you.)

"There be many a journey that have sullied our sails, but this one in particular holds promise of brightening our sails to a grand degree." (Translation: We have dealings with many, but this last one will be immensely profitable in more ways than money can provide.) The queen gloated and continued, "Ta be sure, such good fortune canna be found amongst simple travelers such as yerselves. (Translation: You cannot afford my price.) But before discussin' more 'bout the condition of our trim, I be looking forward to reunitin' with me beloved husband, Billy."

When she spoke, it was with a soft voice but one that carried the threat of a sharp dagger. "Where be my husband?"

There was a murmur throughout the hall but no one answered.

The queen stood and screamed with anger. "Bring me Billy Bragg and I will spare yer miserable lives."

Grandfather was just as shocked as everyone else. Only I knew that Captain Bragg was the husband of the Pirate Queen. I glanced around the room leaning on my mop and I saw Camphoria's face turn white as she heard these words from the queen. I left my mop and went to intercept her before she left the room.

The battle of words was over but as I pursued Camphoria I heard Grandfather deftly deflect the challenge and invite the queen and her men to enjoy the feast in her honor.

"Camphoria, wait!" I yelled as I caught sight of her hurrying towards stairs carved in the stone.

She turned, I could see that tears had stained her face. With a tremulous voice she said, "What be the pleasure of m'Lordship?" She curtsied formally, trying to hold in her emotions in check.

"I heard what the queen said about your father, William Bragg, and I believe that you should talk with him before taking any rash action. I will have the Betty-Lou meet you at south entrance in the lower levels where you and he can talk about this."

Camphoria's ability to retain what she was feeling shattered. "That horrible witch were never my father's wife, nor be she my mother," she clenched her fists in fury and through gritted teeth continued, "My father recounted stories what revealed how vile and vengeful the pirate queen were but failed ta mention any relationship with her. I've been surrounded by naught but lies my whole life! E'n ye pretendin' ta be the all-powerful Fire Lord. Yer just a boy, 'n a liar like the rest 'o them! I've had enough 'o ye hypocrits. Yer no better 'n the Overlord 'n his adjudicators, pretendin' ta be all righteous but hidin' vicious lies!"

"Camphoria, you need to calm down! You can't mean what you are saying. At least withhold judgement till you can talk with your father," I tried to console her and ignore the hurtful jabs.

"Begging yer pardon, yer Majesty, I canna comply with yer wish. I will be talking to me da, as ye suggest, but calmin' down, well that be an impossible task. The south entrance ye say... have a pleasant evening yer Highness," she curtsied again and bustled up the stairs.

<Betty-Lou, please take Captain Bragg to the south lower entrance so that he and Camphoria can have a chat. >

<Already on me way. That were a kindness ye showed her that she'll be not forgetin' soon, though ta be certain, she still holds a bit of spite.>

<Really? I did not notice. Though my heart aches to see her in anguish, I have to turn my attention to other matters. Please protect them both.>

<Aye, laddy, that I'll do.>

CHAPTER 22 SEED PLANTED

(Compiled from the records of the Fire Lord, Gideon Livingston, King of Portus, Protector of the 18 realms.)

I returned to the great hall just as the Pirate Queen and Captain Livingston sat down at the head of the table and the leaders of both groups arranged themselves. I chose a table as near as I could to my grandfather and the queen, but the regular troops, such as I was dressed, were relegated to the undecorated tables on the outskirts near the walls on either side of the central table. It was too far for me to hear clearly what they were saying especially when the puff gourds full of liquor arrived amidst the gleeful outbursts of the soldiers and the pirates.

I clenched my fist in frustration. And growled.

"Arg yeself!" the pirate sailor next to me growled back.

I looked about for a solution and my eyes lingered on the ornate candle holders full of candles lighting the central table.

<Hmm...Maybe if I concentrated on the candle that is nearest them and would be able to project myself into that flame and hear the conversation. As long as they don't look too closely at the flame I should be alright,> I thought.

<It be worth a try,> Betty-Lou stated.

I jumped when Betty-Lou responded, causing the pirate next to me to slap me on the back and say, "If ye can't handle yer liquor, ye should stick ta water. Hah," he laughed loudly at his own humor.

<Ow! I keep forgetting that you are always there. How

do you know when I'm talking to you or just thinking?> I asked in my mind.

<It dunna matter. Either way, I hear it clear as a bell, no matter the distance.> There was a hint of amusement in her voice.

<So that means you can even hear my dreams?> I blustered mentally feeling embarrassed and violated. <Every stray thought... every fantasy...daydream...every...>

<Now hold on laddy. The bridge it works both ways. What do ye hear from meself? Are ye spying on me dreams or be ye bombarded by me personal thoughts?> Betty-Lou countered with a stern tone.

<No, I don't hear your thoughts in my head all the time. What? If it's two ways, I should be able to,> I thought, now thoroughly confused.

<Laddy, it be when ye be formin' yer thoughts inta words that I be able ta hear 'em. Tis only when ye be particularly worried or focused that I be bothered. Most often, I simply choose to not take note if it be a trivial thing,> Bett-Lou mollified.

<But you can only think words, you can't say them. I should hear your thoughts all the time. Why can't I?> I asked.

<I've a bit more practice than yerself. I control what I be formin' inta words. Now ye be satisfied? There be work ta do!> Betty-Lou chided.

<Oh yeah, I was trying to hear a conversation when I was interrupted,> I retorted.

<I'll not be drawn into a piddly argument, get on with yer plan> Betty-Lou said with a smirk in her voice.

When I concentrated on one candle, through a greenish haze, I could see that the Pirate queen was talking. I could hear well enough, even with the noise of the other sputtering red buzzer candles in the ornate candle holder.

"Captain Mejilla claims that the Fire Lord is a magical being of immeasurable power. How is it that you have acquired such an ally Captain Livingston?"

Captain Livingston stroked his beard in thought, then responded, "When a cause is right, the Creator favors the just. We believe and pray constantly for divine intervention and considerable luck."

"My sources informed me that more than mere luck and a lightning storm destroyed the overlord's armada. Rather that the lightning came from that unique ship of yours. I understand that ye arrived here aboard it and that the dragon ship were still in your possession. Where be it now?" The Pirate Queen almost purred her question.

"The Betty-Lou be in fine shape away on an errand," Grandfather calmly replied.

"That be where my husband be. We shall wait for its return, then," the queen said smugly.

"Begin yer pardon yer Majesty. Ye may be waitin' quite a long time. The Betty-Lou's crew will stay away as long as there be unfamiliar ships moored in the dock."

"Then I shall have them withdrawn, so your famous dragon may return unhindered," Cirulea countered in an irritated voice.

"There be no returnin' till the all's-clear signal be given, and that will be at me own hand, when I feel it be safe," Grandfather crossed his arms and sat back in his chair with a defiant look.

"I see that we have no choice but to take ye prisoner and force ye to give the signal," Cirulea was about to snap her fingers and call her guards, but suddenly the candles in the holder shot great gouts of flame like stepping on a nest of fire lizards.

<Whoa, pay attention Gideon!> I growled at myself for losing control. <That was a stupid thing to do!>

<Maybe not so stupid> Betty-Lou replied. <Look again.>

I returned my thoughts to flame.

"Did ye ferget yer Majesty about the minor detail of the Fire Lord bein' on our side an all?" Grandfather said sweetly now leaning forward towards the queen and gesturing at the smoldering candle holder.

The queen's shock and realization of the change of power made her face blush. After she regained her composure she stated in a slightly tremulous voice, "I see that we are at an impasse. What do ye propose?"

"Thanks fer comin' to yer senses, yer Highness. I propose that ye be our guest for a few rotations ta rest yerself from your weariness and travels. T'would be the very least we could offer as a token of friendship," Grandfather lowered his head in a token bow.

The queen smiled unexpectedly. "Ye were always the gentleman and I see that there be no need of hostilities at this point. Will ye be sending the "All-clear" signal any time soon?"

"I can see that ye be anxious to reunite with yer beloved husband and I must obtain assurance that he be not further harmed, he was treated in unkindly fashion when we arrived," steel entered Grandfather's voice as he said this.

"Why should I agree to that? He abandoned me and deprived me of me own flesh 'n blood!" Disdain and cycles of anger could be heard in the queen's voice.

Changing the topic, Grandfather continued, "Ye know, she has yer same eyes and fiery temperament."

"Captain Livingston, I warn ye not to trifle with me. To whom be ye referrin' and why should I care?" Queen Cirulea responded with curiosity.

"Why I be referrin' to yer very own daughter, a right pretty lass," Grandfather teased.

"My daughter? You have my daughter? You've no right to hold her prisoner. Release her at once, or there'll be more 'n liquor spilt at this feast!" Queen exclaimed, hand on her cutlass.

Nonplussed, Grandfather continued, "I could arrange a meetin', should I get assurances of Captain Bragg's safe treatment."

"So be it. Me husband shall not be harmed, though it cost me dearly to not flay him alive. Even still he shall get a tongue lashing that he shall not soon forget. Bring me Camphoria immediately!" The queen demanded.

"Now that we be in agreement, I beg yer pardon yer majesty ye canna meet with her this evening. Yer daughter, knew not who ye were till ye arrived. For her sake, I will arrange a more presentable and private meeting in the mornin'. Till then, I beg you to enjoy the food and spirits and our finest hospitality," Grandfather oozed charm as he said this.

The queen was not pleased but given the resolve of my Grandfather, she seemed to realize that further argument would serve no purpose and gain her nothing but trouble. She appeared to finally notice the food that had been placed before her and picked up her fork and began delicately eating in a manner befitting a queen. Captain Livingston was pleased at her acquiescence and followed her example and began eating as well.

<Whew! I'm glad Grandfather was handling that! Reminds me of trying to get control of a scorpion crab with only a pair of short handled tongs—all the parrying and maneuvering just to get the tongs in the right place without getting stung or nipped! I definitely have a lot to learn,> I thought to myself as I released control of the candle flame.

<Aye Lad, ye do,> Betty-Lou agreed.

CHAPTER 23 FATHER AND DAUGHTER

(Reconstructed from the journals of Captain William Jasper Bragg and the memoirs of Lady Camphoria Bragg Livingston)

Camphoria stomped down the passage way towards the galley on the Betty-Lou where her father, Captain Bragg awaited.

She was furious. "Why did ye not tell me my mother was the Pirate Queen?" she snapped, pointing a shaking finger in his face.

Captain Bragg just sat there, beaming, arms open wide. He finally said, "Ye be just like her. So glad I am ta be seein' ya.!"

This made Camphoria even more upset. "Ye'll be glad ta see me leave when I've scratched yer face 'n kicked in yer shins!" She lunged at her father, arms extended to fulfill her promise.

Her furious attack was met by her father's strong arms holding her wrists, twisting her down so she abruptly sat on the chair that her father had just vacated.

Captain Bragg whispered in Camphoria's ear as he tightly held her hands from harming him, "Now you'll be letting me explain and answer yer question before ye be attackin' yer father. After I say my piece ye may do what ye feel ye must," he let go and jumped back to avoid the wicked jabs Camphoria aimed at his head.

Camphoria remained seated however, and did not continue her attack. The fierce expression on her face showed that she was struggling to control her anger and confusion.

Captain Bragg brought forward another chair from the galley and sat out of reach of Camphoria's punches and kicks, but close enough to speak softly.

He began, "Truth be told, the fault be yer's. Before ye were born, yer mother, Cirulea, and I were happy with our two boys. Twas our thinking that they would follow in my footsteps and become pirate captains and eventually rule the pirate kingdom. But when ye were born, everything changed. I could'na imagine ye livin' the life we did. More 'n anything else, I felt to protect ye an keep ye from it. Yer mother saw things different. She saw in ye the same little lightning stick that she were. That is where the difficulties all began. Now dunna misunderstand me, I love yer mother dearly, ta this day, but she 'n I we disagreed mightily on what to do with our children. When I came to understand that she would never consent to exempt ye from the life of a pirate wench, I took it upon m'self to escape with ye all. Camphoria, ye were just a baby, and the boys, they were just toddlers, so ye would'na remember."

Camphoria took a moment to respond, and in measured words said, "Me whole life, ye told me that ma was killed! Ye lied to us!"

"I could'na have ye be tellin' yer friends that yer mother be a pirate. If ye have'na noticed, folks don't take kindly to pirates. I had'ta keep ye safe," Captain Bragg explained. "Now ye know everythin' and ye can do as ye please with me. It's been a heavy burden and I'm glad ta be rid of it."

Fury and sadness overwhelmed Camphoria she grabbed her knees and she began sobbing quietly. Her father approached her but she batted his extended arm away. "I dunna want to speak to ye ever again!" she screamed.

"I canna abide facin' the fury of both ye and yer mother. I did'na want ta hurt ye. I hope one day ye'll understand," Captain Bragg turned and staggered out of the galley.

(Taken from personal writings of Camphoria Bragg)

I sat in the galley heaving sobs and curses at the empty kitchen. All my life I had thought of my father as a brave and honorable man, doing the best he could as a single parent raising three children. Now I knew the truth. It was all a superb lie. Yes, he was a captain, but a pirate captain- a brigand, a thief...a murderer. Worse yet, the hazy memories of my mother as a beautiful saint were dashed to pieces when I learned that my mother is the ruler of the pirates...the queen.

"What difference do it make ta me...really? I be the same person. Things be much clearer now. This be why me father ne'er spoke of his early life...why he ne'er spoke my mother's name without clenching his jaw...and why topic of pirate were avoided like the plague," I said to the uncomprehending silverware.

I stood up and paced the length of the galley, walking between the four long tables surrounded by benches. I shook my hair and ran a hand through the curly red strands as I was wont to do when I had a problem to solve.

"What be me course now? That were the question of the day," I said to the round portal window as I paused in my pacing.

Nothing could be seen amidst the darkness and the mist of the cloud. I stared out seeking for an answer, but none were found in the swirling void outside of the Betty-Lou. I turned and faced the warm light of the sconces, each with two firestones, forced in close proximity to provide just the right amount of light without bursting into flames.

"Flames," I vacantly muttered the word, "Flames, flames, flames..." as I walked toward the sconces. "I have seen the most wondrous flames...green flames. I recalled my rescue from the Boar Riders and my utter shock at being caught in the invisible net and the relief I felt when I was hauled aboard and saw his handsome green eyes full of concern. "What of the Fire Lord?" I voiced without thinking. Then I slumped down into the vacant chair in which my father had been seated.

"What be I to him...The Fire Lord? Me...a lowly daughter of pirates. Besides, he would not want nor care a whit to be in my company after I treated him so rudely last we spoke. He did seem but a boy, awkward and hesitant. Curse my temper! I've ruined it now!"

I stood up suddenly. "No matter, he'll not deign to see me again. It be forward not back where be my future. If I am to be a pirate, then I'll be a good one."

I walked out the galley door with purposeful strides.

CHAPTER 24 WHAT PIRATES DO

(Compiled from notes, letters and journal entries of Lady Cirulea Bragg)

"How many men defend the fortress?' The queen asked her First Lieutenant while she manicured her nails with a golden file.

"They be no more than 150 men, M'dam," the lieutenant responded with a bow.

"Between Captain Mejilla and the forces we brought, what be the total?" The queen said as she continued examining her long red fingernails.

"Your Highness, t'would be more than 500 men," the lieutenant answered with a grin on his face.

Now the queen turned her full attention to the lieutenant, "We came ta get me husband, capture that demonic airship, and destroy the rebellion. What be ye waiting for?"

"Only your leave to do so, Madam," the lieutenant responded smiling widely, then he stopped as he turned to go, "and the Fire Lord?"

"Leave him to me," Cirulea crooned while she examined her fingers, pleased with the shape of her nails. Each finger resembled red talons of a scrybeast. "I have plans for him. We attack at dawn."

I walked with the gait of a sailor, following my Grandfather as he left the dining hall. He knew I was behind him, yet to continue the ruse, he ignored me. In the great entry hall, he turned left and went up a set of stairs. I followed trying to look the part of a soldier. As I topped the stairs I heard Grandfather hiss, "M'Lord, this way."

From across the narrow hallway I saw him motion to me from an open doorway. I followed and as soon as I entered, he quietly closed and locked the door. I began to speak, but he motioned with a finger to his lips to be silent. He crossed the small room with comfortable embroidered cushions and pillows surrounding a short table. No chairs were in the room. Dimly, as I crossed the room, I remembered my history that some cultures eat while sitting on the floor.

My Grandfather had gone through a hallway rough-hewn out of the mountain, into another chamber, much less opulent than the first. Here there were chairs and a table, at which my Grandfather was seated. He motioned for me to shut the door.

Only then did he speak in quiet tones. "We must be careful. This used to be her home and she has many secret ways of obtaining information. Right be the warning, "the walls have ears". This be a new section of the fortress, hewn after she be gone from here and I feel somewhat safe to converse."

I nodded and bade him continue.

Grandfather spoke in a whisper, "I dunna trust her. She plays a fine part, but underneath, she be wily and cruel. If she says she will wait, then she will do the opposite. We can expect to be attacked this very evening and they outnumber us five to one. She knows this fortress better than we and she has a plan, or she would'na have risked herself bein' here."

"I knew that we must dissuade her from her plan, so I have taken a gamble that may make her change her mind," I explained what I had done with the gold and the crown.

Grandfather threw his hat on the ground, and gritted his teeth as he spoke, trying to control his anger. "Ye know not pirates. Ye have just whetted her desires to attack us even more. She believes that she be in control with more men and weapons than us, and now you have given her more reason to take back her fortress so she can find the rest of the treasure. Pardon me yer Highness, but ye've done a foolish thing," he turned and surmised a painting of a ghostly ship on the wall and took a moment to rub his whiskered chin before speaking again. "Yet mayhaps, this could be to our advantage with the help of the Fire Lord," he said with a wry grin.

CHAPTER 25 THE DREADNAUGHT

(Compiled of court records from the secretary to his lordship, Philbrook McStone. The Dreadnaught remains can be found in the museum at Gran Saline.)

"Report. Is it ready?" the Grand Overlord asked.

The Master Boatwright fidgeted and wrung his hands knowing that the Overlord would not be pleased with what he had to report. "We have made great strides, m'Lord. The work progresses marvelously..."

"T'was a simple question," the Overlord interrupted, "Is it ready? Fail to answer and ye will fail to take your next breath."

The Overlord raised his ceremonial serrated blade to the master boatwright's neck. It was patterned after the famous blade from the original Fire Lord. Wicked sharp teeth lined the curved blade as the maw of the deadly water fish that prowl the seas between the islands. Gilded with gold and silver filigrees along the blade. Encrusted with five sparkling red stones in the pommel. The hilt was of the rough skin of the dragon-lizard to provide a firm grip not prone to slip. From the tip of the hilt dangled a golden tassel woven of hair gathered from the tail of the elusive skyhorse.

"Nnnn'nay m'Lord. Tis not ready," the boatwright stammered.

The Overlord did not lower his sword but gently caressed the quaking man's neck with the blunt side of the blade as he spoke softly. "What be the problem? Have ye not the materials necessary? Be there not enough skilled craftsman? Or be ye simply inept and incapable?"

"We be well supplied, but beggin' yer pardon m'Lord," the terrified man gulped air, "ye have asked us ta build ye a ship that ne're existed a'fore. We be working mightily, day 'n night. It be the strongest ship yet made. It be nigh invisible clad in reflection stones that reflect its surroundings, and also protect it from the deadly rays. It can belch smoke for concealment and discovery of invisible things. It can attack with the deadly talons of a scrybeast. Within its hold be the latest weapons known. It be a beauty to behold...."

"Yet it lacks something? What be that?" The Overlord said as he shifted his blade slicing off one button then the next from the Master Boatwright's embroidered vest.

"It canna fly m'Lord. It be too heavy. The ballast tanks necessary to lift it be so large and cumbersome that t'would be the slowest craft in the skies and shine like a beacon for miles."

"It appears that not only have ye wasted my money but also my time. Ye have built me a useless craft," the Overlord growled, taking another button off the boatswright's vest, " If ye 'n yer men wish to live...ye have one cycle of the moon ta fix it."

"As ye wish m'Lord," the boatwright said as he backed away as fast as he could while he still had buttons on his vest and his neck on his shoulders.

The Overlord smiled as he replaced the uselessly ornate blade in the ceremonial scabbard. It's only redeeming quality was that it was sharp. Heavy and unbalanced as it was, it had its uses. It was fearsome to look upon and drawing it always had the desired effect. Much like the airship they were building.

"They will never make it fly swiftly. But just as the sword, it will strike fear into the hearts of all who see it. None will dare challenge it. Most of all, as rumor spreads, it will draw mine enemy to me."

(Compiled from the Memoirs of the Pirate Queen, Lady Cirulea Bragg)

Cirulea made her way to the opulent quarters prepared for her. She stationed four of her red hatted guards at the door.

"Leave me, but stand guard outside. I do not wish to be disturbed," Cirulea ordered and dismissed the servants with a wave of her hand. They bowed and backed out of the door leaving her alone.

"The fools," she thought out loud. "I know this room and its secrets."

As she entered, her eyes rested upon the beautiful box and embossed message scroll sitting upon a chest at the foot of the sumptuous bed. She walked over to the box and opened it. Within was the most beautiful golden crown she had ever seen. The crown was known to her. She sang the ballads of this crown and the herald queen as a child. A large diamond was the central stone, grasped by two graceful dragon claws of gold, intertwining with golden leaves and gem studded flowers. The band of the crown was formed of the golden body of the dragon, the head meeting the tail under the diamond. For eyes, two green gems sparkled above the vicious looking fangs of the dragon of old.

"It canna be! The crown of Queen Jasmin, the Fire Lord's beloved wife," Cirulea's knees gave way and she slumped to the floor as she said this.

She reached up for the scroll, careful to not touch the crown with a tremulous hand.

She hastily opened the message and read the contents aloud.

"Dearest Queen Cirulea:
Welcome to my home, though for a while it was yours. I offer this token of friendship and trust, knowing that you are not swayed by riches. It is not poisoned nor does it pose

a threat to you in anyway. It is a free gift to garner lasting good will.
I have no quarrel with you, indeed, you have done me a great service in returning my home to me. I do not wish to battle you nor inevitably slay your fine warriors who fight at the behest of others. My wish is to allay your concerns and assure you that my cause is just.
Please know that as I slay the ancient scrybeast and his minions, I would not wish to find you among them. If so, just as assuredly as they shall perish, so must you. Tis foretold and so it shall be.
Captain Bragg and your daughter are safe and well cared for. I look forward to the day in which your family may be reunited in peace.
To cover the expense of your journey here, please take the meager renumeration found in the chest upon which this crown rests.
A hopeful friend,
The Fire Lord"

Astounded and shocked, Cirulea dropped the scroll on the ground, overcome by gifts and the words of the Fire Lord.

"Indeed, he is formidable. There is no treasure in the entire world worth the value of this crown! Why would he offer it to me, his enemy?" she wondered aloud.

She stood and admired the ancient artistry of the crown, hefted its weight and placed it on her head. Looking in the reflecting stone on the wall, she admired herself and its beauty. She immediately removed it saying, "Tis not for me that I shall keep this."

She walked back to the chest and viewed its contents. She gasped as she saw the shining gold bars stacked neatly in the case. She closed the lid and grabbed the handles to pick it up. It would not budge. "Not five of my strongest men could lift this weight."

"This alone would cover the cost of the entire voyage one hundred times and makes the Deputy's payment seem a paltry sum. Add the crown and this voyage has been exceedingly fruitful if we do nothing more. And why not more? Hmmm," the pirate queen purred to herself.

She quickly changed from her formal attire to clothing that covered her completely in the gray of the hewn walls; from the gray bandana and hat hiding her face and scarlet hair to the gray knee length boots she donned. She stood next to the wall and viewed the effect in the reflecting stone. If she remained immobile, she was nearly invisible in the gloomy light provided by stone sconces.

Cirulea approached the ornately framed reflecting stone on the wall and closely examined the carved dragons cavorting all around its edges. She selected a dragon on the right side of the frame and gently twisted its clawed foot. As it swiveled she heard a muffled clunk and the reflecting stone swung open toward her. Behind the stone lay a dark passage. Cirulea pulled a portable light-stone frame from her pocket and adjusted the two stones so they gave just enough light to see, but did not blind her. She held the handle of the frame ahead of her and clambered up and into the passage.

CHAPTER 26 THE FIRE LORD'S PALACE

(Compiled from the records of the Fire Lord, Gideon Livingston. The headquarters is now a museum in honor of both of the Fire Lords. A map of the Palace is in the appendix.)

Filled with doubt, I stealthily returned to my quarters. Dressed as a common sailor, no one paid me the least attention, which for once was a relief. No constant bowing, nor m'Lording. No having to think what this person wanted from their favor. No having to endure the expressions on their faces that ranged from admiration to disgust. As I approached my quarters, I remembered that I had dismissed the guards posted by the door so I would be able to enter without being seen.

"Since my disguise had worked so well, why shouldn't I take the opportunity to go exploring?" I said to myself as I reached for the door latch, hesitated and then kept walking.

<Betty-Lou, you know this place. Where else should I explore?> I thought.

<The upper reaches of the fortress have been abandoned for eons, as ye discovered yesterday. This were the home of the Pirate Queen an' there be many secrets, new an' old,> Betty-Lou responded.

<Lead me to one if you please.>

(Taken from the journals of Cirulea Bragg, mother to Queen Camphoria Bragg-Livingston)

The passage led down through the solid grey stone of the fortress. The man-hewn portions were narrower and rougher, while the natural lava tubes were spacious and smooth. Other tunnels intersected this tunnel and located on either side were obvious spying-ports and reflecting stones at regular intervals.

Cirulea navigated the branches leading off from the main tunnel with the ease of long practice. When she became Pirate Queen, she spent her nights in these tunnels, gathering information, discovering her enemies and eliminating threats. No one expected her to survive a week, yet because of the knowledge and control she gained from these nightly forays, she remained the queen for 18 cycles. She told no one of the existence of these passages and since she only discovered them by accident when she was a girl, she assumed that she was the only one that knew them.

Cirulea's destination was the control center of the fortress. She needed to find out what they knew and any usable information about the Fire Lord. To be sure, she was shaken by the gift that the Fire Lord had given her and for that reason, she had to be prepared when she met him in person.

She arrived at her destination: an oval room with observation holes in the floor and the walls. Cirulea twisted the dial to separate the light stones in her portable sconce and extinguished the light. The room was not completely dark because light emanated from the small observation ports dotting the room. A chair and an odd device were the only things in this room. Cirulea sat in front of the device and placed the odd shaped helmet on her head. She heard a conversation about the horrible food and how cold the fortress was. She reached up and twisted a dial that brought a talk stone on a circular foil dish close to the central stone. There were at least forty such stones surrounding the dish. As the mechanism pushed the two stones together, the vibrations were transmitted to the helmet Cirulea wore and she could clearly hear another private conversation. It took only a few turns of the dial to find the stone she was looking for.

<Go left, then right, then three lefts,> directed Betty-Lou.

<Wouldn't that take me right back where I started?> I chided.

<Absolutely if the passages were not built by a skillful engineer able to hide secrets in plain sight,> Betty-Lou answered with a chuckle.

I followed the directions from Betty Lou: left, right, left, left, and left.

<Perhaps your memory is faulty. I am right where I was just a moment ago. See, it is the same corridor,> I teased.

<Nay, ye be not in the same place. Tis designed to appear the same. Ye be beneath it. To your left be a reflection stone frame just as it appears where ye were, but behind this one lies a hidden stair case. The forward passage returns the traveler to the same corridor above, none the wiser,> Betty-Lou explained.

<Amazing. Hidden in plain sight. How do I open the framed reflection stone?> I asked.

<Find the right-most dragon and twist the claw,>Betty-Lou responded.

The reflection stone frame swung open revealing a thin staircase carved in the rock leading up. I stepped in and saw the green glowing dragon circlet on the wall that I had seen on the Betty-Lou and which was emblazoned upon my chest. I reached out and touched the symbol thoughtfully, and the frame swiveled closed. This left me in darkness except for the glowing symbol.

<Ye seem surprised. Tis an ancient place. We be headed to the upper reaches visited by none for ages. Mayhaps the Dragon Lord himself last traveled those passageways,> Betty-Lou conjectured.

<Does the queen know about these passageways?> I asked, now worried.

<Aye lad, she does,> Betty-Lou warned <Perchance she be in them now.>

<You could have told me that before you led me here!> I huffed. <I'll have to take precautions.>

I concentrated and focused on projecting myself as smoke. I flowed up the stairs that led to another passageway. Seeing no signs, I went right.

<Which way would you have taken me?> I asked.

<T'would be to yer left,> Betty-Lou responded then added <Have a care lad. Ye canna be discovered.>

<Understood,> I answered.

Through smoky haze, I examined the dust on the floor of the corridor as I flowed along and saw that it was not disturbed. The passage ended at an intersecting passage and I could make out foot prints headed to the right. They were smaller, as if made by a woman or child in boots.

I followed the prints until I flowed into an oval room with lighted holes on the floor and walls. Near the opposite wall was a table with a curious mechanism enclosing a circle of stones. Something indefinable sat in the chair. A human form, but difficult to see because it was as gray as the walls of stone with the exception that it was wearing a black lumpy helmet connected to the mechanism by flexible tubes.

"That be odd," Cirulea thought, "I've never seen fog in these passageways...Wait! It smells like smoke. Something is burning! I cannot be trapped in this passageway if there be a fire."

Cirulea quickly placed the helmet on the table and headed up the corridor. As she did so, she pulled out her portable sconce and she dialed the stones closer, allowing her to see with the extra light.

"The smoke is getting thicker," she said and covered

her mouth with the gray cloth of her bandana. She quickly retraced her steps back to her quarters.

<Lets have some fun! What do you say Betty-Lou?> I thought.

<Aye laddy. Tis an opportunity that canna be wasted,> she said with what I imagined was a grin.

I pushed the smoke ahead of Cirulea to make her believe that it was coming from her quarters.

<Betty-Lou, can you guide me to the queen's quarters?> I asked.

<At the first crossing, use the left, then at the next the right. It should be up a dragon hop on the left,> she directed.

I sent the smoke flowing up ahead of the now coughing queen and seeped into her quarters to fill it with smoke. I looked around to see what could be burned. I saw the ornate wooden box the crown was in, the message scroll and the small crate filled with gold bars. I quickly incinerated the three items and melted one bar of gold on top of the pile now sitting on the floor surrounded by ash. I wrote a message with the ash on the floor next to the crown and remaining gold bars:

"BE YE WARNED."

I could hear the queen now hacking and coughing profusely. Smoke filled her entire room and I saw the reflection stone frame swing open. I concentrated smoke to form the life-sized visage of the Fire Lord and at the same time I dissipated the smoke on the floor a bit so she could see the message when she climbed down.

"It canna be! The Fire Lord!", she said between coughs, eyes wide as marsh puffs "How?"

Then she collapsed on the floor, unconscious.

I quickly gathered the smoke and retreated down the secret passageway.

<She'll be alright, won't she Betty-Lou?> I worried.

<Not but a bit of smoke. With fresh air and a new point of view, she will revive a changed woman. Well done lad,> Betty-Lou said and I could feel a sense of pride from her.

<While I have the time, I'd like to explore the upper reaches,> I stated.

< Have at it lad, though ye in truth have little time,> Betty urged.

All the smoke was gone and lit my finger to provide a bit of light. I mounted the stair two by two and turned left instead of right. The way spiraled three or four times and ended at a reflection stone frame. This opened into a vaulted hallway with green dragons in the form of columns lining the walls. Because the light of my flaming finger was green, perhaps everything seemed green, but they seemed so lifelike. At the end of the hall sat a large throne on a raised platform and behind that a painting of a man with red hair and a red beard riding a green dragon. The same man of the tapestry... an ancestor of mine...the Fire Lord. In his hand he held a serrated blade, bathed in green fire. In the foreground of the picture, cowed a scrybeast ridden by a dark-haired man.

<This must have been some sort of judgement hall,> I thought.

I climbed the stairs to the throne and observed the ornately bejeweled and decorated golden throne.

<Tis yours now,> Betty-Lou commented.

I sat down, raising a cloud of dust and triggering another green dragon symbol on the armrest. Without thinking I placed my palm on that symbol. Immediately I heard a rumble beneath me and a scraping beside me. I saw that the panel to my left had slid open. I raised my right hand with the burning finger to light the contents of the panel. I clearly saw, resting on a purple cloth, the serrated blade of the Fire Lord.

The curved blade had wicked looking teeth along one edge and at the base of the blade, just above the guard formed in the shape of a silver dragon was a large white jewel with the familiar circular dragon emblem engraved upon it. The hilt was a gray leather, bound with silver wire. The hand guard glittered with numerous diamonds. I admired the highly polished steel that seemed to magnify the green flame from my finger. Impulsively I grabbed the hilt with my left hand and felt what seemed a lightning bolt run through my hand throughout my body. I raised the perfectly balanced sword and saw that the brilliant green flame surrounding it lit the entire hall with a dancing green glow.

"Amazing!" I whispered in awe…and then the sword became very heavy...and so did my arm. I dropped the sword and succumbed to the extreme weight of my body.

<Aye Laddy, tis amazing that ye held it for that long,> chuckled Betty-Lou.

(As recorded in the Pirate Queen Lady Cirulea Bragg's journal)

All it had said was , "Be ye warned." But if that was not enough deterrent, the green fire surrounding the fortress, making it shine like a beacon, broke the resolve of even the most stalwart of my men.

I myself was shaken to have come so close to incurring the wrath of the Fire Lord. I never imagined a being with such power as to know my every move, to understand my keenest desires, and to be generous on the one hand and merciless on the other.

"Might it be that the prophecies are bein' fulfilled?" I wondered as I quickly packed up my things. "I'll have ta get men ta carry the bullion to the ship. He could'a melted it all and taken back his gift, yet he did'na. How short-sighted I was! I thought to surprise him and find the rest 'o the treasure. I thought me own wisdom to be far surpassin' his. Yet at every turn o' the sail, I be thwarted. I did'na get the Betty-Lou, I did'na get me husband, nor me daughter, aye, 'n I did'na get the treasure!"

I slammed the lid of my trunk and called for my men. I fell back and landed on the bed ta think things through. In my mind I argued, "The Deputy's payment be dammed. The Fire

Lord paid me a hundred times more with just the crown, let alone the gold. And... he asked for me help! Why should I not give it? If this be the prophecy, the Overlord and the two-faced Deputy canna withstand it. T'would be foolish to go against destiny. Me husband, 'n all three 'o me children be followin' the Fire Lord. So must I, though I be incurrin' the wrath o' the Deputy Minister!"

I stood up and scooped up my hat to fling it on my head. "So be it," I said out loud as I viewed myself in the reflecting stone.

When the men arrived at the door I was determined. "Take my trunk 'n the gold to me quarters on the ship. We be leavin' immediately."

CHAPTER 27 THE SWEET DREAM

(Taken from letters written by the Fire Lord, Gideon Livingston to Camphoria Livingston and the journal of Gideon Livingston, the Fire Lord.)

"I remember how I was surprised by the strength of your hands as you helped me up the ladder in the adjudicator's mansion, but now your hands are as soft and gentle as baby river dogs. I like how they feel in my hand," I said softly.

Camphoria took a step closer and I took her hands in mine. She was nearly as tall as I and we looked into each other's eyes. I could feel her sweet breath and felt her pulse quicken in pace with mine. I did not want to shut my eyes to savor this moment longer but just as our lips touched, I closed them, and in that instant, I heard a gasp and Camphoria dropped my hands and stepped back.

It took me a moment to realize what had just happened. I looked and saw that I had burst into green flames. On impulse I slowly extended my hand again and with amazing courage Camphoria extended her hand. When our fingers touched I could feel that she tensed in anticipation of pain, but when none came, her firm grip relaxed. Then I pushed my power through my hand and felt it entering and filling her and I knew her in a way that a kiss could never reveal.

Once again, Camphoria gasped in amazement as she gazed from her feet to her hands and back again. She was blazing green just as I. "How is it possible?" she asked.

"I willed it to be so and so it was," I responded tenderly.

She looked at my hand in hers and smiled, then said carefully, "I saw the terrible wrath these hands wrought on our enemies and I trembled at their power, but now they are warm and caring and I trust them like a she meercat trusts the terrible claws of her mate...Oh, I am sorry your Highness. I did not mean to make allusions to something that a person as lowly as I could not possibly hope for. Please forgive me your Lordship. I..."

I put my burning finger on her lips and re-ignited her flame that embarrassment had extinguished. "I understand the allusion and the message implied. I agree, we need to get to know each other more before such things are spoken of, but until then...we have shared some of ourselves with each other and that is a start to a wonderful friendship and perhaps more."

I extinguished the flames and I led her to a nearby bench and we chatted shared stories of our histories with each other.

We must have been there for quite a while because one of the cabin boys came running into the whey hen enclosure and said breathlessly, "There you are, your Lordship. Captain Livingston has been looking for you for quite some time. No one thought to look here."

"Where is my Grandfather, so I might find him?" I replied with a grin.

"He is topside Sire, upon the forecastle," the boy reported.

"Tell him that I will be there momentarily and please do not mention where you found me. You may go," I placed a coin in his hand to ensure compliance.

"My Lady, thank you for a most pleasant morning, one of many to come I hope," I bowed and left Camphoria smiling prettily on the bench.

A loud knock on the door woke me from my happy dream. "Ah...hmph...Yes, who calls," I said trying to not sound like I just woke up.

"Tis Mr. Pulsey. The pirates they be leaving. Captain Livingston thought you should know."

<Twas an unlikely dream Laddy> Betty-Lou commented. <She be a lass not so easily impressed. Likes ye

she does, but it will take much more ta win her me thinks.>

"Don't I know it," I said groggily as I rolled out of bed. My last encounter with Camphoria showed no hint of any positive regard...if anything, just the opposite.

As I dressed, it occurred to me that I was becoming used to having Betty-Lou share my thoughts, so much so that I didn't even think it strange that she knew about my dream.

<By the way, Betty-Lou, how did I get back to my room? I don't remember anything after dropping the sword,> I asked.

<If ye be thinkin' that I carried ye, tis amusing. Nay, ye made it here on yer own power, but frequently I had to wake ye ta keep ya goin',> Betty-Lou said with some humor.

<Well, thank you for helping me,>I said as I had just put on my boots, <Apparently, I couldn't have done it without you.>

<Twas nothing.>

I was about to grab my customary sword, a well-balanced two-edged sword, and my eyes rested on the scabbard of the serrated sword.

"That's the one that I want," I murmured to myself.

<That be a much-celebrated blade, for good and ill. Be ye certain ye want ta draw attention with it?>

I turned around as if I could see Betty-Lou and shouted as I burst into flames, "I am the Fire Lord am I not? This just completes the image."

<Me thought to dissuade ye gentle-like. Speakin' frankly laddy, ye be not ready for this sword. Did ye not notice what it did to yer abilities when last ye touched it?>

<Yes, it drained me,> I replied sheepishly and let the fire shrouding me evaporate.

<Yeah, that it did, and much more. When ye picked up the blade and it alighted with flames, ye lit up the entire mount. All who be outside the fortress witnessed and with much embellishment reported the great event to all within. The pirates, being superstitious folk, they did quake and be much taken aback by the strange portent o' this sign. This

sword...it takes yer power and it makes it larger, like a far sight stone. But it comes at a terrible cost. It will take yer very life if ye be not careful.>

<So every time I pick up that sword, the power will be taken out of me and there's no limit to how much it takes?> I queried.

<Tis so. Ye nearly died from the few moments ye had the sword. If it had'na been fer left over power in the sword, maybe in the jewels themselves, ye may've died. Ye canna risk it till ye gain more strength, control, knowledge, and ....more power,> Betty-Lou warned.

<How do I gain those?> I asked.

<How did ye learn ta walk, speak, or buckle yer boots?> She responded.

<A lot of practice and consistent use until it became second nature.>

<That be it.>

<I get what you mean now. Thanks,> I said as I picked up my normal sword instead.

It would be a while before I could master the dragon blade, but master it I must if I was to be the Fire Lord.

CHAPTER 28 THE TRAPS ARE LAID

Compiled from records and memoirs of Abigail Stenson, the Secretary to the Deputy Minister.

"She did what?" The Deputy Minister shouted at the quivering messenger

"The Pirate Queen let 'im go," the messenger stammered.

"Incompetence! Must I do everything myself? Arrange a meeting with our dear Pirate Queen and I will force her obedience," the Deputy unconsciously twirled is index finger in his goatee. "Now, leave me and do not return until you have better news... find me that blasted green dragon ship!" The Deputy Minister slammed his fists on his desk.

"Yyyes sir!"

As he watched the terrified man scuttle out of the room. "This is getting out of control," he muttered as he reached for the green talk stone affectionately known as chirp stones.

He placed the stone in the tin dish and made a staccato rhythm on the stone with his index finger. There was no response.

"Arrgh!" He growled, gripped the edge of his desk... paused, took a deep breath. "No, that be the old Forldon--topple the desk 'n play the berserker. Him it is would'a made a right mess'o things." Realizing his speech had lapsed into his native Turrinian dialect, he struggled for composure.

He spoke again, this time in a refined speech. "I am the new Forldon, soon to be the new Overlord and I must behave as such."

Relieved that he had stopped himself from overturning his desk, he replaced the communication stone in its storage slot and stood to leave the room.

"I must prepare a welcome for the queen. She will regret her disobedience," he thought as he donned his black cape and sword disguised as walking stick.

"Cap'n. Bragg! There be a whey hen missing. I've been watchin' the count as I were assigned and when I found 'im missin', I come ta report that someone's been communicatin' without yer permission."

"Well done airman. Which hen be missing?" Captain Bragg asked.

"Tis odd. T'was the bird from the shoals."

"There only be one person it could be then. Camphoria. I best be havin' a word with her. Would'ja mind fetchin' her fer me?"

Captain Bragg's last conversation with Camphoria two day ago had not gone so well and he was not anticipating a better one now. The thought niggled at his brain. "Why would she be tryin' ta communicate with Gavin Rookler? She only met im once, many cycles in the past, when she was but a lass."

Captain Bragg put on his most pleasing face as he heard Camphoria's footsteps in the gangway. "G'day to ya, me sweet darlin'!"

"G'day to yeself. Pirates be sweet darlins ta no-one, not even kin."

"My, what foul wind has entered. Though m'sight be poor at best, I see no pirates about. Early this morning the Queen 'n her ships departed," Captain Bragg tried his hardest to maintain a jovial tone, ignoring the vitriolic gaze of his daughter.

"Ye be the filthy pirate and so be I the daughter of one," Camphoria almost spat that last words.

"Calm yeself Camphy. Ye canna punish me fer tryin' to keep ye from me past. I know the stains ma hands carry 'n the guilt ma heart contains. I've tried ta make amends n' I've made sacrifices ye canna imagine ta keep ye protected. I am what I am. The same as ye've known all yer life. Knowin' 'bout me past changes not a thing. Yer words of spite, canna change how much I love ye."

"If ye loved me, ye would'a told me the truth," Camphoria scowled and crossed her arms.

"Truth is all I told ya, jest not the full measure…'n this were done, in order ta keep ye safe. Could'na have ye speakin' ta yer friends about yer pirate parents, or saying words that reach listening ears about where we might be livin'."

"Words of a coward. Hidin' and sneakin' about. I want no more part o' ye nor yer pretended righteousness. Ye be a hypocrite of the first order. Ye present yerself as all noble 'n brave, but within, ye be a cowardly, conniving, 'n blood thirsty pirate."

At these words, all pretense of joviality disappeared. Captain Bragg's voice took on a deadly tone. "Now, there be none alive that dared call me a coward ta me face. I'll forgive yer insolence cause yer not in yer right mind. I dunna have to excuse me actions to ye nor anyone else. I done what be right, and God be the judge, not ye.

"I am in ma right mind…'n I said what I feel. Now that I am knowledgeable of the truth, I will not cower nor run from it like a coward. If I be born'o pirates, then that be my true heritage and my just destiny."

"There be no destiny in piratin'. That be the first lesson I learned. There be only death 'n sorrow for loss, then anger, then more sorrow … it were a vicious maelstrom sucking me to hell. But when ye were born, I could'na let ye be a part'o that. Tis why I left it all behind. Twas not easy raisin three whelps on me own. A coward would'a placed ye in an orphanage and been done with ye. Bein' a pirate is what I saved ye from. Why do ye think ye have ta be one? Can ye not see that yer words hurt me to the core?"

"Glad ta know I've hurt ya. The truth it hurts, na? Since last night, there be nothin' fer me here but sorrow for cycles lost not knowin', and anger at bein' deceived by a pirate."

Camphoria was crying, her fists at her side clenched. She wiped her tears, straightened her leather apron and looked directly into Captain Bragg's eyes. "Ye sent fer me Cap'n. So what is it ye wished ta discuss?"

Never before had she called him Captain. It was always, 'Pa', 'Da', or 'Pops', but she never called him by his title till today. Captain Bragg sighed and shook his head. "Ye be just like yer mother: fierce, stubborn 'n beautiful. Aye, I did send fer ye. Ye sent a message to the shoals, I'd be curious ta know why?"

"The message be my own business. Anyth'n else?" Camphoria stated defiantly.

"No, jest that ye be endangerin' the Fire Lord 'n everyone else. Ye canna trust Gavin Rookler. Ye barely knew'm."

Camphoria raised her chin defiantly and growled, "Ha, the Fire Lord. A pretentious boy, tryin' ta be the hero of old. Blundering about, unaware of who he hurts with his words and his actions. He be naïve 'n he be the greatest danger to us all."

"Me thought ye had a sweet spot for him. What caused the change?" Captain Bragg now understood the emotions behind Camphoria's words. She had quarreled with the Fire Lord and is lashing out.

"Nay, simply a realization that we be in two different worlds 'n the likes of me could ne'er be with the likes 'o 'im."

"Ye canna tell what the future may bring. There be one truth 'bout mankind, tis our amazin' ability to change. No one stays the same one moment ta the next, whether it be by self will, 'o by circumstance," Captain Bragg looked closely for a sign of hope in Camphoria's eye. All he saw was a grim despondence.

"Thank ye for the advice Cap'n... Beggin' yer pardon fer the bird. Ye must trust that I dinna put any one in jeopardy with the message. If that be all, I'll be attendin' ta me duties above" Camphoria said with a stone face, curtsied, and left the galley.

Captain Bragg could not breath as he watched her go. He put his head in his hands. "I dunna have the strength ta let her go back ta the pirates. After all I've done ta keep'er safe. I have ta do somethin…That be it. The Fire Lord. If there be anythin' ta do, he can do it."

CHAPTER 29 CAMPHORIA'S FLIGHT

(Composed from the journal and papers of Gideon Livingston, The Fire Lord and Captain William Jasper Bragg)

"There she be!" Captain Livingston points to the resplendent green of the Betty-Lou as she emerged from a cloud bank. "That be Betty-Lou. I told ye not ta concern yerself for Betty-Lou. She can take care of herself."

It had been two rotations since the departure of the Pirate Queen (Capitan Mejilla and his crew remained true to their oath and stayed with the Fire Lord's troops), and though I had been receiving updates from Betty-Lou about her progress back to the fort, it was still not fast enough. I wanted to see Captain Bragg again, but more than anything, I desired to see Camphoria's sparkling green eyes and charming smile.

<They be not sparkling now and there be no smile from Camphoria. She did'na take the news 'bout her parentage well. She 'n Captain Bragg are at odds. I'm afraid she be breaking his heart,> Betty Lou interrupted my thoughts. The news only made me more anxious to see Camphoria.

The crew extended the landing planks and quickly attached the mooring lines to the iron rings embedded in the rock. In no time at all, the Betty-Lou was secure and crew members began disembarking.

<I looked at Captain Bragg as he descended the rampart

and thought I saw an old man. What has been done to him?> I mentally asked Betty-Lou.

<That be a man under a terrible burden of grief,> Betty-Lou responded.

<Camphoria did this to him?>

<Aye lad ‘n much worse. She’s turned cold and past feelin’. I’ve seen the grim spirit that attacks ‘er and others, ‘n none survived.>

<There she is and she appears no better than her father. Finding out that she is the daughter of pirates must have been quite a shock but she is taking it too hard.>

My thoughts drift away from Betty-Lou as I step forward to offer my had of assistance to Camphoria as she navigated the gang plank.

She took my hand, but there was no hint of any emotion. “Thanks” she intoned as she stepped to the surface of the mooring pad. She did not look me as she stepped forward.

Abruptly, she addressed me, “M’Lord, I wish to be assigned to my own quarters apart from Captain Bragg.” When she did look at me, I thought I saw anguish in her red rimmed eyes.

“That can be arranged. Is there something else I can do to help?” I offered.

“Naye M’Lord. Much obliged,” Camphoria curtsied, grabbed her things and entered the fort.

Captain Bragg pulled me aside and told me what was bothering Camphoria and begged me to convince her to give up her foolish notion of becoming a pirate. I looked for opportunities to speak with her for the next few rotations, but Camphoria successfully avoided me. I only saw glimpses of her as she hurried elsewhere.

Then she was gone.

Camphoria had taken one of the tiny air skips of the headquarters without even a word of farewell. Desperate and worried for her safety, we sent out search parties to find her. I directed Captain Bragg to get word to his contacts for any clue of where she might be.

"I'm afraid she's been confiscated by pirates what inhabit the shoals. She were communicatin' with one 'o them by whey hen. She intended ta become one 'o them, bein' as that were her last words," Captain Bragg confided, "We'll find her. Though they bein' worse than a pack 'o mongrel meercats, e'en still, they'll not harm her. They'll be seekin' a ransom."

"Then we wait," I replied.

I realized how empty her father, Captain Bragg, must feel. Though he must have been dying inside, he returned to his duties and it seemed that this was just what he needed to get his mind off of Camphoria. He carried himself as a person that has found out that he is terminally ill and determined to make the most use of the time remaining. He worked like a hungry meercat, giving 110% to every assignment. Though he appeared to be cheerful and full of hope, yet I could still note a bit of grief in his eyes.

I likewise, had not given up hope to find Camphoria. To cover my grief of her departure, and since there was little else that could be done, I transferred my rage and frustration into training to be the Fire Lord that everyone thought I was. This left me little free time to worry about the Braggs. Betty-Lou had designed a rigorous training schedule which I was expected to complete, apart from my other duties as leader of the rebellion.

The day that Betty-Lou showed me where the battle room was in the lower levels of the fortress reminded me of what I had experienced in the Noonday's battle room.

<Here be your new quarters. Tis time ye became who ye were meant to be,> Betty-Lou announced.

<It seems like ages since I first took a sword into the light shard training room, but it's only been five cycles. So much had happened,> I thought to Betty-Lou as I looked at the large cavern hewn out of the stone.

I walked around the hall, inspected the weapons in racks on the walls: swords, spears, throwing daggers and even axes and broadswords. Long bows, straight arrows, fire throwers and slings all received my touch as I drifted through the cavern.

<Weapons of death, designed to inflict pain and misery; is this what I am meant to do?> I questioned.

<Nay lad, your kin and your people have had enough o' that. It be your destiny to free 'em from it. A sword be good for two things, strikin' a foe in attack, or defendin' ye'self and others. Tis the duty of the wielder to decide which be the best action. Freedom exacts a high price to be sure. The best blood of Portus has been spilt defendin' it. Be ye more righteous than they?> Betty-Lou accused.

<Spilling blood is not righteous!> I countered.

<That foolishness 's what ye were taught in school. Ye must forget what yer pasty, cowardly teachers taught ye in school about patiently waiting out the bad times. There be no honor in succumbing to evil. Tis evil that causes grief, despair and cruelty. Ye've never been in real battle where it is kill or be killed, but war is ugly, heartless and cruel to all sides. The right demands ye to match evil, blow for blow, till it be conquered. Ye have ta take up the sword to defend yerself, and yea, even attack. There be no other way than the spilling of blood.>

<In my heart I know this to be true, but to kill a man who is just following orders and who may or may not know why he is fighting, does not seem right. I know that evil men in power are to blame. Would that I could punish them directly,> I moaned mentally.

<Ye canna escape getting blood on yer hands 'n soul in war. Focused 'n prepared ye 'll have ta be in order ta free this people. Be it in God's hands to determine if ye did right,> Betty-Lou consoled.

<If that be true, then ye and God are my witnesses, I do not take up arms for any selfish desire and I will spare lives, even evil ones, if I can. I will use my powers to free the people from injustice and cruelty. I will embrace the destiny that God has given me and if by my life or death I can topple

the Overlord and destroy the power of the Boar Riders, I do it willingly,>I vowed.

<Tis a grand speech. Brought a tear to me eye... Save it fer inspirin' yer troups. Now tis time to get ta work!> Betty-Lou snickered.

My training regimen consisted of four areas, politics and war study, mind control through meditation, blade skill development, and physical strength and agility practice. I requested that my aunt, Mercedes Stewart tutor me in politics and war study, Betty-Lou in mind control and meditation, Colonel Hars Cloudjumper, the weapons master, for blade training, and Sir Percival Kendrick, as fine a specimen of a warrior as I have seen, for strength and agility training.

Each day, before the 2nd morning bell, Sir Kendrick trained me on Vorkistad, a brand of fighting requiring the agility of a tree cat, cunning of a clouded fox, strength of a rock serpent and the patience of a predator wasp. The basis of Vorkistad is to anticipate both the beginning and end of each of your enemy's movements and either defend or attack in between.

At the 6th morning bell, I ate. Then, at the 8th bell, Colonel Cloudjumper and I sparred with wooden swords until my knuckles were bloody and my ribs bruised. No matter how hard I tried, nor how quickly I moved, "Cloudy" could always find a way to slip between my defenses and give me a bruise. I hated those first sessions, but I knew I needed them.

I spent the forenoon-watch studying the maps, charts and manuscripts brought by Auntie Stewart while I soaked my feet and hands in a slimy concoction that smelled as bad as it looked. But it took the pain away, so I put up with smelling like the nine-pin changing room. Auntie's favorite method of instruction was to present a nearly insolvable problem and require me to resolve it: politically first, economically next, and strategically last.

Lunch, then audiences and interviews with the rebel leaders, inspection tours, and paperwork filled the afternoon watch. The headquarters was as busy as a rock wasp nest: endless plans for battle strategy, the training of Capitan Mejilla's pirate crew, the construction of hand weapons in the forges, gathering of supplies, storage of munitions, the collection of reports of the Overlord's activities from spies around Portus, the recruitment of rebels, the coordinated attacks on supply depots and storage facilities of the Adjudicators, freeing rebels and innocents from the jails and executions, and the continued search for Camphoria. We had much to do in preparation for the coming revolution.

Once he understood what we were doing, Capitan Mejilla proved to be a valuable source of knowledge about the routes of the Armada, places to land and resupply unknown to the Overlord and ways to help the rebellion fight pirates and the Overlord. His crew enthusiastically integrated themselves and were hard workers, though still prone to be blamed when things went missing. Capitan Mejilla enthusiastically volunteered for dangerous reconnaissance missions, his ship being unknown to the armada.

Most rotations, the first bell of the first evening watch found me on the deck of Betty-Lou in the most grueling training of all. Here, I learned how to maintain concentration on the powers of the Fire Lord, while performing other tasks. For example, she often tried to build my fire-stamina by having me maintain ship invisibility, target wind sprites with smoke balls, and navigate the spikey rock spires of the south by skip jumping the ship from one safe area to another. Betty-Lou loved to see if she could break my concentration by flying upside down, hopping, or simply dead weight dropping. One of the things that I enjoyed the most was when we explored the regions around the headquarter fortress, including the dragon caves on the west of the Island of Melispora- also known as the Tristeza.

After training with Betty-Lou I'd stumble to the mess hall for dinner, drag myself to my quarters and then slip into exhausted sleep by the 5th bell of the first night watch.

As the sun-rises passed and added up to moon cycles, I could see myself changing physically. My body was responding to the demands I was placing on it. I could keep up with Sir Kendrick in the calisthenics of Vorkistad. Colonel Cloudjumper rarely could breach my defenses to land blows. My knowledge grew about how to handle people and strategy, and how to govern centers of power. I learned that by concentrating I could detect body heat and I could tell when someone was nervous or lying. I discovered new talents from the Fire Lord powers and my ability to sustain them grew each day. For example, in the darkness of the Dragon caves, I learned that I did not need light to see if I filled a space with smoke. I could sense the eddies and wisps of smoke much like blind leap frogs used sound to guide their webbed-finger glides from rock to rock. I tried this with Colonel Cloudjumper and found that I could detect movement in the air, identify the shape and size, speed and angles and easily deflect his attacks. In this same manner I found that I could also detect things that were nearly invisible to sight like stinging cloud pods, or mountain peaks covered in fog.

One night, exhausted from my exercises, I lay on my bed and pondered these things. My beard had grown as bushy and red as a marsupial bat's fur. I liked it. I had become stronger and my knowledge and my confidence had grown.

I stroked my beard and had the following conversation with myself.

"I know my destiny is to be the eventual Fire Lord, but all around me consider it a feat that I have already accomplished.

<Ye be the Fire Lord.>

<Thanks, but let me think a bit, for myself, Betty-Lou.>

<Alright, I'm here if ye needs me.>

"To be the real Fire Lord, I need to defeat the Overlord and his Boar Riders and that won't be easy."

~"Duh, it's going to be nearly impossible."

"Agreed. It has to be a total defeat."

~"You are right. You cannot just defeat him in combat, for after the victory, other challengers would quickly arise to replace him."

"That's what I mean. I have to completely eliminate his source of power: the fear he causes to rise in the hearts of the people."

~"Yep! That is where you as the Fire Lord come to save the day. Because the people have no way to withstand his brutality and so they have to comply with his taxes and fees. You liberate them."

"Yes, but in order to really defeat him, I have to make sure that he and his entire regime are completely eliminated."

~"Wait a moments, you can't just kill everyone! That'd be as bad as the Overlord. What you have to do is make sure that he, and all like him, are scorned by those same people who once aspired his favor."

"That's exactly what I am thinking! A mere military victory could not do that. But a rebellion of the people could."

~"Yes! That is it. You simply have to get the seeds of rebellion to grow and spread."

I yawned and turned on my side. "...but how do I do that?"

~"Here's an idea. The people have to see the evil of the Overlord and his corrupt Adjudicators and they need hope that they would be able to overthrow their despotic rule. You as the Fire Lord will have to point out how corrupt the Overlord is and then give the people hope by publicly challenging and defeating the Overlord!"

"It is not as easy as that."

~"Maybe so. Why don't you sleep on it and we'll talk in the morning."

Then the same thought that had entered my brain every rotation for the last three lunar cycles intruded again, "Where are you Camphoria?" Then I drifted off to a fitful sleep.

CHAPTER 30 THE CAPTURE

(Extracted from Camphoria Livingston Bragg's Memoirs)

Heart-broken I was, 'n I knew it'd caused ma' Da' great pain fer me to turn from him. But I were mighty angry! So turned out were I that an unquenchable flame burned inside 'o me, 'n that be the very thing what fueled me to see my foolish plan through. I wanted 'im ta suffer the anguish that I felt at bein' lied to, betrayed and coddled from the truth. I reasoned that if I be a pirate, if it be in m'blood, then I'd be the best pirate 'n fulfill m'destiny. So, I came ta Polgro and sought out Gavin Rookler, knowin' he could tell me where ta find the pirates what infest these skies. I found him in the place befittin' his stature: the Crag Saloon.

"The bartender said ye be Gavin Rookler" I said as I approached the shaggy disheveled man in the far corner of the tavern.

Without looking up he growled, "He be a liar. The fellow ye be huntin' died a might bit ago. Ye be too late."

"Ye knew me father, I'm Camphoria Bragg."

He lifted his head to see me. "Well glory be. I was wonderin' when ye might appear. When I received yer message it made me mighty pleased that ye remembered the likes of me." He looked me over from head to toe and remarked, "Ye've grown to be quite handsome lass. Look at ye! Ye have the air 'o yer mother and the stature of good Capt'n. Bragg hisself."

I frowned and wondered if I should continue. But when I thought 'o the anger that burned within me, I gritted my teeth and pressed forward, "I was'na sure what ta expect when I met ya, but I can tell the fates have not been kind to ye. Can ye help me o' not?" I asked.

"That be it then. Ye still want to be joinin' a pirate crew?" He scratched his shaggy head and looked me in the eyes. "I be owin' Capt'n. a favor and t'would do 'im no justice if'n I did'na warn ye about what yer plannin' ta do."

"I understand there be risks 'n I be not afraid," I lied.

"Well if that be the case, then there be no point in tellin' ye that pirates in these parts be the most cut throat and blood thirsty 'o the lot, nor in revealin' that these here pirates would kill ye or worse just for fun. Piratin' be no place fer a woman such as ye appear ta be," Gavin said with a wicked grin.

"The leader 'o the pirates she be a woman, be I right?" I retorted.

"That be correct young lassy, but ye've ne'er seen a more heartless and cruel witch. Be ye prepared to follow her example?" He said as his grin grew wider.

"She be my mother 'n though she may deserve what ye say, ye've not the right ta malign 'er with yer evil words." I instantly pulled out my sword and put it to Gavin's neck. His smile disappeared. "Tell me where ta find the Red Hand Pirate crew, what I hear inhabit these parts, and I'll let ye live."

"'N if I don't, ye'll kill me?" He slapped the blade away and I felt a sharp point in my stomach. "Now lassy, ye be unacquainted with the likes 'o pirates, so let me give ye one free lesson. Never threaten a pirate unless ye intend to see it through. The next lesson be not free. This blade I hold ta yer mid-section be sharp and ready ta run ye through and under normal situations, I would do it, especially since ye threatened me first. But in this case, I see no profitin' in that. Ms. Bragg meet the Red Hand Pirates! Boys take 'er away."

Strong arms grabbed my sword before I could react. A black cloth was placed over my head and my hands were tied behind my back.

I struggled and shouted, "Ye canna do this! I came ta

join ye, not be made captive! Ma father were yer friend!"

"That be a long time past, 'n to be more specific, ye could call us acquaintances. I simply be fulfillin' yer wishes lassy ... 'n at the same time, makin' a profit," Gavin sneered.

I squirmed, kicked and bit ferociously. I was determined to not make it easy for them. "My mother, when she hears 'o this will tear ye all ta shreds!"

"I'm countin' on her hearin' 'bout this. She'll be mighty interested ta retrieve her long lost daughter," Gavin crooned with glee.

"She's got the strength of a meercat, hold her boys!" a man shouted as they attempted to take me from the room by force.

"She's makin' too much of a ruckus!" another roared over my screams.

I was struck on the head and then the world went silent.

I awoke with a horrendous head ache and an equally horrendous smell. I reached up to touch my head and found that my hands were shackled to the floor. My hand came away bloody from where they had struck me, so I couldn't have been there too long or it would have dried. I looked around and saw that I sat in the middle of a cell with two wooden walls and two made of metal bars. Beyond the metal bars were other cells, all were empty save for the one farthest from me. A man dressed in dirty rags, with hair and beard down to his waist sat in a heap in the middle.

I could feel the floor swaying and knew that I was aboard a ship.

"This be a fine lot I'm in now...not near what I intended," I groaned. "How could've I been such a piglin-head? Gavin Rookler of course would have seen profit in me 'n would'a sold me ta the Red-Hand pirates."

"Dunn'a be so hard on yeself lassy. E'en experienced folk like meself have been duped by those considered friends." The ragged man in the far cell commiserated.

"Who be ye and why be ye in this state?" I demanded.

"It matters not who I be nor why I be here. The better question ye should be askin' is where be ye 'n what's ta become 'o ye." He responded with a dry chuckle.

"Seein' as we be in the same boat, ye mind enlightin' me with some answers?"

"I canna oblige ye seein' as I've been in this cell fer many cycles 'n ne'er once set foot above. A lone sailor he brings stale bread 'n brackish water once at day break. That be all I know. Ye be the first in that cell for many a cycle."

I thought, "It'd be just like pirates to plant a false prisoner in the cell to garner my trust and to get information about my father and the Fire Lord. Too late, he knows that I'm a valuable prisoner, but I shall have ta be more cautious anyhow."

"That be a shame. Fer sure ye must know just from the sounds above what be goin' on." I responded.

"I hear the sloshin' 'o the bilge tank mostly... once in while shouts and noise 'o battle. But where we be, nor when we be, I know not."

"I've told ye 'bout me troubles. What about yers?" I questioned to try to get him to give me some information.

"We've only just met and ye want me ta reveal m'secrets? Nay lassy, we have nuthin' but time, and time will tell what is revealed or not." The wretched man chuckled.

I began thinking, "He believes that I be the false prisoner, and so the game begins."

Only I held no illusions that my time would be long. Sooner or later, base men find a use for young women, unless there is great gain from keeping her unsullied that protects her.

"Then that be it," I thought, "The cell was not my prison, but my protection. Though dastardly as he may be, that Gavin Rookler saved me from my own folly!"

CHAPTER 31 BECOMING THE FIRE LORD

(Recreated from the journals of Ariel Livingston and Sadie-Belle Livingston)

"Laddy, ye've received a whey hen message," Grandfather informed me with a sour look and handed me a tightly rolled parchment sealed with my mother's ring in red wax.

"I know, I should not have sent her a message. I did tell her not to respond, though."

"We best see what be so important ta tell ye then."

I fumbled to open the message from my mother and read the contents out loud.

Dearest Son:

I thank ye fer writin' that letter 'n lettin' me know yer progress, though ye warned me 'bout writin' due to the poor weather. I'm glad ta know yer safe 'n enjoyin' yerself, though I've had a rough time of it along with the folks of Miller's Pond. The weather's been terrible here 'n the wind's been like the adjudicator, pokin' his nose through all the cracks in the house, tryin' ta find where ye be, 'n makin' it right chilly. Good thin' yer on vacation, I says. Folks in Miller's Pond've been fightin' it as best they could but've found themselves at the mercy of the foul winds 'n have ta hide or face its wrath. I ne're seen a storm like this what could jail people inside, 'n as a wild boar, cause 'em serious injury as if fer complainin' 'bout the wind. People say that the wind 'as searched fer any airships what'r seen ta dash her ta the ground. I tell'em that fer 9 solar cycles I've never seen an airship what could withstand such a wind 'n survive. I know ye both battle winds like this fer many a season. When weather like this happens, it makes me glad yer on the right side 'o the wind.

I'm fine fer the most part, puttin' rags in the chinks ta answer the cold wind. I know my last words were unkind, 'n my behavior was worse ta boot. Ye've my blessin' ta be gone from this wind. I miss the warm weather 'n company. I be keepin' busy sortin' through boxes'o lithographs, drawin's, school papers 'n such that I kept ta make a memory book for ye. I'd ne'er wish this wind on anyone. Ye take yer time 'n I'll see ye when I see ye.

With Love,

Yer Ma

"What a strange letter. Why was it so important to tell me about the weather?" I asked Grandfather.

"Did ye not understand it? Tis nothin' ta do with the weather, it be a warning. I knew yer mother had an idea of what I 'n yer dad were about, and this be the proof! Here, let me read it again to ye so ye's can understand it. Tis written so as ta appear innocent, but tells another message entirely. Here. She says the wind is like the Adjudicator. That be the key."

Dearest Gideon:

I know your last message said ta not return a letter, but I felt I needed ta inform ye 'bout things occurrin' in Miller's pond... Since ye 'n my da' left, there be terrible things happenin'. The adjudicator's been puttin' people in those horrid sewers he calls jails.

Anyone what speaks out, gets clobbered 'n worse, by those infernal Boar Riders. They been askin' bout yer granda' 'n all I tell 'em is that ye be gone on a vacation. They say that they've witnesses what've seen the Betty-Lou. I told 'em that I'd not see the Betty-Lou fer 9 cycles. I know what purpose yer granda' has taken ye on this trip ta do. I'm proud 'o ye both fer doin' the right thing.

I'm fine. I know my last words were unkind, 'n my behavior was worse ta boot. Ye've my blessin' ta be gone with yer granda'. I miss ye both, but wish ye were here. If I dunna see ye again, dunna forget me. I wish ye ta be safe from harm. Dunna come home till it be over.

With Love,
Yer Ma

(Compiled from the personal papers possessed by Torrance Cloudjumper and the journal of Gideon Livingston, the Fire Lord)

In a lull in the lesson, I turned my mind to the letter my mother had written. "Maybe I can borrow a whey hen from another ship and send that bird? No, I can't do that. If she were to answer, and it were intercepted, it would put that ship in jeopardy."

"Pay attention! Attend to yer surroundin's!" Colonel Cloudjumper barked and rapped my knuckles for good measure.

"Ow! Was that necessary?" I yelled.

"Shut yer fire off. This be about skill not power," Colonel Cloudjumper shouted back, as I had lit myself in flames in anger.

"There's more where that came from should ye continue ta lose focus. Now parry this!" Colonel Cloudjumper shouted as he lunged forward with his wooden pole while keeping perfect balance on the rope strung over the water in the shallow lagoon of the island.

I parried, shouted triumphantly, “Ah, ha!” and then promptly lost my balance, plunging into the cold water.

Underwater, I felt anger for my inability to maintain balance, this being the fifth plunge into the frigid waves. As I struggled to the surface, I noticed bubbles all around me. I stopped swimming and observed that the bubbles seemed to come from me. Then I noticed the green flames close to my skin. I was covered in green flames and I was cold no longer. Not only this, but I was not sinking, but staying motionless. I opened my mouth and instead of water, warm moist, air filled my mouth. I breathed it in and exhaled, then repeated. I thought, “Since fish breath water, there must be enough ‘air’ in the water to breath to keep them alive and that is how I am breathing underwater!”

“I can breathe underwater!” I shouted to no one. “I’m boiling the water around me and it lets me breathe!”

I looked around me, noticing that the shallow lagoon dropped off to deep water just a few ship lengths away.

<I wonder if I can use this to help me swim,> I thought and then concentrated on putting more fire at my feet and hands.

Slowly I could feel pressure on my head as I began to move through the water to deeper water. I willed more heat at my feet and felt the speed increase.

I exhilarated in the way the water rapidly flowed past me and how I could maneuver as well as any water dog by moving my hands and feet. Before I knew it, I was in deep water and the lagoon was far behind me. I realized my danger too late, for directly in front of me was a leviathan of a fish. It was as long as the Betty-Lou, with shimmering silver scales the size of my hand. Its pointed nose was crested with a blue fin the size and shape of the webbed dragon-wings of the Betty-Lou. It lazily moved its long muscular body back and forth and then I saw its eye, the size of a serving dish swivel in my direction. When it saw me, it turned with a powerful jerk of its tail and it shot in my direction like a razor disk. In awe at its size I did not move as its narrow, toothy jaws gaped wide to engulf me. At the last second, I did the only thing I could do. I put all of the energy I could into my feet and hands and shot directly upwards. I heard the underwater chomp of those massive jaws and the immediate swoosh of the water as the beast followed me to the surface. I knew that I should not look back as that would cause me to lose the forward momentum and direct me closer to the fish.

I broke through the surface of the water and urged even more energy to my feet and hands. I heard the enormous splashing of the giant fish as it catapulted out of the water in pursuit and then the enormous splash as it plunged back into the water.

I made the mistake of looking down and saw that I was hurtling through the air, three ship-lengths above the water, ten or so ship-lengths from the lagoon. Of course, the act of looking down changed the direction of my flight and I plunged back into the water, nearly colliding with the waiting leviathan who had been following my progress from beneath the waves. I zoomed through the water, leaving a trail of bubbles as I headed for the lagoon, with the monster at my heels.

I broke through the surface to see a worried Colonel Cloudjumper on the beach.

"Oh my! Be ye alright?" he shouted from the edge of the beach.

His and my surprise continued as not only I left the water, but right behind me, shot the incredibly large fish as well. At the last moment before the monster crashed into the water, I heard a loud snapping and grinding as the large fish gnashed its teeth in frustration. When the giant fish landed in the water, it sent a wave of water that smashed into me. Not able to control the fire from my hands and feet, I skipped across the surface of ocean towards the shallow lagoon like a stone thrown on a smooth lake. I sensed the anger of the water beast at not being able to follow me into the shallow lagoon and made the mistake of looking at my pursuer which caused me to spin in tight summersaults in the air. I straightened up my body and used my hands to try to stabilize my flight, but I began zigzagging above the beach uncontrollably.

"I need to stop this before I get hurt or run out of power and then get hurt," I thought.

I concentrated on putting less heat at my feet which slowed my dizzying speed, but also brought me closer to the beach. I tried steering using the fire in my hands and then turning my head as a rudder. It worked to some degree in that when I finally stopped, I was mostly in the water, which absorbed most of my fall.

Colonel Cloudjumper came running over, splashing in the shallow water and looking much relieved.

"Wahoo!" I shouted, "Did you see that monster? Not only can I breathe underwater, and swim faster than the leviathans, I can fly... well sort of, it needs some work, but I can do it! Isn't that amazing?" I grinned as I sat in the knee-deep water of the lagoon beach.

"Aye yer majesty, it nearly ate ye. The birds 'n the fish have much ta be wary of now that ye be in their territories." He said with a grin. "Now quit yer playin' around and let's get back ta work!"

"Ok already. I'm coming." I complained and with a thought instantly dried my clothes as I walked toward the ladder for the tight rope.

(Taken from the personal journals of Camphoria Livingston.)

Rises turned into lunar cycles and each sun appeared no different than the last. The light became shorter and each nightfall colder. The ragged man and I came to a truce. We did not have to reveal anything about ourselves, so we stopped trying to wheedle information from the other. Without realizing it, though, in this simple way we learned more about each other than we would have with interrogation.

"What be yer favorite color?" he asked.

"Tis the lavender of briar thistles in bloom on a crystal-clear mornin' at the start 'o spring. And ye?" I returned.

"Used to love the color of the sunrises, bright 'n cheery, but now me favorite color be that of silver, as in the silver rays that perchance make their way to this wretched place. It be yer turn ta ask."

I shared what I thought would be a difficult question, "What be the most important thing in the world?"

He sighed and replied, "That be easy, freedom it be. Freedom to move about and do as ye please. Freedom to say what be in yer heart without fear. Freedom to work and gain rightful reward. Freedom to love and hate who ye may. Freedom to strive and to suffer failure 'o glory in victory. Freedom to worship the God of creation. Freedom to choose right or wrong and reap just recompense. So that be it, lassy... Freedom."

I could not disagree and told him so, "Ye be right. Tis the greatest thing that we have been deprived. Ye more 'n me since ye've been here many cycles. I ache for ye and yer family who must think ye dead."

The wretched man sobbed, though I could not see them, I knew there were tears also.

"For whom do ye weep?" I asked.

He continued to sob but did not answer.

CHAPTER 32
THE HISTORY OF BETTY-LOU

(Extracted Directly from the Personal Log book of Gideon Livingston, the Fire Lord)

<Betty-Lou, I remember when I first boarded you, I felt a surge of power from my feet and hand on the rail. Then it happened again, but more forcefully when I first found out about my powers at Noonday. I felt a tremendous surge of power starting from my feet going up to my chest. If the power comes from me, then why did that happen?> I asked as I rested at the octagonal table on Betty-Lou's deck.

I was resting because Betty-Lou had given me a particularly grueling mental work out. She had me juggling balls of flame, while trying to keep myself, cross-legged, hovering on a cushion of flame, one arms-length off the deck, all while whistling the tune of "Oh Valley, Oh ".

I had done pretty well until that wind sprite suddenly flew at my face and I tumbled to the deck in a heap.

<Why be ye askin' this?> she responded. <What be troublin' ye?>

<No troubles, just that for what I will need to be able to do, I am concerned that I cannot contain enough power to be able to do it. Are there other sources of power?> I questioned.

<That be where ye be misunderstandin' and tis time I told ye everything. Both yer powers 'n mine come from the

same place. The power be not yours nor mine. We be just conduits or containers fer it,> she explained.

<So, if I do not generate the power, why would I be affected and die if I do not have enough for the sword of the Fire Lord?> I asked.

<I did'na say that ye have no power 'o yer own, I said it dunna belong ta ye. There be a difference. Mayhaps tis time ta tell ye 'bout me history 'n how I came ta be. Then ye may well understand what makes ye special and unique in this world. It began three hundred cycles afore ye were born. I were built in Gladewater ship yards by Gunda Hilderbert. He were a master shipbuilder the world's ne'er seen hence. Ahead of his time he was, and for this, he was ridiculed and scorned. At the time, I were but a ship with no knowledge of meself. No captain would fly me, and no banker would buy me 'cause 'o me unique design. Yet one young man saw the value in me and offered to be the captain. He was poor and made arrangements with Hilderbert ta pay installments. He flew me well and soon became wealthy enough to buy me outright. His name was Clarence Elder and he was a kind soul. He had a daughter, Betty-Lou, after whom I were named the day he paid for me in full. That same day, as we traveled on a celebration voyage and a vacation, brigands attacked, and Clarence's darlin' wife and daughter, that were me, were killed. He fought them off, suffering many wounds. But this tragedy were too much for him ta bear, so he traveled the world and came to the maelstrom. In that storm he thought ta find his final release and so he headed straight into it. In the maelstrom, though, he found anguish equal to his own and howled in unison with the winds, but it gave him no release. That be my awakening. As the spirit of his daughter, Betty-Lou, I came alive in the dragon ship. Then the maelstrom spit us out on Asombre where there be then only a few small towns. There we dwelt for many rises.

I tried to console Clarence and I tried ta communicate with him who I be, but he took no notice. Grief still had its hold of 'im. As time went on, little by little, he began ta see what I were. He noticed how I moved of my own accord. How I resisted the winds that would take me away from him. He finally boarded me and he saw how I was able to move anything on board ta help'm: a chair when he wanted ta sit, raise the bed when he wanted ta sleep, or with a bed cord, pick up a brush for his hair. One day, he were lookin' at a lithograph 'o me. I frantically tried ta tell'm that twas me. I moved the bed cords ta point at the picture then I picked up the writing stick to write a message on the painting. 'I am Betty-Lou' I wrote. Finally, he understood and first in his dreams and then when awake, we were able ta communicate as you and I communicate. With me, his daughter at his side, Captain Elder became a fearless sky merchant, daring ta go where others feared ta venture. Nothing could stop us...or so I thought.

Then war broke out and we were conscripted ta serve the king. There be a picture 'o me in that war in yer cabin. Battle after battle we fought and it became known that Elder's dragon ship were unbeatable. Clarence told no one that I be alive.

Due to his success and fame, he became well-known 'n admired. But as always happens, jealousy arises in human hearts and one fateful day, the same brigands that had killed his wife and daughter were hired ta kill Clarence. He fought valiantly, but were handicapped by the fact that his dearest friend be the one who conspired against 'im. He could'na believe it, 'n at the last before he died, his false friend told 'im he had also paid to have his wife and daughter killed. All this so that he could obtain the ship. My fury knew no bounds and I unleashed the gates of hell upon that man and the brigands. I made sure that they would kill no more. My rage and grief continued and I flew off, not caring where. I were found by a man who I let take possession 'o me. After that, fer hundreds 'o solar cycles, I were bought 'n sold and were the airship of many a captain, some good, some bad. I did'a care. I withdrew ta m'self 'n let 'em fly me as if I were a normal airship. When I were tired of it all, I came alive 'n flew as if I were broken: twistin', jerkin' 'n endangerin' the crew 'n captain, flyin' upside down, 'n doin' circles in the sky. The last captain and crew escaped 'n were glad fer their lives ta be rid of me. I drifted without aim, nor destination. Fate brought me to the floating island of mist where I met other lost ships who were possessed of grieving human spirits just as I. Born of tragedy in the Maelstrom. There I stayed among my own kind for two hundred solar cycles till your father took a chance on me 'n ye know the rest 'o the story,> Betty-Lou stopped her narration.

<Can any ship become like you and the other lost ships? >

<Nay, tis not the ship that be main concern. Tis the tragedy that befell the human soul on the ship. The Maelstrom be what caused the tragedy fer most 'o them ships, but some, like m'self, had other tragedies befall us, 'n then in grief 'n anguish entered the Maelstrom. All the souls posessin' them ships were connected with the ships by headin' in ta the Maelstrom.>

<Wow. This is unbelievable! You are the daughter of Captain Clarence Elder?> I asked.

<Aye lad. Cursed or blessed to travel the skies forever in the form of a ship. So if ye've been listening, what be the source 'o me power?> Betty-Lou asked.

<It can't be the Maelstrom. Ye once told me that Portus is an angry planet and that that anger fuels the Maelstrom. The power must come from the planet itself!> I guessed.

<Right ye be,> Betty-Lou confirmed. <Ye owe yer powers ta the planet Portus, 'n can draw upon them ta replenish yer own if it be her wish. The planet be alive, 'n free ta choose. Ye be at her beckoning, ta fulfill her wishes and follow her course. Ye just need the stamina 'n will ta demand that Portus help ye. Without that, ye be usin' yer own power, which be easily diminished.>

CHAPTER 33 UNEXPECTED REVELATIONS

(Reconstructed from the Lady Camphoria Livingston Bragg's memoirs and journals)

I couldn't take the untrusting game any longer so I just asked my cell mate, "We both've been together at least five cycles and chatted we have 'bout many things. I trust ye to know who I be, 'n in some ways ye know me better than anyone alive. I be Camphoria Bragg, daughter 'o Cirulea, the Pirate Queen. Who be ye?"

The ragged man laughed and responded, "That explains why ye be here protected from those mangy rascals above. They want a ransom, or several ransoms for ye. If what ye say be true, I feel in ma bones that our time be short. I knew and loved yer father, Billy Bragg, and I knew ye as a babe. I be Robert Livingston, son 'o Ariel Livingston. Pleased ta make yer acquaintance again, Camphoria. Ye can call me Bert. My, what a lovely lass ye've turned out ta be!"

Now it was my turn to cry and sob. The man I had scorned and realized that I loved since first I met him, he had lost his father long ago and t'was I what had found him, but neither of us would see Gideon again.

"Lassy, what be the reason fer yer tears, if ye'd be please ta tell me?" Bert asked in a timid voice.

"Oh Bert!" I cried. "I know yer father and yer son, 'n love

'em both dearly. Like an angry, spoilt child, I ran away from 'em. Ta spite my father fer lyin' ta me, I intended ta become a pirate like me mother and that be how I ended up here." I cried even more as I stated what was in my heart.

"How be they? What say they 'o me?" Bert eagerly asked.

"Robert, I mean Bert, there be so many things I need ta tell ye. They be fine and highly engaged in the rebellion. They think ye be dead, though yer son talks 'o ye often as if ye still be alive. On several occasions he mentioned his desire ta find what became of ye. And, I must tell ye one other thing. Yer son, I love him, though when last we spoke, I was cruel ta him. He be the Fire Lord reborn," I confessed through tears of grief and remorse, "and I shall see him no more."

With that I cried even the more piteously. I heard Bert crying also. We cried together for several moments.

Then Bert spoke up again, now in control of his emotions, "My son, be the Fire Lord Reborn? How can that be?" he asked.

"Tis true. I have seen his terrible power. He rescued me from certain death by turnin' the Betty-Lou invisible and shooting flame at me oppressors. He be kind and wise, yet merciless to his enemies. Ye should be terrible proud ta be his father." I shared through teary eyes, wiping them with my sleeve repeatedly.

Bert was on his knees and earnest, "That be grand. My baby boy has grown ta be a man, and not just any man. He be the prophesied Fire Lord and the future king of all Portus. I can tell that ye love 'im." He paused, searching for words, "Now lassy, ye be young, ye must have hope. There be a loving God in heaven and he has brought ye to me and he be watchin' o're us. If my son, he be the Fire Lord, 'n given that ye be not just amazingly beautiful, but kind and gentle, I guarantee that he, with God's help, will find a way to save ye and me from the pirates. Ye will see 'im again," Bert consoled.

I awoke to the sound of pounding on my door.

"Sire! We have news of Camphoria!

"Come in!" I commanded.

"M'Lord, one of the messengers has returned and brings news that Camphoria went to join a pirate crew ported near the Shoals. They be the Red Hand lot and never a group of meaner rascals ever existed. Instead, they took her captive. They want a king's ransom--ten thousand pieces of gold in exchange for her release." Sir Percival stood at the door after delivering the message.

"Thank you. Call Captain Bragg to my quarters immediately. I wish to tell him the news myself. Also raise the alarm, and rouse the crew. We head for the shoals immediately." I ordered.

<Heaven's be praised. We've found her at last!> I thought to Betty-Lou as I jumped out of bed and quickly dressed.

<I know what ye intend ta do, and ye be not ready,> she warned.

<If you had a chance to save your father, would you not risk everything to do it?> I countered.

<Aye, lad, I would and I'll risk everything ta help ye rescue the girl ye love, because I love ye both dearly,> Betty-Lou said, and I felt the glow of her love.

<I feel the same about you, and thank you,> I responded, brushing away the tears that had sprung into my eyes.

CHAPTER 34 THE WRATH OF THE FIRE LORD

(Extracted Directly from the Personal Log book of Gideon Livingston, the Fire Lord)

We were all boarded, gear stowed and provisions garnered before the first afternoon watch bell rang.

"Captain Livingston, is all prepared?" I asked.

"Aye, yer majesty, we be ready to cast off at yer command." Grandfather responded with a crisp salute.

"Make the call to cast off then."

"Sir. Kendrick, make all haste to the southern shoals. First Mate, take us through the maelstrom. Captain Livingston, gather the war council in my quarters immediately." I made the orders and headed to my quarters to prepare them.

I had no intention of paying the ransom and I am certain that Cirulea felt the same. These pirates would pay dearly for harming Camphoria. I thought of options and scenarios while I prepared the captain's quarters. I lowered my bed to make the conference table and got the drawing frame ready.

"Come in!" I pronounced just as I finished.

The leaders all came in. I noticed Captain Bragg's aspect had changed. He was energetic and enthusiastic in his manner, though his gaunt appearance still persisted. Worry does not lend to good eating and sleeping. It pleased me greatly to see his improvement though.

"Thank you for coming so promptly. Have a seat. Before I begin, I want you to know that I believe that in this room we have the finest minds on Portus and that if we pool our intellectual forces, we can find solutions to anything. Having said that, this meeting can only be effective if all ideas are considered equally, regardless of who it came from. Let me be more specific. I do not presume to know everything, and just because I am the Fire Lord, does not mean that my ideas are more important or better than yours. After all the ideas are presented, we cannot leave here till we all agree on a course of action. Do we all agree?" I asked and looked for a response from each person at the table.

"Good. We all agree. Now let's get started. I am going to write three questions that I think need to be answered and if you wish to change or add questions feel free. 1) What do we know? 2) What do we not know? 3) What are we willing to do?

The conversation began with me asking particular people for their opinions. As they saw that I was serious about free discourse, they began to speak more freely about what they believed. The tempo of the conversation increased and the solutions and possible actions started flowing. By the time we had exited the maelstrom, we had decided on a course of action. The rest of the conversation dealt with details and assignments.

One of my assignments was to get a message to the Pirate Queen to tell her to not respond to the ransom, that the Fire Lord would take care of the problem personally. I thought, "I can't use whey hens because I don't have one from her ships. I can't use my powers because don't know where Cirulea is."

I paced the deck and kept thinking, "She has the gold and the crown. In order to see in the darkness on the way back from finding the crown, I had forced my power into the diadem in the crown just as I had done to the ring I gave Camphoria. I wonder if like the serrated sword, there might be residual power in the diadem? Cirulea has the crown and would keep that close to her. If I could project a different kind of flame power through the gem, then I would be able to communicate with her, wherever she is! I could reach out to her through the diadem."

"Can I detect that residual power?" I asked myself.

I concentrated, imagining the beautiful crown, and I reached for the residual power left in the diamond when I last used it for light. Several moments passed and I extended my search further and further in concentric circles. Then I found it, a bright spot of green. I focused on that and as I did so, a hazy green image of a room appeared in my mind. It seemed to be her sleeping quarters and no one was present. I extended a trail of green smoke to go under the door. I formed the green mist into the shape of the Fire Lord. Just in case anyone should notice the mist, I wanted them to know that it was the Fire Lord and not just some strange smoke. I passed frightened pirates who all ran in one direction. I followed, thinking that they were headed to the Queen. The wooden corredors and narrow passageways told me that was aboard a ship and that this was Cirulea's airship.

"They must have received a ransom also and that is why they were traveling!" I mused to myself. I followed the airmen out onto the deck and there found the Queen.

"Good day, Cirulea." I spoke in the deepest voice I could muster. I waited for her to respond. Through the green haze, I could make out her shocked look and the frightened look of her crew.

She stammered, "Ggg'day yer Lordship." Then she regained her composure. "How may I be of assistance to ye?"

"I share your concern for your daughter's safety, though nothing can match the feelings a mother has for a daughter. I know that you are on your way to the Shoals to confront the Red Hand Crew about your daughter Camphoria." I guessed.

"Why, M'Lord, we be but takin' a trip ta Ladaso ta complete business transactions." She purred, pouring on the charm.

Because of my training in lie detection, even as a smoky apparition I could sense that her temperature was rising and I could feel her increased heart rate. She was lying, though she gave no outward appearance to that fact by just looking at her.

I sent a burst of green flames around the image and shouted, “Do not lie to me! You cannot deceive me!”

The crew fell to their knees and trembled. The Queen took a step back and was about to speak.

“Silence!” With another burst of flames, I cut her next lie off before she could utter it. “Out of respect for your mother hood I have come personally to give you this message. Do not go to the Shoals and interfere. Be at ease about your daughter. She will be freed, but will be in my care. Forget your plans to use her as leverage to get to your husband. Ye be warned.” I repeated the warning that I had given her the night before she left the headquarters.

I dispelled the image of the Fire Lord but lingered as mist to see what the Queen would do.

“What ye be wait’ fer. Ye heard ‘im. Turn about ‘n take us home!” The queen commanded.

With smug pleasure, I released the connection to the crown.

By the time we reached the shoals early that evening, we were ready. We knew that our presence at the shoals was noticed because not a ship was in sight. They were watching, but they were not nearby, yet.

In our war council, Captain Bragg had shared, “For certain they will keep their prize on board, but they’ll keep ‘er out of reach. They will send spies ta determine our strength even though they knows our weakness.” He explained, “Demandin’ ransom for a pirate were never just ‘bout treasure. Tis ‘bout complete control. They haves what we wants and if we shows up, that reveals our desperation ‘n our weakness, and with that, they know that they be in control and they win it all."

The consensus of the group was to eliminate our weakness, i.e. get Camphoria before they can press their advantage. Colonel Cloudjumper had the answer for this one, "Every magician knows that controlling the attention of the audience makes the trick work." Colonel Cloudjumper held up a coin which he threw high into the air. All eyes watched the coin's straight rise and fall. When it was caught, it was not Colonel Cloudjumper that caught it. In the place of the Colonel was Sir Kendrick, smiling. They had switched places without us even knowing, so intent were we on the coin. In his new spot, Colonel Cloudjumper continued, "I suggest that we do a bit of sleight of hand. Undoubtedly, the pirates are aware of some of the powers used to defeat the Overlord's armada" he said, "We just have to make them think that they know where we are. I propose, if I may be so bold, that the Fire Lord surround the Betty-Lou in green smoke when we arrive, then he turns the ship and crew invisible, free to leave the cloud and retrieve Camphoria."

Percival asked "How do we retrieve Camphoria if we dunna know where she is?"

I had the answer for that, "I gave her a ring that I hope she still wears. I will use the Fire Lord powers to locate that ring focusing on the residual power in the ring from the last time I used it."

Now that we had arrived at the Shoals, we had to start the plan in motion. I concentrated on Camphoria's ring as I did with the diadem on the crown earlier. After a few moments of intense concentration, I knew that I had made the connection because I could visualize a green haze. But it was all dark and I could not make anything out. I focused on trying to hear what was going on. I heard random noises: loud rhythmic thumping, creaks, shuffles, sloshing of the bilge tank, etc... I spoke in a whisper.

I heard a woman's stifled scream and a man's concerned

voice. "What be the problem lassy?"

"Me thought I heard the voice of the Fire Lord. As if he were standin' next ta me. Twas but a whisper." Said the voice I recognized as Camphoria's.

Who else is there with her? I wondered.

I spoke again, a little louder. "Don't be frightened. I am here to rescue you, well sort of."

She jumped a little bit and I could tell that her temperature was rising.

"Ye be here yer Majesty?" she whispered and I heard her begin to sob. I could hear her breathing quickening. "Be it true? Ye've come ta fetch me out of this horrid place?

"Why can't I see anything?" I thought. "Is that her heartbeat? Why can hear her heart pounding so loudly?"

She whispered, "Where be ye? I canna see ye."

"I'm connected to the ring I gave you. I'm glad you didn't get rid of it." I said softly.

"Oh my!" I heard her say and then suddenly there was light.

I projected my image to be in front of her. She was smiling and was holding up a ribbon still tied around her neck from which the ring dangled. Then it was my turn to say, "Oh my! That's where I was...er the ring was! Forgive me! I did not know that's where you kept the ring."

"M'Lord, I had ta hide it, bein' among pirates." she said now grinning wide, "I did'na know that I truly did carry ye near ma heart. Twould've given me great comfort these long rotations ta know that ye were there." Now she became serious, "Please forgive me fer bein' so unkind 'n thoughtless. I must tell ye now before I burst, 'n please dunna think less 'o me 'n forgive me fer assumin' I could even feel this way but..." she paused and took a deep breath, "I love ye, 'n I've known it since we first touched hands in Noonday."

No words could have shocked me more, and yet been the very words that I had been yearning for. I responded, "Camphoria. I feel the same about you, but we will have to save this conversation till I get you back aboard the Betty-Lou. I heard you talking to someone else. Who is with you?"

"Ye will'na believe it, M'Lord. Tis yer father, Robert Livingston!" she told me, tears streaming down her smiling face.

Now it was my turn to sob and I nearly lost the connection. "My father, Bert?" I asked.

"He be right there." She said as she pointed to a man with long shaggy hair, dressed in rags.

"Hello father. I am Gideon, your son. I can't believe that you have been found after all these cycles! I'm come to get you out." I said, tears now streaming down my face.

"Son! Words canna tell how much I've missed ye 'n yer mother. I canna believe how ye've grown, and ta be the Fire Lord Reborn ta boot!" He said as he kneeled, letting the chains dangle from his arms as he raised them to the heavens. "Blessed be the God of all heaven who has answered m'prayers!"

"Dad, I have little time. I must explore the ship a bit. Ye will see a green mist, that'll be me. We are on our way to come get ye both!"

I dematerialized and flowed to the top of the stairs where a locked door barred the way. I flowed through the keyhole and out into the ship proper. I got my bearings as to where the prisoners were. They were in the bottom most section, aft, Camphoria in one corner and my father in the other.

"I've got to give a signal to the Betty-Lou as to our whereabouts," I thought

I flowed over the deck and then overboard onto the side of the ship. I looked around and saw that we were in a cloud bank and there would be no direct line of sight. I could not tell where the Betty-Lou was nor she the pirate ship.

I thought, "Maybe I could signal her by sending a shaft of green flame up into the sky, but that would alert them."

Then I realized, "Eventhough men flew in the skies, in

three dimensions, it is difficult to not think in two dimensions. Besides, they'll not be looking under the ship."

I sent a shaft of green flame directly downward beneath the ship, hoping that the crew would be able to see it from the Betty-Lou.

I could not stay long. Someone was bound to see the green mist trail sooner or later. I followed the green shaft down until I exited the cloud. I concentrated and burned the side of the hill directly beneath us just in case they had not seen the green light. I retraced my path back to the brig and my father and Camphoria.

"Ok, it is done. Be patient and we will be here soon." I projected my image again and gave them the biggest smile I could muster. I waved good bye and broke the connection.

<Betty-Lou, did they see it?> I asked.

<Aye Lad, and we be only waitin' fer yer next part 'o the plan. Ye've found yer father! Blessed be.>

"Captain Livingston! We found Bert!" I called as I poked my head out of my quarters.

"M'son Bert be alive? Glory be!" Exclaimed Grandfather.

"Are we ready for the slight of hand?" I asked.

"Aye, aye, Sire. We be ready." Grandfather saluted me and grinned. "This is goin' ta be utterly enjoyable! I owe a few things ta that Red Hand lot and fer Bert's sake, I mean ta make'em pay dearly. They won't know what hit 'em."

I returned to my quarters to sit at the comfortable reading chair by the desk. I concentrated on enveloping the Betty-Lou with a thick cloud of smoke. Since it was dark, the pirates wouldn't notice that it was green. While keeping the cloud of smoke in place, I turned the ship invisible.

<Thanks Betty-Lou. Your bells of practice are coming in handy!>

<So, now yer not complain'n! I just hope it were enough, we be dependin' on ye.>

<Don't worry. I've got a lot riding on this too! I won't fail them, or you. Take us to the Red Hand ship Betty-Lou.>

<Hang on ta yer hats. Here we go!>

She wasn't kidding. I nearly fell out of the chair, the jolt of speed was so great.

<We should be there 'n back again afore they know it,> Betty-Lou stated with a hint of glee.

As to how we would get them out of the ship, we had a plan for that too.

This is what happened. We snuck up, still invisible, to the bottom aft of the ship. Through her ring, I informed Camphoria and my father to stay away from the burning holes that appeared in the bottom of their cells. Then we freed them from their chains and quietly lowered them down to the Betty-Lou. Once we had them safely aboard, I projected a ship-sized image of the Fire Lord in the clouds and appeared to be looking for the ship while Betty Lou returned to the smoke cloud as fast as she could.

In my deepest booming voice I shouted, "Aha! There you are!" and I pointed to the ship with my serrated green sword. I held just a stick in reality, but they didn't know that. "Where be yer cowardly captain?" I demanded, knowing that this would rile them up like nothing else. The worst thing you could call a pirate was a coward.

As expected, the captain smugly swaggered into view.

"Release the prisoner and I will not destroy yer ship and crew." I demanded, emphasizing the words with gouts of green flame from the sword.

He looked at me, smiled and said, "No."

"What? Ye dare to defy me order?" I was having too much fun with this.

"Give me the ransom I be askin' for 'n I may not kill the lass." The pirate captain said, unconcerned.

"What be yer name so as ta know who will suffer my wrath?" I demanded.

"Ye canna make demands ta me. If ye want ta see the lassy alive, ye must do as I say." The pirate said confidently.

"Insolent cur! If ye will not give her ta me, I will take

her!" I turned my sword into a fiery snake that went straight for the cocky pirate commander. He ducked as well as did all the crew. I made the snake circle the ship horizontally, burning all the sails, then I made it go beneath the ship and come up the other side. I changed the snake back to the sword again and moved the image of the Fire Lord's face to almost touch noses with the captain. "Captain no name, ye think that we be finished with this. If I ever see you again, you will wish that I turned ye ta ashes this night!" With that I dissipated the image but lingered as mist just to see what would happen.

The pirate captain shouted to his crew, "Put out those fires and you, check on the prisoner."

The pirates had buckets of water ready and went into action.

A moment later the pirate came running up from below deck. "Cap'n Easely, the Queen's daughter 'n the other prisoner be gone. Two holes burned right through the bottom 'o the ship!"

Captain Easely ripped his hat off and threw it on the ground. "Damn the Fire Lord!"

I broke the connection and mentally returned to the Betty-Lou. She was visible but still hidden in a cloud of smoke. I addressed the crew. "Our plan worked flawlessly. Well done all!" I cheered. "Not only did we rescue Camphoria, but also my father, without single injury or loss of life. The rebellion cannot succeed based on my powers alone. Today, a united resistance overcame a cunning a wiley foe. Tonight we place a spark of doubt in them and tomorrow we will fan the flames until everyone knows that we can fight against pirates and the Overlord!"

Amidst handshaking, backslapping, and congratulations I worked my way to the galley where we had decided that Camphoria, and now my father also, should first go to get a decent meal. I had taken one step into the galley and a jubilant Camphoria rushed up to me and embraced me. I returned the embrace and we stood there for a few moments, oblivious to the onlookers in the galley…indeed, oblivious to the world.

Finally, I looked down to see what the pirates had done to Camphoria. She was thin, ragged and careworn, but through the dirt and grime, she was still beautiful.

"Did you eat your meal already? I asked as we disengaged but still held both hands.

"Nay, we've been waitin' fer ye. Come join us." She said and pulled me to the table.

For the first time, I realized who the other people were at the table. Captain Bragg, though haggard and thinner, was as happy as before. My father, Robert Livingston, was sitting next to his father, Ariel Livingston, both beaming and smiling joyfully. I sat next to Camphoria who sat next to her father.

"You all must be famished! Dig…" I was interrupted by my father.

"Yer majesty, beggin' yer pardon, may we say grace upon the food and thank the Lord above for his kind mercies in returning myself and Camphoria ta ye'all?

"Of course, father. Will you do the honors?" I asked.

We all held hands and bowed our heads as my father poured out his thanks to God. Not a one of us had a dry eye at the end of the prayer, but all were smiling.

Twas a gran night, full of laughter, sharing of news and remembrances and joyful beyond measure. I knew that Camphoria and my father would need to wash and put clean clothes on and have a good night sleep in a bed, so I sent them to their quarters, though they complained fiercely. The rest also I sent to their quarters because we would have another big day tomorrow.

CHAPTER 35 FAN THE FLAMES

(Extracted Directly from the Personal Log book of Gideon Livingston, the Fire Lord)

At the Shoals the next morning. We expected Red Hand to seek retribution. So we waited, alert. We traveled to Asombre knowing they were watching us. We arrived at the city of Polgro in the late morning. We wanted witnesses to what was going to happen and we also had some business to take care of.

I went with Captain Bragg to visit Gavin Rookler at the Crag Cantina, his favorite hang-out. We found him slumped in the corner in a disheveled heap. He apparently had not heard what happened with Red Hand or maybe he did but didn't care. Either way, he had to have known that Captain Bragg would be seeing him.

"Mornin' Gavin." Captain Bragg pronounced. "Mind if we 'ave a seat?"

"Wha,?" Gavin raised his drunken head. "Oh, tis only you Jasper."

Captain Bragg turned to me and asked, "Be that him?"

I nodded.

"How ye been these few cycles?" Captain Bragg asked.

"Between you, me, 'n a dragon's backside, its been bad, except for the last few cycles," Gavin shared and winked.

"You mean about six cycles ago, when ye sold me daughter ta the Red Hand pirates?" Captain Bragg accused.

"Yes, that be right....Oh, my. I didn't mean ta say that. What I meant ta say is that I came upon some good fortune." Gavin's aspect changed. All of the sudden he wasn't drunk anymore. "And good fortune continues ta favor me. It's brought me two 'o the most wanted persons on Portus!" Gavin said looking mighty pleased with himself.

We drew our swords but Gavin already had both of his swords in our bellies.

"Ye see, I knowed ye would come 'n when the Betty-Lou appeared, I knowed ye would come ta see little o'l me. Now we can do this the easy way, or the hard way. Which be it boys?"

Captain Bragg said, "The hard way suits me best." He and I then batted Gavin's blades on to the ground and ran our blades through his jacket, pinning him to the seat making sure he could not use an escape hatch like the Captain's Keel had.

He simply smiled and said, "Come 'n get 'em boys."

We heard boot steps behind us but never took our eyes off of Gavin. Several men approached behind us and as they neared, Gavin's smile faded when he saw our men and not his.

Captain Bragg commanded, "Bind this poor excuse for a rodent 'n take'im out inta the court yard for all to see!"

Already tied to the flag pole were the seven pirates who had been laying in wait to ambush us and take us prisoner. Captain Bragg stood on the podium next to the flag pole.

"Tie him to the fence up here on the podium. You there!" Captain Bragg said to a young boy watching the proceedings. "Go ring the bell and call the whole town to the square. Be quick about it." He tossed the young man a coin.

The boy caught it deftly, then ran with pleasure and gusto straight to the church. In a few moments, the bell was clanging loudly and folks came scurrying out to see what the ruckus was.

The mayor and a group of armed guards came bustling out of the largest building across from the church. They pushed through the gathering crowd of people and the mayor immediately began shouting, "I'm the may..."

"Shshshsh," Captain Bragg held up a finger to his lips. "Wait till they be all assembled."

"How dare you! I'll put you in chains, I'll..." the mayor blustered, but was interrupted by a circle of green flames surrounding him and his guards. Little by little the flames continued to tighten, forcing all of them into a small knot of bodies.

"Wait!" cried the mayor. "I didn't mean it. I am please ta see ye'all 'n thank ye fer apprehendin' that evil man 'n his henchmen, Gavin Rookler and the Red Hand pirates!"

I stopped the circle of flames from tightening and left them tight enough to singe their toes but not to burn them.

As news of what was happening spread, more and more people entered the square. Faces looking expectantly at Captain Bragg, the eight men tied in the middle, and the mayor and his guard encircled in green flames.

As if on cue, a pirate ship appeared above us. I noticed they had done a poor job of patching the two holes I and my crew had burned in the bottom.

A pirate shouted through a simple voice amplifier composed of a splayed wooden tube so all could hear, "Captain Bragg, release Gavin Rookler 'n our men. Ye have no right ta attack this here town 'n the lawful mayor. Release them ta boot. At the count 'o ten I'll start shootin'! One, two, three, four, five, six, seven, eight, nine...."

Also on cue, I heard a gasp from the crowd as the Betty-Lou appeared over their heads.

Colonel Cloudjumper who had the most booming voice shouted through an ornate dragon shaped voice amplifier, "Belay that command. Under orders of the Fire Lord, I arrest ye, Gavin Rookler, his men, the mayor 'n his guard fer kidnapin', lawlessness, malfeasance, theft, bribery, 'n many more crimes constitutin' conspiracy ta commit high treason against the people of Polgro in the continent of Asombre.

There were immediate cheers from the people, but the pirates shot anyway. The people screamed in terror. They were safe, though they did not know it. I had placed a barrier of superheated heated air between the pirate ship and the people on the ground. The metal balls exploded in the air harmlessly.

The Betty-Lou fired a cannonade full of salt-rock, knocking the crew of the pirate ship to their knees in pain.

"Pirates of the Red Hand. Surrender now, or the next shot will'na be salt-rock." Colonel Cloudjumper threatened. The crowd cheered extatically.

All while this was happening, I watched the face of Gavin Rookler transform from smug satisfaction when the pirate ship appeared to that of dismay when the Betty-Lou appeared.

Another cheer arose from the crowd when they saw the white flag run up the pirate's mast.

"Pirate ship of the Red Hand. Stand down 'n prepare ta be boarded." Colonel Cloudjumper commanded as the Betty-Lou pulled aside the ship and attached boarding grapples and a boarding plank.

All of us watched the proceedings with interest craning our necks to catch glimpses of what was occurring up there.

"Is all secured?" Captain Bragg shouted up to the ships.

"Yes, Captain Bragg." Replied the crewman. "... exceptin' that the captain 'o the Red Hand pirates be not aboard." The crewman shouted down.

"Good people of Polgro. This be the reason the captain 'o the pirates be not above, he be right here!" Captain Bragg exclaimed and pointed his sword to Gavin Rookler, "Be that not correct captain Easely?"

Once I had seen Gavin Rookler, I knew of a surety that he was Captain Easely, but according to Camphoria's description of her capture, we knew that Gavin was connected with the Red Hand in some way.

Gavin's face was bright red from fury. "Damn the Fire Lord!" he spat out.

"These men be the reason that ye be sufferin'." Captain Bragg pointed to the tied men, the mayor and his guard and the pirates above. "They've threatened, robbed, killed, 'n kidnapped ye fer too long. Three cheers for the Fire Lord!"

The town erupted with shouts, "Hurray, Hurray, Hurray!"

Then there fell a silent expectation and whispers, "Where be the Fire Lord?"

I took my place on the podium and signaled my father to come up to join me and Captain Bragg. Bert was clean and shaven and though new clothes and a bath helped, it could not erase cycles of suffering that shown in his skinny, malnourished frame.

I pulled out the serrated sword and held it aloft. Green flame surrounded it, me and everyone on the podium, then shot a beam high into the sky. The people gasped in amazement. I quickly put the sword away because I could already feel it draining me and I did not want to lose the mayor and his guard yet.

People of Polgro, even though you have not directly felt the tyranny of the Overlord and his Boar Riders, you know of it, and you have felt its effects right here. Your mayor has been in league with the Red Hand pirates and their captain." I looked scornfully at Gavin Rookler and the mayor. "What the pirates have stolen from you, the mayor received a portion for allowing it, and for not executing the law, but ignoring your pleas for justice!"

The people erupted in angry shouts, raising their fists and farm instruments. "Kill 'em!" they shouted.

"Let me finish, then ye can decide what to do with them. This man over here is my father, wrongfully imprisoned 16 cycles ago by his best friend. His crew and his ship were stolen and he being in a locked cell all this time, his friends and family thought him dead." I again pointed to Gavin Rookler. "But Gavin Rookler, nor Captain Easely, they are not his real names. His real name is Granger Rockland, born and raised on the island of Noonday, and he is the one man that has terrorized your town and many others, and that spitefully betrayed his friend."

The crowd growled with anger. More shouted, "Kill 'im!"

My father looked closely at Granger and I saw comprehension flood over him like a windstorm. He clenched his fists, and gritted his teeth for only a moment, then I saw him relax.

"With far less evidence, your Mayor, or the Overlord would have, without a moment's hesitation, done as ye ask. He would be executed, in other words murdered. You see though, if we do the same, that makes us no better than them. No better than those pirates who were only able to be pirates because evil men, like your mayor and others, allowed it." I paused to let my words sink in. The crowd was silent and pensive.

"Did you notice that in today's battle, not a single person got hurt or killed? Yet we won an undeniable victory. How did we do it? It wasn't just me as the powerful Fire Lord. We did it together, coming up with a plan, deciding what most needs to be done, and then doing it together. Killing is not what solves problems. Good laws and law-minding folks, like yourselves, are what solves problems."

If ye will permit me, I will take Granger Rockland here and give him 16 cycles in a cell with bread and water and straw for a bed as that is what my father had to endure. Look at my father." I signaled to him to step forward. "He could have chosen to be bitter and vengeful about his fate, but he is at peace because he knows that there is nothing he can do to Granger that will give him back the 16 lost cycles of his life. He knows that he must move forward rather than look behind. I propose that you all do the same. We will remain here for three rises to help you to choose good men and women to be your leaders to root out the evil that still remains. Some of those evil people are packing their things as we speak. I will let you deal justly with them, the mayor, his guard, their crooked friends and the pirate crew. Until you have decided what just punishment they deserve, lock them up. Remember that the laws must be enforced to be effective. To enforce laws you must be strong. Evil preys upon the weak, so be strong Polgro! Three cheers for a bright future for Polgro!"

"Hurrah, hurrah, hurrah!" The people chanted.

I motioned for quiet to be able to continue. "In this battle against evil in whatever form it takes, pirates or the Overlord, we need good men and women willing to strive against it. You have three rises to make your decision to join the resistance. All who wish to make a difference in this world must be on the ship the morning of the fourth rise from today. If you cannot go, but would like to help, we need stores and munitions for which we will pay with our own gold. We will be leaving on the first bell of the forenoon watch."

I released the mayor and his men as well as all the pirates, including those aboard the ship to the people of Polgro. We emptied the treasury of the mayor and the pirate ship and the hoard that Granger had acquired and gave it to the new Polgro leadership to distribute to the people of Polgro. We confiscated the pirate ship and cleaned and refitted it to make it habitable.

The people of Polgro selected a council of men and women to govern and execute the laws. News of what happened at Polgro spread throughout Asombre, and assuredly, beyond. At Polgro we picked up 50 volunteers who I was careful to interview to determine if they spoke the truth using my ability to detect falsehood.

We traveled to all the major cities in Asombre and Montora and had Polgro's own witnesses share what happened. Over all, we garnered 450 new volunteers for the resistance and both ships were full and well stocked. But we only had two ships.

Over the next four cycles we secretly visited over 30 cities and towns across the 13 kingdoms, arriving and departing invisibly. We told them about what became known as the Victory at Polgro. In every city we established or strengthened an underground movement and trained them how to be secret and safe but still recruiting resistance volunteers. We gave them chirp stones that they could use to communicate with us and us with them and a call sign to make sure that only those with the call sign could utilize the stone. I placed fire in a jewel that each leader possessed just in case I needed to immediately communicate with them.

CHAPTER 36 THE CALM BEFORE THE STORM

(Recreated from council reports and the memoirs of Fenworthy Stonebrow)

"Report!" Commanded the Overlord.

"We hear rumors, yer Majesty. The Fire Lord be recruitin' an army. Our spies see increased agitation among the people. The adjudicators are tryin' to stop it by puttin' the suspected rebels in prison, but that only has increased the anti-government sentiments," the spy reported.

The Deputy Minister, Forldon McWhorter, listened to the information with glee though he showed no indication of his happiness to the people present in the room. This is exactly what he was hoping to hear. It's been nearly a full rotation since the defeat of the armada and finally, now all his plans were coming to fruition.

"This is dire news, your Lordship. You must move to quash the malcontent of the people and their anti-government sentiments quickly." The Deputy Minister insisted. "We can use the completed Dread Naught ship with a display of force to strike fear in the people to show them that resistance is futile."

"Didn't you hear what this man said? That's what the adjudicators are doing and it's making it worse!" The Overlord countered. "What other ideas does the council propose?"

"We could arrange a truce meeting with the Fire Lord

and the resistance leaders and then capture them and make a public execution." One minister proposed.

"What about staging a bow and arrow competition to draw out the Fire Lord and then capture him for a public execution?" A senior minister offered.

"How about sending out a rumor that we are staging a crack-down on Gran Saline. The Fire Lord being a heroic figure will not be able to resist coming to save the people. Then we capture them for a public execution." A junior minister suggested and everyone nodded, especially Deputy Minister Forldon McWhorter.

<My plan worked perfectly. When I spoke with the junior minister, he jumped at the opportunity to increase his standing and he said exactly what I told him to say,> The Deputy Minister thought and allowed a nod and a smug smile of approval to flicker as the junior minister looked his way.

"That's no different than Forldon's plan. Force is not going to work." The Overlord refuted.

"You are correct yer Lordship. Force may not be the answer. We can send messages to the adjudicators for them to ease up on regulations, taxes and punishments. Have them show leniency for a time. We could have a public celebration of a new kinder, more empathetic and inclusive government and sign a decree to begin a new era of peace and prosperity," Fenworthy Stonebrow, the oldest minister proffered.

There was stunned silence.

"What about the capture and public execution, Fenworthy?" the Overlord sneered.

"There would be no need. The people would be mollified that we are listening to them, and they would view the Fire Lord and the resistance as rabble rousers and war mongers just wanting to cause trouble." The old minister responded.

Before the seed could take root, the Deputy Minister interceded, "What an utterly worthless plan. People will begin to think we are weak. The treasury will be depleted and worst of all, the people will think that we are accountable to them!" Forldon laughed and the others waited, watching how the Overlord would respond.

After a moment, the Overlord laughed, then the rest joined in, except for the old minister.

"Four cycles from now we will make Gran Saline an example for all the other cities that harbor rebel scum. We will break their spirits with a show of force at their most important celebration- Summer Solstice. We will spread the rumor everywhere, but not in Gran Saline, that the dread naught will destroy their city and the resistance. This will not be just a rumor though. We will do it whether the Fire Lord comes to rescue them or not. We will have the entire armada and the Boar Riders army hidden and ready and if the rebellion shows up, we will capture the Fire Lord. In a public execution, we will show the people of Portus once and for all that rebellion will be dealt with severely." The Overlord raised his hands and all but one minister cheered.

CHAPTER 37 THE FIRE LORD'S ARMADA

(Taken from the journals of Gideon Livingston, the Fire Lord.)

<This is too slow. We only have 12 resistance bases established so far. Our volunteer recruits are signing up, but we only have two airships. We do not have the fighting power to face the armada and the army of Boar Riders together. This cannot be just my battle. It has to be the battle of the people. If I defeat them alone, the people will view me as just another despot,> I mentally complained to Betty-Lou.

<The people be too poor to leave their workin' ta go ta war. They've not got ships ta donate nor arms ta provide. Ye are doing all ye can, but ye be right, it will'na be enough.>

<Leave their work, too poor...> the thought niggled at my brain. <If they are too poor to leave their work, what if their work was to build ships, and make arms? What if we approach Asombre, who the Overlord does not rule, so they can make weapons and ships for us. We have plenty of money from the dragon treasure. We could pay them to get us ready for the rebellion.!> I shared, relieved that there might be a solution.

<Aye lad, tis a gran idea with possibilities. I've another that may be of interest to ye,> Betty-Lou offered <What about the lost ships? I am sure that many 'o them would join ye and they be in prime condition. We just need ta provide captains ta be their companions.>

<Do you think you can find them?> I asked.

<I lived amongst them fer 100 hundred cycles, I know where they might be. With a little huntin' we can find 'em.>

<Excellent! I love it when things come together. I'll talk to Captain Livingston to set up the factories in Asombre. Then I'll talk to Captain Bragg to see who has airship experience and is captain quality and get volunteers to go with us to find the lost ships.>

Dear Fire Lord.

I am a senior minister in the counsel of the Overlord. I fear greatly for my life and for the future of Portus. They have lost all compassion and desire to serve the people, which was their first duty. The Overlord and the other ministers, especially the Deputy Minister have all gone mad. They would rather see the people destroyed than lose power over them. They will not see reason. I see you and the rebellion as the only salvation for Portus.

I must warn you. In four cycles, at the summer celebration, they plan on attacking Gran Saline and destroying the city and all the inhabitants as an example for the other cities. They hope to lure you into their trap to capture you and execute you. You must not come to Gran Saline.

Signed,
Fenworthy Stonebrow
Senior Minister

I read the message over and over. "Do I go to Gran Saline to save the people only to fall into the Overlord's trap, or do I let them be destroyed to further anger the people?" I said to myself in a whisper.

<Ye canna use the Overlord ta arouse the people by sacrificin' innocent souls. I know ye know this, so what be botherin' ye really?>

<I know what I need to do, I doubt if I'm ready and I feel that the people are not ready either. There's just so many things to do!>

<Me thinks ye be underestimatin' the will ta fight that glows strong in this people. Ye said it yerself to the people of Polgro, 'n they believed ye! They'll rise ta yer expectations if ye give 'em a chance.>

I hated being away from the war preparations on a mission that may or may not result in success. We had only a general idea of where the Floating Mist Island may be and it could take us full lunar cycles to find it.

<'n it could take us only a blink of an eye,> Betty-Lou interrupted my thoughts

<Thank you. My world would be bleak without your optimism!>

<Dunna mention it. Glad ta oblige,> Betty-Lou responded cheerfully.

I asked Betty-Lou, <Is there no way of contacting them?>

<I be in contact with them at all times.>

<Well ask them where they are, please.>

<What does that mean ta someone what dunna care where he be? They could'na tell me where they be, 'cause they dunna know themselves. They be lost, remember?>

<Fine! We'll keep searching blindly,> I retorted, exasperated.

A few more rotations passed with no sign of the floating lost islands or the ghost ships. Then Betty-Lou informed me, <We've found 'em!>

I ran topside and sure enough, we were approaching a bank of mist. Normal pilots would avoid this if they saw it.

I nodded to Captain Bragg who looked at me with, "Should we go in?"

"Approach at slow speed Mr. Pulsey and take us right into the mist." He commanded.

We entered the mist and it became dark, even though it was bright morning. The normal noises of wind and sail were eliminated as I got darker and darker.

"Man the light stone, and shine 'er round 'bout." Captain Bragg ordered.

Nothing but more mist was seen for a few moments. Then we saw some eddies and darker shadows.

"Full stop Mr. Pulsey."

<They be all around us,> Betty informed.

<Can you talk to them?> I asked.

<Aye, but ye need ta do it, not me.>

I requested the loud speaking tube that Colonel Cloudjumper used in Polgro. "If you can hear me. I am Gideon Livingston, grandson of Ariel Livingston whom many of you met when he was my age. He was chosen by one of you, the Betty-Lou, on which I stand before you. I have two hundred fine captains aboard this airship. I know you seek companionship and release from your long wait. We need your assistance in fighting the injustice and malice that brought you here and that still threatens the world. We have the will and determination, but we lack the means to make it happen. If Captain Sorenson be among you please make yourself known." I put down the tube and we waited.

I was annoyed by the whispering noises, but no one else seemed to be affected.

About two bells passed before we were approached by a ship. It was an old-style ship, hanging from a large buoyancy tank painted to look like an eagle in flight.

I greeted the ship with a smile. I said as heartily as I could, "Welcome. Thank you for responding!"

In my mind, as if Betty-Lou were talking to me, I heard these words. <I be Johnathan. Captain Sorenson died several cycle past. We will help you. Present yer captains and we will choose.>

"I will bring the captains and their crews one by one to be presented to you." I responded out loud for the crew's benefit.

All of the sudden I heard a commotion of talking <He

can hear us!> a woman's voice sounded in my head. An old woman cackled, "No one 'as been able ta hear us a'fore,> A deep man's voice said <He be the one foretold,> A child's voice said, <After so many cycles, he is here!> Many other voices were talking excitedly all at once.

<Stop!> I shouted mentally. <I cannot understand you if you all talk at once. Please take your turns talking to me.>

There was shocked silence then I heard a familiar voice. <I think I can help ye with this. If ye'all would be so kind as ta talk with me, a'fore ye direct yer comments ta the Fire Lord, I think t'would help relieve the burden.>

I heard many "gladly's and "of course's and there was silence.

<Thank you Betty-Lou!>

She smiled. How I knew she smiled, I'm not sure. I guess I just felt it.

I lined up the captains and their two or three crew members on the deck and had them circling and taking turns presenting themselves at the boarding entrances on each side of the Betty-Lou. I thought moving the men would save time instead of having the ships do the circling. The men introduced themselves one by one until a ship accepted them and they boarded and the next ship pulled along-side the Betty-Lou. This process took us till the second dogueral watch when the last of the Captains boarded a ship. We had manned a full 200 ships with fine men and women captains.

<How many ships be there without a captain?> I asked. I heard a multitude of replies all at once.

<There be fifty three still not manned m'Lord> Betty-Lou responded. She had never called me anything other than lad or laddy.

<If you wish, those who are able to choose a captain but have not, may follow us to our fortress. There we have many men and women from whom you can choose,> I offered.

I heard many assents of approval.

It was a grand sight to behold. We left with one ship and returned with 254 ships. Shouts and cheers were heard all over the fortress as we arrived and resistance volunteers flooded out to the ample mooring rock to help attach all of the ships.

When we moored them all, I had Captain Bragg choose good volunteers to be presented as captains of the 53 remaining ships.

Captain Livingston reported that the people of Asombre were tired of the pirates that inhabited the Isles of Montora. They wanted to be able to defend themselves and were eager to create the weapons that we required. They had already begun to create, shafts, razor circles, crossbows, slings and other projectile weapons. There were two factories that could produce the larger weapons such as the flame throwers, harpoon launchers, and sulfur cannons.

Would we be ready in time? I wondered.

CHAPTER 38 FINAL CONFRONTATION

(Compiled from records obtained from the Gran Saline Historical Archives, rebel forces documents discovered in the house of George Sandstill, excerpts from the personal journal of Gideon Livingston, the Fire Lord, and the journal of Camphoria Livingston.)

It was the last rise before the Summer Solstice celebration at Gran Saline. Our spies had told us that the Boar Riders and the Armada were hidden all around the town. Of course, we had a large resistance in Gran Saline and the ranks grew even larger, especially after the news of the Overlord's plan became well known. The local resistance force was given the task of helping the women and children leave the town without alerting the town leaders. This mass exodus occurred under the very nose of the Adjudicator, since the very day I received the letter from the senior minister. I personally connected with the leader of the resistance to have him inform the townsfolk, without the Adjudicator finding out, and get the women with children, the old and feeble out of town immediately. I even sent a message to Cirulea, the Pirate Queen to ask for her aid on that day.

All the remaining men and women had three cycles to prepare the parade celebrations and the fireworks show. All our men, ships and equipment arrived one full cycle ahead of the Boar Riders. The Armada and the dreadnaught showed up only two rises ago.

It had been an absolute pleasure having my father work

at my side the last few cycles. Each day he looked healthier and younger. While we worked, I spent the time talking with him and telling him about my life and how my mother and I had got along. I shared with him all of the amazing things that had happened over the past solar cycle. He listened avidly and ask many questions. His time in captivity had made him strong, not in a physical way, but spiritually. He constantly referred to God as a loving Father who he knew personally. From my father, I gained a new perspective that destiny was not up to chance, but was guided by our loving creator.

I also found time to work next to Camphoria. She had blossomed and was fully recovered from her time in the cell. She was more beautiful than ever. In the limited times we had together, she did most of the talking and I loved to listen to her talk about her favorite things, her challenges and what she liked to do. We also talked about the future and what was in store for both of us.

"Ye canna think that life will return ta normal. What be normal now? When the resistance be over, and ye be the king, will we not be e'en more busy than now?" Camphoria asked and held my hand after I put down the paint brush.

"Everyone expects me to be the king." I enclosed her in my arms and continued, "I'm not sure that is what the people need. I might be a good king, but my sons and grandsons may not be, or may be overthrown by some other power-hungry man or woman. Remember when you told me what was most important to my father? Freedom will make all the difference, freedom to govern themselves. Freedom for us will mean that even if we are busier than ever, it will be our choice, and that will bring happiness."

We stood there for a while, holding each other. I spoke up, "I want you to know that whatever happens tomorrow, I will always love you. You are the light of my life and the joy for my soul." I looked down at her and saw tears in her eyes. No more words were necessary. We kissed gently and picked up our paint brushes.

We had finished just before dawn. All of our plans were laid. I sat next to Camphoria, taking a rest, I recalled the words I had said to the original crew at Noonday. They were never more true than today. I had them written and given to the commanders of each group to read this morning. I stood up and gathered my little band and quietly read the words.

> *"We are facing the entire might of the Overlord's armada. For some of us this is our first battle. I know you feel fear. Courage is not the lack of fear, it is the domination of it. The will to keep struggling and fighting when facing a terrible foe is the essence of bravery. We have something they do not. Our cause is right. We fight for our freedom, for our families and our children. And that my dear comrades, makes all the difference, for the God of truth and right will help us and send his angels to watch over us. Do not falter! Do not hesitate in performing your duties. I promise you as Fire Lord, I will fight to protect each and everyone of you with my last breath. What say ye? Will ye fight beside me?"*

All in the warehouse raised their brooms and paintbrushes high and mouthed a silent cheer.

"Now go eat, take a nap, build up your strength. At midday, blend in with all of the other people when night falls, take your positions." I shooed them all off with a smile.

(Reconstructed from the writings of Racheal Piedrelle, then personal secretary to the Mayor of Gran Saline)

"Any sign of the traitors yet?" the Overlord asked.

"I know they will be here. They think to surprise us, but we are ready. I have look-outs stationed on all the buildings around the town. I have troops hidden in strategic places. The entire armada is hidden in a nearby forest. They won't know what hit them." *And you won't know what hit you,* The Deputy

Minister said and thought. The anticipation of seeing the look of surprise in the Overlord's face when his own Deputy Minister becomes the new Overlord was hard to bear.

(Taken from journal and personal memoirs of Jacobus Hleghter, of Iron Feld, survivor of the battle of Gran Saline.)

We waited silently in the dark caves and grottos underneath the city of Gran Saline. We had been given strict instructions to not come out until we heard the signal. Few knew of the existence of these caves, and fewer knew that they connected to nearly every part of the city. But the Deputy Minister knew of them. That is why he chose Gran Saline for his take over.

At the signal, we were to flow out of the secret entrances in the city of Gran Saline, and kill anyone not wearing a boar rider uniform. In return for this slaughter, Ironfeld would get a seat on the council and each individual warrior would get a sack of gold.

(Extracted Directly from the Personal Log book of Gideon Livingston, the Fire Lord)

The people were out in the streets at midday, all dressed up in colorful costumes and masks. Everyone headed toward the center of Gran Saline where all types of food and beverages were sold and the people played games of chance and skill in hopes of getting a prize. There were singers, choirs, dancing groups, theater troupes, minstrels, and jugglers everywhere. In the very middle of the town sat the raised pavilion where the Overlord and his ministers would most assuredly be. There were no children, or old folk however, which gave me great comfort. They were safe.

I and Camphoria spent time trying some food and playing tossing games in which, she was much better than me. We both wore masks, crowns, and colorful flowing robes of a king and queen. We saw many of our comrades doing the same as us, staying alert, but enjoying their time. In fact, most of the people on the street were part of the resistance. And the Overlord and his underlings had no clue.

As soon as darkness fell, the parade started. Fireworks lit the night sky to shouts of glee and awe from the people. 200 large, delivery-hog driven carts slowly made their way down the center of the main roads with their loads of decorated floats. They came from the highest part of the city to the center, which was the lowest. The theme for the parade was obvious, "Airships Through the Ages." Cart after cart carried full-sized painted airships from the very oldest kinds to the most modern. They were all painted, some in bright oranges, greens and yellows. Some had clouds painted on them with flocks of birds flying through them. One was a night sky studded with stars and all sorts of sky creatures. Others depicted pastoral scenes of red flowers in the fields, or majestic forests. Others were of pure fantasy showing clouds of fairies, dancing nymphs and gnomes playing musical instruments. Each was a masterpiece and brought cheers of delight from the crowds watching the spectacle. As they passed the central pavilion, even the nobility were amazed and awed.

Everyone was in position and I hurried to get Camphoria and I into our positions. We had to be directly in front of the central pavilion with an unobstructed view.

When half of the airships had passed the central pavilion, all the carted airships stopped moving. In unison, they rose up from their carts into the air one ship length in height.

The crowd cheered in delight. Then the fireworks began from the highest part of the city. Lighting the airships and making the scenes painted on them come alive with color and movement. The sky was full of the colored rockets, booms, sizzles and cracks. No one noticed that there were other booms, sizzles and cracks happening in the forest to the south of the city.

When the colored rockets were depleted. The central

airship lowered to the ground while the others remained aloft, making a circle around the central pavilion. Light stone projectors lit the ship brightly. The gang plank was lowered and a green glowing Fire Lord descended with his serrated sword extended toward the Overlord.

One of the light stone projectors from the ships lighted the Overlord as he stood and shouted, “Arrest that man!”

Troops from all sides, seemingly out of nowhere, ran with bayonets to comply with the Overlords command.

The man quickly took off his beard, his shiny outfit and threw his glittering wooden sword on the ground. He then bowed and the audience erupted in laughter, cheers and applause.

The Boar Riders surrounded the terrified man and were ready to take him off when the Overlord laughed loudly. “What a funny joke! Leave the fellow.” And the Overlord applauded, at which time all of his ministers and the nobility of the town did also. The man who pretended to be the Fire Lord was none other than our own Deputy Navigator, Granite Pulsey.

With the light still shining upon him, the Overlord shouted, “Bring them forward.”

The crowd gasped in dismay as a group of 20 Boar Riders came forward, each guiding bound prisoners with black sacks over their heads.

“Adjudicator, pronounce the charges!” The Overlord commanded and there were cries and sobbing heard.

The white wigged adjudicator stood and commanded the troops, “Remove the head coverings.”

A woman’s voice rose above the nervous murmuring, “Please no, dunna hurt ‘im!”

He then held out a parchment which he began to read, “For crimes against the Overlord, treachery, treason, and subterfuge. For seeking the overthrow of the legitimate government of Portus. For harboring fugitives, for smuggling, for possession of illegal arms, for unauthorized gathering…”

I searched the faces of the people bound. I recognized three of them as members of the resistance in Gran Saline. One was a member of my crew. And there in the middle, was Camphoria. I looked to my side and she was gone. They must have grabbed twenty random citizens, not knowing that most of them were not citizens.

While the adjudicator droned on, I thought to Betty-Lou <Is the armada destroyed?>

<Yes it is, m'Lord 'n we had some help.>

<Help? Never mind, come quickly and quietly and surround the town.>

<Yes, right away, dunna fear, she will be alright!>

"...for these and many other illegal acts, these people are sentenced to immediate death."

The crowd shrieked and cried, "Murderer!" "Ye canna do this! It be evil!" "They be innocent!" "You foul monster, filthy Overlord!" and more.

"Ready, Aim, Fire!" shouted the adjudicator.

CHAPTER 39
HIDDEN ARMADA

(Compiled from the log book and personal journal of Commander Jennifer Cragg, surviving member of the Armada.)

"This is going to be a glorious victory!" I mused.

"All is prepared Commander Cragg," my Lieutenant reported.

Hidden in the forest, outside of the city, the entire armada of the Grand Overlord waited for the signal of the red fire rockets to begin their attack on the forces of the Fire Lord. So far, no sign of the rebel forces had been seen. Over two hundred airships of all sizes, were moored amongst the tall trees, ready to cast off and race to the city center. My ship, the dreadnaught, and my squadron of 75 airships was assigned to take down the demon dragon ship at all costs. One third of the airships were to engage the Fire Lord's ground troops dropping explosive stones and fire sands on their heads, while the last third was to enter the city from all sides, low enough for their contingents of Boar Riders to slide down on ropes to surround and engage the Fire Lord troops.

All was prepared, but for me, worse than the fear and terror of battle, was the waiting. I was uncomfortably standing at attention on the forecastle of my airship, the Lightning Bolt, searching the skies for the red rock sparklers, and trying to stay focused on the task at hand. We had arrived a full cycle before the celebration and within a few rotations had hidden all the airships in the forest. Not one ship could be seen from the air as the tops of our ballast tanks had been painted with color of green leaves of the forest and shaded by the enormous old-growth trees.

"All that we have waited for will come to fruition tonight," I shared.

"Yes Commander. Your name will be recorded in history as the great Commander Cragg that destroyed the Dragon," the Lieutenant responded.

I smiled at the thought. Too long had the Dragon been free to taunt our forces with the humiliating defeat at Noonday. It ends tonight.

(Reconstructed from the journals of Captain Ariel Livingston.)

Captain Livingston reflected as he waited for evening to come, low to the beach, knowing that the armada could not see them through the trees, <I be aboard the Betty-Lou and Sir Percival Kendrick aboard the Penelope Stalwart, whose be captain Abrielle Lunafiel. Fifty three ships will follow us into battle. All these ships be positioned ta attack the armada.>

<That be correct Ariel,> Betty-Lou confirmed.

<With the element of surprise, though the Overlord's armada be larger, I believe that the odds of winning will be in our favor, especially since our plan will not let them get off the ground,> Captain Livingston mentioned.

<It must be a completely coordinated attack. There canna be mistakes,> Betty-Lou responded.

<When ye informed the other ships 'n their captains 'bout the plan, they all understood 'n be ready?>

<Aye sir, they be ready.>

<So as soon as the first sky crackers and rock sparklers go off, we commence the attack.>

<They will'na see us comin'!>

(Taken from the journal of Abrielle Lunafiel and Sir Percival

Kendrick.)

"Captain Lunafiel, is all at a ready?" Sir Kendrick asked.

"Yes sir. For the one hundredth time. All is ready," she replied, "Everything will go as planned. Trust us."

"Then why do I feel that something is going to go awry? The plan is sound, we have the element of surprise, and we have the high position of attack. What could fail?" Sir Kendrick wondered.

"We've got perfect weather, the troops are rested and they are well trained. Nothing can go wrong," Captain Lunafiel encouraged.

"The sun is descending, broadcast to the other ships that they should be at the ready."

"As you wish sir."

(Compiled from the log book and personal journal of Commander Jennifer Cragg, surviving member of the Armada.)

"Commander! The first sky sparklers have been set off," the lieutenant exclaimed and pointed in the sky over Gran Salina.

"It should be anytime now that the red ones are used. Patience, Lieutenant."

An insistent buzzing startled me and drew my attention away from the show in the sky, to the chirpstone sitting in the metal resonator. "Commander! We are under attack. Hundreds of airships approach from the sea! We could'na see them until the sky rockets went off."

"Lieutenant, light a red fire rocket and attack the airships."

(Compiled from the log book and personal journal of Sir Percival Kendrick and the journal of Captain Lunafiel.)

"What's that over there?" Sir Kendrick asked.

"It's only red sky sparkler being shot out of the forest," responded Captain Lunafiel.

"Why the forest? Why not the city?" Sir Kendrick questioned.

"Look Sir, the armada is rising from among the trees! See how the sky sparklers light up their ballast tanks?...Oh no! That means that we are as visible to them as they are to us! We didn't think of the light from the sky rockets!"

"Tell all ships to attack immediately! Don't let them clear the trees!" ordered Sir Kendrick.

"So much for surprise! It will be a hard-fought battle and we'll be lucky to survive," Captain Lunafiel pointed out, then shouted, "To battle stations! Fire at will!"

(Compiled from the memoirs of Lieutenant Jonathan Trueweather and the logbooks of Commander Jennifer Cragg.)

"Look Commander. There be the Dragon ship!"

"Fire all cannons. Fire the grappling hooks! Pull her down!" Commander Cragg shouted.

Multiple explosions belched from the side of the steel-clad dreadnaught, but the swift dragon zigged and zagged through them all with no harm, except one of the grappling hooks had found its mark. The dragon struggled to break free. Without the ability to maneuver, she was an easy target.

"Bring her down!" clamored the commander.

But even being attached to the dreadnaught, the dragon was able fly in circles, and amazingly avoid the barrage of sulfur bombs shot at her.

Then the dragon began a new tactic. It flew straight at the dreadnaught, performed a roll at the last moment, circled in on itself and flew away at top speed. The firing of weapons had ceased, so astounded we were at this maneuver.

"Fire you idiots!" shouted Commander Jennifer Cragg.

At that moment, we felt a huge jerk, heard a tremendous grinding, and then a loud crack. We looked over the side of the ship and found that the dragon ship had ripped a hole in the side of the dreadnaught and where the grappling winch was housed was nothing. We looked to see the dragon ship once again hurtling towards us, then at the last moment veer away.

"What does she think she is doing? Trying to intimidate us? This ship is impervious to even her lightning bolts. She cannot harm us!" Commander Cragg laughed.

Then to our horror, we saw what the dragon ship was doing. Flying towards our ballast tank above us, at the end of the grappling chain, was the heavy grappling winch which the dragon ship had whipped with tremendous speed, like the tail of a snap dragon whips a bug out of the air. The concussion completely ruptured the ballast tank, throwing the dreadnaught into a slow descending spiral to the ground.

(Taken from the journal of Abrielle Lunafiel and Sir Percival Kendrick.)

The sky rockets from the city lit the sky along with the sulfur cannon blasts and exploding ballast tanks of the armada. Just as the first airships of the armada cleared the trees, another set of ships dropped down from above. These ships rained down loads of fire sand and explosive stones upon the unsuspecting armada ships. The air above the armada became filled with deadly razor discs and explosive sulfur bombs launched from ships above.

A cheer went up from the rebel vessels as ship after ship of the armada sank to the forest on fire or crippled.

The resistance ships, rained destruction upon the Overlord's ships that tried to escape, staying out of the line of fire of the ships above them and preventing any armada ship from escaping.

"Ahoy there!" came the call from the lead ship from above. "We saw ye needed assistance! Be there more we can do?" As the ship descended, the pirate flag was clearly visible in the glittering sparks from the rockets.

"Sir, the Betty-Lou has relayed a message from the Fire Lord. They be under a fearsome attack in the city and request our aid!" Captain Lunafiel exclaimed.

"Let the pirate ships know to go to Gran Saline and aid the Fire Lord!" Sir Kendrick directed.

CHAPTER 40 THE BATTLE OF GRAN SALINE

(Extracted directly from the Personal Log book of Gideon Livingston, the Fire Lord)

All the flying crossbow bolts directed at the 20 bound prisoners hit a wall of superheated air and turned to ash. Then the crossbows of each Boar Riders burst into flames. The first sword that was raised melted into slag and severely burned the Boar Rider's hand. That is when I ripped off my costume and on jets of flame, flew between the prisoners and the Boar Riders. Hundreds of Boar Riders rushed from all sides. I pulled out the serrated sword and called upon the fury of Portus. It boiled up from my feet and I concentrated it into the sword. I shouted to the prisoners, "Lie down now!" They immediately fell to the ground as I swung the sword in a tight circle. Green flame gushed from the sword circling every Kingsman that came to attack me with ropes of green fire. I raised the sword in the air and 150 Boar Riders rose off the ground. I disarmed them and their weapons rained to the ground. I shouted, "You have dishonored the royal seal of the scrybeast for the last time!"

I was so angry I could have crushed them, but I heard Camphoria cry, "No, m'Lord, they be followin' orders."

I slowly set them down and said, "Be gone!" Amidst bows and "Thank ye"s all of them ran away.

Hundreds of my resistance fighters rushed from the streets and from the ships to the center pavilion area to aid me and to free the prisoners. One by one as they were freed each of the twenty ran over to pick up one of the swords of the runaway Boar Riders.

Camphoria cried again, "Beloved, behind ye!"

I turned just in time to see a sword deflected by my father, Bert's blade. "I'll take the Deputy Minister, go get the Overlord."

The Overlord's guard was ready for me. I dare not use more power from the serrated sword for fear of fainting so I put the blade away. They grinned and advanced. I melted their blades as they raise them to attack, then they turned and ran screaming while holding their burned hand.

While I chuckled as I watched them flee, the Overlord attacked. Instinctively I pulled out the serrated blade to protect me and instantly I was surrounded by an impenetrable barrier. The Overlord's sword-strike simply bounced off of me with a loud clang. I hit the Overlord on the chin with the hilt of the sword. He slumped down in an unconscious heap. I put the serrated sword away and the protective barrier disappeared.

I ran over to my father, who was still in a fierce sword battle with the Deputy Minister. Both were expert swordsmen, though it was obvious that my father was out of practice and tiring rapidly.

"My turn!" I picked up a sword from the ground and easily stepped between my father and the Deputy Director and picked up where he left off.

"I hope you are a better swordsman than your father. It will be my pleasure to kill you both." He said and lunged.

I deflected and swatted him on the rump with the flat of my blade as he passed. He turned and tried every attack possible and was met with my blade and a slap with the flat of my blade on the hand, side, hip and arm. Colonel Cloudjumper had taught me well.

I smiled, which infuriated him even more. He attacked with all the speed and fury he possessed. I parried easily and one by one relieved him of the buttons on his jacket. I parried and cut his left cheek, another parry and his right cheek. I needed to end this, so I spun his blade around pretending to disarm him, for which he was prepared. What he was not prepared for was my foot in his midsection. He dropped the blade as he was propelled backward.

"You think you have won! You will die tonight! Fire Lord!" Forldon McWhorter groaned, then before I could get to him, he pulled a stone out of each pocket and crashed them together. Immediately the pavilion upon which the unconscious Overlord lay erupted in an explosion.

I was thrown backward, landing hard, knocking the breath from me and making my head ring with the force of the explosion.

"Bind him would you please." I requested of my father, who had been knocked down as well.

As my hearing returned, I sensed other sounds that came to my ears. Much clanging of metal and shouting. I looked around me and the fire of the ruined pavilion lit the scene eerily. I saw my men locked in battle with the remaining Boar Riders and it appeared that we were winning.

I looked for Camphoria and saw her in combat with a much larger Boar Rider. She expertly parried and attacked, which surprised her opponent who undoubtedly did not expect her strength. In that moment of hesitation, she disarmed the Boar Rider, who then knelt and pleaded for his life. She socked him in the face and he fell unconscious.

I ran to her and called, "Camphoria!" just as a crossbow bolt struck her.

"No!!!" I screamed and turned to see the man in black who had shot the bolt. In fury I willed him to instantly burst into flames. I ran to Camphoria and felt relief when I saw that the bolt had missed her vitals and only hit in her shoulder. She looked at me and said, "It hurts like the sting of a wind floater, but I'll be fine, just take me ta yer father. Ye canna help me, go lead yer troops. They need ye."

I nodded reluctantly. I dared not leave her side, but she was right. I picked her up and carried her to where my father had tied up the Deputy Minister. "Please tend to her." Then I was about to give the signal to gather by sending a bright green shaft of light into the air, when I was attacked by several swarthy men dressed in black, with hundreds more following them. I had to protect Camphoria and my father so I surrounded them with a ring of fire and I tore into the mysterious black invaders. I barely had the time to wonder, "Who are you?" before I had to defend myself slashing, punching, kicking my way to higher ground, all the while holding the circle of flame around Camphoria.

There seemed no end to the number of black warriors that attacked us. Seeing the reinforcements had emboldened the remaining Boar Riders as well. After dispatching a black-clad enemy, I raised the serrated sword and shot a green light into the sky to rally the resistance forces. I saw the haggard and wounded men and women of the rebellion rush to gather around me, their swords ready. I concentrated as a flurry of crossbow bolts flew in our direction from all sides. They hit the superheated barrier and turned to ash instantly. I saw that we were less than 300 rebels surrounded by thousands of men in black clothing. Even with the aid of the planet's fury, I could not hope to keep all of us protected for long. We could not be surrounded and survive. "Follow me!" I shouted and hoped to break through the enclosing circle of mystery fighters. I lit myself with green fire as I rushed towards the wall of black. I vaporized cross bow bolts that rained upon us and then swung my sword and ten black opponents were sliced in two. Before I could bring my sword back, ten more took their place and a hammer blow knocked the serrated sword from my grasp.

I dove upon them, using every ounce of strength and agility that Sir Kendrick had taught me. Black clad men fell from my blows, left and right, to then be rendered unconscious by the resistance fighter that followed me. I avoided, a vicious blow from an axe and used the momentum of the man's swing to steal the axe and throw him to the ground. I swung the axe in a deadly half circle, and pushed ahead, slicing, bashing and hammering my way to the interior corner of the high wall surrounding Gran Saline. My fighters rushed behind me and formed a quarter circle with their backs to the wall.

"Too many have fallen!" I observed with anguish, and fierce anger boiled my blood, but I did not have the serrated blade and could only depend upon my own strength, which was fading fast. I kept the flaming circle around Camphoria, but did not know how much longer I could stand in my exhausted state. As the black clad enemies attacked, their bodies piled up in front of our circle, restricting our movements. One after another of our fighters succumbed to exhaustion, and wounds.

I could not bear it any longer. I called on all the strength within me, and from the anger of Portus. I held the two-headed axe in both hands in front of me and roared as an explosion of flame burst from the blade, shattering it into a thousand pieces striking hundreds of on-rushing men in black and knocking them and hundreds more to the ground with the shockwave. I collapsed to my knees for I had spent all of my energy.

I saw the wall of flame around Camphoria flicker and disappear and I saw my father valiantly protect Camphoria from the on-coming attackers.

In this moment of deepest despair and anguish, I saw dark shapes above in the sky and at first thought Betty-Lou and her flotilla had arrived. But they were not our ships. My hopes plummeted as I saw black clad men running to attack us again. I had only postponed the inevitable for a few moments.

<All ships. Be prepared to fight!> I thought to warn Betty-Lou and the other ships.

Then the ships let down ropes and hundreds and hundreds of pirates slid down and began attacking the men dressed in black. The resistance fighters in the ships with Betty-Lou also slid to the ground and attacked.

<That be the help I mentioned,> Betty-Lou shared.

<Protect Camphoria and my Father!> I pleaded.

<That I'll do!> Betty-Lou promised.

<What is that you are dragging behind?> I asked Betty-Lou.

<Tis an interesting tail!> Betty-Lou laughed at her own joke. <I'll tell it to ye when we be done.>

Somehow, I and the remaining resistance men and women found the energy to get up and continue fighting. We fought like meercats backed into a corner. So vicious and unexpected was our response, added with ferocity of the pirates, and the bombardment from the ships above, that soon the men in black clothing, threw down their weapons and pleaded for mercy.

I went to check on my father and Camphoria and was surprised to see Cirulea kneeling by her side holding her hand. Tears were gushing from both mother's and daughter's eyes. My father limped up to me, bleeding from a number of cuts, but was alive.

"Thank you for coming to our rescue Cirulea," I told her as I supported my father with an arm around his waist.

She smiled as she looked at me and replied, "Tis the least I could do for the Mighty Fire Lord...and my future son in-law."

Captain Bragg ran up and said, "Be she well?" Then he noticed that his wife was there also. "Hello Cirulea. This be quite a reunion!" then he kneeled down and gave her a kiss on the lips, which she did not resist.

CHAPTER 41
EPILOGUE

(Taken from the personal journal of Captain William Jasper Bragg)

Throughout the night and come morning we looked for survivors and counted our dead. Over the next rotations, we cried and mourned for them as we buried their bodies. We also buried all the other dead, and mourned them too. Over five hundred resistance fighters and pirates had died, with hundreds more severely wounded. Over one thousand black clad combatants were killed, and including the Boar Riders aboard the armada ships, nearly a thousand of them were slain as well.

The people of Gran Saline returned to find their city center in ruins, but were overjoyed to discover that the Overlord was no more and that the evil Deputy Minister would be put to trial and punished.

Everyone who had been on the pavilion had instantly died, including the Overlord and all his cabinet, except one: the senior minister who warned the Fire Lord of the trap and who had declined to come to Gran Saline.

When we questioned the prisoners, we discovered that the men dressed in black were mercenaries paid by the Deputy Minister. They came from the little-known land of Ironfeld in the Southern Marches. We sent them back to their country and informed their leaders of their part in the bloody coupe. Later we sent delegates and opened formal relationships with their leaders to add them to the newly formed republic.

My daughter, Camphoria, recovered from her shoulder wound after a cycle of rest and recuperation. We, meaning my wife, Cirulea and Camphoria, as well as the Fire Lord and his Grandfather, mother and father, took up residence in the Overlord's palace.

The pirate airmen, now called Freemen, took over the Boar Riders barracks and what was left of the armada. Of course, they had to be retrained to uphold the law instead of ignoring it, but the deep desire to grasp and protect freedom was what fueled that transformation, as well as strict punishments from the Fire Lord for those that would not behave.

The 253 captains and their companion airships, became ambassadors of good will throughout all of Portus. The ships that were painted for the grand parade at the final battle retained their striking colors as a reminder of the sacrifices of blood spilt on that day and became iconic symbols of freedom everywhere. They were led by Sir Percival Kendrick and their mission was to help each town, city and region recover from the despotic rule of the Overlord, evil adjudicators, Boar Rider Legions, wicked town and city mayors and corrupt judges. They carried the template of Polgro and offered assistance in choosing new people-accountable governments.

Gideon Livingston, The Fire Lord, was crowned King of Portus, with a representative government council granting equal say to all 16 regions (Ironfeld, Asombre, and Montora were added to the realm). Each town was asked to do what Polgro did and selected righteous men and women to execute the law and then judge the former oppressors, adjudicators and Boar Riders according to their crimes. All towns in the region would send their representative to the region center to choose a representative to be on the Fire Lord's Council.

The Fire Lord assigned his father to seek out spiritual men and women to establish churches and places of worship to succor the needy, strengthen the weak, and establish virtue, honesty and trust in God as the foundation of Portus' new era. He also established schools and universities in every continent, even Asombre and required that the history of Portus, and the new laws and principles of government be taught to every child, youth or young adult.

When Camphoria was fully healed, she and the Fire Lord were wed in the grandest celebration that Portus had ever seen. The city of Scryberg was decorated with flaming yellow and orange banners. All were invited to attend, not just the rich or noble. On the day of the wedding, which took place in the center of the town, Gideon Livingston and Camphoria Bragg stood before Bert Livingston to pronounce their vows. The Fire Lord wore dark blue military jacket emblazoned in gold with the crest of the scrybeast on one breast and the dragon on the other. Camphoria wore a dress of white wind wisp silk quilted with iridescent buttons made from sea shells.

"Lord Gideon Livingston, do you take for time and all eternity to be your lawful wife Camphoria Bragg?"

"I do."

"Lady Camphoria Bragg, do take for time and all eternity to be your lawful husband, Gideon Livingston?

"I do."

"By the power vested in me, I pronounce you man and wife. You may kiss the bride and exchange rings."

They kissed amid cheers and greetings of good will. Then they exchanged rings. Camphoria placed a simple band of gold on Gideon's finger and Gideon placed a familiar silver ring with a white jewel, now resized on her finger.

Then Gideon motioned for Cirulea to come forward with an ornately decorated wooden box. She opened it and Gideon removed a dazzling golden crown formed of a single dragon holding a large diamond in the center, with curtains of golden chains ending in diamonds on either side. Someone shouted, "Tis queen Jasmin's crown!" Camphoria was overcome with emotion as Gideon placed the crown on her head. The people erupted in shouts of joy and happiness as Gideon roared above the noise, "Behold, Queen Camphoria Livingston!" Truly, there could have been no woman more beautiful and radiant than Camphoria Livingston.

The parties and celebrations went on for a full lunar cycle as newly chosen leaders came to give their respects to the happy couple and their families.

Betty-Lou took the married couple on their wedding trip as her last voyage and then retired for good, sailing off to parts unknown.

TABLE OF REFERENCES

Mejilla, E. (14, 7,1989): "Volumes 1-7: The Fire Lord Reborn" Asombre Publishing Company: 1525 Bragg St., Polgro, Asombre

McBride, F. (7,35,2025): "Pirates Through the Ages." Wendover House S.A: 87 N. Keel Ave, Noonday, Scryberg.

Livingston, C. (3,12,2023): "Personal Memoirs of Her Highness, Camphoria Livingston." Steelbrow Publishing: Scryberg, Scryberg.

Livingston, G. (3/12/2023): "Personal Memoirs of His Lordship, Gideon Livingston, Fire Lord." Steelbrow Publishing: Scryberg, Scryberg.

Livingston, A. (7/20/1835): "Memoirs of Captain Ariel Livingston." Handwritten document archived in the National Museum of Asombre.

Stonebrow, F. (13/15/1829): "Personal Communication to Gideon Livingston, the Fire Lord" Handwritten document archived in the National Museum of Scryberg.

Bragg, W.J. (5/21/1830): "Personal Journal of Captain W. Jasper Bragg" donated by the Bragg Family Incorporated.

APPENDIX A A BRIEF HISTORY OF PORTUS

Landing (0-100)

Legend hints that the inhabitants of Portus came from another world. The location of the landing is believed to be in the area of Asombre. It also hints to some relation to the Maelstrom whether the Maelstrom interfered with the landing or the landing caused the Maelstrom, no one knows. Ethnographic studies suggest that the immigrants were of varying races based on skin color and language preferences. Portus means door or port in one the ancient languages called Latin. Either as a rejection of their technological past or through cataclysmic loss of technology, the inhabitants of Portus had to depend on what they could make and produce with limited tools.

Age of Exploration (100-400)

The people of Portus discover the variety of helpful stones that form the base of their technology. They also discover the xeoxyn gas and develop methods of traveling in the air to avoid the deadly seas. The eight continents are discovered.

Age of Expansion (400-800)

Air travel is further developed to be more reliable and safe. The eight continents begin to be colonized. Trade routes are established. Wealthy individuals rushed to claim as much territory as they possibly could. Territorial wars abounded.

Age of Conquest (800-1300)

Wealthy men and women begin to subjugate those less wealthy. A caste system was established where birth determined your status in life. Indentured servitude and slavery became rampant. Trade guilds kept strict control over who was allowed into the guild and who could advance. Large landowners proclaimed themselves kings and queens. Air travel became dangerous because of the large number of pirates.

Reformation- The first Fire Lord (1300-1400)

The economic situation for the lower classes became dire. The poor suffered from lack of health care, proper nutrition and education. Weir rats infested buildings and carried diseases. The wealthy lived ignorant and oblivious to their suffering and instead, imposed heavy taxes on the working poor. A farm boy named Sam from Meridian became the Fire Lord and rallied the people to overthrow the nobles. Fire could not hurt him and he became known as the Fire Lord. He became king and set up a royal army called Boar Riders.

Age of the Overlords and Boar Riders (1400-1829)

When the Fire Lord stepped down, he set up an Overlord and ministers to run the kingdom. For two hundred cycles, this worked well for Portus. It was a time of peace and prosperity. After the death of the Fire Lord, a bloodthirsty Overlord took power through conquest. This despot appointed wicked ministers and became king. He, his sons, grandsons and great grandsons ruled Portus with an iron fist. Once again, all people without money or land suffered.

Age of the Fire Lord Reborn (1829-1872)

The Fire Lord Reborn overthrew the evil Overlord, Octavious Rumford, III. The Fire Lord, Gideon Livingston, was crowned king and led the effort to set up a representative government that exists today that limits the power of the king or ruler. It is now called the Portus Republic, PR, and boasts of an executive council composed of representatives from each of the eighteen independent nations.

APPENDIX B
PORTUS TIME

Passage of time in Portus is measured in Rotations- approximately 452 solar rises (or just rises), and 15 lunar cycles (or just cycle). Each lunar cycle is approximately 30 rises of the sun. The current date is a running count of the number of rotations after the landing (*al*). Gideon Livingston, the Fire Lord was born in the 3rd cycle of the 1812th *al* rotation on the 15th rise.

Portus time is based on 7 maritime watches, each lasting 4 bells, except for the Dogueral watches that last two bells each.

Time is kept by the ringing of bells- eight per watch. One ring means the first watch bell, two rings, the second watch. Change of watches is announced as follows:

First Watch, After sundown to midnight- one extra bell, four times separated by the count of 4.

Middle Watch, Midnight to pre- sunrise- two extra bells, four times separated by the count of 4.

Morning Watch, Pre-sunrise to mid-morning- three extra bells, four times separated by the count of 4.

Forenoon Watch, Mid-morning to mid-day (noon)- four extra bells, four times separated by the count of 4.

Afternoon Watch, Noon to mid-afternoon- five extra bells, four times separated by the count of 4.

First Dogueral Watch, Mid-afternoon to evening- six extra bells, in rapid succession.

Second Dogueral Watch,.Evening to after sundown- seven

extra bells in rapid succession.

(By means of the Dogueral Watches, the watches can be changed every day, so that each watch gets a turn of eight bells rest at night. Otherwise each member of the crew would be on duty the same bells every day.)

APPENDIX C LIMITED BESTIARY OF PORTUS

Piglins:

Small domesticated mammal no more than three hands tall, equipped with porcine features such as a flat snout for digging roots and tubers and long curly tail. They are prized for their white curly fur suited for the colder temperatures of northern Portus which is collected every spring and used for weaving cloth and the plush furry leather is used for jackets, vests and boots. Piglin meat is also a delicacy. When startled, piglins jump up to 3 arms lengths and squeal in an extremely loud and high pitch to ward away predators. This makes it difficult to pen them and hearing protection must be worn when caring for them. Their main predators are the Meercats and the Weirats, though Rockweasels, and Rock Serpents often attack them, as well.

Rock Serpents:

Vicious constricting serpents that grow up to two times a man's height in length. They are cold blooded but inhabit the high reaches of the rock strewn mountains of Bergland and Sky Forest. They are the same color and texture of the rocks among which they dwell and are extremely dangerous because they are often not noticed until too late. These serpents dwell in communal holes, crevasses and caves preferring the geothermal vents for warmth. They are often seen basking in the sun but on cold rotations, they are prone to warm themselves by using their great strength to create extreme friction by wrapping themselves around a boulder and scraping their tough scales in alternating patterns on the rock. This leaves curious circular marks on the stones and creates highly prized sand used in polishing gems. Rock serpents eat anything that invades their domain by either swallowing them whole if small, or squeezing them and eating them at their leisure. Because of their tough heat resistant hide, rock serpent skin is valuable rock smiths and firemen's protective gear. Man is their only known predator.

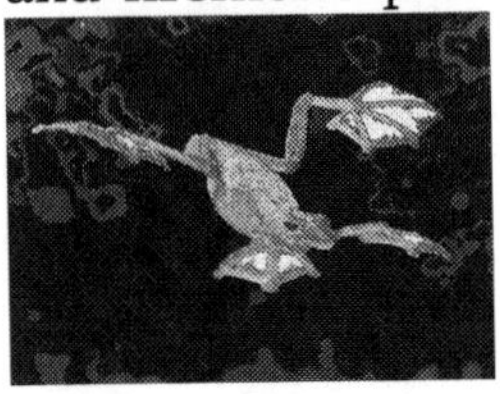

Blind Leap Frogs:

These colorless sightless amphibians begin life in the dark cave waters hatched from eggs. The first phase of their existence is as an elongated fish with external gills. As they mature, they develop lungs and four limbs and exit the water to live on land. Each limb terminates in elongated, five-fingered webbed feet. The bling leap frogs eat flying insects, birds and mammals, by jumping and gliding with their webbed feet extended. They capture their prey with their long tongues that contain sticky poison. They navigate their dark environment and locate prey by high frequency chirping which sound bounces off objects painting an audio picture captured by the amphibian's sensitive skin.

Meercats:

Not really a cat, but more like a rockweasel. About four hands tall and ten hands long (including the tail), these fierce mammals widely inhabit wilderness forests of Portus but often enter inhabited regions in search of food. They are curious and extremely intelligent creatures that cause havoc among farmers trying to protect herds of piglins, musk deer, or delivery hogs because the meercats long claws allow them to dig under any fence, or climb nearly any protective wall. They are omnivorous and will eat nearly anything but particularly love honey from rock wasp nests. Elongate whiskered snouts allow for a considerable array of fangs and teeth. They have pointed long ears, similar to tree cats, elongated bodies and their tails are twice as long as their bodies and aid in jumping, climbing rocks and trees and defense. They are covered in a thick, shaggy black fur with white rings around the long tail that protect them from rock wasp stings. Known for their fearlessness in protecting their life-long mate and offspring. When startled they have glands under their tails that spray, with extreme accuracy, a foul smelling and stinging liquid that causes even the most daring creature to flee in agony.

Tree Cats:

These nocturnal creatures inhabit the humid, tropical lowlands of central Portus. They grow to be five to seven hands tall, have large eyes and ears and dwell in the tallest forest trees. Their fur is spotted yellow and black. They have powerful retractable claws that allow them to climb vertically and they have powerful legs that allow them to spring up to a stone's throw in distance. Their twin tails are used for balance and are prehensile and able to grab objects and aid in navigating tree branches and holding their young. Only descending from the trees on rare occasions, they live their lives entirely in the canopy, eating birds, rodents, reptiles, amphibians and tree mollusks. They obtain their water from water gathering flowers, branches and leaves with their long tongue that they can form a drinking straw to extract water from deep crevasses and plants. Stealthy hunters, they can jump and climb trees silently. Though rarely seen, the night skies of the forests are filled with their loud purring songs and growls.

Rockweasel:

These creatures are long and thin to aid in entering rodent burrows and snake holes. They are found in most areas of Portus and are considered a nuisance, though some ingenious farmers have domesticated them to keep the rodent population down on their farms. They have cat-like ears, short muzzles and large eyes for nocturnal hunting. Their nimble front paws can open nuts, rock clams and rock worm eggs. Their fur is short and brown except for the tail which is as fluffy as a wind floater tendrils, making it highly sought after for fashion accessories such as scarves, hats, and belts. They are marsupials that bear their young in pouches until they are old enough to fend for themselves.

Delivery Hogs:

These are large domesticated creatures used for hauling large wagons of goods long distances. Their strength and docility make them useful in transportation as well as construction. They stand 20 to 25 hands tall at the shoulders and weigh 1000 to 1500 stones. They are docile, loving creatures that are covered with curly brown or black fur. Their snout is flattened to aid in digging for roots and tubers, yet they also will scavenge and eat nearly anything. Wild hogs inhabit the plains of Idylwyld and Granberry and are fearsome beasts when provoked, but spend most of their rotations either cooling off in the mires or sleeping in the shade. In mating season hogs use their tusks to fight with other hogs over the most desirable females. The tusks for delivery hogs are removed at birth.

Scrybeasts:

Scrybeasts are a rare creature once inhabiting caves and grottos in remote mountains of Fernland. Standing 15 hands tall, and 35 hands long (including the tail) with a wingspan of 25 hands, this is a magnificent beast. It stands on four feline shaped legs ending with paws with red razor sharp claws. It is covered with dark, spiky scales from its marsh hawk-like beak to its knife-like tail similar to a swamp lizard's. Even the wings of 20 hand wingspan sport protective scales. These wings can be folded for swift travel on land or in the water. Equally at home on land, water or air, this beast has no land enemies, though swift enough in the water to avoid the smallest leviathans, it is no match for the large ones, nor can it match the ferocity and speed of the sky devils though there have been tails of terrible battles in which the scrybeast was victorious. Scrybeast are swift and strong fliers, able to carry off juvenile wild hogs. Its main source of food are rock serpents, fin fish and cloud reapers. This beast appears in many legendary tales and is used as a symbol of strength by the Boar Riders, a military force that once served and protected the king but retained the name when the age of the Overlords and Adjudicators began. scrybeasts were hunted to near extinction. The Fire Lord discovered that they are sentient and communicate through their screech speech.

Underbeasts:

Are small, four to five hands in length, and live underground. They have large front paws and large incisor teeth for digging and eating through roots and tubers. They have dark brown fur much prized for its ability to shed water and maintain heat. They are nearsighted and use their acute hearing to locate their favorite food: rockworms. They dig tunnels over large stretches of ground, even through rocky ground and cause much consternation for farmers and builders whose structures sink or fall because of the tunnels. These creatures are fierce fighters and use their sharp claws to penetrate between the scales of the rockworms. Over the cycles farmers have preferred the underbeasts to the rockworms which indiscriminately destroy acres of farmland.

Springlet 

Springlets are grass eating animals domesticated for milk and cheese. They stand ten hands tall due to their long legs and neck, but they are only five hands long and five hands wide, nearly round in girth and width. They have long ears, slender snouts and the males have two curved horns used for protection and mating battles. They use their long prehensile tongues to grab grass as they spread their legs, or by extending their necks they prefer to eat the low hanging leaves of the red bean trees. They have short-haired, spotted or striped brown hides, often used in clothing, shoes and bags. The females produce a rich creamy milk excellent for butter and cheeses often called spatter milk. 

Marsh Hawk

A predatory bird that inhabits most of Portus. This bird stays in the lower altitudes and hunts small rodents, reptiles and other birds. With only a wing span of four hands it is a nimble flyer and excellent hunter. It has a sharp curved beak and sharp talons. Its upper feathers are dark while its under feathers are white. This bird is recognizable due to its extended wingtip feathers, two long tail feathers and feathers that appear as horns on its head.

Swamp Lizard

Are small reptiles that infest the swamplands of Marshton, and Asombre. They are three to four hands in length including the tail, and are green colored, making them almost invisible in the green waters and swamps. They are rarely seen on land, only to make their nests. If you see one swamp lizard, know that there are hundreds more nearby. They are communal hunters and take down much larger prey, by their sheer numbers. They swim using their long vertically flat tail using a side to side undulation of their bodies. They can sustain their breath for bells at a time underwater, but most often rest on the surface of the water with only their eyes and nose broaching the surface. Their thin long snouts contain hundreds of blade-like fangs used to quickly tear flesh from larger foes. A swarm of swamp lizards can reduce a fully grown wild hog to bone in moments.

Horned Adder

Horned adders infest the deserts of Turrin and Stonehold. They are called horned adders because they are serpents with eyebrow ridges that extend behind the head in the form of horns. They are extremely poisonous and nocturnally hunt rodents, and lizards. They hide during the day under rocks, logs, bushes or anything that can provide shade from the burning sun. They come out in the early evenings to hunt and since their vision is poor, they use their forked tongue to sense heat and movement. Horned adders eat their prey whole and unhinge their jaw for larger than normal meals. These snakes are fearless and do not give warning before they strike, making them extremely dangerous to humans and domesticated animals.

Rock Wasps 

These insects are valuable for their agricultural benefit as pollinators but they are fiercely protective of their honey. Each insect is approximately a thumb's length and can not only sting multiple times, but can also bite with their mandibles. If they sense no threat, they will ignore most animals and humans (except for meercats). They build their paper nests in hollow trees, sheltered rocks, crags and caves. Nests are black ovals three hands long and two wide. They are colored red and yellow stripes for an apt warning of their danger. Only the meercat is able to successfully collect this honey. Attempts have been made to domesticate these insects, but once a nest is robbed of honey, they depart the nest and make a new one over a league distance. The only known enemies are predator wasps that attack the nest and set up residence with a new queen. 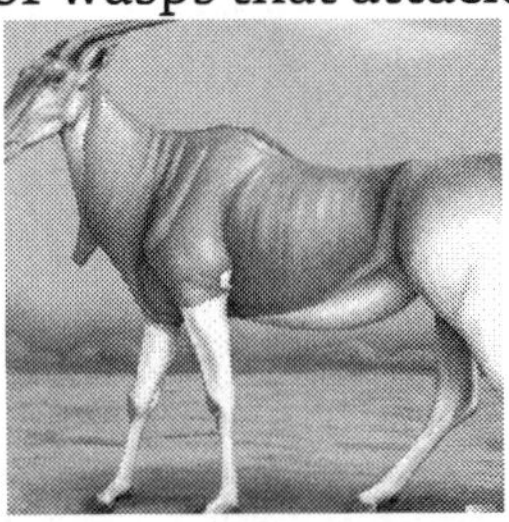

Musk Deer

Musk Deer are domesticated animals used as livestock for meat and skins. They are about eight to ten hands in height. They are short legged animals with elongated flexible nostrils used for foraging for food. Their skins are very durable and thick of rusty brown color. Males have various types of straight or curved spiral horns that are removed at adulthood. Musk deer are named for their fondness of aromatic plants found in the flatlands and central plains region of

Portus. 

Predator Wasps

Are easily recognized by their red wings, aerodynamic shape and black furry thoraxes. They are approximately two thumbs lengths and have large mandibles and antennae. They scavenge for food, mainly from dead animals but are often found near refuse bins or garbage dumping grounds. They are nuisance pests that ruin picnics and outings where there is food. They are aggressive and easily provoked. Their sting is potent enough to cause swelling and severe pain. Unfortunate humans and animals have been killed by multiple stings when they unintentionally uncover the nests. The name predator wasp comes from the frequent practice of positioning themselves by the entrance to the nest of rockwasps and patiently attacking the host one by one as they exit and taking over another nest of the less aggressive wasps. Predator wasps make their nests in any protected space, especially in dwellings and buildings that allow easy ingress. Fire and smoke are the only things that will scare them away.

Cloud Reapers

Live in the mid stratospheric clouds in all of Portus. They are large bulbous creatures that are nearly transparent but for their short stubby wings which are dark orange. They are shaped like a green sweet beet but the size of a small cottage. They have a cavernous mouth that they use to gather the nutritious gases and microbes which are found in clouds. Cloud reapers travel by flicking their translucent rubbery tails the size of a bed sheet folded into a triangle back and forth. They gather the xeoxyn gas that keeps them afloat in their skin in bulging transparent bubbles. It was these creatures that helped men discover the xeoxyn gas and its ability to lift great weights in the air. While cloud reapers are no threat to humans, they have been known to inhale entire flocks of birds and navigators keep a wary eye out for them to avoid collision.

Whey Hens

These are fat stubby birds that do not appear to be able to fly, but are able to fly quickly great distances. Their keen sense of direction makes them indispensable for communication. They will always return to where they roost so they are valuable as messengers. They vary in size from two hands to three hands with a wingspan of four hands. Their eggs are a delicacy, but are extremely valuable and are not consumed regularly due to their messenger skills. All the great houses and sky merchants have flocks of these birds raised in different parts of Portus for easy communication.

Weirats

Weirats are everywhere on Portus and have proven to be a dangerous threat in several periods in history. The weir rats are two hands long and have a thick armored hide that makes them extremely difficult to kill. They reproduce at 9-week intervals and if left unchecked will overrun any community. They eat anything but are particularly voracious grain eaters. Only foods stored in metal or rock containers are safe from them. There are several types of traps designed to kill or capture them, but the weir rats soon learn to avoid them. Fortunately, dragons, rock serpents, meercats and Clouded foxes keep the numbers down. Weir rats are nocturnal and have large eyes and long pointed ears. When frightened they tuck their limbs and head in and form a ball with their hard shell, often rolling away from their enemy.

Dragons

These reptiles are five to seven hands long (including the tail) and are covered in glossy smooth black and red scales. They have long orange tongues that from a distance could look like flames, hence the name dragon. They are extremely fast and able to catch weir rats. The index claws on their front feet are elongated to be able to pierce the weir rat's protection. Many people keep dragons in their store rooms and cellars to protect their food. Dragons, however, do not make good pets as many a bitten owner will attest. Historical records report of a species of dragon that was much larger and able to fly. Ancient tapestries depict this creature as a friend to man, but it is not understood if this is figurative or actual.

Rock Lizards

Rock Lizards are the predominant reptile on Portus. They can be found anywhere there is rocky terrain. They are one hand in length, including the tail. They are found sunning themselves on rocks but are hard to see because they can change their color to match the rocks or trees they hide on. Rock lizards also have hard rock-like scales. Rock lizards eat all sorts of insects and small mammals. Their favorite is the wasp. They position themselves near the entrance to a nest or mound and as soon as the insect emerges, they flick their sticky tongue out and capture the insect. Rock lizards are impervious to wasp and ant stings. When pursuing an insect, a rock lizard is capable of great leaps and is known to catch predator wasps ten hands in the air.

Wind Wisps 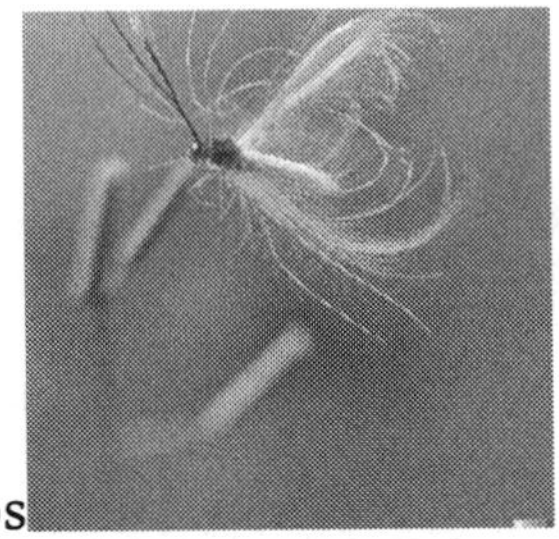

Wind Wisps are small, six legged insects that have two unique characteristics. The first is that they are shaped like the long fluffy seed pods of the trees they inhabit. Their wings are fixed on long stems that extend from their thorax. They are incapable of long flight by themselves but utilize the wind to flit from tree to tree. The second defining characteristic is that when startled or mating, their abdomens glow bright red. On breezy summer nights it is quite a treat to see all the red spots of light in constant motion with the wind.

Clouded Fox 

Also known as the gray fox inhabits the central temperate regions of Portus. It is between seven and nine hands long (half of that being its tail). It is a shy nocturnal creature known for its creative hunting techniques. It has large eyes, oversized pointed ears and sleek fur. It also has tufts of fur around each paw to dampen sound and increase stealth. Its long tail is slender with a puff of fluffy fur on the end. Often the fox will climb low hanging branches, leaving its tail puff on the ground. The tail puff contains a gland that excretes tantalizing smells for rodents. It will twitch the tail once in a while. When an animal comes to investigate, the clouded fox will pounce from its hiding place. These animals are hunted heavily for their beautiful silky furs but recent efforts have been made to protect them. 

Wind Sprites

These bird-like creatures inhabit watery regions near rivers, marshes, lakes or beaches. They are capable of hovering motionless due to their rapidly beating wings and xeoxyn gas bladders that make them look like floating balls. They are curious creatures and will investigate anything entering their domain. They can flit quickly and are nearly impossible to catch. They have long tubular beaks that allow them to drink from a variety of flowering plants. Normally playful, but when angered, their pointed beaks serve as spears and can inflict severe puncture wounds.

Sky Devils 

(Also known as Guardians of the Wind) These dangerous creatures inhabit the upper stratosphere and glide effortlessly above the clouds and maintain their altitude by large bladders of xeoxyn gas located in their wings.. They are triangular in shape with their rubbery wings extended. The largest recorded was thirty hands long with a spiked three-prong tail extending another twenty hands. They possess a wide mouth full of razor sharp teeth. The eyes are below the mouth and to the sides for better views below. Their main food are cloud reapers but will also devour entire flocks of wind floaters and windlings. It propels itself using its wings in an undulating pattern. The sky devil will dive from extreme heights and attack its flying prey without warning. It uses its barbed tail to whip and stun prey and to defend itself from scrybeasts, the only creature capable of countering its attacks. Sky merchants have reported that the sky devils will frequently follow their ships and upon occasion attack them, causing severe damage and destruction. Guardians of the Wind are sentient and gentle, unless they are threatened or attacked. They are highly intelligent and communicate through telepathic methods.

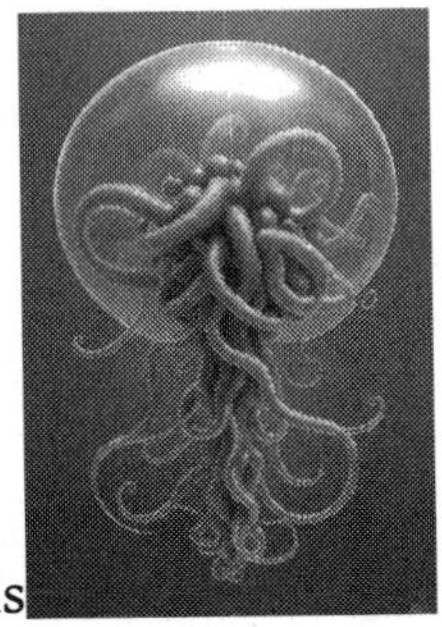

Stinging Cloud Pods

These creatures use a balloon-like sack of xeoxyn gas to float at low altitudes. Their body is five to eight hands in circumference and is completely translucent. Their many translucent tentacles dangle beneath the spherical body another ten to fifteen hands. Unwary birds are caught in the tentacles and brought up to be digested in the spherical body. This is the only time that they are clearly visible, after they have fed. Great masses of the stinging cloud pods have been reported in the southern marches. A touch of the tentacle will cause a severe localized paralysis and excruciating pain.

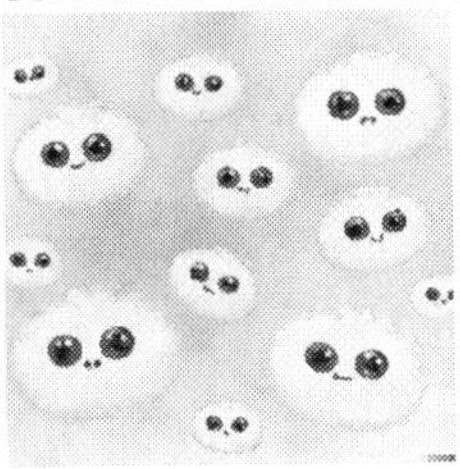

Wind Floater

These are similar to stinging cloud pods but are much bigger. The wind floaters inhabit higher altitudes but still well below the stratosphere. They are difficult to spot due to their blue undersides and dark topsides. Similar to stinging cloud pods, these creatures float using bladders full of xeoxyn gas. Wind floaters have undulating wings on the sides. They prey on larger flying creatures unwary enough to be attracted to the fluffy tipped tentacles that look similar to windlings. They get tangled in the translucent tentacles and are hauled up to be devoured by grinding teeth at the bottom of the white spherical body.

Windling

Windlings look like gentle, fluffy white puff balls that float randomly in the air but this is a false impression. They travel in swarms of ten to fifty and have distinct patterns of flight. They are three hands in circumference and the fluff hides a large xeoxyn bladder, two small limbs, a beak and sensory organs. They constantly search the air for flocks of small birds that they trap with walls of sound that confuse and disorient the birds. The birds get tangled in the sticky fur and are guided to the sharp beaks by the small limbs.

Rock Worms

Rock Worms are from six to eight hands long and one hand in circumference. They are covered with rock-hard scales and have a three prong beak that allows them to dig through soil and soft rock and cement. They eat the soil and digest its decayed matter and minerals. They are beneficial in that they churn the soil but in large numbers, they can cause significant damage to farmland and buildings.

Fin Fish

These fish are some of the only sea fish available to humans because they dwell in great schools on the surface of the oceans and can easily be snagged or retrieved from the air. Even this is dangerous because of the large sea creatures that are able to leap from the depths to great heights above the water. Fin fish are recognizable due to their white color and their large webbed dorsal fin that protrudes above the surface of the water and catches the wind. The fish below the water is about twenty hands long and has a large mouth that engulfs small crustaceans and schools of small fish as it is propelled by the wind. Large predatory fish that dwell deeper in the ocean do not bother these peaceful fish because of the defensive measures of the many sharp spines in the fins, tail and along the dorsal line. 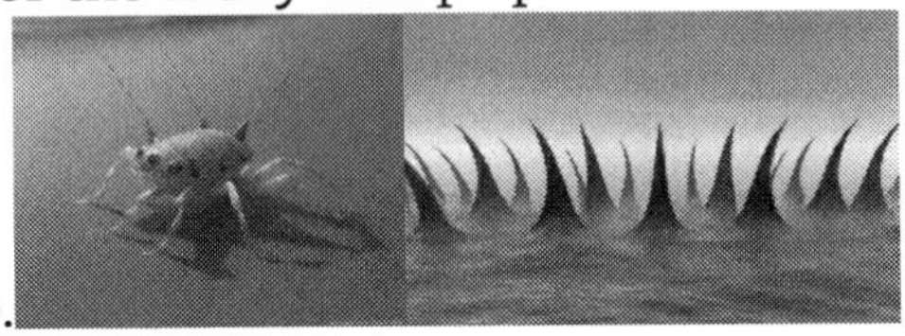

Sea Fleas

These small creatures inhabit the beaches of Portus. They are crustaceans that are one hand in size, round and with six legs and two pincers. Their eyes are on antennae-like stalks and they also have longer antennae. They burrow into the sand and wait for the high tide in which they can search for smaller crustaceans, and seaworms. Unwary beach goers my step on a sea flea and receive a nasty pinch or a poke. Sea fleas are a delicacy when steamed over hot rocks. Removing the hard shells reveals tasty white meat.

Leviathans

Not much is known about these sea creatures because of the dangers of ever seeing one up close. Some reports that say that these creatures are simply extremely large fish 200 hands or more in length. Other say that they are much larger and can swallow an airship whole. All accounts agree that they are extremely deadly and dangerous and for this reason no successful attempts have been made to float ships on the sea. 

Sea Monsters

Tales of strange creatures seen in the waters from above report that some beasts have long necks, four large flippers and a long tail, while others are ravenous mouths surrounded by spiked tentacles. Eye witnesses claim that there are beasts similar to the sky devils but much larger. Another beast was reported that was armored with pincers the size of wild hogs battled with a swarm of fish with long sharp swords for mouths. 

River Dog

Water loving mammals are covered in soft green fur. Flippered forefeet and flippered hind feet. Able to swim quickly and change directions rapidly using their flippers as oars when on top of the water, and undulating the hind legs for propulsion and using the fore flippers for steering. Often seen sunning themselves on the rocks. Only found in freshwater rivers and streams. They eat mollusks, fish and water insects. Much prized for their soft, water repellent fur. 

Marsupial Bat

This nocturnal mammal lives in the upper canopy of the trees and hangs from the upper branches from his prehensile tail. The wings are five hands across but the body is only one hand while the tail is two hands. The body is covered with white fur and the leathery wings are black. Each night the marsupial bat flies in search of insects. The bat has keen eyesight and keen hearing, using high pitched screeching to locate prey. When born the babies instinctively crawl into a pouch on the mother's abdomen where they attach to a milk pap until they are large enough to fly.

Squabbler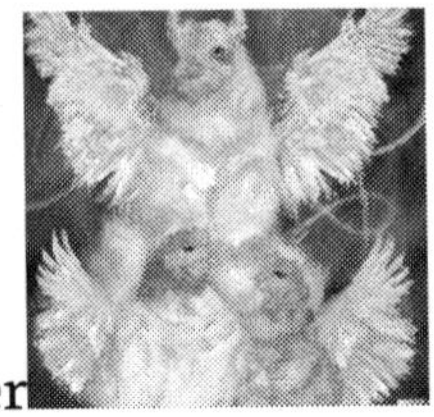

As the name suggests, a noisy roosting bird of two to three hands in length and up to four hands tall. Their legs are long and spindly, allowing them to run extremely fast. In the wild, these birds can be found in swamps and marshes. There are many varieties of squabblers, but the most common is covered in red feathers from beak to toe. These birds have been domesticated and are used to harvest their daily eggs, or for their meat.

APPENDIX E STONE TECHNOLOGY OF PORTUS

Light Stones (also known as glow stones)

These stones are smooth and nearly white and the higher quality stones are translucent. The stones come in all sizes and are found throughout Portus. The people of Portus discovered that these peculiar stones when placed in close proximity begin to glow. The closer they are the brighter they glow. After continual use in close proximity, considerable heat is generated and care must be taken so as to not crack the stones seeing as light stones are far less capable of handling heat as heat stones. The wealthy families of Portus have replaced their candles and torches with light stone fixtures that allow the distance between the stones to be adjusted. Portable light stone fixtures have been made using the same principle. Most airships are equipped with a large light stone projector. This usually uses a number of light stones in a circular frame, which by reducing the circumference, or by introducing a central light stone, create a powerful beam of light when channeled through a shaped clear stone. (Warning, prolonged exposure to light stones may result in skin discoloration, diarrhea and loss of hair.)

Heat Stones (also known as fire stones and hearth stones).

Heat stones are rough, dark gray to black and much heavier than light stones. Similar to light stones, when placed close to each other, they begin to glow red and generate heat. The closer they are, the more heat they create. Used generally for cooking, especially on wooden airships where uncontrolled fire is a real hazard. Often used by wealthy families as braziers to heat individual rooms during periods of cold. Wood and coal are still used to cook, and heat. (Warning, prolonged exposure to light stones may result in skin discoloration, diarrhea and loss of hair.)

Explosive Stones (also known as pop stones, or demolition stones)

There are two varieties of explosive stones: direct contact, and indirect contact stones. The direct contact stones are extremely dangerous because any sudden impact will cause it to explode. They are useful in demolition projects where they are placed around the foundations of the structure to be destroyed and someone with a good aim throws a rock or shoots a projectile and strikes one stone from a distance, causing it to explode and thus causing the other stones to also explode. A more rare variety of explosive stones are the remote or indirect contact stones. They are a pair and if one receives an impact, it activates the other to explode.

Spark Stones

A very hard stone, reddish in color. When struck against another spark stone, or a piece of metal, large sparks are created. Useful for making fires or igniting fire sticks.

Lightning Stones

Crystal-like stones able to hold electric charge. When brought close to another lightning stone with a charge, the stones combine their charge and release it in a spectacular show of electric plasma similar to lightning. Recent discoveries show a lightning stone may be charged by rubbing it on a lodestone.

Death Stones

These stones are extremely dangerous but fortunately, they are extremely rare as well. They are called death stones because even short exposure to the baleful purple glow of these stones proves fatal after rotations of agonizing pain, loss of teeth, blindness, and dehydration.

Navigation or Location Stones

Navigation stones are orange and smooth. Their interior structure aligns strongly with the planetary lines of force at the place that they were formed. Used extensively in navigation, by themselves, these stones always point towards their birthplace. Navigators use calibrated devices that identify direction of travel to chart courses, even in inclement weather. Used in combination with a sister stone (one forged in the same location), one being fixed and the other moveable, when calibrated with a map of Portus, the moveable stone shows the current location and moves in unison with the travel.

Loadstones

These stones are dark gray, dense and extremely attracted to iron metal. Used in retrieving tools and other metal items from deep pits and lakes. Also used as quick-release safety couplings for carts and horse harnesses. With the use of metal filings, scientists have discovered attraction fields emanating from these stones. Frequently used in the game of stones to disrupt other specialty stones in play.

Floating Stones

Floating stones are white, porous stones found in areas with high concentrations of xeoxyn gas. The stones are used for marker buoys and decorations. These soft stones can be carved easily into any shape, but are quite delicate and can be broken easily. They are found in volcanic regions and areas rich in xeoxyn gas. Though mining operations extract the xeoxyn gas contained in these rocks for airship buoyancy tanks, most of the xeoxyn gas comes from wind floater harvesting.

Reflection Stones

Reflection stones are found in all parts of Portus and are of many colors but all contain a high quantity of reflective crystals. The highest quality reflection stone, when polished, appears almost metallic. Reflection stones are polishable stones and after the grinding and polishing process are able to reflect images accurately. While metal can also be used as a reflection stone, its scarcity makes it too expensive for most people.

Viewing (sight) Stones

Portus scientists discovered that certain transparent stones found in the mountains of Granberry, change the way light passes through them. Some stones magnify the image while other stones diminish the image. By grinding and polishing these stones into convex or concave shapes, oculists are able to both see great distances, and send light great distances.

Twin Stones (also called Chirp Stones or Talk Stones)

These stones have the unique characteristic of harmonic vibration in response to sound. When one stone is activated because of a sound, it causes its twin stone to vibrate regardless of how far apart the stones are. These stones are found mainly in Fernland and are usually green, orange or yellow in color. Large stones can be broken up into several smaller stones with exactly the same quality.

Cutting Stone

These stones come in all shapes, colors and sizes from darkest black to clear as crystal. Early inhabitants of Portus used the brittle black stone chips to form spears and cut animal skins. Today, the larger of these stones are used for protective measures by being inserted in the top of fences to deter entrance by animals and thieves. The hardest stones are clear and are used to cut metal, or engrave on metal, or stone. Also used for decoration and jewelry.

Grinding Stone

Grinding stones are rough stones that are easy to form into grinding wheels, grinding blocks or sharpening stones. Coarse stones are used to shape reflection stones and metal, while fine-grain stones are used for polishing and sharpening. Also when two large, circular grinding stones are put together, they are able to mill grains into powder used in cooking.

Polishing Stone

Almost always white, gray or light brown, these stones are

used to take a rough surface and make it smooth. Most often used to polish reflecting stones or viewing (sight) stones. The initial step is to use a rougher polishing stone and keep increasing the smoothness of the stones until the surface is smooth. The final polishing is done with polishing paste and water.

Gaming (and power) Stones (See chapter 14)

The game of Stones is a simple game of skill in being able to accurately hit other stones that have been identified beforehand. If the prediction is completed, then the thrower gets to keep all the stones touched. Stones can be heavy, light, rough, smooth, and any color or form. The only restriction is that they cannot be larger than the palm of your hand or smaller than the first digit of the thumb. Stones can be simple, or extravagant. They can be decorated with gems, or they can be inherently valuable; made of a precious metal like gold or silver. Given these few restrictions, the insertion of power stones, or stones with special properties, the simple game of "Stones" becomes a game of strategy and deception. Power stones can behave differently when thrown, spun, struck or rubbed. Some power stones are attracted to other stones, or repel other stones. Part of the deception comes from some stones being made to appear to be certain power stones and the skill used when they are thrown in order to fool the other players into making impossible predictions.

Gemstones

These are stones that are translucent or clear and come in any color. The most esteemed gemstones are able to be cut so as to reflect light from all angles. Lower quality gems that cannot be cut, are mounted as decorations. Gemstones are valuable, and in many cases used as currency. Wealthy individuals use the stones for jewelry and decoration on their clothing, property and even teeth. Properties of some gemstones, combined with lightning stones and sight stones have produced powerful beams of destructive light.

Sound Stones

These stones are almost always clear, except for the larger sound stones that are hollow and shaded pink or red. When struck with a metal or wooden mallet, these stones produce a variety of loud tones. Musicians use these stones, arranged in tonal quality and pitch to play local tunes and popular melodies in street bands, or musical festivals. Often used on door frames to announce the arrival of a visitor. Sometimes used as paving stones for security or amusement and found frequently in toys and household decorations.

PRAISE FOR AUTHOR

Testimonials
One preview reader commented on the book, "This is a real page-turner. I couldn't put it down!"

Another preview reader stated, " I loved how easy it was to follow the story. The author's use of different dialects makes it easy to imagine the different characters.

"This is the kind of story that they make block-buster movies out of!" stated another reader.

- PREVIEW READERS

BOOKS BY THIS AUTHOR

The Fire Lord Trilogy: The Last Voyage Of The Betty-Lou

The Last Voyage of the Betty-Lou tells the life of Gideon Livingston and how he became the fabled Fire Lord. Faced with battling a despotic Overlord, the machinations of a power-hungry Deputy Minister, and pirates with their alternate moral code, Gideon must use his untested powers to lead the underground resistance movement inspired by the dragon.

The Fire Lord Trilogy: The Dragon And The Maelsrom

The Dragon and the Maelstrom recounts the history of how Gideon discovers the secrets hidden within the Maelstrom. To free a people from bondage, he battles the power-hungry Gran Cadiz who can control water like Gideon can control fire. Gideon learns that the dragon symbol on his chest is more than just a symbol. Curiosity nearly kills him as he explores the dangerous oceans and discovers an ancient evil there.

The Fire Lord Trilogy: The Battle For Portus

The Battle for Portus follows Gideon as he maintains and expands the representative government. He finally confronts the foretold 'danger from the West' and must fight against an ancient underground organization that threatens to destroy his family and ultimately, freedom on the planet Portus. To help him in this heroic effort, he finds unlikely allies.

Better Questioning For Better Learning: Strategies For Engaged Thinking

Learn how to ask deeper questions and develop better questioning habits with this important resource. Author Benjamin Stewart Johnson takes you step by step through the key considerations and brain- based research to keep in mind when developing questions.

Teaching Students To Dig Deeper: Ten Essential Skills For College And Career Readiness

What does it really mean for students to be college and career ready? In this new edition of Teaching Students to Dig Deeper, Ben Johnson identifies the ten attributes students need for success, according to key research, the College Board, the ACT, and rigorous state standards.

Teaching Students To Dig Deeper: The Common Core In Action

This important new book identifies the skills and qualities students need, based on the Common Core State Standards, to be really ready for college and careers.

A Parent Guide For College And Career Readiness

A 'must read for parents of all aged children who are interested in improving and enriching their student's learning.

A common-sense approach to learning, that makes it

understandable for anyone.

How To Be Successful At Elementary Home School

Learn the fundamentals of how to set up a successful elementary home learning program. Dr. Johnson will help you identify the unique nature of home schooling and help you firmly set in your mind what kind of home school environment you wish to have.

How To Be Successful At Home School For 12-15 Year Olds

Creating a successful learning environment in your home requires a bit of forethought and a clear understanding of what "learning" really is. How to be Successful at Home School for 12-15 Year Olds provides insight into the junior high and middle school minds and how to help them focus on learning.

Made in the USA
Columbia, SC
23 August 2024

41014720R10180